Hitler's Assassin

a novel by

David Bergengren

Hitler's Assassin
Copyright © 2016 David Bergengren. Produced and printed by Stillwater
River Publications. All rights reserved. Written and produced in the United
States of America. This book may not be reproduced or sold in any form
without the expressed, written permission of the author and publisher.

Visit our website at **www.StillwaterPress.com** for more information.

First Stillwater River Publications Edition 2016

ISBN-10: 0-692-60190-2
ISBN-13: 978-0-692-60190-7

Library of Congress Control Number: 2015960192

Publisher's Cataloging-In-Publication Data
(Prepared by The Donohue Group, Inc.)

Names: Bergengren, David.
Title: Hitler's Assassin / by David Bergengren.
Description: First Stillwater River Publications edition. | Glocester, RI, USA :
    Stillwater River Publications, [2016]
Identifiers: LCCN 2015960192 | ISBN 978-0-692-60190-7 | ISBN 0-692-60190-2
Subjects: LCSH: Germany. Heer--Officers--Fiction. | Jewish journalists--Fiction. |
    War crime trials--South America--Fiction. | Official secrets--Western countries.
    | Hitler, Adolf, 1889-1945--Assassination--Fiction. | Cold War--Fiction. | Espi-
    onage, Soviet--Fiction.
Classification: LCC PS3602.E74 H58 2016 | DDC 813/.6--dc23

1 2 3 4 5 6 7 8 9 10
Written by David Bergengren
Cover Concept by David Bergengren. Cover design by Dawn M. Porter.
Cover photo of clouds by Jim Gipe/Pivot Media
Author photo by Holly Angelo
Published by Stillwater River Publications, Glocester, RI, USA

The author thanks
Jon Bergengren, Holly Angelo,
Stan Freeman, Fred Contrada,
Suzanne Strempek Shea, Tommy Shea,
Adam Trott, Joe Pennell, Professor John Adams,
Ellen Levine, Erica Spellman-Silverman,
Steven and Dawn Porter
– and his parents, for their lifelong support.

With a special thanks to
Steven Spielberg
for the inspiration of his
magnificent film version of
Thomas Keneally's
"Schindler's List"

For Holly

"I raised my head. The offing was barred by a black bank of clouds, and the tranquil waterway leading to the uttermost ends of the earth flowed somber under an overcast sky – seemed to lead into the heart of an immense darkness."

Joseph Conrad

"After all, who remembers the Armenians?"

Adolf Hitler

22 August 1944
Salzburg, Ostmark

There was a good chance he was about to commit suicide, Johann Richter knew. He checked and rechecked the rifle a dozen times, noting the irony of its American manufacture.

His father had never shared Hitler's down-the-nose attitude toward Americans and their products and had kept the weapon in excellent condition. The more likely problem would be his own marksmanship. His target would be well over a hundred meters away, at a long downhill angle. It would be a difficult shot. He would need luck, as well as a firm hand.

Finally, shortly after 5:45, with the sun still strong, a motorized escort pulled into the parking lot of the train station. A double cordon of SS men flanked four limousines as they disgorged a small torrent of military VIPs. Richter held his breath to flatten out any potential shakiness. This was not the moment to falter. He tried to pick Hitler apart from the rest with the Remington's sniper sight. When he didn't spot him, he had to force himself not to panic. He could hear his own strained breathing. Each time he inhaled, he grew more nauseous at the smell of gun grease from the well-oiled firearm cradled against his cheek.

The first of the high-ranking officers were already nearing the station building. From out of nowhere, Adolf Hitler suddenly appeared in Richter's sights. He took steady aim at the instantly recognizable profile, asking God to forgive him for what he was about to do. His body relaxed and an immense feeling of relief flooded through him. It felt as if a force outside him had taken control of the rifle.

But as he touched his index finger to the trigger and slowly, carefully increased the pressure, the telescopic sight abruptly turned fire-red. Hitler's profile had been replaced by the brick wall of the station building. Richter had missed his chance. Maybe his only chance. He was furious, frantic.

Then very quickly it appeared he would have one more opening, as Hitler's entourage began moving out from the protective cover of the building and down along the open platform toward the rear of the train.

He scanned the crowd of uniforms. Hitler was about to board the train but had stopped to confer with a Kriegsmarine admiral. This time the Fuhrer was facing Richter directly. He looked somehow different. Heavier, perhaps, more jowly. Aiming at the bridge of his nose, Richter experienced one last wave of doubt. He remembered what Heinrich Mueller had said about aiming at a live target. Palms sweating, fingers icy, unable to make the final irrevocable decision, he pictured all he had lost because of this man and finally let his finger move against the trigger.

For a split second, perhaps hearing the gun's report, Hitler stared straight up the sniper sight, a look of startled recognition on his face. . .

CHAPTER I

She opened her mouth to scream, but nothing came out. The SS officer was belting her with a leather whip, raising ropes of blood across her bare back. The crack of the whip was the only sound. The woman was stretched over a large metal drum. Her eyes screamed, but not her voice.

Michael Cohen watched, helpless, locked in a familiar impotence that terrified and enraged him. The SS man took the woman by the hair and forced her to her knees to beg for mercy. When she refused, he laughed, put a boot to her chest and shoved, knocking her to the feet of another man.

This part was new. This man's face was blank. He took the woman into his arms – gently or roughly, it was impossible to tell. Her face, too, was unreadable, but Cohen sensed this second man might be trying to protect her, and his fear and anger were twisted into an unexpected pang of jealousy just as he surfaced from sleep.

His forehead beaded with sweat, Cohen stared out the window of the plane trying to jettison this all-too-familiar nightmare. The sensation was one of floating, and he tried to set his mind free, let it wander out beyond the tips of the wings, out above the soft white clouds pierced here and there by a stark shadowed pinnacle shooting up from the Andes.

He felt a little dazed. He knew almost nothing about South America. The city of La Negra was a total mystery to him. It had been a long trip. He had left New York yesterday morning. Tomorrow he would be in a courtroom looking an accused Nazi war criminal in the eye. The thought made him as uneasy as the nightmare had.

"Please fasten your seatbelt, sir. We are starting our descent into La Negra." A tall bottle-blond Pan Am stewardess was addressing him. She held her hand out for the half-filled glass of blended whiskey he was drinking. He drained it and handed it to her.

The passenger cabin of the old warhorse Lockheed Constellation felt cramped after nearly four hours in the air since a stop in Caracas, but the flight, most of it at 20,000 feet, had been remarkably smooth. He had overheard this stewardess tell a passenger the plane had been used by the U.S. Army Air Corps during the war. Maybe he had seen it before, over German skies. One more layer of irony – or perhaps absurdity – to add to his mission.

The stewardess, distracted now by a passenger flirting with her on the other side of the aisle, seemed to him somehow out of place here. His eye caught the name-tag pinned above her right breast, "Ariel." He couldn't make out the last name, but its mere configuration, many-syllabled and ending in "i," was enough to strike a vague chord in him. It made him think of Israel, and of Rachel. With effort, he put clamps on the thought.

"Excuse me, sir. Your seatbelt," she repeated as she turned and found him neglecting her instructions. He obediently snapped his seat-belt in place. Still the good German. In spite of everything. She smiled patiently and moved on down the aisle reminding other passengers, "We are starting our descent into La Negra."

Cohen stared back out the window. Catching his own reflection in the window glass, he looked away self-consciously. He had strong, sharp features. Women seemed to like him, but he thought little about his appearance.

This trip for some reason reminded him of how he had felt leaving Germany and arriving in England after the war. With nothing. No family, no money, no country. Nothing but what his British handlers had in mind for him. He had never quite gotten comfortable during his time in London. He felt better now that he was living in New York, near his German-American roots. The city's bubbling melting pot of anonymity suited him.

Needing something to do, he took a newspaper clipping from his shirt pocket and examined it. There were two photos, supposedly of the same man, at the top of the carefully folded story. In one the man looked like a prep school student of the 1920s or '30s, young, chiseled and confident. In the other he appeared to be perhaps in his late thirties, graying at the temples, with tired, intelligent eyes. A thin scar cut across the cheekbone under his right eye.

The item was from an edition of the *Times* of London of several months earlier, dated 24 January 1952, the sidebar to a daily news story. For about the twentieth time, Cohen reread it:

While researching background material for the upcoming South American extradition hearing of former Wehrmacht colonel Johann Richter, this reporter came across a related story published by the Times nearly six years ago about his father, General Karl Richter.

Though of potentially substantial interest – to historians, if not to the present Conservative government – the questions it raises appear never to have been followed up.

The story was printed without a byline. Attempts to uncover its author have been unsuccessful.

Dated 21 July 1946, from London, it reads as follows:

Oxford University professor Robert Edward Klinesmith yesterday asserted Great Britain may have played a role in the 20 July 1944 effort by German army officers to assassinate Adolf Hitler.

Speaking at a Royal Historical Society commemoration of the second anniversary of the nearly successful assassination attempt, Mr. Klinesmith said any role played by Her Majesty's Secret Intelligence Service branch MI6 most likely would have been facilitated by German General Karl von Richter.

"Von Richter was a high-ranking member of the Wehrmacht's General Staff, and I believe him to have been an early and rather prominent member of the German military clique that opposed Hitler from 1933 on," Mr. Klinesmith said.

Mr. Klinesmith claimed he had seen copies of top-secret British Intelligence memoranda that made it quite clear SIS – commonly known as MI6 and responsible for intelligence operations overseas – had made contact with von Richter beginning as early as the late 1930s.

"This contact was for the purpose of encouraging a political opposition to Hitler and the Nazis inside Germany," Mr. Klinesmith submitted. The intent might even have included promoting the possibility of political change through an assassination of the German Fuhrer, he said.

This latter hypothesis was the object of a good deal of skepticism during the question and answer portion of Mr. Klinesmith's programme. Particular doubt was expressed over the likelihood British Intelligence would have promoted the assassination of Hitler as early as September 1938 when then-Prime Minister Neville Chamberlain was dealing so liberally with him at Munich and elsewhere.

Mr. Klinesmith conceded the available evidence was sketchy. He pointed out, on the other hand, the implications to be drawn from the actions of Karl von Richter's son Johann, who attended public school in England in the 1930s and spent the first half of the war here. During the early war years the younger von Richter secretly lobbied Whitehall in pursuit of support for a military coup d'etat in Germany, Mr. Klinesmith maintained. He also interrogated captured enemy fliers for MI6 and its domestic counterpart MI5, Mr. Klinesmith said.

Johann von Richter disappeared from London, returning to Germany via an unknown escape route in June 1943 after he had become the prime suspect in the notorious and still officially unsolved murder case of Christine Johns, 27-year-old daughter of Tory M.P. Lord Neville Johns, Fifth Earl of Darbyshire. In early 1944, as a newly-minted Wehrmacht *oberstleutnant*, he relieved the infamous Gerhardt Gruning as commander of the German garrison in the occupied French city of St. Sentione, north of Lyon.

His ultimate fate is as yet unknown. Despite several unauthenticated sightings in South America over the past few years, it is generally assumed he died in the aftermath of 20 July, Mr. Klinesmith said, exhibiting a short obituary to that effect published by a Berlin newspaper in September 1944.

Professor Robert Edward Klinesmith, who taught at Magdalen College, Oxford, had been researching a comprehensive study that sought to unravel, as he put it, the many mysteries of the military life, customs and personalities of the Third Reich.

Before he could publish the results of his investigations, Mr. Klinesmith died at the age of 55, in London, on 3 March 1948, his death a presumed suicide. He apparently destroyed his papers before taking his life.

One mystery, however, has now been cleared up. Johann Richter survived the war. He was found last month, living on a farm in the South American jungle under the name "Eric Altmann."

Richter was taken into custody and is scheduled to appear before an extradition hearing in the capital city of La Negra next week to determine whether he will be brought to trial in England and France on charges of murder and possible genocide. Prosecutors are also investigating an alleged connection Richter had with SS Standartenfuhrer Heinrich Mueller, commandant of Kaisenher, a satellite camp of Dachau.

Efforts to elicit comment from anyone in the Churchill government or in MI6 have thus far been unsuccessful, though one source who wished to remain anonymous questioned whether Mr. Klinesmith would have had access to top-secret documents.

It was this extradition hearing and the possibility Richter had had dealings with Heinrich Mueller that was bringing Michael Cohen to La Negra. Postponed nearly three months, the hearing was now scheduled to start tomorrow. Cohen's mission was personal, but as a journalist, despite his better judgment, he had also agreed to write about the proceedings, and about Richter. "Let the reader know what makes this guy tick," were his marching orders.

Something began to shake his thoughts out; landing wheels on concrete bumping him back to earth.

The plane coasted, stopped. Cohen, waiting for the aisle to clear, was the recipient of what he took to be a veiled smile from Ariel. The look seemed somehow different from the ones she was doling out on automatic pilot to the other deplaning passengers. Or was that just him, the lack of trust he always felt in the presence of a smile? Any smile.

"We hope you had a nice flight sir," she said, the smile beginning to fade.

CHAPTER II

El Morro Prison
La Negra

Today was Hitler's birthday. April 20, 1952. He would've been, what? Sixty-two? No, sixty-three. An old man almost.

At the moment, Johann Richter felt like an old man himself. The wound in his left side, which hadn't bothered him in years, had started acting up again when he was tossed in prison. He wasn't getting much sleep. One more day and he would be in court, his fate hanging in the balance.

He stared through the bars of a long rectangular window that opened out across a short field at eye level then dropped off toward the ancient center of La Negra. His cell was a fortress dungeon, cold at night, but the barred window had no glass or screen in it and let in a good deal of sunlight, particularly in the morning. They had given him writing materials. He had a few of his books. All was not lost.

He sometimes wondered what it would have been like if Hitler had won his war. Could it have been much worse than it was now? Stalin would have been gone years ago, consigned to the dustbin of history where he belonged. Hitler would've backed Chang Kai-Shek or the Japanese in China. He would never have allowed Mao Tse-tung to seize power. Communism would be dead, instead of threatening to devour the globe. There would have been no war in Korea. No six Soviet armored divisions in East Germany. Who knows? he thought.

It might have been a more peaceful world. And one without nuclear weapons had the war ended soon enough.

His father had been right: For better or for worse, the Fuhrer had changed the face of history. Forever. Even in defeat. If he had won, once he had gotten everything he wanted, he might have been generous, magnanimous even, with his defeated foes. On the other hand of course there would have been a price to pay, and the Jews and the Slavs would already have paid it.

Such musings inevitably led to thoughts of Elena. He could not fend them off. It was painful. He tried not to think of her except at night, when he tried to sleep. Her absence left an emptiness at the core of his being. And in the final analysis, he knew, even more than his father and his own family, she was why Hitler had had to die.

He was not looking forward to being in court. He stared out across the rocky fields again toward La Negra. No matter how optimistic he tried to be, he saw little hope for himself out there now. Only the bars of a prison he would never escape.

He turned around. He had been so preoccupied, he hadn't heard Father Felipe Hidalgo, the prison priest, being ushered into the cell.

He managed a smile for his frequent visitor, whose presence he welcomed. "So tomorrow it starts, Father," he said.

"It does, my son. But there is nothing to fear, if you feel settled in your heart."

Father Hidalgo took his customary seat in a chair at the foot of Richter's bed, while the prisoner did likewise at his desk. The priest was an older man of medium height, a little flabby. With eyes that reflected an unpriestly sophistication.

"No one, I'm afraid, can feel truly settled at heart, Father. Certainly not I," Richter said, placing his elbows on his knees and resting his chin in his hands.

"I think you know what I mean. If you are truly innocent of what they accuse you, it will show–"

"We shall see," Richter interrupted the priest. "I'm worried about my family."

"They seemed fine when I was out there. They miss you, of course." Richter's wife, a young German woman named Elena who Father Hidalgo had known for several years, possessed an impressive strength of character he had confirmed during the day he'd spent with her a week earlier. She was holding up bravely. The couple had a baby girl and a son too young to understand much of what was going on with his father.

Richter looked away. Father Hidalgo felt as he often had before with the prisoner. He seemed basically a good man, but there was an unbridgeable gap between them, an emotional moat that surrounded the younger man for which the drawbridge was broken. Richter had, on the other hand, confided bits and pieces of his personal history since Father Hidalgo had first met him and his family nearly four years ago in the jungle outside Riberalta – that he still regretted the death of a woman he had loved during the war; that his father had fought in both world wars, and had been on Hitler's general staff; that just before his capture he had felt as happy with life, his time with his wife and children, as he could ever remember.

He was a handsome man, Father Hidalgo had always thought, with a thin, jagged scar slicing dramatically below his right temple and per-haps contributing to the slightly droopy eyelid on that side. Angular features and thick brown hair that was graying slightly and had not been cut recently. A tall man. At present somewhat worn down, pre-sumably by all he had been through. But still given to sudden unex-pected bursts of energy.

"I don't know, Father. All we wanted was peace, some of us. It was not allowed. Not for Germany. And now, I suppose, not for me." His English had a slight British inflection and was better than his own, thought Father Hidalgo, who had sharpened his delivery as a student at Notre Dame University in the U.S. years ago.

Richter reached into a bag, tore a piece of coca leaf from its stem and put it in his mouth. He started chewing it with an absentminded air. Father Hidalgo did not approve, but had broken down and helped him smuggle the coca into his cell a month ago, swayed by a heartrending plea from Elena that Richter had become intensely de-pressed since his capture and was in pain from a wound he'd received during the war. He needed any remedy he could find, she said. The priest consoled himself that without being processed into cocaine, the coca needed alcohol or some other booster to give it any real kick. And Richter wasn't likely to be drinking much alcohol in here.

Time was short today. Father Hidalgo picked up a tiny silver bell and shook it. Its ring echoed out of all proportion down the dim empty corridor outside the cell. "I must go, my son. I will be back tomorrow after court." He turned toward the sound of someone approaching. "Ah, Frederico. You are always so prompt. Muchas gracias."

A dark, heavyset jailor jangled the door open with a huge set of keys and extended the priest a respectful smile. "Everything I drop when a man of God calls for me."

Father Hidalgo stopped outside the cell door and looked back at Richter, whose attention was still focused elsewhere. The priest took a deep breath, let it out, and walked away with the guard, who acknowledged the prisoner with an abbreviated salute.

Richter took note. Frederico's presence always reminded him of the war. The man was of Italian blood, born in La Negra of parents from the old country. Siena. His sentiments had been torn during the war, from what Richter could gather. He wanted to emigrate to the United States with his family someday and had rooted for the U.S. and her Allies to win. But he had wanted just as much to see Italy survive intact. Each time his chosen country had plunged the dagger deeper into his native land, he had felt the pain deep inside, he'd told Richter, who within a few short weeks inside El Morro had won an exemption from Frederico's hatred of Germans. The guard had turned out to be full of good cheer and small kindnesses. He regularly snuck Elena's letters by the prison's censorship apparatus and delivered them to Richter unopened.

As the echo of footsteps from Frederico and Father Hidalgo died away, Richter felt more alone than ever before. Tomorrow he would be forced to start reliving his past. It was a journey he had hoped never to have to make again. In private, in fact, he had been making it since the moment he'd entered this hellhole several months ago. At the start, the effort had only made him feel like Marlow's Kurtz. All he could remember was the horror. But after a while it had begun to come back to him, and it was not limited to the parts of his past that might be relevant to his defense.

Clearest of all were memories of his father, Karl von Richter, the product of an old Prussian military family with aristocratic roots, one of the youngest members of the Army General Staff. His father had been a distant, often absent but revered figure during Richter's youth. Tall and commanding, he wore a black patch over his left eye, a memento of British shrapnel from the First World War. Imbued with an unshakable belief in himself and the future greatness of Germany, he had rapidly ascended the Reichswehr hierarchy. In 1924 he was posted to the *Truppenamt* of the *Heeresleitung* office, the Army's disguised general staff organization, and the family moved south from its sprawling estate outside Tilsit in East Prussia to "Orienbad," a smaller property near Zossen, still in the countryside but not far from Berlin.

Johann's mother, Frau Gerta Richter, the youngest daughter of a prosperous Tilsit merchant, held a belief in Germany's inherent greatness as strong as her husband's. His two sisters, Ellen and Gretchen, bore names more English than German because Karl Richter thought German names too harsh for females. A French governess named Marie Renault helped look after the children. While most Germans struggled in a devastated economy, these were good years for Johann. There were open fields, icy streams, and a rambling old house to explore and re-explore, to fortify, attack and defend with or against the hordes of imaginary invaders that constantly preyed upon it. He attended a small schoolhouse nearby and his mother granted him an occasional tutor in history, English and literature, the subjects he favored.

Johann was a natural horseman. He could ride at the age of six and was an accomplished rider by the time he was ten, as smooth almost as his father, who had been a cavalryman during the war. Karl Richter made certain his son learned another cavalryman's skill as well. Along with a horse he named Sacha, Johann was given his own rifle, taught to clean and care for it and how to shoot it. How to hunt with it. His marksmanship improved in tandem with his horsemanship.

As he looked back now, it was not difficult to remember when he had first heard of Adolf Hitler and the Nazi Party. It was 1928, he was ten and riding Sacha through the morning fields of Orienbad with his father, something the two of them enjoyed doing together. The elder Richter, in the serious tone that always frightened Johann a little, had very deliberately announced, *"Johann, it is time you and I talked of things more serious than the health and feeding habits of Sacha. . . Do you understand anything of what I have been doing for the past six years?"*

"You are in the army."

"Is that all?"

"You are fighting the enemies of Germany."

His father gave him a curious glance, a quick smile of adult indulgence. "And who are these enemies?" he asked.

"Those who forced us to sign the Treaty of Versailles." Johann looked up at his father.

"But we're not at war with anyone," the elder Richter said, the wry smile lingering. "Who are we fighting?"

"Our enemies inside Germany. The ones who made us lose the war," Johann said.

"And they are. . .?"

"The Jews," he concluded proudly, thinking his father would be pleased at his knowing about the Jews, something he had never taught him. Instead, Karl Richter abruptly reined in his huge, dapple-gray mount and stared down at his son, surprise giving way to something more ominous. Johann, terrified and confused, reined in too and waited in anguish for whatever was coming.

"Who told you this about the Jews?"

He had overheard friends of his mother's, in conversation with her, say this about the Jews. She had said nothing to contradict it. The harshness of his father's implied accusation triggered an instinct to protect his mother. Nervously, he lied. "Eric Hesse told me," he said. The first name that had popped into his head.

"And who is Eric Hesse?"

"A friend of mine."

"You will never speak to him again. Is that clear?"

"Yes." Eric Hesse, thankfully, was not such a close friend.

"The Jews are not the enemies of Germany, and those who think they are, are not only ignorant, but dangerous. Our friends, the Liebermanns. You know the Liebermanns, Johann. Herr Liebermann won the Iron Cross in the war. They are as much true Germans as you and I. Do you understand that?"

"Yes sir." Johann was confused, but this was obviously not the time for uncertainties. He hadn't even known the Liebermanns were Jews.

"Have you ever heard of a man named Adolf Hitler, and this political party of his, the 'Nazis'?" his father asked him.

"No sir." Johann felt as he did in the schoolroom after having made a wrong answer.

"They're a good example of what thinking like your friend Eric Hesse can lead to. A motley bunch of misfits with no talent for anything but street fighting. They're not even very good at that. The Jews were responsible for our losing the war, they say, so they preach that only people of what they call the 'Aryan race' are true Germans and that the Jews and Slavs are meant to be our slaves. This is the logical order of the universe, they say – an absurd idea that's not only wrong, Johann, but immoral. The Jews are not the subhumans, as they call them. If anybody is less than human it's the Nazis."

His father had reached a kind of low-keyed crescendo in his argument, staring straight at Johann while he spoke. Now he looked away across the open fields and said, as much to himself as to his son, "Some of their ideas are good – they hate Communism, for instance. But it doesn't matter. This racial insanity of theirs makes them worthless. . . Do you understand what I am telling you, Johann?"

His father's tone had softened, and Johann wanted only to please with his answer. "Yes Father. That Adolf Hitler is a madman and I am not to hate the Jews and Slavs like Eric Hesse and the Nazis do." Johann watched first a loving, amused smile, then a faraway, distracted look, traverse his father's battle-scarred face. He wondered if his reply had been satisfactory. His father seemed to be mulling its worth.

"Just remember to stay away from Eric Hesse. He is to be your friend no longer." The elder Richter's order had an abstracted air about it, and without awaiting any unnecessary confirmation he wheeled the huge dapple-gray around and began riding away. Johann, puzzled by all that had just passed between them, gave Sacha a light kick and trotted along behind his father, not wishing to catch up for the moment.

This memory blended with thoughts about the early months of his schooling in England, at the start of 1933, and how much he had worried about his father when Hitler was named chancellor. He had been right to worry, he thought now. By 1933 Karl Richter's staff work was with the highest echelons of the German Army. The new general was becoming an important man in Germany, as were all generals, and Johann had instinctively worried about the sudden accession to power of a man his father disliked and distrusted. He knew his father might somehow be endangered by this development and had felt totally powerless to do anything about it.

As the extradition hearing in La Negra neared, he had mulled over this and many other parts of his past in an effort to prepare. He had committed a lengthy narrative of memories to paper to help guide him in court. In a general sense, he felt all right about how he had acquitted himself during the war. There were specifics, however, of which he was not so proud. One in particular still filled him with guilt.

Now everything would be reopened in public, and it would not be pleasant. He would have to walk a difficult tightrope to salvage anything for his family. For himself, it was already too late he thought.

But then again, perhaps not. Father Hidalgo today had brought him a glimmer of hope. A dim one, but a ray of hope nonetheless. He lay back on the bed and shut his eyes. It was going to be a long day and a long night. He wished it could be longer.

CHAPTER III

Stepping off the plane, Michael Cohen was slapped across the face by a cold bitter wind. His left leg ached from the long flight, and his limp felt exaggerated as he crossed the tarmac. He felt dizzy, disconnected, short of breath. It was two o'clock on a Sunday afternoon. The La Negra airport was at thirteen thousand feet.

Moments later he found himself sitting dazed in the backseat of a taxi, watching the local panorama sweep by the windows. La Negra was nestled in a huge mountain valley surrounded by a massive, heroic topography that was barren and forbidding. The sky was close enough to touch, a chalky white, unreal, not like anything Cohen had ever seen before. Against it, the city's mountain sentinels stood out in stark relief, their impressive ring broken only by several giant plateaus, one of which supported the airport. The plateaus swept out into broad flat plains that seemed either to run up against more snow-capped peaks in the distance or to drop off into space.

His taxi began descending into the earthen bowl of La Negra. The first thing Cohen noticed, off to his right, was the famed Lake Tocqual sparkling out to the horizon, far reaches lost between the distant mountains on its opposite shore. On a nearer shore, further to his right, the capital city's only modern high-rises gleamed bone white in the midday brightness.

People began to move past the window in front of him. Mestizos. Dark Spanish-Indians, poor. Many of the women sported white panama hats. All of them wore bright-colored dresses made of heavy cloth. Some of the men were in military uniform – olive green, with red stripes down the trousers, peaked caps. In closer toward the bottom of the bowl, bars, prostitutes and other merchants appeared; open marketplaces, dogs prowling below food carts.

The Hotel Miranda, an ancient four-story pile of crumbling stucco, was at the very edge of this part of the city, its back jammed up against the side of a steep hill. Inside, a surprisingly luxurious red-carpeted lobby led to a bar and a dining room, an elevator that was out of order, and the staircase. After a puffing, oxygen-hungry climb, Cohen stepped inside his two-room "suite" on the top floor. It was so stuffy he could hardly breathe. As he plunged, feeling nauseous, across the room and out onto a balcony, he made a mental note of the bright red resuscitator sitting in one corner.

The shock of cold fresh air cleared his head. He began to refocus. The view was startling, out over the rooftops of La Negra to the mountain peaks and huge lake that lay on the city's far side. In local lore, Cohen had read, Lake Tocqual was where creation had begun, where God had emerged from the waters to make the sun, the moon and the stars, and ordered the sun to travel east to west in its daily arc. Where too His subjects would eventually seek to appease His perceived whims with human sacrifices.

Etched against the mountains and blank sky, the lake's surface was an off-shade of turquoise glimmering in the late afternoon sun, so placid it seemed an illusion. The cityscape was a cold combination of less inspired hues – whites, blacks, greens and blues. Cohen shivered and limped back into the room, shutting the sun-drenched balcony off behind him.

He had forgotten the short dark boy with blazing white teeth who had introduced himself in the lobby and helped carry his bags. Cohen took out his wallet and handed an American dollar bill to the boy, who received it eagerly.

"You feel not good, Señor? I have a help." The boy produced a small bag from beneath his shirt, took out a wilted green leaf, tore it in half, popped it into his mouth and chewed. "Coca," he said. "Good for the mountains." He handed a leaf to Cohen, who nibbled at the edge out of curiosity. It tasted bittersweet and numbed his tongue.

"Two dollars, American." The boy held out the bag.

Cohen, amused, said "No. Gracias." Alcohol was his numbing agent of choice. He went into the bathroom for a drink of water. When he returned, the boy was gone.

Cohen explored his rooms. They looked the same, were connected by a bathroom with shower. He had to duck his head to clear the doorways. Each sparsely furnished room had a large creaky double bed pushed up against one wall and a brightly colored oval throw rug in the middle of the floor. One room had a large easy chair and a desk, the other a small couch. Cohen, deciding to headquarter in one room, moved the chair and desk in with the couch, then sat down in the chair and promptly fell asleep.

* * * *

When he awoke an hour or so later he felt better. In the bathroom, he splashed water on his face and combed his thick unruly hair. He stood out on the balcony, bathed in the dull light of late afternoon, and took a few deep breaths. Suddenly restless, he descended the stairs, received directions from the Miranda desk clerk and struck out through a maze of streets that wound and twisted with no discernible order.

His leg felt better, but he found he had to pace himself against the thin air. It occurred to him he hadn't spotted another European or American since the airport. At his retarded speed, it took nearly an hour to find his way to El Morro, as the prison was called, a Seventeenth-Century Spanish fort stuck high up on a bluff near the center of town. The heavy mound of stone and iron bars was sunk deep into the hill it dominated. Its forbidding air was due in part to its empty look, as if it were deserted. The hill it sat upon was surrounded by narrow alleyways lined with dingy bars and decrepit flophouses.

Cohen stared at the prison and tried to imagine the man inside. Thirty-four years old. Not much older than he. A fellow German, though Cohen identified himself more as an American now. Richter had been some kind of Nazi spy it appeared. Commandant of the German garrison at St.Sentione during the final days of the occupation of France. Cohen had researched him as best he could, but aside from his fellow traveler in folly Terry Harper's secondhand account, little information had been available, not even of Richter's years in England. Only news clips on the murder of Christine Johns.

He felt an odd blend of emotions. Repugnance at the very thought of the man. The idea of confronting Richter made him feel physically sick. But the man's life, what he knew of it so far, raised compelling questions. Primary among them: What was Richter to Heinrich Mueller? And had he had anything to do with Mueller's Kaisenher, sister camp to Dachau? If the answer to that one was yes, Cohen had no idea what he would do about it. But he had to know.

Strangely enough, he felt a sense of connection as well. As improbable as it seemed, his own life in some ways mirrored Richter's. Ultimately, he supposed that was why he was here. As if all the terror, all the guilt, might somehow find an explanation inside the walls of this prison.

He reminded himself this man was almost certainly a killer. One clever enough to have escaped the Nazi Gotterdammerung. There were supposedly others in the neighborhood: Bormann, Eichmann, Mengele – Klaus Barbie, "The Butcher of Lyon," who had held a position in France similar to Richter's. Cohen knew from personal experience how tenacious the Israelis and their Nazi hunters could be, but these men were not easy to bring to justice. It gave him a vague sense of hope that this one, at least, had been run to ground – that in spite of a local government sympathetic to Nazis, here he was, behind bars and about to go on trial.

He wondered if he could really write about this guy. Jack Ames, his editor at *World Horizons*, thought he could, but Jack Ames didn't really know him. He had only freelanced for the magazine. When he'd told Jack he was going to La Negra, Jack had used all his considerable powers of persuasion to talk him into writing about it for *WoHo*, as the prestigious monthly was called, sometimes affectionately, by insiders. Cohen had even allowed himself to accept an advance, because he needed it. But could he really write about the man in this prison with any objectivity? He doubted it.

He had not told Jack Ames about Terry Harper. There was, he thought, too much an element of absurdity in what had brought him to this spot, standing outside this prison in the middle of a strange city, in the middle of a strange country and continent. Sent here from beyond the grave by an old man he hadn't even known all that well, and now would never know any better because he was dead.

Terence Harper-Smythe was a transplanted Englishman whose roots had taken so well in the New World that he had dropped the "Smythe" from everything but his byline, pulled for the Yankees and talked more like a New Yorker than the Oxbridge man he had once been. He'd been a curiosity, something of a mysterious figure – no family, no close friends, and writing projects that took him to distant corners of the globe and that no one knew anything about unless they happened to see the end result in print. Which was not often, because Harper was secretive, a freelancer who published primarily in sleazy periodicals. He had written for the London tabloids before he had transferred his skills, quite logically and with purple prose intact – *Reardon was called "The Hawk," not because of his prominent beak, but for his skill at the toughest of all blood sports, hunting his fellow man* – to American magazines with names like "True Adventures" or "The Mercenary Monthly."

He and Cohen had become friends, or at least friendly, Cohen had always suspected, largely because of Harper's obsession with the war and his fascination with Cohen's angle on it, including his German-American pedigree.

It hadn't hurt either that Cohen had once played a role, however minor, in the Israeli War for Independence. The Englishman had frequently asked him about it. Cohen never told him much. Never, for instance, that he'd been sent to Palestine by the British to infiltrate Haganah, the Jews' primary fighting force there. In spite of his British background, Harper, Cohen had always suspected, would not have approved.

Harper had plenty of secrets of his own. Two months ago, though, he had sought Cohen out and raised the corner on a curtain that cloaked one of his biggest ones. In the best tradition of widescreen melodrama, Harper had entrusted him with a thin manila envelope, which he made Cohen swear never to open unless and until he knew Terry Harper was a dead man.

Trying not to laugh, because Harper's sensitivities were notoriously hair-trigger, Cohen had agreed. "You're the only one I can trust with this," Harper had told him. "I fully expect to live long enough to retrieve it from you, but in the meantime I feel better that you have it, old boy. You may consider this a sign of respect. If you ever have to open it, you will know what I mean."

Two weeks later Terry Harper had taken a spectacular nose dive from the nineteenth floor balcony of his apartment in Brooklyn Heights. A suicide, it was ruled. The next day Cohen had opened the envelope. Inside was a key to a safe-deposit box and a note revealing in which bank the box resided.

The safe-deposit box had yielded a manuscript and another brief note:

Cohen, the story in here, such as it is, is about a man named Johann Richter. I met him during the war while I was assigned to MI6, a branch of British Intelligence. He was in England on a rather bizarre mission, which is explained, to the full extent of my knowledge, in these pages. When he was accused of murder, in 1943, he escaped back into Germany. By the end of the war he had disappeared and was presumed dead. But not by us. We had reason to believe otherwise.

In the late '40s, on assignment for a magazine – a legit rag, by the way – I tracked him down in South America and met with him in La Negra. It took me awhile to bring him around, particularly because he knew me from my days with MI6, but eventually he told me quite a lot about himself. He is an interesting chap. He implied at one point, for instance, that he had shot Hitler, that he himself had shot Hitler, sometime late in the war after the infamous botched assassination attempt in '44. I asked him if he was trying to say he killed Hitler, and all the bugger would do was smile. I could not wring anything more out of him, try as I might.

From South America, I went to England and the continent to find several of the characters mentioned in the pages enclosed here. I got in deeper and deeper, fascinated, started to put it all together and write it up, but I realized I would have to see Richter again. When I returned he was gone. This time there was no finding him. I came back to New York and made a stab at finishing the story, but it didn't click. Too many connections were missing. It was all too incredible. It sounded like a bloody schoolboy concoction. "The Fables of La Negra" I thought I might call it. But I wasn't writing this one for the tabs, was I. Eventually I gave up. Terribly disappointing. Nothing was ever published.

Last week I found out Richter had been picked up, taken without a struggle it was said, by the authorities in La Negra – actually it seems he was bagged by Shin Bet, or one of your other Israeli Nazi-hunting groups, and they bollixed getting him out of the country. Now apparently there is to be an "extradition hearing" or some such non-sense down there. I would love to attend. Unfortunately a few dodgy

*political complications left over from last time are holding up my visa.
In the meantime, some strange thoughts have come to me. This manuscript has been seen by people on both sides of the Pond, and there
is some sensitivity, governmental sensitivity, toward this man here and
in Britain. I think my old colleagues in MI6 may be shadowing me.
Want to catch me with my wanker in my hand. Maybe I'm being paranoid. If you're reading this, however, perhaps not.*

*My thought is that you might be interested in giving all this a go
yourself. If you decide to look into it, be on your guard. Why, or for
exactly what, I don't know. Just keep an eye out, dear boy.*

Good hunting. Terry Harper

Cohen was well-acquainted with MI6. Nothing they might do
would surprise him. Including heaving a former colleague off a nineteenth floor balcony.

Harper's manuscript, a combination of narrative and random
notes, was in essence the story of Johann Richter's life. Incomplete
but full of intriguing tidbits. Some of them seemingly unrelated to
Richter. It was full of hints about wartime conspiracies – by Hitler,
against Hitler, by British Intelligence and the Americans' Office of
Strategic Services. Harper believed that Communists, Stalin's men,
had infiltrated MI6 during the war. Mentioning the two British Foreign Office officials, Guy Burgess and Donald Maclean, who had defected to Moscow just the year before, he theorized the Soviets' pil-
fering of atomic and other secrets had simply shifted after the war
from Nazi Germany to the U.S. and England, with the unwitting MI6
used as cover both times.

Harper said he had it on good authority that someone higher up
was suspected as well. He even had a candidate of his own, a marginal
acquaintance from his days in MI6, one Harold "Kim" Philby – "a
Cambridge man I never quite trusted." Philby was a former head of
the Secret Intelligence Service's anti-Soviet section, who had since
become an MI6 liaison officer with the American CIA and FBI in
Washington, D.C. A man with a background intertwined with Burgess
and Maclean, perfectly placed to be a Soviet mole, Harper wrote.

It was difficult for Cohen to assess how grounded the many suspicions and instances of finger-pointing in the manuscript might be.
The posthumous gift from Harper muddied the waters more than

cleared them, but had helped hook Cohen into taking a look for himself.

The cold wind was picking up again as twilight came on. Cohen turned away from the prison. He zipped his jacket up and trudged on. There seemed to be no horizontal in La Negra. Traversing one hill was only prelude to the next, and his exerted breathing grew louder. He passed no other *norteamericanos* or Europeans in this part of town. No one looked at him; no one but the street urchins, who didn't bother to put out a hand for money. He thought some of the locals looked strange, kind of glassy-eyed and detached from their surroundings. But then maybe he looked the same. That's how he felt, glassy-eyed and detached.

He navigated by the setting sun rather than ask questions. His leg starting to hurt, feeling a little dizzy again, he finally succumbed to the lure of a small cafe. It had round wooden tables and sturdy metal chairs and opened out onto a side street. It did not, unfortunately, serve liquor.

Cohen bought a Coke at the bar and took it to a table. He was the only customer. As he sat in the gathering mists sipping from the familiar-shaped bottle labeled "Disfrute Coca-Cola," the waitress, a dark petite woman of indeterminate age, approached.

"You are American?" she said after he had ordered.

"Uh, yes, I guess I am." It was the simplest answer. And he *was* an American, technically. Born in New York. An American mother, American passport. Now back in New York again. It pleased him she took his accent to be from the U.S.

He decided to take an impromptu poll. In his feeble, halting Spanish, he asked the waitress what she thought of the extradition case against Johann Richter.

She looked at him blankly.

"Eric Altmann," he corrected himself.

Her answer surprised him.

"Ah," her eyes lighted up. "Señor Altmann. In El Morro. I am told he is a good man, a farmer. A friend to the people. Do you know him?"

Cohen shook his head. The woman seemed disappointed. She brought him his food and left him alone.

A few lingering rays of orange still haloed the mountain range to the west beyond Lake Tocqual, as Cohen, halfway back to the Miranda, welcomed a second wind into his gut and began to feel like his feet were touching ground again. Then all at once the dying mountain light was extinguished, as streetlights flared on all around him. A sudden brightness lit the naked ugliness of the city and darkened the mysterious beauty of the jagged peaks and open plateaus that surrounded it.

For an instant Cohen felt a trill of loneliness shudder through him, the kind of loneliness that excites, though, rather than dulls, the senses. The other kind of loneliness he knew all too well. He thought he could hear the rumble of thunder building somewhere out in the darkness and hurried his pace a bit.

Two blocks short of the Miranda he stopped to catch his breath. As he did, he happened to look back and notice a tall, bearded white man tailing about fifty feet behind him, looking in his direction. When Cohen stared at him the man quickly glanced away and turned a corner out of view.

Cohen took a few more deep breaths and moved on.

CHAPTER IV

Monday morning, Cohen awoke early to a cold blue sky so heavy it seemed to seal in his Miranda balcony. He dressed, decided against breakfast, and struck out for the courthouse. The walk took him half an hour, but his leg held up okay. He arrived about fifteen minutes before the extradition hearing was scheduled to begin.

The courthouse was a 200-year-old stucco building with an eroding facade of bland color and unremarkable design. The visitors gallery could hold a couple of hundred people. There were about twenty-five present when Cohen arrived. As he walked down the middle aisle, his attention was drawn to the massive bench that dominated the front of the courtroom. More suited to the Spanish Inquisition than to a modern court of law, Cohen thought, it loomed above the spectator seating and emanated a threatening, magisterial air.

He took a seat on the right-hand side. Looking around, he saw no familiar faces.

A short, wiry man made his way down the middle aisle carrying a 16-millimeter movie camera. He was followed by an older man with sound equipment. The two set themselves up toward the front of the room, over to one side, the camera on a tripod, the sound equipment on a wooden table out from which several microphones dangled freely into the air.

Cohen took out a notebook and started doodling in it, a habit he'd picked up during the war. He sketched the two-man camera crew and their equipment.

"Pretty good." A man on his right was addressing him. "Your drawing, I mean."

"Who are they?" Cohen asked.

"BBC crew," the man said. He stuck his hand out. "John Weaver, *Baltimore Sun*. You and I seem to be the only reporters here. Real ones, anyway." He nodded toward the BBC crew. Maybe in his mid-thirties, he wore wire-rimmed glasses and a smile Cohen, as usual, did not entirely trust.

Cohen wondered if it were really that obvious he was a writer. He felt no need to disabuse this guy of the notion he was a "real reporter," but qualified his status with, "I'm just freelancing."

"Oh yeah? Who for?"

Cohen was not interested in conversation. "Nobody, really," he said.

His interrogator was undeterred. "Freelancer, huh. I've done my share of that. Tough work. No leverage."

Cohen smiled noncommittally.

"Where you from?" Weaver said.

"New York."

"The Big Apple, eh? I lived there for a while, right after college. Great town."

When Cohen said nothing in reply, Weaver pushed on. "I'm just happy this thing's in English," he said with a flick of his hand that indicated the trial. "I'd never have gotten this assignment if they'd done it in Spanish. My editor would've said 'adios muchacho,' thought he was being Milton Berle, and that would've been that."

On the bench between Cohen and Weaver was a four-day-old *New York Times*.

"Would you mind if I took a look at this," Cohen said, patting the paper.

"Be my guest. The Senators lost. I'm done with it." Weaver looked a little disappointed. Maybe it was the Senators, Cohen thought. The *Times*, in its inimitable fashion, managed as always to reduce the chaos of world events into a smooth if somewhat dry libation for its readers. Cohen couldn't find anything on President Truman's recent decision not to seek re-election, or on rumors General Eisenhower might run for president. Maybe too much else was happening. There was the stalemated war in Korea, fighting between France and the Communist Vietminh in Indochina, and several stories on domestic Red-baiting featuring Senator Joseph R. McCarthy and the House

Committee on Un-American Activities. Secretary of Defense Robert A. Lovett was warning the American Society of Newspaper Editors, "We must stop World War Three before it starts."

A page two story caught Cohen up short. Stalin, it said, was believed to be speeding up his efforts to get the hydrogen bomb through espionage. The *Times* investigative reporter pointed out that two months following the pronouncement of death sentences for Julius and Ethel Rosenberg, for allegedly handing atomic secrets to the Soviets, two former officials of the British Foreign Office, Guy Burgess and Donald Maclean, had defected to Moscow. British Intelligence and the American Central Intelligence Agency, he wrote, were now pulling out all the stops to find a "Third Man," another Soviet infiltrator reputed to have been spy master for the defectors.

Terry Harper's notes had mentioned Burgess and Maclean, Cohen remembered. As well as another British operative Harper thought was suspect – Kim Philby, the Cambridge man he didn't trust.

He put the newspaper down and looked around the courtroom. There were three or four more new faces in the visitors' gallery.

"Pretty grim news, eh?" his uninvited companion observed. "If you really wanta be depressed," John Weaver said, "check out the sports pages. Your Yankees lost worse than my Senators did. Or are you a Bums fan?"

"I don't really follow baseball," Cohen said. He once had, though. When his family had left New York for Germany twenty years ago, to join his father there, he'd been about to try out for Little League. He had loved the Yankees. But now these things seemed part of some ancient world.

"Careful. They'll be hauling you up before the House Un-American Activities Committee," Weaver grinned.

Cohen conceded a grudging smile and went back to the news. Buried on the back pages, he found a brief mention of Johann Richter's extradition hearing in La Negra. It included nothing he did not already know.

On the facing page, Israeli Prime Minister David Ben-Gurion was quoted as telling a Manhattan fundraising event that his young nation, not yet four years old, remained surrounded by Arab states that refused to make peace and was beset by "enormous difficulties, internal and external."

An understatement, Cohen thought. That Israel was playing David to the Arab world's Goliath was a given. But on top of that, there were the British, who for years had done everything in their power to help Goliath crush the pesky David. And to his lasting shame, he had helped them. The British had been liberators, from where he had stood at the time. But the liberators of the Jews of Europe had been their oppressors in Palestine. It had just taken him too long to see it. By then–

Cohen's daydreams of Zion were interrupted by a sudden commotion at the back of the courtroom. He turned just in time to catch an imposing man of perhaps thirty-five or forty, tall, with broad, slightly stooped shoulders and freshly trimmed dark hair, on his way down the aisle trailed by two guards with holstered pistols. Unshackled, the prisoner kept his eyes pointed straight ahead. With the hint of a smile on his face, he looked much as he had in the more recent newspaper photograph – fine features, a high forehead and trim physique. The scar below his eye was thin but purple and more dramatic than in the news photo. Even dressed in a suit coat that had seen better days, and no tie, he possessed an upper-class aura that belied the tag of simple farmer the waitress had bestowed on him last night.

The little entourage took their places at the front of the courtroom, on the left-hand side, the prisoner sitting behind a table perpendicular to the rows of spectator benches. Beside him was a squat, balding man paging intently through a thick black book that lay open in front of him.

Facing the defendant across the room was the prosecutor's table, behind which the chief prosecutor and an assistant were flanked by one legal representative each from England and France, who were in turn each flanked by an Israeli lawyer, the latter officially acting only as informal advisors in the case.

In spite of his antipathy toward Richter/Altmann, Cohen couldn't help feeling the opposing lineups were unfairly balanced.

The judge entered the courtroom from his chambers behind the Bench. Everyone stood while he ascended to his lofty perch, then sat in unison at his direction. From where Cohen sat, he was an impressive head full of gray hair setting off a huge pair of impassive eyes, slack neck disappearing into flowing black robes.

The prisoner and his lawyer were summoned to stand before the Bench. The defendant stood a full head taller than his diminutive defender.

Cohen primed himself to catch anything that might connect this man to the concentration camps.

"Eric Altmann, you have been accused by two sovereign nations" – the judge's voice was deep and powerful, but softened by its Latin cadence – "that of Great Britain and that of France, of having committed high crimes of international law within their respective jurisdictions during the 1939 to 1945 World War. This hearing will seek not to determine your guilt or innocence, but rather whether enough evidence exists against you to obligate this court to order your extradition to either of those countries, or both, to stand trial for your alleged crimes."

The judge's English was excellent. His deep intonation and sing-song cadence lent his speech an almost religious dimension, Cohen thought. The absurd height of the Bench added to the on-high sense of the proceedings.

He caught only snippets of the hearing's first exchange, as the proceedings veered into the technical realm. The gist was that there would be no jury and no appellate court. Whether extradition would occur was solely up to this judge. There was no further explanation of the charges.

In a high-pitched, almost falsetto voice contrasting with the judge's, Richter's lawyer, a Mr. Hiram Benevides, readily acknowledged his client was not "Eric Altmann." The accent was distinctly British – heavier than Richter's, who followed with an even, crisply articulated response to the judge's question of why he had been using an assumed name. "Because I have been hunted," the defendant said, a subtle undercurrent in his voice deflecting the implied accusation.

"Then you have had good reason to assume you might one day be brought to task for acts committed under the name of Johann von Richter?"

"If it please Your Honor," Mr. Benevides interjected. "We prefer simply 'Johann Richter.'"

"Very well. Mr. Richter?"

The prisoner did not respond. He looked away and rubbed the scar on his cheek, as if contemplating something.

The judge paused, his eyes turning more intense as they searched Richter's. "Let us proceed then," he said finally. "Be seated."

The rest of the morning was given over to procedural questions, as more spectators continued to file into the courtroom.

The judge ruled that witnesses, particularly since there were so few, would be allowed to tell their stories without interruption. Within reason, at any rate.

"As this is an extradition hearing, not a trial, we want to get as much truth out on the table as possible," he said.

During a late morning recess, from what Cohen could pick up, the only general agreement among the courtroom audience so far was that Richter's fate was already sealed, that he would definitely be extradited, convicted and executed. The local regime would not have permitted this hearing otherwise.

At the noon break for lunch, as Cohen ducked out for a bite to eat, John Weaver invited himself along." Are you all right?" Weaver asked, his eye on Cohen's limp, which had returned after the long morning of sitting in the cramped courtroom.

"I'm fine. Just a little stiff." Cohen knew Weaver wouldn't buy this explanation, but he didn't care.

* * * *

"It's a setup, you know, this trial," Weaver said. They held down a table at an outdoor cafe, almost literally, a stiff breeze tempering the sun's pleasantly warm glow. After Cohen shook his head "No thanks," Weaver lit up a Camel.

"How is that?" Cohen said.

"It's very accommodating of them to stage it for us in English, but there's a reason for that. This is a show trial for the rest of the world. You might have noticed we've already been joined by more press. The regime here is trying to prove this is not a haven for ex-Nazis."

"Is it?"

"Let's just say they look the other way down here. Especially if a man can pay his way."

"The people running this trial don't appear to be locals," Cohen said.

"Raoul Zamora, the prosecutor, qualifies. Up from the streets. A La Negra boy made good. He is, in fact, very good, but his English is not the best. Since the specific charges against Richter involve Brits, they'll most likely have 'Sir Tony' – Anthony Wilde – handle most of their case. The defense lawyer, Benevides, might as well be British. Has dual citizenship through his father. Used to practice in London, but has more or less retired to La Negra. He's handled very few cases down here, and this is by far the biggest. The judge studied in the States. Went to some college in the Midwest like Ohio State, then Harvard Law. He hates the Commies."

Cohen looked at Weaver, amazed at the details apparently at his fingertips.

Weaver took note. "I've been doing a little prep work," he said.

"So Richter will be acquitted, you think."

"I doubt it. It's still a show trial. They've still got something to prove." Weaver stubbed out his cigarette and called for the bill. "Let me pay this," he said. "The company will cover it."

* * * *

"Your Honor, the prosecution will show. . ." Cohen and Weaver returned just in time for Raoul Zamora's opening remarks. He was a thin man, with small dark eyes and slicked-back hair. As he spoke, his battery of lawyers alternately studied documents and whispered asides to one another behind him. His Spanish accent was much heavier than the judge's.

". . .that this Johann Richter, he is guilty of having committed at least two murders not recognized as legal war killings by the rules of internationality of the Geneva Convention. We are confident to prove these two crimes beyond any shadow. Certainly beyond what is required here. At this extradition hearing."

Listening to Zamora's syntax, Cohen predicted Weaver's supposition that the prosecution team would rely on its British lawyer would prove correct.

"We are also investigating how much Mr. von Richter," Zamora continued, this time ignoring the earlier request from the defense to drop the title, "participated in 1944 in the Nazi brutalities of occupation in the city of St. Sentione, in France."

The prosecutor paused for effect, then concluded, "By the end of this hearing, your Honor, you will know of the personal viciousness of this man and his crimes. That he must be extradited to Europe to answer for his past, will be known by everyone in this courtroom. Respectfully including the Bench, your Honor." With a slight bow toward the judge, Zamora returned to his seat looking pleased with himself. For good measure, as he sat down, he fixed an accusing glare on Richter that he held perhaps a beat too long for proper dramatic impact.

Nothing yet about the death camps.

While he awaited the next development, Cohen studied two people John Weaver had pointed out to him – Clay and Anne Wheldon Johns, the brother and sister-in-law of the woman Richter was accused of murdering just before his wartime escape back into Germany. They were sitting five aisles in front and slightly to the right of him in a special section reserved for witnesses.

Clay Johns, portly and prematurely gray, appeared lost in thought. He had a wistful, worried air about him. He was said to have been Richter's closest friend in England before the war. His wife looked more alive, if only because she looked angrier, more defiant. Harder. As if put together by the hand of a perfectionist. Impressively sculpted, smoothed and painted, every hair in place on her carefully coiffed bouffant.

Absentmindedly, Cohen began to sketch the English couple in his notebook. With a wry grin, he pictured what Jack Ames might think of him illustrating the trial with a series of *New Yorker*-style cartoons for *WoHo*.

There would be no opening statement for the defense, Mr. Benevides announced.

The prosecution's first witness was called.

"Marie Renault. Take the stand please."

A compact woman perhaps ten years older than Clay and Anne Johns arose from the bench just in front of theirs and headed for the witness stand.

Cohen wondered again if he would be able to write about all this. Getting a handle on Johann Richter was going to be a challenge. He hoped he was up to it.

EDITOR'S NOTE

The following is excerpted from "Killing Hitler,"
the remarkable story of Oberstleutnant Johann Richter
and the German Army's
attempts to assassinate Adolf Hitler,
written by Michael Cohen and serialized in
World Horizons Magazine beginning January 1953.

Written in memory of Terrence Harper-Smythe,
who provided the inspiration
and preliminary research

"An English Education"

In his adolescence, Karl Maria Wilhelm Toller, Count von Richter, future member of the German Wehrmacht General Staff, had spent two years at the Whitby School, an English public school designed to prep young men both socially and academically for going up to Oxford or Cambridge. His stay at the school, on the outskirts of St. Albans thirty kilometers north of London, had broadened his understanding of a people he admired. He thought his son Johann should have the same experience.

Johann Richter began his own Whitby years in the fall of 1932 feeling uprooted and apprehensive. His father had told him to try one year in England, promising that after that first year he could make his own decision as to whether he would continue at the school.

The year was not yet over, but Johann had already decided to stay. Not that it had been easy so far. The teachers were stern. Early on, he'd received a caning for failing a test in Latin declension, setting a precedent that had made him a target for discipline. But his classmates were the roughest on him. He was the school's only new fourth-former, and foreigners were not looked upon kindly at Whitby, a rigorous institution founded on inspiration from the Eighteenth-Century voyages of famed explorer James

Cook. He was "Boche," "Kraut" – even a "bloody papist" – to fellow students smug behind their native Anglicanism.

To his great good fortune, his roommate was Claiborne Smythe-Osborne Johns, scion of a prominent family, in line one day to become the Sixth Earl of Darbyshire. Clay Johns was talented and self-assured, a social force to be reckoned with at Whitby. Eventually Johann learned his good luck had been the direct result of paternal protectiveness. Karl Richter had known Clay's father, now Lord Neville Johns, at Whitby. Had played rugby and polo with him. Without informing Johann, the General had asked his old friend to look out for his son. Rearranging room assignments had not been difficult.

But all that hardly mattered anymore, Johann thought now as he stood with Clay on a crowded platform of the train station at Henley-on-Thames, each of them a head above the rest of the assembled throng. The two of them had hit if off immediately, and Clay had quite willingly, as far as he could tell, taken him under his wing. An inseparable pair, they seemed well on their way to becoming the King and Crown Prince of their class. They even looked a little alike, though only superficially, with blue eyes the common denominator. Clay, with his broad shoulders, wavy blond locks and substantial, solid-looking features, had the look of a second-row rugger. A man who would be good in a scrum. Johann was slightly taller and wirier. With his straight well-groomed brown hair, piercing glance and refined, angular features, he looked more the English aristocrat than his aristocratic friend did.

In spite of his problems with Latin declension, Johann was more intense, more the scholar of the two. He had begun to hone his love of literature at Whitby, enamored particularly with expatriate writers – Joyce, Conrad, Hemingway and the like – and their fresh, often incisive way of looking at the world. Clay was more the socializer, already building up an old-boy network for future use. Two of the school's best athletes, they were both fiercely competitive, but so far had managed to avoid locking horns with one another.

Johann was suddenly knocked from his reverie by a high-pitched whistle followed immediately by the 4 p.m. express chugging into sight. It rumbled into the station like some ancient behemoth, heaving out a final locomotive hiss that quickly gave way to the lower rumble of voices on the platform. This was, Johann thought, the perfect entrance to the world of Croyden Castle, the Johns' sumptuous ancestral home to which he had been warmly welcomed earlier that day, his first visit with Clay's family. The station was like a Victorian Age stage set that had survived into the England of 1933, a colonnaded pile of bricks perched atop a putting green surrounded by wooded thicket.

The train was ten minutes late, and conductors hurried alongside the cars pulling down exit ladders. Johann, not knowing who to look for, watched as Clay actively craned his head this way and that searching for the mystery girl he referred to at Whitby as his "sweetheart."

The flow of debarking passengers ebbed after a few minutes. "Hope she made the train!" Clay shouted to Johann above the clamor.

"Clay! Over here, darling!"

They turned in unison toward the voice, Johann a little startled by the reference to his friend as "darling." He spotted two young women, obviously traveling together, standing twenty yards down the tracks surrounded by bags. One of them, the taller of the two, waved, while her companion simply stared.

The tall woman held Johann's attention as he and Clay approached the pair. In close-up she was attractive, though not a conventional beauty. She barely seemed a grown woman. Her body was fully rounded, but her long dark hair framed the face of a little girl, bright confident eyes, small flaring nostrils and pouty lips. Her family, he knew, was prominent and wealthy. And for all her girlish look, she was nearly two years older than he and Clay.

"Hel-lo! How delightful to see you again!" Clay did indeed seem delighted. He kissed and then hugged the tall girl with a certain formality, while Johann continued his own perusal. Over Clay's shoulder, her eyes suddenly riveted on his for the first time. Not a little girl's eyes. They bored right through him. He stood at

least six inches taller than she, but her stare – which he interpreted as disdain – immediately cut him down to size. He felt himself automatically resisting her, fascinated but repelled.

Clay introduced them. They exchanged greetings with a lack
of enthusiasm that was obvious, while Clay, baffled, interrupted
their locked stares with, "Anne, you haven't introduced us to your
friend."

Anne Wheldon slowly and pointedly turned away from Johann to perform her duties. As she turned, her personality seemed
to turn with her. Her introduction was almost buoyant. "Forgive
me. Clay, this is my very good friend, Emily Hardewicke."

Clay smiled. As Anne did not continue, he was forced to take
up the slack again. "Pleased to meet you, I'm sure, Miss
Hardewicke. And this is my friend, my roommate at Whitby, Johann Richter."

Johann, stung by Anne Wheldon's obvious disapproval,
acknowledged only with a terse "Hello."

Emily muttered something about how pleased she was to meet
them both then returned abruptly inside her shell. She was of medium height and on the thin side, with tousled, mouse-brown hair
worn shoulder length. She had an undistinguished but softly attractive face, dominated by a pair of shy eyes that lent a touch of
intrigue to her quiet persona.

Johann and Clay each picked up a large suitcase and valise
while Anne and Emily collected their numerous smaller pieces of
luggage. As they walked back down the station platform toward
the chauffeured Bentley, Johann felt uncomfortably fused to the
two women by mutual distrust. He began to have his doubts about
the prospects of the vacation that had begun so well such a short
time before.

* * * *

Two days had passed since the meeting at the train station.
Anne and Emily had been inseparable, playing tennis together,
swimming in the pool, taking long walks, horseback rides, sitting
and sunning, reading. Whatever they did they did together, or together with Clay.

Johann, contrary to his earlier fears, was becoming more comfortable as life on the Johns estate – a life to all appearances unhampered by the world's economic woes – began to settle into a routine. With Anne avoiding him, and Clay seemingly at her beck and call, Johann was free to enjoy the amenities of Croyden Castle, often on his own.

Earlier that afternoon, Clay had been chauffeured in to the London docks to collect his older sister, Christine, returning from a Mediterranean cruise. He for some reason had wanted to meet her alone. He'd always been reticent about Christine whenever her name came up at Whitby, it seemed to Johann, saying only that she was "popular," particularly with men. At Croyden Castle, mention of her was treated in similarly circumspect fashion. Lady Eleanor's reference to her the night before as "impetuous" was about as far as anyone had ventured. "Perhaps Johann will be a calming influence on her," the lady of the manor had smiled. Johann had thought this an odd remark, and had smiled back, slightly embarrassed.

Lord Neville had taken Clay's younger sister Samantha on an outing somewhere. That left no one around the house but Eleanor Johns, Johann and the servants. Lady Eleanor was directing preparations for the evening's formal dinner to celebrate the spring holidays and the increasingly rare occasion of having all her children home at one time.

The sky was clear blue, the air cool and refreshing. Johann decided to go riding. The green of early spring dominated everything – velvet-smooth lawns, immaculately trimmed hedgerows, trees just starting to bud. The dark green stables and garage blended in. Behind him, the magnificent late-Restoration mansion looked like something from the notebooks of Sir Christopher Wren. By comparison Johann's home outside Berlin was an overgrown farmhouse. Orienbad. He missed it.

Selecting a large brown mare, already his favorite mount in the Johns' stables, he felt ecstatic as they galloped across Croyden Castle's long stretch of open acreage toward the forest up ahead. He had kept up his superior horsemanship at Whitby, but had often felt a lack of freedom in the stiff riding courses and overtrod bridle paths of the school grounds. Riding wild and free gave him a joyful release. He had the old unharnessed feel of the German fields again as the powerful horse jumped smoothly over a small brook and made for the woods. The muscular movements of the mare beneath him was generating a familiar excitement. The motion was hard, too hard to be sensual, but the heat it produced was a reminder. As an undefined anticipation began to build, his thoughts turned to Marie Renault.

*   *   *   *

She had been the Richter family's governess for six years before Johann had awakened to her at the age of fourteen. By that time, early 1932, though she was really only governess to Johann's younger sister Gretchen, Johann began to find more excuses for being in her company.

Marie Renault was then in her late twenties and effectively cut off from significant contact with people her own age. Most particularly from men, who weren't included in the few social gatherings she attended with any regularity. She enjoyed Johann's companionship as much as he did hers.

She was from Paris. Her German was more fluent than Johann's French, but they usually conversed in French, or sometimes in English, for practice. She loved to read, and provided added inspiration for his continued interest in literature. Marie was an excellent horsewoman. She would ride with Johann as long as he didn't bring guns along. They made her nervous. During her free hours the spring and summer of Johann's fifteenth year, the two of them would often explore new territory beyond the reaches of Orienbad, racing their mounts out over the open fields in laughing, eager competition and occasionally stopping to rest in some newly discovered mead or thicket.

These moments were a special treat. They allowed Marie and Johann to extend their relationship beyond the bounds of governess and charge. From the moment they would dismount, a subtle change would come over them. He, already the taller, seemed to grow older while she grew younger; he taut and lean, she with an almost childish plumpness to her figure, rosy cheeks, short brown curls dancing around her ears. He felt a mysterious excitement being alone with her this new way. It scared him a little as well.

On one such ride in the late June of that year, in a tucked-away meadow surrounded by forest west of Orienbad, the inevitable had happened. After a picnic lunch and a bottle of wine, they had begun an innocent horseplay that soon turned to something else. A gradual shedding of clothes and, for Johann, an accelerating surge of desire like nothing he had ever experienced. The beauty of her unfolding nakedness took his breath away. Her heavy, almost labored, breathing aroused him to exhilarating heights. What followed was intoxicating, the building tension, the spasms of release. He wanted to do it again and again.

After the third time, Marie laughed at his eagerness to continue and patted the blanket for him to take a rest. Lying beside her, an oddly detached feeling came over him. It reminded him of hunting, after the kill. The irresistible pull began to dissipate. He felt a new sense of power.

As his mood shifted, so did hers. She suddenly looked him in the eye with what he took to be a new seriousness between them.

"Your father must never know," she said.

* * * *

Johann and the brown mare had been wandering through the alternating fields and forests out beyond Croyden Castle for nearly an hour now. There were longer stretches of woodlands here than anywhere else in this part of England, Lord Neville had announced with pride at dinner the night before. A bit of foresight on the part of his ancestors, he said. Avid hunters all, they had been determined to have a genuine forest in which to hunt, and hundreds of years ago had replanted many acres of trees to that effect.

Johann could not shake the memory of Marie Renault. Though a part of him knew theirs was an impossible relationship, he still longed for her. He did not believe his parents had actually known about him and Marie, but he knew they had suspected. Shortly after he had been sent to school in England she'd been dismissed and had returned to her native Paris.

He had received one letter from her since then, a cryptic farewell that had cited what she called their vast differences in "age and circumstance" as the reason they must remain apart. There had been no return address. He had no idea what Marie felt toward him now. Nor really he toward her, for that matter. Only that he wished she were with him right now.

When Johann finally awoke from his memories, he and the mare were winding along a primitive overgrown path. Thick branches brushed against his legs and the horse's flanks. The afternoon air had grown cooler in the dense underbrush and the sun's shimmering game of hide-and-seek above the treetops was doing little to alter the temperature for a horse and rider on the forest floor. The thought crossed Johann's mind that it might soon become difficult to find his way back, but a perverse instinct kept pushing him on. He told himself he could always give the mare her head and she would rescue them both.

He heard the faint echo of a laugh.

At first he thought he was mistaken. He reined in and listened. The stillness cracked again with a distinctly human sound. There was no mistaking it this time. It was a woman's laugh. Johann started to call out and announce himself but something inside him cautioned against it, as if the unfamiliar environment required stealth of him. Instead he dismounted and made his way quietly toward the sounds.

At a part in the thicket, he froze, at first disbelieving what he saw in the small clearing just below where he stood. Anne Wheldon's friend Emily was reclining on a large flat rock that caught the sun directly. She was laughing softly to herself. Her body was mirrored in the pool of a stream that bubbled along behind the rock, and she appeared to be throwing pebbles at her reflected image. She was naked. Barely developed. Half girl, half woman.

Johann's thoughts of Marie rekindled at the sight before him now. He felt the familiar tension building up inside, wanted somehow to announce his presence, perhaps even join this enticing tableau, but realized his entrance would spoil the scene and simply embarrass Emily. He shivered at the cool breezes that whispered through the bushes around him, and envied her her patch of sun.

Emily stopped laughing. She peered intently down at the pool behind the rock she was lying on. Johann wondered what she was looking at, until Anne Wheldon, also naked, emerged from the water. His mouth was dry; he could feel his heart pounding against his ribcage. Anne's body was all woman, long, lithe, milky white, its suppleness giving sensuous play to her slender flanks and ample breasts.

His arousal quickly gave way to confusion, however, as Anne began moving her hips in a kind of dance for Emily, who watched every move with an unmistakable lust. He looked on in fascinated guilt while Emily slid down the smooth rock on her back and Anne, on all fours, crawled her way into a position above her, straddled her and held her friend's head up to her own body. Shortly, Anne began to moan and spasm and they both tumbled to the soft grass beside the rock and lay still, breathing heavily. Johann could not reconcile the reactions surging through him, just as he could not take his eyes off the two women.

Then suddenly without warning his mare, munching grass in total oblivion of the unfolding human drama, rustled through some short bushes with a noise the two lovers could hear. They jerked their heads up in unison, startled does caught by the hunter.

Johann snapped out of his trance and reacted quickly. He grabbed the horse, gently holding her snout and restricting her movement. He could hear the two women scrambling about – for shelter or their clothes, he presumed. He led the mare carefully back down about fifty yards of path, mounted her in one smooth silent move and made his escape.

CHAPTER V

"I first met Johann Richter when I became his family's governess in 1926. I took care of Johann and his two sisters, and tutored also each of them in French, English and several other subjects. Johann was eight, I believe, when I first joined the Richter family."

"And when did you leave the Richter family's employ?"

"In November of 1932. After Johann left home to attend school in England."

"Miss Renault, were there any, ah, extenuating circumstances to your dismissal from service in 1932?"

Marie Renault, her dark brown hair pulled into a tight bun, looked away from Sir Anthony Wilde, who had taken over for the prosecutor, and straight at Johann Richter for the first time since she had taken the witness stand that afternoon. The severity of her hair and dress was offset by a softness, almost a kindness, in her eyes.

Cohen couldn't read the look she gave Richter, but the defendant returned her gaze with what appeared to be a sympathetic one of his own. Finally she looked away and began speaking clearly, but haltingly, to no one in particular. "Yes, I believe there were 'extenuating circumstances' involved in my dismissal. Johann and I, you see, had become lovers while he was still quite young."

There was suddenly complete silence in the courtroom. "I think his father somehow found out about us," she continued with only a trace of French in her accent. "Perhaps he simply realized. . . In any event, Johann's father, who had never much cared for me in the first place, turned even more against me after Johann left for England. It must have been because of what was happening between Johann and me. I believe that was the real reason for my dismissal."

Sir Anthony, a tall, impeccably dressed man of assured bearing, nodded his approval. He permitted himself a barely perceptible grin that conveyed confidence in the tack he was taking. After delivering a few more leading questions, he appeared satisfied to step back and let the witness tell her story.

"When I left Germany in 1932," she began, "I returned to France, to Paris, where I became a school teacher of young children. With what was beginning to happen in Germany at the time I was glad I had left. I missed Johann and his sisters, but very little else from my Orienbad days.

"I continued in my teaching position, and lived in the same three-room flat on the Rue des Jardines, right on into the war. There was a brief interruption of activity when the Germans occupied Paris in 1940. But as with many others who had not fled the city, and those who returned after the Armistice, I soon resumed the same job, the same routine, more or less. It was not really the same, of course. But then it was, in many ways. We received directives from the Germans or their French stooges now and then about what to teach or not teach, but for the most part we did as we always had done.

"Day-to-day life, however, became more difficult as the war went on and shortages grew. And as for a personal life. . . Physical movement in the city was often restricted, and people didn't visit with one another as much as they had before. Some of my closest friends who had fled at the first had not returned. I had no real personal life, as such, anymore."

The witness appeared distracted, as if remembering more than she was saying.

"And?" Sir Anthony arched an expressive eyebrow.

Marie Renault looked up. "And," she said, "my existence went on this way up until Christmas of 1943. . . I must explain that I was by this time thirty-eight years old and single, with no family of my own. My parents had both died in the First War. In spite of my children at the school I was very lonely. I suppose that was why I allowed myself to go to a German party that Christmas Eve. There was no other place for me to go.

"The Germans often gave parties they encouraged French women to attend. Alone, of course. I had never attended such an event before.

This one was held in the grand ballroom of the Hotel Abelard, on the Champ de Elysees. It was quite a lavish sort of affair for those times, for German officers only, I believe.

"At first glance, I thought it seemed an attractive enough gathering, the men all in uniform or formal dress, the ballroom all lit up and decorated. A band was playing music, soft music, for the dancers. But as soon as I had checked my coat, I noticed a noisy group of officers gathered off to one side. They were standing in a circle cheering encouragement at someone. I caught a glimpse of a woman dancing with the top of her dress pulled down. She wore a black brassiere the officers were grabbing at. I was immediately ashamed for having come. I had never felt the humiliation of defeat so much as at that moment.

"I noticed two men on the fringe of the circle looking at me. They laughed at something between themselves and started over in my direction. I turned to flee them, to flee this ugly place, but my way was suddenly blocked by another officer, young, very tall. A nasty scar on one cheek. I was terrified. I asked him to please step aside so that I might leave. He acted surprised, and said something like, 'Don't you recognize me?'

"At that, I looked at him, at his face, really for the first time, and told him that I did not and begged him to let me pass. He could not seem to believe I didn't recognize him. He asked me to look again, subtract four inches from his height and about fifty pounds from his frame.

"His voice was beginning to sound familiar to me. He had a commanding presence. The other two officers looked at him and turned away, and my panic subsided a little. Less distracted, I did as I had been asked to do, looked at him again, and suddenly found myself face to face with Johann Richter for the first time in ten years."

"The defendant," Sir Anthony clarified for the record.

"Yes, the defendant," Marie Renault parroted with a touch of irritation. "I wanted to hide, did not want him to find me in this dreadful place. But I could do nothing except stand there and gawk at him until he realized I had finally recognized who he was. He didn't say a word, just picked up my coat and helped me on with it, took my hand and led me outside.

"We walked through the snow for maybe an hour or so, reminiscing about the old days, talking about what we had each been doing since we'd last seen one another. It all seemed so strange. For many reasons, of course. Aside from the war, and all that had brought about, it seemed strange, I think, because we were both adults this time. And the balance had clearly shifted between us.

"We eventually wound up back at my flat that night. We built a fire and drank hot tea. He told me a few of his experiences in England during the first part of the war. He seemed tense, very angry and depressed about things. Not so much about the Germans doing badly in the war. It was more that Hitler, who Johann criticized quite openly, and the Nazis had dragged Germany so low. It seemed a relief for him to finally have someone to listen to his true feelings."

"And what happened next, Miss Renault?" Sir Anthony wanted to angle his witness toward something more specific, sensed Cohen, who had noticed John Weaver's ears prick up at mention of the word "Hitler."

"Johann told me that on New Year's Day he was to be reassigned to the army post at St. Sentione to the southeast. Occupation duty. He asked me if I would join him there, as soon as he could arrange quarters for me. I agreed to go. I knew I was taking a chance, that my countrymen would likely see me as a traitor. But I didn't feel like one, and I didn't really have anyone else, you see. And neither did Johann, not in France, and I still felt a loyalty, an instinct to protect him, as absurd as that may sound."

"When exactly did you join Mr. Richter – or perhaps I should say, *Oberstleutnant* Richter, in St. Sentione?" Sir Anthony said this with a sarcasm that won a sharp glance from the witness, who paused as if debating whether to continue.

"I joined him," she said, "about a month later, quite surprised to learn that he was not simply assigned there, he was their new commander."

"Please tell us what you saw and heard about the occupation of St. Sentione, Miss Renault." Sir Anthony's voice now held a mildly placating tone.

"The people of St. Sentione were terrified of the Germans, much more than the people of Paris were. They had good reason to be. Johann was replacing Gerhardt Gruning, an SS colonel known to be sadistic far beyond the needs of his post. Many thought him worse than Klaus Barbie in Lyon."

Something jogged in Cohen's memory. He had read about Barbie, "The Butcher of Lyon," of course, but he had also heard of Gerhardt Gruning. Like Barbie, the man had fled Germany at the end of the war. But unlike Barbie – or Adolf Eichmann or Josef Mengele – who had disappeared, Gruning had been accepted quite openly into one of the smaller South American countries like Paraguay or Bolivia, as Cohen recalled. He was doing quite well in some business or other in his host country, the head of which had also benefited handsomely, it was said, for having granted asylum to the former SS standartenfuhrer. It was rumored Gruning, like other Nazis, was being shielded by the CIA and MI6 for fear he could jeopardize anti-Communist spy networks if he were arrested.

"When I first arrived in St. Sentione," Marie Renault continued, "the townspeople didn't know there was any connection between Johann Richter and me. He had used a surrogate to arrange an apartment for me on the top floor of a small inn on the northern edge of town. For a short while I was accepted as a Frenchwoman there to meet relatives who had yet to arrive. In this role, I exchanged confidences with my new neighbors. Johann was a big improvement over Gruning, they said. He had already removed most restrictions on movement about the town. There was much less harassment now, they said.

"It was good to hear such things of Johann, from people who were to be expected to hate him for his very existence. They were still suspicious, of course. It was said by some that he was trying to soften them up. That in the end he would be even worse than Gruning. They remained wary of him. But any German would've produced that response from them, no matter what he did–"

"Quite so, Miss Renault. Point taken. Thank you." Sir Anthony cut her off in mid-sentence. He had evidently heard enough apology for Johann Richter. To change the flow, he now paused – somewhat melodramatically, Cohen thought – and said, "Tell us everything you know, Miss Renault, about the death of Yvonne Duchamps."

The courtroom audience came alive. *Who was Yvonne Duchamps?* Marie Renault darted an unhappy look at her interrogator. He turned away, demanding an answer by his silence.

"The 'disappearance' of Yvonne Duchamps, you mean? No body was ever found."

"If you prefer," he amended, facing her again.

"I don't know much about it," she said. "Only what I heard and could guess. My only real regret about going to St. Sentione is that it was through me Johann met Yvonne."

"Go on, please."

With an audible sigh, the witness complied, speaking more softly now. "It didn't take long, of course, for the people of St. Sentione to find out why I was really in their city. I'm sure most of them thought I was Johann's lover. I had half expected that to become the case myself. But Johann, I think, was still in mourning for the woman he had lost in England. The one he was accused of killing – unjustly, I am quite certain."

Sir Anthony shook his head at this last line. "May that be stricken from the record, your Honor. It is strictly hearsay. The witness is drawing her own conclusion."

"Agreed. Strike that last answer from the record," the judge said. "Proceed, Miss Renault."

"In any case," the witness picked up with an accusatory glance at Sir Anthony, "Johann was forced to provide me with a guard, wherever I went. I lost all friends but one because of my connection with him. That one was Yvonne Duchamps.

"Yvonne had moved to St. Sentione just after I had. She had three rooms at the same inn, on the floor just below mine, the third floor. We became friends very soon after she arrived. She was as lonely as I was. Johann visited me only when he had the time, no more than two or three times a week."

"What else do you know about Yvonne Duchamps, Miss Renault?" Sir Anthony coaxed, perhaps sensing the reluctance in his witness.

"She was French, or at least had a French father," Marie Renault dutifully continued, her voice fading to a monotone. "I think perhaps her mother was English. She said she'd lived in England for quite some time earlier in her life. Her husband was a French army officer, a prisoner of war somewhere in Germany.

"She hated the Germans. She had come to St. Sentione, from Paris, because her husband's family lived on a farm nearby, she said. She went out to see them occasionally. Her father-in-law was supposedly in the Resistance. I don't know. I never met any of these relatives."

"What was she like, as a person," Sir Anthony said.

"She was slender, with long dark hair and extraordinary blue eyes. A wonderful smile, not often on display. About twenty-five, I should say. Emotionally quite a strong woman, it seemed to me. She had a young child, a three-year-old girl. She often took the girl, Yvette, out into the country and left her in the care of a sister-in-law, an older widow who apparently loved to look after her. I offered several times to look after the girl myself but Yvonne always said she didn't want to trouble me."

"And the defendant, where does he fit into all this?"

Marie Renault shot Sir Anthony an icy look, but answered the question. "I suppose the real trouble started one day when Yvonne was up in my apartment, taking afternoon tea with me, and Johann walked in unannounced. It was awkward. Nobody said a word. You see, instead of simply deserting me as the others had, when she found out about my relationship with Johann, Yvonne had tried to reason me out of it. We had talked about him a good deal, but I hadn't told Johann about her at all. I'm not certain why. Her possible connections with the Resistance, I suppose, perhaps. I don't know.

"This was the first time, then, that Yvonne had actually seen Johann. I think she was a bit shocked to see her abstract argument with me suddenly appear in the flesh. Johann Richter in 1944, as I have said, was a very impressive, imposing man. A handsome man. He and Yvonne stared at each other for what I thought was an uncomfortable length of time. It made me nervous." Marie Renault laughed softly. "Maybe even a little jealous. . ."

"Do continue, Miss Renault. Please do continue," Sir Anthony said.

CHAPTER VI

At first Richter had tried to laugh it off. He felt like Mr. Dickens' Ebenezer Scrooge: characters from his past lining up to parade by with their accusations. As he entered the courtroom he had tried to catch Clay's eye. But it was Anne Johns who had stared back at him, and it was with a look of hatred.

Sitting at the defendant's table, he was less concerned with Marie Renault's testimony than he was about the state of her health. She looked unwell. He imagined her life since 1944 had been difficult. The friend and intimate – as she said, probably the presumed lover – of a Wehrmacht officer, of a man who had overseen the occupation of a French city. That's how she would've been seen. She would have been lucky if she'd only had her head shaved and been paraded through the streets. More likely it had been worse than that. He felt sad, and not a little guilty, to see her like this.

And now, on the stand, she was talking about Yvonne Duchamps and the memories were flooding in on him from a corner of his mind he had managed to block off for years.

Yvonne Duchamps had been a striking woman, her beauty not of the usual order, almost Eurasian-looking – more exotic than Christine Johns, but like Christine possessed of an aura cold for a female. It was that coolness, ironically, rather than her beauty, that had driven him to seek her out in St. Sentione. On that first day, after Marie had introduced them and Yvonne had left, Marie had told him Yvonne's French husband was a prisoner of war and that she hated the Nazis. Richter had needed a confidant, an ally, someone he could trust, and while Marie too may have hated Hitler, she had also hated Richter's father too much to take a chance with her.

Yvonne Duchamps, he had thought, might fill the bill. He had approached her two days after that first meeting in Marie's flat. Though she had appeared surprised to find him on her doorstep, he thought she had half expected it. He invited himself in. She shrugged her shoulders and opened the door. A lovely little girl stared up at him from where she was playing on the living room floor. A miniature of her mother, the same straight brown hair and big blue eyes. Yvonne immediately sent her off to the bedroom.

Richter chose a chair and sat down, without invitation. Yvonne remained standing.

She asked him why he was there. When he didn't answer, she told him – quite boldly, under the circumstances, Richter thought – that she knew why. She assumed, she said, that he had come to propose some sort of bargain. Her husband's good health, possibly even his freedom, for her body. Her "sexual favors," was how she put it, her voice as hard as she could make it. Richter laughed and assured her that was not the reason he was there.

What was he doing in her apartment, then, she asked, finally taking a seat on a couch halfway across the room and lighting up a cigarette. The aroma sparked an old memory in Richter but he squelched it. This was going to be a real shot in the dark, he thought.

"What do you think of the Nazis?" he said.

The question appeared to catch her off guard. She looked uneasy again. "What is it you really want?" she said.

"First I need to know what you think of the Nazis," he repeated. "I'm not one of them. I am not a Nazi," he added, to ease her fear. She had to commit herself before he could.

She simply stared at him.

He tried a different tack. He told her he understood, from talking with Marie, that she hated the Nazis. That she was a loyal French patriot. That she followed De Gaulle, not Petain. Was that a fair assessment?

She studied him intently for a moment, hesitated, then finally committed herself with a slight nod of her head.

"Good," he said, "because I need your help."

"My help?"

"We are going to kill Hitler, and we need all the help we can get." Now he was as committed as she.

She looked at him as though he were a madman. He laughed. He felt like a madman. He did not know yet that "fool" would have been the better description.

* * * *

". . .And so people put two and two together" – Marie Renault sounded old and resigned on the witness stand, light years away from her original emotions – "Myself included, though at Johann's urging I had left St. Sentione for Paris several days before it all happened. Yvonne Duchamps had vanished; her little girl simply left behind, found on the steps of the St. Sentione prefecture. Johann Richter, her lover – something that was common knowledge by then – was also gone.

"What would anybody make of it? That he had killed Yvonne Duchamps, or had her killed, and then dropped out of sight, is what most people thought. As it was, they happened to disappear just after the attempt had been made on Hitler's life by one of his own officers. So Johann was not the only German officer to disappear without any evident reason during those days. Hitler was having his revenge on a lot of them.

"I myself was questioned at length by the Gestapo just after my return to St. Sentione. I told them virtually nothing; but then I knew virtually nothing. They threatened to torture me, but never did. It turned out they did me a favor. Their interest in me helped convince my compatriots after the liberation that I was not a collaborator. Not a bad one, anyway. My transgression with Johann, our friendship, earned me some punishment, some ostracization, but it was mostly from people who meant little to me."

"And what had happened with the defendant and Miss Duchamps?" Sir Anthony asked. "Where were they?"

"There were all kinds of theories," Marie Renault said. "Not everyone thought Johann had killed her. Some thought he had simply been transferred. Or cashiered, punished. Most likely for his leniency on St. Sentione. A few had the romantic notion the two of them had run away together, gone underground to escape both the Allies and the Nazis. Others said they had been killed by the Resistance or the Gestapo, or maybe by the British, or even that they had committed suicide for some reason or other.

"No one, of course, really knew. Though a lot of people certainly thought them both, one way or another, dead."

"And you, Miss Renault? What did you think?"

This time Sir Anthony seemed to be the one asking for a conclusion from the witness, Cohen thought, but no one objected.

"Me? I thought Yvonne Duchamps was indeed dead – though I certainly didn't say so to the Gestapo. I could not imagine any other explanation for her disappearance, leaving her child behind like that. Somebody from Paris took the little girl in, but Yvonne's sister-in-law, no relative, ever showed up.

"Johann had been extremely moody during our time together in St. Sentione, sometimes frighteningly so. He would recover his good humor a little now and then, but always succumbed again to something, some inner tension, it seemed to me, soon afterwards. He wouldn't tell me what was bothering him. I never thought him dead, though, after he disappeared. He could have been killed, I supposed, by us or the Germans, but that wouldn't likely have explained the disappearance of Yvonne Duchamps. And Johann, you see, was not the kind of man to kill himself. Not for any reason."

"So again, Miss Renault. What did you think happened?"

Marie Renault stared, her eyes downcast, as if she were inspecting the railing of the witness stand. "Frankly," she said, "though here again I didn't tell the Gestapo, I assumed he killed her. He would've had to have had good reason. And perhaps he did. I always felt Yvonne was using him for something – not just to protect her husband, but for something more. I told Johann this, but he never seemed to believe me.

"So you thought him capable of murder?"

Marie Renault seemed uncomfortable. She looked down at her lap. "It wasn't like him. He would've had to have been provoked. But yes, he was capable of it I believe. Particularly if it were to protect his father."

Johann Richter, who had kept his eyes on the witness throughout her testimony, now looked away and shook his head, his fingers again stroking the scar that traced a jagged line across his cheek.

Sir Anthony stared at his witness. He must wonder, Cohen thought, why she assumed Richter did not kill Christine Johns but did kill Yvonne Duchamps. To probe further, though, would challenge the judge's ruling that the witness should not draw conclusions. To push the issue might cost more than it was worth.

Sir Anthony evidently drew the same conclusion. "No more questions," he said, and headed for his seat.

* * * *

Michael Cohen picked at some sort of chicken concoction while John Weaver continued to regale him with stories about the *Baltimore Sun*, life on the Chesapeake, the women in his life, his views on world politics, and his alma mater, Williams College.

They were seated outdoors at Miguel's, a hole-in-the-wall with an open courtyard that squeezed ten tables snugly around the perimeter of a stone fish gurgling a small column of water toward the sky. To the east the view was blocked by stucco, but to the west a range of majestic Andean peaks were dimly visible beyond the lamp-lit early evening streets.

His leg aching, feeling a little dizzy, Cohen sat back in his chair and chewed absentmindedly on a coca leaf from a small bag of them he had found in his jacket pocket – a promotional sample his bellhop had left him, he assumed when he had found them. It wasn't booze, but it did smooth out the jagged edges a bit. He offered one to John Weaver, who smiled and shook his head.

Cohen let his mind wander. He had gotten absolutely no feel for Johann Richter yet. Would he ever? It was early, but already he had his doubts. Though there had been nothing to confirm a connection between Richter and Heinrich Mueller, the commandant of Kaisener, Cohen still held the same negative stereotype that had made him hate the guy in a general sort of way from the start. Marie Renault's testimony was convincing, in spite of a primness of delivery that made it seem almost scripted. But at the end, her portrait of Richter had taken a strange turn for someone seemingly so in sympathy with him during most of her time on the stand. Was she simply a jilted lover, snatching a final chance at revenge? Or was he indeed capable of having killed this Yvonne Duchamps?

The picture Terry Harper had painted, however disjointed it may have been, had made Richter seem more complicated, as Cohen remembered it. Marie Renault had praised Richter for his treatment of St. Sentione, but Harper had hinted at other redeeming features. He had Harper's manuscript with him in La Negra. He'd have to reread it, he told himself.

He sighed. He had not given a thought yet to writing anything down. Had taken no notes. The tape recorder he had lugged along was still in his suitcase. His task here was starting to look impossible.

So what had he expected?

John Weaver was talking about another woman. But this one, Cohen suddenly realized, was a woman connected to Richter.

". . .It's mostly rumors about her, though. I'm not even sure she really exists."

"Why don't you find out?" Cohen said.

"Ahh, I haven't got time to go traipsing out into the jungle on a wild goose chase. Frankly, you'd be a better man for the job."

"Oh? Why is that?"

"I, uh, have to confess a little something to you, Cohen," Weaver said, sounding a bit sheepish. "I know you're down here for *World Horizons.* Your editor Jack Ames is an old friend of mine. Well, 'old acquaintance' might be more accurate."

"Jack told you about me?"

"No, not directly. I have some contacts at good old *'WoHo.'* The place leaks like a sieve. Always has."

It disturbed Cohen that this virtual stranger knew even this much about him. It raised a red flag. For the moment, however, he was more interested in something else. "So, about this woman," he said. "Just what is she to Richter?"

"She's his wife, they say."

"They?"

"My sources."

"I see," Cohen said, knowing Weaver wasn't going to reveal any more than he wanted to reveal. "And where does she live?"

"She's supposedly living on some farm or something, way up beyond Riberalta someplace."

"Where's that?"

"Northeast. Way out there. Rebel territory."

"What else do you know about her?"

"I've heard she's young and pretty," Weaver said, a twinkle in his eye. "You'd think that would get me up off my ass. Guess I've seen enough pretty women I don't need to go chasing through jungles to find'em anymore. Must be gettin' old." Cohen smiled, but he wasn't thinking about John Weaver. He felt a sudden surge of purpose again. He was going to have to deal with Richter face to face at some point, but he wasn't looking forward to it. A preview would be helpful. He washed down the residue of coca with a long slug of beer and bid Weaver a good night he hoped was not overly abrupt.

Walking alone back to the Miranda, shoulders hunching his jacket collar up around his ears, his breath a white mist, Cohen felt vaguely uneasy again over Weaver's knowing about his *World Horizons* assignment. Halfway home he heard what sounded like a clap of thunder, an echo of the night before. It rumbled somewhere off in the distance, but there was no lightning and no rain came.

He wondered if this was to be a nightly occurrence in La Negra. Tonight it seemed appropriate accompaniment to his having learned about the Richter woman. He warned himself not to let his hopes climb too high. She could turn out to be as difficult as he imagined Richter to be. She might have nothing to offer him. The very possibility she existed, however, gave him reason to hope.

Up in his rooms, he stepped out onto the balcony and stood for a moment, listening. The distant explosions had stopped. The city was almost as dark as Lake Tocqual, whose darkness swallowed up the far side of town. It was cold. Cohen shivered. His leg felt better, but he still felt disoriented. He imagined the Miranda, perched high up on its slope, wavering on creaky hinges above the depths of the city. Shivering again, he returned inside to seek the sanctuary of dreamless sleep, the now-stilled rumble of La Negra continuing to echo faintly through the back of his consciousness.

"Christine"

The evening's dinner had been planned as a small, formal homecoming affair. All of the Johns including Samantha, who usually dined with her governess, were to be there. As well as the three house guests at Croyden Castle that week, Johann Richter, Anne Wheldon and Emily Hardewicke. But at the last minute Anne Wheldon had pleaded a headache and had not appeared. Nor had Christine Johns. Everyone else was present, including Emily, displaying a demureness Johann would never have noticed had he not seen her with Anne in the woods that afternoon. He watched her now for any hint that she knew he had seen them. She avoided his eyes, but he couldn't tell if it were anything more than her natural shyness.

Johann was still obsessed with what he had seen that afternoon. It had startled him. But thinking back on it, he realized he'd probably been naive. He was already familiar with the homosexual dalliances of his classmates at Whitby. It was not that unusual. Older boys often treated younger ones with a kind of Victorian era romanticism. Many of these relationships were platonic, but some were not. So Emily and Anne shouldn't have surprised him so much. What perhaps bothered him most, he thought, was the strength of his own reaction. He could not get the two young lovers out of his mind.

He wondered if Clay knew about Anne. He doubted it.

In a conscious effort to escape this uncomfortable preoccupation, Johann focused on his surroundings. It was his first meal in the main dining hall. The cavernous space dwarfed the intimate gathering. Fires crackled softly at opposite ends of the long room and waves of flickering candlelight lit the broad expanse of snow white tablecloth,

turning the table into an isle of light in a sea of darkness and soften-
ing the stern faces of ancestors that lined the walls. As Clay wound
up a well-edited version of their winter term at Whitby, Johann
watched the elongated shadows pursue the liveried men serving dinner.

Suddenly all attention swiveled to a new arrival. Christine Johns.
She was shown to a seat directly across the table from Johann. He
was at odds with himself not to stare at her. Her deep Mediterranean
tan set her apart from the smooth paleness of the other two women
at table. He tried to be discreet but could not take his eyes off her.
When he did, she appeared to blossom more each time he looked
back again.

She was tall, maybe five feet ten, with a striking figure on a slender frame, a finely chiseled face and shoulder-length dark blond
hair. Dressed more casually than the rest of the dining party, in a
skirt and a top that bared her shoulders, she seemed to Johann as
formal as her beauty.

He laughed to himself, wondering if Hitler would consider this
extraordinary specimen inferior to the typical German *machden*.

Christine at once began to dominate the dinner conversation,
talking about her cruise and peppering her family with questions
about the local gossip she had missed while away.

"Was Capri absolutely delightful?" Emily ventured in her timid
manner.

"Beyond delightful. Smashingly delightful! The water is so clear
you can see the bottom of the ocean from the ship."

"And Greece? Did you enjoy Greece, my dear?" said Eleanor
Johns, a statuesque woman with dark eyes and an unusually deep
voice, visibly pregnant, who had already won Johann's allegiance by
refusing to shorten his name to "Joe" as his classmates at Whitby
did. "How frightfully dreadful!" she had said. "'Johann' is much the
nicer."

"Greece was lovely." Christine smiled. "But tempting. I did
something very naughty on Mikanos."

"Perhaps that should remain confidential," her mother suggested.

"No, tell it!" Samantha demanded.

Christine looked at her mother, who lifted her eyebrows, but
only slightly.

"One simply could not resist. Gerta von Flossenburg and I snuck away from the others and found a beach where we could take our bathing costumes off."

A sound burst from Eleanor Johns, half laugh, half snort. "My dear! Not at table!" Synchronized with it was a "Good show!" from Clay.

"Didn't you wonder about my tan, Mother? I'm all brown. All over."

Eleanor Johns averted her eyes, as if she dared not take this in. She passed an indefinable look to her husband.

Johann for his part sat mesmerized, riveted by every word from this goddess-like creature.

"Did you visit Captain Hardy while you were at Malta?" said Neville Johns, a trim, fiftyish figure with dark hair graying at the temples of a sharp-angled face governed by a pair of worldly, perceptive eyes. Lord Neville was a sometimes controversial member of the House of Lords, Johann had heard. But sufficiently modern to have solidified his inherited wealth in the transport business. And evidently modern enough not to be ruffled by the idea of his exquisite young daughter sunbathing in the nude.

"Yes, of course, Father. One could hardly neglect Captain Hardy, now could one." She gave her father what appeared to Johann a rather coy smile. "And I of course gave him your regards. As requested."

"Was Anders there?" said Emily, the hint of a tease in her voice. It was the first time Johann had seen her smile.

"Yes, dear old Anders was there, all atwit about going up to Oxford in the fall," Christine replied, lowering her eyes almost shyly. When she raised them, she eyed Johann, then quickly averted her glance to Emily, with whom she appeared to have some special sort of understanding. Perhaps on the subject of this Anders fellow, Johann thought.

Mention of Captain Hardy and Anders, apparently his son, brought the conversation back around to local gossip. Finding himself on the fringes of this talk, Johann tuned out and lost himself in daydreams of Christine Johns. She had dropped out of some fancy school, he had heard, and was trying her hand at being a photographer's model or fashion model, something along those lines.

It was not difficult to see her in that line of work. His thoughts, with a mind of their own, posed her in front of a photographer, then a painter, then drifted to her on Mikanos with her girlfriend, stripping off her bathing suit in a secluded cove and stretching out in the hot sand. The friend gradually dissolved and Johann placed himself in the scene, emerging from the water, walking up onto the sand toward the naked reclining figure and–

"The lamb is really quite excellent, don't you think. . .? Mr. Richter?"

Reality abruptly intruded. Christine appeared to be directing a question at him. He stared at her blankly. She was indeed addressing him.

He had to think for a moment to even recall what she had asked. Staring down at his plate, he remembered. "The lamb," he said, inspecting the remains on his plate. "Quite excellent. Yes."

"Would your Fuhrer approve, though?"

"I beg your pardon?"

"Herr Hitler. Isn't he a vegetarian?"

It surprised him she had heard of Hitler as Fuhrer. The Nazis called him that. Not many others did. "Yes, I believe he is," he said. "He has not taken to dictating diets for the rest of us, however," Johann smiled politely.

"Not yet, anyway," she countered. "And of course they say he eats like a pig. Simply shovels the food in."

"Give it a rest, Christine," Clay warned his irrepressible sister.

"I'm simply trying to balance some of that beastly little club-footed Goebbels' propaganda about the 'master race' and its fearless leader," she said. "I'm terribly sorry, but any government so keen on putting its own people into 're-education camps' must have some fundamental flaws."

"They call them 'KZs' now – Konzentrationslagers – from our Kazetlager camps in South Africa during the Boer unpleasantness," Clay said.

"Bravo, *mein bruder*. At least the Nazis have learned something from us," Christine returned.

Her next question was more conciliatory. "So. Righto, then. How did you decide to study in England, Mr. Richter?"

"The decision was made for me. By my father."

"Johann's father and I schooled together at Whitby before the war," Neville Johns interjected in an amiable tone.

"I see," Christine reflected. "And what does your father 'do,' may I inquire?"

"He's an army officer." As always, Johann could not keep an edge of pride out of this pronouncement.

"He is a general," Lord Neville amended. "A highly respected one, I'm sure."

"So he was in the war."

Christine's candor this time put the rest of the dinner party visibly on edge. Neville Johns, who had served with some distinction himself in the Great War, started to politely intervene, but Johann, feeling challenged by Christine, cut him off. "Yes. He was a cavalryman. He–" He was about to say his father had had half his face blown away by British artillery, but drew back, balancing his sensitivity for Clay's feelings against the emotion of the moment. "He was also a farmer for a while. Right after the war." Johann thought of the Tilsit estate, where he had spent his first six years, and felt sad. His father was still absentee landlord of that land. Perhaps one day they would return there.

Christine persisted. "Is he a Nazi?"

"I say, Christine, that is quite enough." Clay gave his sister another warning look.

She remained unruffled. "Please stay out of this, Claiborne. This conversation is between Mr. Richter and myself."

"It's all right Clay. I don't mind." Johann understood he was being interrogated, but he felt more aroused, and perhaps a little embarrassed, than angry. "No," he said. "My father is not a Nazi."

"Why'd he return to the army then?" she asked.

"I don't know."

"Where was your farm?"

"In East Prussia, near Tilsit. It's still in the family."

"A large farm?"

Johann shrugged.

"How big is it?"

"Twenty thousand acres, perhaps." As soon as he said it, Johann realized he had tacked on a few thousand extra acres. Out of spite, he supposed. He knew the grounds of Croyden Castle couldn't be more than five thousand, at most.

"But that's an estate, not a farm!" Emily exclaimed, incredulous enough to put forth her views on the matter.

Christine was poised to trumpet a counterattack, but this time Neville Johns interrupted more firmly. "Come to think of it now, I do seem to remember Karl was heir to a rather large estate somewhere in Eastern Prussia. I had forgotten all about it." His eyes, focused steadily on his daughter, decreed an end to the conversation. The table gathering fell silent. Johann and Christine eyed each other warily, while Clay somewhat anxiously eyed them both.

The talk returned to more mundane topics, but Johann no longer paid attention. He was thinking about his parents. Over the past few years his father's remarks had softened toward the Nazi leadership. And his mother, who had been sympathetic toward the Nazis since the party's early days, now took less trouble to hide her feelings. Karl Richter seemed to think there were too many controls on Hitler to allow him to put any of his crazier ideas into practice. That maybe some of his better ideas were worth a try. Johann had once told that to a classmate at Whitby, and the boy's response had been, "Like getting rid of the Jews?" said with an aristocratic sarcasm that made it difficult to gauge his seriousness.

By the time he returned his focus to the dinner party, dessert was being served.

For the next few days at Croyden Castle, Johann consciously assumed the role of outside observer. He was increasingly disturbed by the influence Anne Wheldon appeared to exercise over Clay, who was not himself in her presence. She made him appear anxious, even nervous at times. The age difference gave her an edge in sophistication. She dominated him, Johann thought, and worse yet, Clay seemed to accept the fact. He acted totally different from the way he handled himself at Whitby. Johann felt almost a stranger to him whenever Anne was around.

Anne and Emily continued for the most part to avoid Johann. Whether they suspected he had seen them together in the woods, he couldn't tell. With Clay's attentions absorbed by Anne, he spent much of his time alone, or with young Samantha, who loved to ride but was only allowed off the immediate grounds with an adult, a role

Johann was deemed to fill. He enjoyed the company of this young-ster with flaming red hair and bright green eyes, so lightweight she needed a special saddle. On occasion Christine, who appeared per-versely drawn to his company, would join them. She seemed not so much friendly, as simply comfortable with the teasing give and take they fell naturally into.

All in all, after it was over, this first visit had seemed to him in many ways successful despite the jolt he'd received that first day out in the woods. By the end of spring holidays Johann felt accepted, at least by most of Clay's family, and had been cordially invited to re-turn.

* * * *

Johann Richter did return to Croyden Castle many times during his ensuing three years at Whitby, spending long stretches of his sum-mers there. He became a familiar household figure at the Johns' es-tate, a special favorite, Clay told him, of both Lord Neville and Lady Eleanor and a great pal to Samantha, who loved to ride with him. When given the chance, he enjoyed helping care for the Johns' new baby boy, Elliot, usually under the watchful eye of a nanny.

After their first encounter, Johann's and Anne Wheldon's stays at Croyden Castle seldom overlapped. On the other hand, he saw Chris-tine Johns there often enough the two of them gradually built up a kind of antagonistic rapport that bordered on something more. It did not become something more in part because it was understood Chris-tine was seeing this Anders Hardy she had visited at Malta, who was now at Christchurch College, Oxford. Though he was not to meet the man until several years later, Johann eventually came to resent his intrusion into his own fantasies about Christine, which had never abated since the first night he met her.

In early May 1936, shortly before Johann and Clay were to com-plete the upper sixth at Whitby and move on to university, Johann made his last visit of those years to Croyden Castle. On the Sunday he and Clay were to return to school, Clay spent the morning with Anne Wheldon visiting mutual friends in nearby Wallingford. While his friend was away, Johann walked along the Thames with Christine. The air was laden with the heady fragrance of newly planted gardens.

To their left, the river ran by, broad and slow-moving. An eight-man crew pushed a racing shell against the current. To their right, thick hedgerows crisscrossed broad expanses of greensward sloping majestically up toward huge old homes. No worldwide depression here, Johann thought.

When they reached a regatta in progress, they watched as set after set of muscled boats glided by in what seemed from shore unruffled competition. A small crowd along the banks – the women in colorful delicate frocks, the men in crisp white slacks, blazers, caps or boaters – sipped champagne and occasionally recognized the racers with a short cheer.

The beautiful morning soon enticed them to climb a steep bluff overlooking the river where it curled around the village of Henley-on-Thames far below. A little out of breath from the exertion, Christine arranged herself on the warm grass at the top of the hill, her skirt tucked up under her, the wind blowing her hair back from her face. She was smiling. She seemed to Johann more relaxed, more accessible, than usual. He sat down slightly above and in front of her, on a large smooth rock that reminded him of the one he had once seen Emily Hardewicke lounging on. From here, the crews racing on the Thames looked like tiny water bugs skimming the surface.

Christine took a Murad from the folds of her skirt and waited for Johann to give her a light. It had become something of a ritual between them. The smell of pungent Turkish tobacco laced the breeze.

"Look here Richter," – she loved to call him by his last name – "let's be honest with each other just this one bloody time." Christine was looking down the hillside as she spoke.

"About what?" He tried to follow her line of vision. It was aimed toward the river.

"I'm talking about us. All of us – you, me, Anne, Clay. It's worse than my crowd in London. We've all been playing some dreadfully silly game with one another since we first met, haven't we."

"Have we?" he said rhetorically. Though he had grown accustomed to her often surprising candor, her brusque prodding on this subject made him distinctly uncomfortable.

"The question is, what is it?" She looked at him, resharpening her usual intensity.

"I don't know," he said.

"Yes you do. We both do."

"Then suppose you tell me what it is." There was an unintended anger in his tone. She looked away from him, took her second drag on the cigarette and flicked it away.

"All right," she said. "I think we've been competing against one another. All of us. I think, for instance, that your major interest – quite platonic, I'm sure – is toward Clay. But Clay is absolutely lost over Anne. There's no mistaking it, dear boy. He's already told me he intends to marry her one day."

This was news, though not very surprising news, to Johann.

"Anne, believe it or not," Christine said, "wants me to be her friend. Her 'best friend,' as she puts it. Unfortunately I don't particularly care for her." Johann wondered how to interpret the slight bitterness he thought he detected behind these words.

"And me, I suppose I'm attracted to you. Though for the world of me I can't imagine why." She looked at him again, then lay back in the grass and stared at the sky.

Johann, startled, gazed up with her at the clouds floating by, trying to think this through and wondering what Christine was after. He couldn't be sure she wasn't baiting him. She had done it often enough before, though never on this subject.

When he looked back down at her, she was staring at him. He could see the challenge in her eyes, as well as a delightful hint of alarm, a vulnerability he had never seen there before. A tremor of excitement shot through him. Without thinking, he found himself on his knees, then was pinning her against the grass, his mouth hard against her lips, his hands meeting no resistance as they explored her body. She met him with a fiery power of her own that consumed him until he began to sense something mechanical in her movements and opened his eyes. Now her stare held only an icy disdain. He shuddered and recoiled. Lay back in the grass and let the sun bask his eyelids in a soothing warmth. He thought of Clay. He felt guilty.

Still breathing hard, Christine sat up. Johann rolled his head toward the movement. The grass that clung to her disheveled hair was like a renewed invitation, a tempting reminder of what he had just missed. But when he met her eyes again, he knew the initial invitation had not been real, was tainted somehow. He also knew, for the moment at least, that to reject her had given him more satisfaction than taking her ever could have.

But that didn't stop him from feeling a regret that bordered on sadness. The faint taste of tobacco on his lips lingered as a reminder.

Johann stood up. Christine ignored his proffered hand and got to her feet without help. Her eyes had regained their customary self-control. Neither of them attempted any further communication as they worked their way back down the hillside toward the river and the regatta crowd.

* * * *

Johann never told Clay much of anything about what had developed between himself and Christine. Nor did he ever tell him of the scene he had witnessed between Anne Wheldon and her friend Emily in the woods of Croyden Castle. He rationalized that perhaps it was only a one-time thing, a meaningless encounter similar to what occurred between adolescent boys now and then. And in a way, it was none of his business. Or so he told himself. In truth, he shrunk from telling Clay. Without anyone else knowing about it, he thought, it somehow seemed less real and more like a disturbing dream.

In late June of 1936, at the St. Albans train station on the banks of the River Ver, he and Clay parted as best friends, Johann headed for the University at Heidelberg, Clay going up to Oxford – "to any college but Christchurch," he had said in a swipe at his prospective brother-in-law Anders Hardy.

It was as hard for Johann to part with Clay now as it had been for him to leave Germany for England three and a half years earlier. Clay's eyes reflected the unhappiness in his own. Both of them stood emptied of graduation-day small talk. Their hands met, held, dropped apart, and Johann climbed aboard the train. He took one last look back at his friend standing on the station platform and wondered if this might not be the last they'd ever see of one another.

Johann Richter would not, as it turned out, see Clay Johns again for another three years – and then only under circumstances neither would have believed possible on this beautiful summer afternoon that marked the end of their youthful days together.

CHAPTER VII

Five o'clock Wednesday morning. Clear skies, crisp air. Court was not in session. Cohen, slightly groggy, caught the early train north. Tuesday had been a brief, mostly procedural day in court. Mr. Benevides had wrapped up his cross-examination of Marie Renault in short order, only attacking her conclusions about who killed Yvonne Duchamps, which were no more than pure speculation, he pointed out.

After Marie Renault's testimony no new witnesses had been called. Cohen had taken the opportunity to poke around and find out what he could about Richter's jungle woman. He had found out very little, but an assistant in the La Negra prosecutor's office, swearing him to secrecy, had at least confirmed that she in fact existed and lived somewhere up above Riberalta.

He still had no clue as to John Weaver's motivation in tipping him off about the woman. In spite of the casual way he'd done it, Cohen doubted Weaver had done it inadvertently. The *Baltimore Sun* reporter did not strike him as a man too lazy to follow up a great lead. His "getting older" excuse had not rung true.

The train was mostly empty. A few mestizos in simple rural dress, and Cohen. While he tried unsuccessfully to sleep, the train wound its way northeast over the Las Yungas Range, down onto plateaus and into valleys, north along the line of the Beni River. Over and over, to the *clack-clack-clack* of steel wheels hitting steel rails, he wondered who Richter's woman could be. He had little to go on. Only that she was European. Or so the assistant prosecutor had heard. German, according to John Weaver. And young. That was about it.

He wondered if she could possibly be Yvonne Duchamps. A long shot, to be sure. Not German. But she had been Richter's lover apparently. And she'd disappeared, Marie Renault had said. What better place to disappear to? On the other hand, of course, she was also supposed to be dead. Her murder, after all, was one of the charges against Richter. The prosecutor had said he would prove it.

Could Richter's woman perhaps be one of his English acquaintances? Cohen had no idea. None of the angles he came up with made much sense.

By the time the train had left the mountains he was engrossed in Terry Harper's manuscript and notes. They did indeed, as he had remembered, paint a more multidimensional picture of Richter than he'd yet received from anywhere else. With an emphasis on Richter's ties to the anti-Hitler plotters, the narrative seemed generally sympathetic toward him. Richter apparently believed the July 20 plot had been undermined, but refused to tell Harper why or by whom. His escape from England in 1943 was a complicated affair, he told Harper, but the complications were not explained.

From his notes, Harper, Cohen was reminded, appeared to have met with Richter in La Negra. There was nothing about a home in the jungle, no mention anywhere that Richter might be with a woman in South America. And – like the extradition hearing so far – no mention of Richter with Heinrich Mueller. Nothing about Kaisenher. Cohen wondered if Harper, wherever he and his unfettered soul were wandering now, was looking on, wishing he could explain it all better.

Finally, by mid-afternoon, the train arrived at the lowlands town of Riberalta at the juncture of the Beni and Madre de Dios rivers. The air was hot and wet. There were few people on the crude gravel streets.

Not a bar in sight.

Cohen entered several shops and one sparsely furnished eating establishment before he found someone he could communicate with, someone who was also willing and able to give him directions to where Richter had lived before his capture.

At first the man would not talk to him. When asking for "Eric Altmann" got him nowhere, Cohen quickly dropped that ploy and said he was a friend of Johann Richter's, with a message for Richter's wife. This lie was a gamble. In making it, Cohen could not be sure whether he would gain an ally or an enemy.

He was in luck. The man was immediately friendlier and drew a map on the back of a menu. Vague directions at best, but Cohen figured other locals could probably interpret them.

"What is the best way to travel there?" Cohen asked the man.

"Taxi," the man said. "En el zocalo."

"Gracias," Cohen said.

At the town square, an ancient beat-up Chevrolet that looked held together by chicken wire appeared to be the only option. In his makeshift Spanish, Cohen managed to more or less convey his wishes to the driver, and between them they deciphered the map. As Cohen climbed into the front seat beside him, the man took a pistol from the seat and shoved it in the glove compartment. He had a machete on the floor beneath his feet. "There are rebels in the jungle," he announced, displaying more English than Cohen had realized he possessed.

They drove further north, along another, smaller river that flowed toward the village of Rio Negro. Here the countryside alternated between open plains and thick jungle, the sun seeming to beat down hotter with every mile the cab progressed. The heat, the primitive road, reminded Cohen of Israel. His mind wandered. This could be a total wild goose chase, he thought, caught between blaming John Weaver or himself for listening to Weaver.

But he didn't mind postponing a showdown with Johann Richter. It wasn't that he feared Richter, the man. What he feared was the past. Confronting the past. All of it. The Nazis, his family, the camps, what happened in Israel, all of it. He was aware of this, but had never studied the idea too closely for fear of confirming something he didn't want to deal with. In confronting Richter, he would be compelled to search for answers. His real fear, he supposed, was that he would find answers he did not want to find. Or perhaps worse, no answers at all.

The final lap of the trip, for five or six miles after they had turned east from the smaller river, was on a pathway that hardly deserved the name "road." The road along the river had been dirt, but at least had been cleared of most obstacles. This one was also dirt, but looked like it was under cultivation. Vegetation grew at every angle out of its hot steamy ruts. It appeared not to have been driven on in months.

The heat sticking to Cohen's skin began to prickle and itch. His driver was growing nervous. At each new bend in the road he became more hesitant. He drove slower – his way of saying he didn't want to go any further, Cohen thought. They saw no one. He had said at the start it would cost extra to go this far into the jungle. Cohen had paid the extra.

Now, with the worsening roads, the driver mentioned the rebels again and started talking about turning back. "Rivera is out here," he said. As the subjects of danger and money came up, his English continued to improve. This gave Cohen hope. He promised the man a bonus. They drove on. Finally, with Cohen nearly ready to concede the effort himself, the cab abruptly bounced its way into a clearing in the undergrowth. He prayed this was it.

The clearing was bounded on one side by a shaded stream that seemed to have emerged from nowhere. The water bubbled along only twenty yards or so in back of a small, neat, stucco dwelling that supported a thatched roof with low overhanging eaves. Trees crowding in close around it provided a thick canopy of shade and shelter. The house and the grounds that surrounded it were immaculate. There was a sense of orderliness about the place. In contrast, a couple of scrawny hens squawked out of the way as the cab wheeled into the front yard. Chickens were wandering around everywhere, the only immediate evidence of life. Against the wall of jungle on the far right-hand side of the yard stood a row of four or five huts and feeders for the birds.

Cohen gladly escaped the suffocating heat of the cab. He climbed out and unlimbered the knots his muscles had tied trying to countermand the jostling they'd been getting back on the road. He suddenly realized he was being observed. A small dark-skinned boy was standing naked in the shade of the house's open doorway, giving him a careful inspection. The boy had a head of strikingly blond hair. This must be the right place. It appeared Richter had more than just a woman out here.

The driver said he must return to Riberalta. Now. Cohen asked him to wait, just for ten minutes, but he refused. Cohen tipped him generously and said he would be even more generous if the man would return no later than noon tomorrow. The driver, happier now, agreed. Cohen shook his hand with a reassuring smile meant to reenforce their pact. The smile faded as he watched the man drive away, the Chevrolet's loose driveshaft bouncing up and down along the road. That was the last he would ever see of him, Cohen figured. A little belatedly, he wondered how unfriendly the rebels might be.

Meanwhile, he hoped Richter's woman, whoever she was, would be a good host. At least give him a place on the floor for a night. His first objective was to find her. As Cohen approached the front door, the young boy fled back into the house. He knocked on the open door. Called out. No one answered. He didn't feel comfortable entering the house unwelcomed, so he decided to explore outside a little. Her boy was here. She had to show up eventually.

Sweaty and thirsty, he headed for the stream.

As he rounded the corner of the house, he was brought up short. Twenty feet in front of him stood a woman. She was cradling a long rifle loosely, familiarly, between her arms, its muzzle pointed off to one side. Cohen had the feeling she had been aware of his presence all along. They both stood stock still, two animals in the wild evaluating each other.

She must have been swimming or bathing when she heard the cab arrive, he concluded. Her black, shoulder-length hair hung together, wet, clinging to her neck and dripping water onto a white sheath that was all she was wearing. The sheath stuck to her body where it was damp. She was dark and statuesque. Here, her darkness seemed to Cohen more Indian than European or Arabic, with strong, high cheekbones highlighting her features.

But he had seen women like this in Palestine as well, eyes dark and intense, with rugged limbs accustomed to hard outdoor work. She looked in fact something like Rachel, which disconcerted him.

The woman finally addressed him, in Spanish.

He brought both his palms up slowly in spread-fingered incomprehension. "No comprende. Habla Ingles?"

"Who are you?" she said, her English thick with Bavarian accent.

He thought for a moment to address her in German, then decided against it. He would leave that up to her. "Are you the wife of Johann Richter?" he asked in English.

She nodded almost imperceptibly.

"Good. I have been looking for you."

"Why?" She had not moved the rifle in her arms, but Cohen had the sensation she was coiled to strike.

"My name is Michael Cohen. I've been at your husband's trial."

"Why are you here?"

Good question, he thought. He wondered if he could make it clear to her.

"Well, I–" He was interrupted by a small monkey bounding up to him and jumping into his arms, nestling up around his neck. The creature was light as a feather and seemed content to stay where it was, firmly snuggled in. Cohen laughed, and petted his new friend.

The woman, however, did not appear to be amused. She was staring at him intently, with a queer look on her face. He still felt a little unnerved by her resemblance to Rachel.

She took several steps closer. "Your arm," she said, making a motion for him to show her his arm.

He held out his right arm, knowing it was not the one she meant, but wanting somehow to meet her demand with some small initiative of his own.

"No, the other one," she said.

He shifted the monkey to his right arm and held out his left, palm down. She reached out and turned it over. "From where?" she said, giving his wrist a gentle tug.

"Dachau," he said, as always feeling a sense of shame for having survived to say the word.

The woman was silent for a moment, looking at his arm. She appeared to have forgotten the rifle.

She held out her own left arm, palm up. "Kaisenher," she said, putting the numbers etched deep in her skin alongside his. He was confused, as if she had suddenly dropped in from a different planet he had never expected to visit again. She didn't belong here.

This was the wife of Johann Richter?

"Come inside," she said. "It is cooler."

Inside, the house seemed more substantial than it had from outside. The main room was large, soothingly dark. Though it had only two windows, the larger one gave an impressive view all the way down to the stream that flowed behind the house and to the jungle beyond.

"Thirsty?" she said.

He nodded. "Very."

"Just a moment." She left for another room, presumably the kitchen.

Cohen put the monkey down and it scampered off.

He felt distracted. Disoriented. Was it that Richter's woman was a survivor of the camps – and of Kaisenher, in particular – or that she looked like Rachel? Or both.

Finding no traction for these thoughts, he explored his surroundings. The floor was covered with several old Persian rugs laid over a layer of wicker matting, under which was probably dirt. He could feel the earthy coolness emanating from beneath him and dying out on its way toward a ceiling that opened all the way up to the inside of the thatched roof. Flat boards had been placed over rough-hewn rafters to form a small loft storage area, to which a ladder nailed to the wall gave access. The walls of the room were hung with original paintings, most of them landscapes that appeared to be of local scenes.

The woman returned with two drinks, gave one to Cohen and sipped from the other herself. The drink tasted like lemonade with bitters added.

"Sit down," she said. He sat on a long, low, roughly stitched couch.

"My name is Elena Stein," she said.

"Michael Cohen," he reminded her, understanding now why she had been in Kaisenher, and taking note there was no "Richter" attached to her name.

"Welcome."

They sipped their drinks in silence. She appeared to have rubbed her hair dry, he noticed. Even dry, it had a glossy sheen.

"So. You are here, why?"

His first impulse was to lie. He couldn't believe he had not thought this out in advance. The truth tumbled out. "I need to know," he said. "I need to know why it happened. Who they were, the people who did it. Who *he* is."

"I understand that," she returned. "But Johann is not one of them. He is never one of them."

Cohen thought for a moment to tell her about his magazine assignment. Maybe later, he decided.

They fell silent. Still feeling unsettled, he let his eyes wander again. "Who is the painter?" he said, scanning the art on the walls.

She stood up and pointed to three landscapes, in oils. The colors were rich and vivid. The style was realistic, very detailed. "Johann's," she said.

She moved to the far side of the room, where two watercolors were hung. The colors were nearly washed out. The brushstrokes were broad and sweeping, the opposite of detailed realism. Cohen didn't know what they were meant to portray, and yet they pulled at him in some basic way.

"Mine," she said.

"They're good."

"Thank you." She returned to her chair.

During the brief silence that ensued, she appeared to Cohen to be composing a question for him. When she finally spoke the words, she showed the first signs of emotion he had heard from her, other than her muted reaction to his having been at Dachau.

"Johann," she said. "Can you tell me about him? You have talk with him? He is. . . How is he?"

"I don't know," Cohen said. "I haven't talked to him."

She searched his eyes. "He is not a bad man."

"To be honest, I, uh—"

A baby cried out from another room.

Elena Stein got up. She started to say something in English, then Spanish. "I am sorry. Un momento, por favor." Still no German. Cohen understood why, now.

She left the room. When she returned, she was carrying a small baby in her arms. Sitting only a few feet from Cohen, she casually dropped the top of her dress and gave the baby a dark nipple. The baby went at it hungrily. More startling than the nakedness was a deep purple scar that ran from her shoulder to just above her right breast. From Kaisenher, Cohen assumed. His doubts were eroding. Perhaps she did belong here somehow.

Elena remained focused on feeding her baby. She seemed comfortable with the silence.

The young boy, wearing shorts now, advanced shyly into the room. Elena introduced Cohen to him. His name was Tomas, she said.

Tomas looked a question at his mother. She said something reassuring-sounding to him in Spanish. The boy walked over to Cohen with small, shy steps, looked up at him with big brown eyes, uncertain. Cohen felt a stab at his heart, remembering a similar pair of eyes from years ago. Unfamiliar guests were rare here, he imagined. On impulse, he reached out, caught Tomas under the arms and flew him up into his lap.

The sudden movement seemed not to startle the boy at all. He put a chubby little hand on Cohen's cheek and pulled it across his face, exploring, then looked back at his mother, who smiled encouragement at him. Finally satisfied, he turned back to Cohen and bestowed upon him a beatific smile.

Tomas settled in and soon drifted off to sleep in his lap. As Cohen watched the baby suckle at Elena's breast, the woman and child gradually melded into one inseparable being for him. It seemed so peaceful here. Somehow this depressed him. He felt overpowered by a sense of loss. Nonetheless, as he sat there, he felt a surge of gratitude toward an unexpected quarter. *Thank you, John Weaver, whatever your reasons were,* he thought.

"Heidelberg"

The eight-hour train ride from Berlin to Heidelberg in October of 1936 gave Johann Richter a chance to reflect on the new Germany he had returned to after nearly four years in England.

Hitler, like some inevitable force of nature, had consolidated the power he had won in 1933. Once secure in that power, he had withdrawn Germany from the International Disarmament Conference and the League of Nations. He had accepted the Saarland back into the Reich through plebiscite, had remilitarized the country and reoccupied the Rhineland in direct defiance of the Treaty of Versailles. With Mussolini, he had begun sending military aid to the fascists who were rebelling against the Republican government in Spain.

Shortly after Johann had begun his second year in England, the leadership of the Nazi Sturmabteilung, the irregular troop SA, the brown-shirts, had been wiped out during the "Night of the Long Knives," so-called because of the symbolic dagger associated with the paramilitary group. Himmler's fledgling SS did the dirty work. Hundreds of SA leaders had been executed during the 24-hour rampage and Erich Roehm – who as head of the SA had held power rivaling even Hitler's – was no longer alive to exercise it. The SA's challenge to the Reichswehr for military supremacy was over. Besides Himmler, the newly ascending stars in the Nazi galaxy were named Hess, Goering, Heydrich, Goebbels and Bormann.

A month later, on 2 August 1934, Field Marshal Paul von Hindenburg, the hero of Tannenberg and president of the Reich, died. Hitler had the office of president abolished and himself named Fuhrer, a Caesar-like figure of chancellor, president and supreme commander of the armed forces all rolled into one. He now demanded an oath of personal loyalty from all officers and men of the Reichswehr. The German military's traditional independence from the head of state, maintained even with the Kaiser during the World War, was at an end.

Hitler was credited with putting people back to work, food back on German tables. He was a hero to many, but not to all. Johann sensed that a new caution, a new fear, had crept into many of his countrymen's lives. The Nazi Party was inserting political officers into all aspects of life, and was indoctrinating the country's youth through the Jungvolk and Hitler Jugend for boys, the Jungmadel and Bund Deutscher Madel for girls. The party was trying to undermine the traditional role of educators, church groups, labor unions, and other political parties or interest groups. Its goal was to smooth out class differences and mold the nation into one state of mind.

"To what end?" Johann had asked his father.

"To go to war," the General had answered.

His father's attitude puzzled him. Some aspects of Nazism, Karl Richter now admitted, held an attraction for him.

"The Fuhrer hates Communism, and is uncomfortable with capitalism," he told Johann. "He wants to recast the German man and German woman in the heroic mold. He wants them to rise above the insignificant role the modern world has cast for them. He and Mussolini both. It is a potent myth he wants to build. Look at the SS, even many of their general officers. They are young; some of them very young. Hitler has struck a chord with them. He wants to change the world, and he is willing to gamble everything for his beliefs. If he wins, his mark on history will be a significant one."

"And if he loses?" Johann asked.

His father paused and stared out a window. "That is, of course, one of the risks," he said. "Whether the man is a madman or a genius depends on your perspective. He could bring us glory. Or he could destroy us."

Johann was dismayed, but he could understand why his father had made at least a practical accommodation with the Nazis. Hitler knew how to keep the army happy. He had followed up his personal loyalty oath decree by replacing the Reichswehr, with its manpower cap of a hundred thousand imposed by the hated Treaty of Versailles, with a new, broad-based national army, the Wehrmacht. Compulsory military service was reinstituted. Secret training exercises, particularly in the Soviet Union, had given the new Wehrmacht several years head start, Karl Richter told Johann, but now the buildup would be much easier and out in the open.

He had even considered joining the Nazi Party, if only for pragmatic reasons, his father told him. What had stopped him, it appeared, was an issue on which his convictions had never wavered. He scoffed at the Nazis' recently announced Nuremberg Laws that aimed to limit the rights of Jews, Slavs and others. This policy to eradicate from German life the economic, intellectual and social influence of non-Aryans was a calamitous mistake, he believed. Indefensible both morally and practically.

The General did not hesitate to express this view quite openly to his guests, usually close military friends, at Orienbad. He'd recently joked with one such gathering, for instance, about a mutual nonaggression pact being prepared with the Japanese, who were to be declared "honorary" Aryans for the occasion. It had won him a hearty round of laughs. At such moments Johann, who happened to be present, felt a renewed pride in his father. He felt on this point as his father did, and more. To him, Hitler was still the madman, ready to lead Germany toward genocide and disaster.

The few months Johann had spent at home after his graduation from Whitby had been a jubilant time for the nation — in August the Nazis had whitewashed Berlin to showcase the XI Olympiad, a stunning propaganda triumph — but they had also been personally difficult. Though Johann had been admitted to the University of Heidelberg, his father was against his matriculating there, favoring instead his entering the Wehrmacht and aiming for a slot at the Army's General Staff College at Berlin-Moabit.

Staff College, founded by the legendary General Karl von Clausewitz in 1810, was Germany's answer to England's Royal Military College at Sandhurst and like Sandhurst was the key that unlocked doors to the upper echelons of command. At Heidelberg, Karl Richter believed, Johann would study too many irrelevant subjects and graduate into the ranks of the army anyway. He would fall behind his peers in the battle for command-level promotions in the years ahead.

But Johann, who wanted to study in Heidelberg's world-renowned departments of history and philosophy, had argued vehemently for the venerable 550-year-old university. Not particularly adverse to the idea of an army career himself, he had tried to placate his father with visions of his spending long hours with some of the best instructors in Europe, studying German history and the military campaigns of past wars. Johann's mother had supported him. Her father had graduated from Heidelberg and had emerged "quite respectably" as a top German general in the World War, she pointed out.

Father and son were at heart too empathetic to come to a serious breach over the matter. The General finally acceded to his son's wishes – though not to his wife's, as he had pointed out to them both in as close to a joking tone as he ever used. Johann appreciated his mother's efforts on his behalf. At the same time, he'd experienced a twinge of guilt when she had backed his side against his father's. He saw his father, for all their differences of opinion, as his more natural ally.

The gentle rocking of his compartment signaled the train was slowing. Johann, as he stared out the window, wondered vaguely if his father might not yet impatiently interfere with his studies at Heidelberg before the normal four-year tenure had run its course. Then the train suddenly rounded the curve of a hill, and he could see the Neckar River and the distant parapets of the famed Heidelberg Castle arching toward a gray sky. The panorama was so enthralling he didn't notice the banner posted just before the station – *Fuhrer, Volk, und Vaterland.*

* * * *

In Heidelberg, Johann took a room on the second floor of the town house of Frau Ida Kampmeier, an elderly widow. Her only rule was no smoking in the half-timbered house. He settled quickly and easily into the life of a first-year university student, a "fuchs." And yet there was something disturbing about that life. By 1936, more than forty Heidelberg faculty members had been dismissed or forced into early retirement during the previous three years for racial, religious or political reasons. Several professors with Jewish wives had been expelled from the university's teaching staff.

The former position of "Rector" was now referred to as "Fuhrer," and as such was appointed by the Reichsminister for Education rather than elected by the Faculty Senate. Members of the Senate, an academic governing and advisory body, were now nominated and removed by this Fuhrer, rather than elected by the Faculties, as had been the case in the past. Instructors could be transferred in and out of the school on short notice, negating the protection and security of tenured professorships. The teachers who remained were either pro-Nazi or politically inhibited. Largely for these reasons, most of the universities of England that year had rejected an invitation to join Heidelberg in celebrating its 550th anniversary.

Contrary to his father's concerns, Johann promptly began receiving a good deal of compulsory military training. Drill time was required of all students and he was given the opportunity to show off his skills in marksmanship. Political orientation, however, received the most emphasis. National student associations had been organized around several of his academic subjects. Each local group had at least one Nazi representative, and much time was spent monitoring and discussing the character and conduct of professors.

Abstract theory was now held in generally low regard, with the emphasis being placed increasingly on technical studies and applied research. In Johann's major fields of concentration, history and philosophy, the curriculum was beginning to lean toward the revisionist and doctrinaire lines of Germany's new leaders. Military history was not ignored in explaining the country's defeat in the World War. But that the Fatherland had been the victim of "Dolchstoss," treacherously stabbed in the back by traitors on the home front, particularly Jews, was now presented as established fact.

In philosophy, many of the obscure, misinterpreted postulations of men like Nietzsche were now being pushed to the forefront, with increasing attention given to the parts that proved readily malleable to Nazi dogma and supportive of an Aryan "master race." Anti-Semitism was running rampant throughout the university, a virulent disease that met little resistance. Students and professors Johann might otherwise have liked and respected were infected along with the rest. For a while, he argued with them. Eventually he learned to keep his heretical thoughts to himself.

He found an exception however in Erich Borchers, a classmate from Stuttgart. Borchers was an active young man with an equally active intellect. He had been influenced by the Heidelberg circle of renowned poet Stefan George. Before he died in 1933, George had preached the emergence of a new German man. He taught the Greek concept of the inseparability of body and soul, had touted action as a way of life, and told his followers they should be prepared to accept moral responsibility for their actions in service to their fellow man.

The Nazis had tried to claim George as one of their own. He used the swastika symbol, espoused the Fuhrerprincep, taught the heroic ideal and believed in a sort of mystical primacy of inherited traits over learning, of intuition and instinct over intellect. But in "The Seventh Ring" he also wrote of Der Widerchrist, the Antichrist who brings destruction along with his miracles, and his disciples tended to look toward Hitler when they referred to the idea.

Borchers was dark and of medium height, with earnest, searching eyes of light blue. A wolf's eyes, but with empathy. He and Johann, who shared several classes, would debate politics and philosophy far into the night. During these discussions Borchers often referred to the von Stauffenberg brothers of Stuttgart, who had also been followers of Stefan George. The three brothers, whose father Count Alfred Schenk von Stauffenberg had once served as senior marshal in the court of the King of Wurttemberg, were particularly adept pupils of George's, Borchers said.

Especially the youngest, Claus. Borchers would often repeat arguments Claus von Stauffenberg had once made to him, throwing them now into support of his debates with Johann. Claus was already a captain in the Wehrmacht and making a name for himself at General Staff College, he had heard.

Sometimes, Borchers said, he wondered how Claus was doing so well in the army. He had a sensitive nature and was not prone to putting up with fools, or with foolish ideas. For example he would never have countenanced the anti-Semites at Heidelberg, Borchers said. He would have confronted them, in spite of the odds.

The daily dose of anti-Semitism made Johann wish he had a Jewish friend with whom he could talk. At the university in late 1936, the only Jews known to him were a few shopkeepers he patronized. He had no real perspective on what being a Jew, particularly a Jew in modern Germany, was all about, and he knew it. He promised himself if he were ever presented the opportunity to find out, he would grab it without hesitation.

* * * *

After only a few months at Heidelberg, Johann came to realize that in many ways he'd had more in common with his former English classmates than he now did with his peers in Germany. In spite of its sometimes callous eccentricities, English public school life began to take on a pleasant afterglow in his memory. He longed for his old friends. In particular, Clay Johns. And oddly enough he missed Christine Johns as well. His memories of her grew all the sharper as it became increasingly apparent Heidelberg would not provide him a substitute. Women were in short supply at the university, and his encounters so far had not progressed beyond a meeting of minds.

But he did have Heidelberg acquaintances besides Erich Borchers. Some he was comfortable enough with to join for an occasional evening of beer-drinking at a studentenlokal, where the entertainment often emanated from the sputter and crackle of a wireless blaring banned jazz from the BBC, and the talk would always turn, eventually, to politics. Sometimes they would do their drinking and arguing at Sepp'l, the official biergarten of the five Heidelberg dueling corps. Johann and Borchers were studying the art of fencing and had been invited to join several of these groups. At first they had declined, put off by the fawning brotherhood fostered by the corps life, as well as by the idea of gaining stature through the bloody use of a sword on someone else, with scars worn as status symbols. Eventually, though, they had joined one and began to develop into superior swordsmen with epee and foil.

Borchers refused to fence with Johann. They were both relentlessly competitive, and he didn't want the formal matches, which could be intense, to come between them. Nor did he want to fight a Mensur – the once-outlawed student duel brought back into vogue by the Nazis – with his best friend. They had opposite fencing styles. Where Johann was reckless, prone to risking all with his aggressiveness, Borchers was more deliberate and strategy-oriented, masking his quickness until just the right moment to strike. Johann's style, and his willingness to use the saber, eventually won him a sliced-open cheekbone below his right eye. As it was being sewn up by a Heidelberg doctor, he said a silent prayer of gratitude that his eye had not been damaged as his father's had been.

His only concern in the aftermath was that the tiny but clearly visible stitch-marks left him with a slightly sinister look. On the positive side, his fencing friends were properly respectful of the scar, which had been earned in a Mensur with the best fencer at Heidelberg, whom Johann had fought to a draw. They considered it a badge of honor. Borchers on the other hand – proud to be one of the few dueling corps members with no scar to show off – teased him unmercifully about it.

The corps became the center of Johann's social life at Heidelberg, but he was also something of an habitué of the bar at the Europaische-Hof, the city's largest hotel. Popular with non-students and often packed, the place offered a degree of anonymity and privacy. It was here he initiated his few close friendships other than Borchers, drinking Schmolles, exchanging toasts and the unfamiliar form of address *sie* for the familiar *du* in the traditional ritual of attained comradeship.

Johann did not give up his love for horses and riding while at Heidelberg. He had little trouble talking his father into the funds to buy a highly spirited black stallion and to rent space for it at a nearby stable. When the books became blurry and tiresome, or when he just needed to get away, he would saddle up and ride out through the fields and forests around the city. He always took a rifle with him, but rarely hunted, preferring to target practice on inanimate objects just to keep his hand in.

Riding was an activity Erich Borchers didn't pursue, and Johann thought perhaps that was fortunate. It was his chance to be alone. After the first snows came, he would ride the ancient frozen countryside dreaming dreams of long-lost worlds so real to him at times it felt as if he had once inhabited this land himself in some earlier life.

It was on such a ride his fuchs winter at Heidelberg that he first met the family of Elena Stein.

CHAPTER VIII

Elena Stein took the baby from her breast and carried her back to bed. When she returned to Cohen, she suggested, with a nod toward the darkening sky, they take a walk outside before the sun was gone. "Teresa, she always sleeps at least one hour," she said.

Tomas skipped out of the house along with them. The air was warm, but not the soppy hot of before. Elena warned Cohen there would be insects. They descended toward the stream and took a rickety handmade bridge across to the other bank. Beyond the trees here, the land opened out into a wide stretch of fence-enclosed field. They climbed the crude rail fence and headed toward a distant curve in the river where it had been diverted to make a small pond. Cohen could see four or five horses congregated about the water. Tomas ran on ahead.

Cohen felt transported into another world. Clouds of shimmering particles hovered above the fields. Horizontal rays of sun illuminated this dust or pollen into millions of airborne crystals that parted in graceful waves as they passed through.

Without prompting, Elena repeated that Johann Richter was a good man, and launched into why that was so. "The first time," she said, "I ever see him is in 1936. He is eighteen. I am only six." She alternated looking down at the ground, up into the crystal sky, as she spoke, her voice softer now. "My family, we live near to Eberbach, a village maybe twenty kilometers from Heidelberg. My father is a carpenter. We are one of only a few Jewish families in Eberbach.

"One time in December – in the evening, very cold, there is much snow on the ground – our supper is interrupted by a young man coming to the door asking a shelter for his horse. It is Johann. My father shows to him our old abandoned barn, for his horse, and invites him to stay the night. Johann is not the first at our door in this way. We live out in the country and sometimes have visitors we do not expect.

"By the time they come back from the barn it is snowing again. Johann, he is shaking his clothes off on the steps, then he is stepping inside and I remember flakes of snow melting in his hair. Even so young as I am back then, he is very handsome to me."

Elena Stein glanced at Cohen with a little smile. "He is such a big mystery to us, me and my brother Gerhardt. He is not like any of the others. He is from Heidelberg, the famous university; he is living near Berlin, going before to school in England. Gerhardt is only eight years old. We ask Johann so many questions, but he is very patient with us. He tells us stories of his 'adventures,' he calls them. To us they are like fairy tales. My mother finally makes us leave Johann alone that first night.

"We enjoy him so much that my father, he invites him to come back. And he does come back. At first not for two or three months, then every month or so, and finally every few weeks. He is lonely at the university, I think.

"Gerhardt and I, we wait for Johann's visits with great eagerness. When he visits he brings us little presents. And always, because he knows we are poor, some food to replace what he eats in our home. We listen to his stories, ride on his horse, sometimes play sports or games with him. I think for him too it is enjoyable. He even joins us for our holidays now and then. Especially Purim and Passover he likes. For two years, he returns to see us many times. Not only for me and Gerhardt. He has long talks with my mother and father. I hear him one time asking my father about the Jews, how it is for them. For us.

"For Gerhardt, he is like an older brother. For me, he is a childhood fantasy. Often I dream of him in my sleep. I dream I am a woman old enough for him. I do not know how he thinks of me. Or if he thinks of me. I am sure I do not always understand the things he says to me, or how he looks at me, or talks to me."

They had reached the pond, which glittered in the setting sun. Cohen stroked the back of a large chestnut mare Elena said was named Sacha after a horse her husband had loved as a child, as it nonchalantly swished at flies with its tail. Tomas was wading in the water. The oppressive heat of the day was only a memory. Rich wet jungle smells assaulted the senses. Elena walked halfway up a shallow knoll that rose above one side of the pond and sat down in the grass. Cohen followed and sat beside her.

He couldn't quite believe she was handing him Richter's story so easily. He didn't want to say anything to break the spell. They remained silent, contemplating the glowing horizon.

"After he leave us for the last time," she finally went on, "we keep hoping he will come back, but he never does. He has warn my parents about the Nazis, but Gerhardt and I, we do not know this until much later, after our father is gone. . .

"The war start. In our village, there is not much done against the Jews. We hear of 'Kristallnacht,' the Nazis' big night of attacking the Jews before the war, but my father says it must be a story. That it can not be so bad as we hear. My father, he thinks all of the terrible stories we hear can not be true. That it is too horrible to be true.

"But by the third year of the war, the start of 1942, he is worried enough to go to Frankfurt, to the home of a cousin there, to find out whatever he can. While he is in Frankfurt, we hear one time from him. My mother, she talks to him by telephone. That is all. She tells us, but not until later, that he says to her it is worse even than we hear. He says he tries to get us out of Germany soon. But we never hear from him, or see him, again. Or the family of his cousin. Mother hears they are put onto trains one night, with many other Jews in Frankfurt, and are sent to the east somewhere. But that is all she can ever find out."

"Nacht und Nebel."

"Yes. 'Night and fog.' People disappearing. So we stay in our village. There is nothing else to do, my mother says. That summer the Nazis finally come for us. My brother, he tries to protect us. He is killed in front of us. My mother and I they take to a temporary camp near Stuttgart, then a few weeks later to Dachau, near Munich – I am sorry, you know that; you know about Dachau. The first day there, we are line up with hundreds of prisoners and they divide us into two groups. Most who are old or very young are put in one group. The rest of us go into the other. The first group they send to the gas chambers at Auschwitz, but we do not know this. My mother is in this group."

Cohen winced. Elena's story hit too close to home. His own introduction to Dachau had come the following year. In nightmares, he was still there. It was something he tried not to think about.

"I am with the others," she said. "They send us to Kaisenher, a smaller camp near Ulm. A labor camp. We live there in barracks surrounded by barbed wire and guards. I am put to work in a factory that makes ball bearings."

Cohen's focus, already intense, zeroed in at the word "Kaisenher."

Elena Stein stared at what was left of the sunset, lost in another world. "Things happen there," she went on, her voice even softer now.

"The commandant of the camp, he takes me to his bed. I do not know about such things. I am only thirteen or fourteen at the time. At first I want to kill myself, but after losing already my father and brother, my mother maybe, I cannot do it."

Rachel, Rachel, Rachel. The two women were blending into one for Cohen, stunned by the parallels. They flowed through his defenses, flooding him with anger and guilt.

"Instead, I kill everything inside me." Elena spoke now as if in a trance. "Everything," she said, staring at Cohen with eyes that seemed less focused on him than on the memory. "Even for my fellow prisoners, I show nothing. I have my own world. The rest I can barely remember."

She gave him a quick sideways glance. "You, I think, will understand all of this." Then she looked away again. Cohen understood better than she could ever imagine.

"Finally, the commandant, he gets tired of me. He sends me back into the camp. Because of him, I think, I am treated a little better by the guards. Many of the other prisoners do not like this, so they do not like me. But they are afraid, I suppose, to attack me, so they just ignore me. I am very lonely.

"Even with the better treatment, by this time my mind and body are giving out. Death is always in the air now, and every day it looks better to me. By now, at Kaisenher too, they are sometimes killing with the gas those who can work no more. I am nearly there, I think. . .

"But then something happen. God, maybe, change His mind, I think. One night, a soldier – not a guard, but a soldier – he takes me from my bed to see the doctor of the camp. Dr. Roark gives me a medical inspection. Afterwards, a clean dress to wear. He tells me not to be nervous. I listen, because he is not such a bad man. He is kind to me before. To my surprise, he and the soldier take me from the camp. We go to a large hotel in Munich. The soldier stays in the hall while Dr. Roark takes me into a room. He tells me to wait, not to worry. Then he leaves.

"I wait. I wonder if I am to sleep with someone again. The commandant, maybe. It is hard to believe, I am so skinny and ugly. Either way, it does not matter to me. Nothing matters to me anymore.

"The room is filled with antiques. I cannot sit down, I think. After maybe ten minutes, an officer walks in. I do not look at him. He leads me over to a sofa and makes me sit down. When he takes off his hat and sits on the edge of a chair in front of me, I still do not look at him. I stare at his uniform. It is dark and shiny. Frightening, in spite of how I feel.

"Then he puts his hands over his face. As if he is crying, almost. I think right then I know he is Johann. When he finally looks at me again, he says, "I am sorry." That is all he says. It makes me start crying too. Johann, he moves over onto the sofa and puts his arms around me. We sit together in this way for a long time. I think maybe I fall asleep for a while, even."

This was hardly how Cohen had envisioned Richter to be connected to Kaisenher and Heinrich Mueller. Could all this be true? And was that it? The whole story? He almost felt disappointed.

Elena paused, her eyes on Tomas, still playing in the shallows at the bottom of the hill. As she picked her story back up, she dropped her gaze to the ground just in front of her. "I spend four nights with Johann at the hotel," she said. "Very innocent. Not as man and woman. That does not happen between us until much later. His only concern with my body during that time in Munich is how thin I am. He has food brought in and makes me eat as much as I can. He has a doctor he knows and trusts come in and look at me. Then medicines and clothes, he brings in for me.

"We do not talk much to one another. When we do, it is usually about the little things, like what we are eating. But I do tell Johann what I know about what has happen to my family. He tells me he wants to send me to his home, which is near Berlin. Only his mother is there now. And she will welcome me, he says, as long as she does not know I am a Jew.

"He has already obtain false papers for me, saying I am 'Helga Schumann,' born of Aryan parents in Vienna. He warns me if his mother finds out who I am she will turn me in. And if that happens, he says, he will be in danger too. It can even harm his father, the General, he tells me."

The sun's final slanting rays skimmed across the pond's surface, streaking it with light. Sitting beside Cohen, Elena Stein seemed to have reentered the past, her eyes staring unfocused down into the dark water below the hill. "The next morning, an officer who is trusted by Johann is going to take me to Berlin, where Frau Richter is to meet me. Just before I leave, I ask Johann what he will do now. He looks at me with the same smile he does when I am a little girl, and says he will end his role in the war with as much honor as he can. He laughs, and says he will probably have no more future after that.

"The officer arrives, a man named Borchers. He takes me to Orienbad, where Johann's mother treats me well. I am afraid my physical condition gives me away, but she says nothing about it. I never tell her I am a Jew. She is so kind sometimes that I nearly tell her, but I always remember Johann's warning.

"At Orienbad, after a while, my strength begins to return. I walk in the woods, read books, just sit and think. Or try to, because my mind, it is full of too many things. Borchers visits from time to time. He is a good man. Most of the time, though, I am alone. I prefer it that way. My best friend is Sacha, Johann's old horse he asks me to look after. Sometimes bombers from England, they fly over us on their way to Berlin. But I try not to think about the war."

Elena Stein looked again at Michael Cohen. She appeared to be assessing his reaction to her story. "So you see, I owe Johann. My life. Everything." Her look, he thought, appeared to be inviting some kind of acknowledgment, but he said nothing. Her story had triggered unwelcome memories. All he could think about was Rachael Stern, and how he had let her down. At Dachau, Rachel had told him how she had been shipped there by Heinrich Mueller after she had been eyed and pawed at by the Kaisenher commandant for weeks and had frustrated him by managing to stay out of his bed. Cohen had wondered why Mueller hadn't simply raped her or killed her. It was well within his power. At the time, it had seemed part of the randomness of life in the camps, this mystery that would eventually be cleared up. For the moment, though, it was shoved to a back burner as Rachel and Cohen soon found a new reason to hold onto life.

Rachel Stern's family had once moved in high society, her father a banker, her mother the only female professor of economics at the University of Berlin. Like all Jews, their status had not protected them long once National Socialism took over. Her father was one of the stubborn ones, much like Cohen's. He refused to acknowledge the new realities, would not give up everything and leave Germany. So he, along with Rachel's mother, wound up dead, and their young daughter wound up first at Kaisenher, and then Dachau. She and Cohen had met on a rare work detail outside the walls of Dachau. They'd both been very young, Rachel even younger than he. After spending the day together, digging trenches, they had pledged to meet again. It had taken months, but they had finally managed it. Twice. The second time, using a torrential rain for cover and because they knew there might be no third time, they had consummated what they hoped was their love. It had been an act of despair and abandonment, wedged beneath the one barracks at Dachau that included a nearly enclosed section of foundation wall, a desperate drive overriding the dwindling strength of their half-starved bodies.

Their fears had proven correct. There was to be no third time. Before the Americans liberated Dachau near the end of the war, Rachel was transferred to another satellite camp, a death sentence for virtually everyone who made the trip.

Cohen, his emaciated body weakened by disease, could not search for her. He was transferred to a British field hospital. For months, in a fevered half-hallucinatory state, while the doctors and nurses put him on the mend, he had dreamed of her almost constantly. At his prodding, the accommodating British had run innumerable inquiries into her whereabouts, all to no avail. Gradually, the dreams had faded, and gradually he had given in to the idea that Rachel was gone. All evidence pointed to it. She was in good company. So many had died. But still he fought it. She had been his life buoy. The acceptance of her death, he knew, would extinguish a vital spark in him, a spark he was not sure he could ever get back.

That what was in store for him would be even worse, he never imagined.

Focusing again on Elena Stein, Cohen tried to shed the fog of his past. Here was another remarkable woman who apparently had survived Heinrich Mueller and Kaisenher. He was amazed she had revealed so much. In spite of her story, picturing her and Richter together, particularly as lovers, depressed him.

Elena appeared to recognize he had been absent during the last part of her story. She didn't seem inclined to pick up the thread again. As they sat in silence, the sun finally dipped below the horizon and the air chilled slightly with its departure.

She suggested they return to the house. With Tomas in tow, they walked back without another word.

She gave him a tour. They had built the house room by room, she said. It now had five, including a bathroom with an ingeniously juryrigged version of indoor plumbing. The kitchen was more primitive, equipped only with a wood-burning stove and an old-fashioned icebox.

A generator pumped running water from a well into the house, but gas lanterns rather than electric lightbulbs were still used for lighting. The one bedroom had two large double beds in it, one on heavy wooden legs, the other resting directly on the floor. When Cohen looked inside, he saw the baby sleeping on the floor-bed. A study with comfortable chairs and walls lined with books led back into the living room.

He had already told her about the taxi. Without a word, she seemed to accept that he would stay the night. Cohen helped her prepare dinner, simple food served somewhat surprisingly with a good Chilean claret. As they ate he asked her about John Weaver. She said she did not know such a man.

After dinner, they put Tomas and Teresa to bed and Elena helped him prepare the living room couch for sleeping. When she excused herself for bed, he stripped to his shorts, stretched out on the couch and quickly dropped off to sleep in the cool night air.

Sometime during the night he had a familiar nightmare. He saw his mother, his sister and baby brother standing in a long line of people on the far side of a raging river. They were waiting patiently for something, showing no particular emotion. Cohen, however, knew where the line was taking them and was overcome with dread. Over and over he shouted warnings to them. His shouts were drowned out by the rushing water. His family could not hear him, though they each, in turn, looked right at him. He knew he was responsible for them, that only he could save them. But he couldn't cross the river. Finally Jeremiah, his little brother, appeared to recognize him, smiled and waved. Cohen was overwhelmed by helplessness and guilt. His shout turned into a scream, but still nothing happened.

He dreamed he was awake. It was the middle of the night. A wind had arisen and was whipping through the open windows, billowing drapes and filling the room with whispers. It felt warmer, but Cohen was bathed in a chilling sweat. Unable to fall back asleep, he got up and stepped outside into the balmy night air.

For a moment he stood completely still and let the night invade his being. The deep rich scent of jungle filled his nostrils. He listened for the customary thunderclaps, but heard none. Only the music of nature. The wind licked drily at his skin and soothed him in a tickling caress. The moon was nearly full. He tread its glow down to the stream behind the house and tested the water by wading in a few feet. A refreshing cold cascaded around his legs. He took off his shorts, threw them back onto the shore and waded out into the current. Sparkling white bubbles engulfed his body in slow motion.

When the water hit his waist, he dove in and stroked the twenty yards or so to the shallows of the far bank. As he emerged from the stream, the warm air kissed his cool skin. He stood on the shore feeling whole and free in his nakedness, staring out at the shadowy fields that lay before him, drinking them in. The ghost of a horse floated past him in the darkness. He had a sense of déjà vu.

Finally, when he had his fill, he turned back to the stream. A stark white figure stood on the far bank.

Cohen was startled, but not embarrassed. Her presence did not seem strange to him. He walked back into the water and swam toward her. When he stood up waist-deep in the stream, he expected her to toss him his shorts or turn away so he could emerge and put them on. Instead she lifted a towel and held it out wide with both hands, inviting him to enter its folds. She wrapped the towel around him and patted him dry, like a mother fondling her baby. When she was finished she led him back into the house, to the couch, where she gently cradled him back to sleep.

Near dawn, he awoke fitfully, unable for a moment to separate dream from reality. Feeling the emotion of both. The burden of both. He remembered the woman by the stream. Had it been Elena Stein? Or Rachel? He wasn't sure. Now he was alone. All around him was quiet. Only the birds and insects outside. He could not imagine what would come next. La Negra had more layers than he would ever have guessed.

He lay there and waited for the sun to rise.

"The Mission"

After his sophomore year ended in July of 1938, Johann had planned to remain independently at his studies in Heidelberg for the summer. He enjoyed the relative quiet and was engrossed in the current progress of his work. He was very much surprised when his father, for the first time ever, paid him a visit late in August. The General arrived unannounced on a Wednesday, at six in the morning. Johann, who had been sleeping and was dressed in night clothes, greeted him feeling a little sheepish. He felt a touch of pleasure that he was now slightly taller than his father, dressed in a dark civilian suit that set off his eye patch more dramatically than his more customary Wehrmacht uniform did.

The two men shook hands. Karl Richter sat down in the room's only easy chair, a scrounged piece of dubious craftsmanship with the stuffing ready to burst its seams. Johann sat on the edge of his bed, the sheets still warm with sleep. His father kidded him about the room's bare furnishings, asking him how he spent the "huge" allowance he was receiving every month. He pretended to look under the bed to see, as he put it, if Johann were hiding an expensive woman under there. They both laughed.

"The good Dr. Goebbels once studied here, you know. I hope you are not learning the lessons he did."

"No, but I am becoming a fencer so I can challenge Heydrich to a duel someday. I am told he was good enough he could have been an Olympian in '36."

Johann was only joking, but the mere mention of Himmler's SS crony brought a frown to Karl Richter's face.

"If you plan to take on Reinhard Heydrich, you had better not let your guard down as you evidently have recently." He gestured toward the as-yet-unhealed scar below Johann's right eye, the first indication he had even noticed it. Johann gently rubbed the raised scar tissue with his fingers, an instinctive gesture already becoming something of a habit.

"Heydrich is not a man to be trifled with, even as a joke," his father said. "We are only fortunate the Gestapo and SD have no technical jurisdiction over the Wehrmacht – though it didn't stop them from bringing down Blomberg and Fritsch, two of our best generals from the old school. Heydrich may sound like a miserable pipsqueak when he opens his mouth, but he is dangerous. More dangerous than Himmler. He's more intelligent. More devious. He recruits for his SS secret service at places like this. Himmler's fanatics are ignorant bully-boys. Heydrich's are far more clever."

"Yes, I know. I was approached once. It was like being rushed for a club. I turned them down. I'm probably in their files now. A potential enemy."

"You undoubtedly are." The concern in Karl Richter's eyes was genuine. The bantering was done. He got down to business.

"Johann, it is very good for me to see you again but I did not, of course, come here only to visit." Johann had assumed as much. "I came here today out of a concern for, among other things, your future." Johann braced himself, on edge now that something important was obviously on the way. "As you have probably guessed by now, my work on the General Staff gives me access to planning information few others possess. I have in fact a good idea of what the future holds for all of us."

The General paused, looked out the window and then straight at his son. "Johann, we are going to war. Very soon. Perhaps before the year is out."

A tingling sensation swept over Johann's skin, left him feeling cold and numb. Among the students, the possibility of war was much discussed. But this was something different. For Johann, this made it definite. He didn't stop to question his father's assumptions. Horrifying things he had heard about the last war filled his thoughts. The personal consequences had not yet occurred to him. "To war?" was all he could muster in reply.

"Hitler set it all out for us at Hossbach last winter. He has plans to conquer most of Europe. I raised the only objections, and he did not appreciate it. Perhaps Frederick the Great was right, perhaps only Prussian Junkers should lead the Army. We have become too soft, too weak-kneed, to handle a Hitler."

Johann felt a flicker of hope that his father's brief honeymoon with the Nazis was over.

"The man has won us some incredible victories, with barely a drop of bloodshed, but he's not done," Karl Richter continued. "Czechoslovakia is next. Taking Czechoslovakia will not be as simple as Anschluss with Austria. Hitler thinks it can be localized, but it will explode in our faces. We are headed for war. A big war, maybe even bigger than the last.

"Which is the reason I'm here, Johann. If you remain at Heidelberg even one more semester, you will be drafted into the Wehrmacht. That's if you do not become a pet project of our Fuhrer, who would like to see you become a member of Sepp Dietrich's Leibstandarte SS Adolf Hitler, his personal bodyguard. This is a great honor in his eyes. I have had to very carefully evade him on the subject. He is a difficult man to say no to, and I will not be able to do it much longer. So we must act quickly."

The idea that he could be dragooned to become a bodyguard to Hitler was a shocker to Johann. The one time he had ever seen the Fuhrer, at a rally outside the Hotel Adlon in Berlin, he had been chilled by the man's presence, even at a distance.

"I have a suggestion," his father said, "as to how you might discharge your responsibility in the most useful way, both to Germany and yourself. And, if you like, to me as well. If you are amenable, I have arranged for your entrance into the Wehrmacht officer training school at Mainz. When you complete the training there you'll be posted to an officer's billet in military intelligence."

"The Abwehr?"

"That is correct."

"When would this school start?" Johann's stomach was tied in knots.

"On Monday next."

His negative reaction was so apparent his father hastened to address any objections. "Don't condemn the idea before you've heard it fully," he said. "This school is the best of its kind anywhere, inside Germany or out. You would be trained well. When you finished your training, because of your language and schooling background, you would quite naturally be assigned to an English-speaking country. Most likely England itself. If necessary, I will see to it."

Johann turned away from his father. Through the window, he could see the sun beginning to rise. Down the hill the slow waters of the Neckar were still dark. "I would be a spy?"

"No. You would be assigned as one, true. But your most important mission would be a personal one for me. And for Admiral Canaris, head of the Abwehr."

"Canaris is a strange man I am told," Johann said.

His father smiled. "You're not as cloistered here as I feared," he said. "Canaris is very private. A secretive man. But a good man. We ride together in the Tiergarten from time to time. I have gotten to know him as well as anyone ever does. He does not reveal much. But just enough, if he trusts you. I cannot explain it all to you now, but for good reason he has taken me into his confidence. Somewhat, at least. He also persuaded me that I needed to upgrade my resume for those who surround Hitler. To do that, I have joined the Nazi Party."

Johann could not hide his astonishment.

"Don't be upset. It's only a maneuver. I must have the trust of those who have Hitler's ear. Canaris convinced me, and he is a man who plays the game with consummate skill. In the power struggle within Hitler's inner circle he's a balance to Heydrich. And whatever else he may be, he is a paragon of virtue beside Heydrich."

Karl Richter shook his head. "Berlin has become a cesspool of intrigue. A very dangerous game is going on right now among those close to Hitler. I have been on the fence, but I won't be much longer if current developments continue. Again, I cannot explain it to you now. It would not be fair to you and it could endanger others. You are going to have to trust me." This time he did not smile. Johann said nothing.

"There are some things I can tell you, however. This must remain strictly confidential. If it leaks out, it could be the death of me, as well as many others. I know I can count on your discretion."

"Of course." A perfunctory response from Johann, still too stunned to think straight.

"Because Hitler is leading Germany toward possible destruction, there is plotting against him, even among the High Command. This high-level opposition to the Fuhrer has been trying to convince the British he means to make war – by attacking Czechoslovakia; perhaps even Poland. Churchill, it is said, is the only one who listens, but he has little leverage in the British government right now. Meanwhile, their prime minister flies off to Berchtesgaden to placate Hitler, which could ultimately destroy the opposition movement. **France won't help. The Soviets and the Americans won't either.**

"I cannot tell you anything more specific right now. Only that I need you as a contact in England. I can assure you that you would be doing nothing there that would compromise your beliefs." Johann could sense an unfamiliar urgency in his father's tone.

"You and I have never been as close as we might have been," Karl Richter said. "That is largely my fault. But our ideals, I believe, are not so far apart. I hope not, anyway. You're more qualified than you might imagine for this assignment. Besides being my son, you are well-acquainted with my old schoolmate Lord Neville Johns, who holds an important post in British Intelligence."

Johann stared at his father in disbelief.

"No, I presumed you never knew. With the English, intelligence work is a task of the upper classes. Neville came to it shortly after he finished at Oxford. Your being able to make contact with him so easily would be an invaluable asset to me. I have been in touch with some of his friends over the past few years, but I'd like to have a more direct contact – your contact, preferably – with Lord Neville. I need someone I can trust without question."

"You expect us to go to war with England, then?"

"I expect England to go to war with us."

"Because of Czechoslovakia."

"Or whatever follows it."

The General stared out the window at a sunrise just now clearing the steeples, spires and rooftops and beginning to wake Heidelberg. "You know, Hitler once wanted to be a priest. Even before he wanted to be an artist. He took his swastika from a monastery's coat of arms. But now he sees himself more as a god, a god of history, a Frederick the Great on the eve of the first Silesian War. The only man with the will to act. The only man who can redeem Germany."

Karl Richter returned his attention to Johann with a wistful smile. "I have learned the only way to look at Herr Hitler is at an angle. If you look too directly, you are blinded by his aura. If you view him from the corner of your eye – or at a distance, through his deeds perhaps – you can better see him for what he is."

Johann breathed a nervous sigh of relief. His father had not sold his soul to the Devil after all.

"You don't think we can win, if it comes to war?" he said.

"That depends upon many factors. But I would not follow even Frederick the Great himself into another world war. That's one reason I want you in the Abwehr, and preferably in England. Just in case. What do you say, Johann?"

In spite of his misgivings about the proposal, it made him feel reconnected with his father. "Do I have some time to think about it?" he said.

A flicker of the old sternness lit his father's eyes. "You have until tomorrow. I have business in Munich today. I will pass through Heidelberg again on my way back to Berlin tomorrow morning. I will need your answer then."

Karl Richter took his leave. Johann listened to the General's boots echoing on the staircase as he descended back into his own world.

It was as if he had been left with a huge weight on his chest. He crawled back into bed, pulled the sheets up around his neck and tried to draw the same comfort from the warm cocoon he had felt before his father's arrival. It did not come. He shivered as the morning's first direct rays of sun hit his bedcovers.

* * * *

When Johann began to collect his wits about him again, he sought out Erich Borchers and walked with him to a private place along the Neckar to talk. He told his friend what his father had told him, leaving out only the part about the resistance to Hitler inside the Wehrmacht.

Borchers was sympathetic. His intense blue eyes locked onto Johann's. He said the news did not much surprise him that war was imminent. They would all be faced with decisions similar to Johann's soon. It would be a test of each man's moral compass, Borchers said. When Johann asked him what he would do if he were in his shoes, Borchers thought for a moment, staring down at the sluggish current of the river. "It all depends on your father, I suppose," he said. "What you think of your father."

After Borchers left, Johann walked along the river by himself. The Neckar had seen a lot of armies in its time. From the legions of Rome to the imperial troops of Napoleon. Would it soon see more?

He went over and over all that had happened that day. His thoughts kept returning to the one brief meeting he'd had, nearly a year ago now, with Borchers' friend Claus von Stauffenberg. Erich had been right about Stauffenberg's charisma. There had been other people present at the gathering at a local rathskeller, and the political talk had been guarded, but Johann had felt the man's power and sensed his integrity. A Wehrmacht officer, Stauffenberg had been dressed in civilian clothes that night. He had said nothing against Hitler or the Nazis, but had made it known the KZs must be eliminated as soon as possible and that he rejected the campaign against the Jews. His own religious beliefs, he'd said, would never allow him to accept what was happening to the Jews. Johann had found himself hoping the army had other officers of this man's caliber.

Stauffenberg evidently felt he could change things from inside the Wehrmacht. Perhaps he was right, Johann thought.

That afternoon he saddled up his horse and rode out to the Steins'. It was a beautiful late-summer's day, the woods green and alive, the fields bright with sun. With the ill tidings he carried, he felt like an unwelcome intruder into another world.

In Eberbach, he took Elena and Gerhardt's father Julius Stein aside and confided in him the essence of his own father's report concerning the possibilities of war. Among students at the university, Johann told the elder Stein, some argued that a war would likely mean a diminution of the plight of Jews in Germany. But Johann said he thought it might well bode just the opposite, that he could easily picture German Jews being impressed as laborers for war industries, if not worse.

Julius Stein accepted this intelligence in silence. He thanked Johann for his concern but was skeptical of his young friend's bleak assessment. He found the imminent likelihood of war a difficult idea to grasp. In any event, he didn't think there was much he could do about it, he said, as poor as he was and responsible for four people.

Johann said he would gladly scrape some money together to help, but Julius Stein smiled warmly and firmly declined the offer. The only commitment Johann could talk him into making was that if war did break out, he'd take it as a sign Johann had been right and would try to get his family out of the country. In spite of this, Julius Stein said he did not want to leave Germany. Johann told him that might change.

Johann said his good-byes to the rest of the family. He assured them he would try to visit again as soon as possible, but confessed he could not be certain what the future held for him. When he kissed Elena, just turned 10 years old, good-bye, the tears rolled down her face and stabbed right to his heart. He prayed he would not be betraying these people if he joined the Abwehr.

He spent the rest of the afternoon alone in the woods near Eberbach, where he dismounted and sat leaning against a tree, his horse grazing nearby. Analyzing his emotions as honestly as he could, he realized he felt a responsibility, a loyalty, and that it was more for his father than it was for Germany. This was the first time his father had ever come to him for help of any kind, albeit the request had been a veiled one. There seemed very little of the rational upon which to base a decision. In the end, his mind spinning uselessly for more concrete justification, he knew he would simply have to trust his father, knew this was what he had been going to do from the very start.

His focus shifted to Neville Johns. An agent for British Intelligence? Maybe it wasn't such an incredible notion after all. He was a man of substance, certainly a man well-connected in the British power structure. Johann suddenly realized he might see Clay again soon. And Christine. For a moment these thoughts lifted his spirits. He could feel the tree at his back, the brightness of the forest all around him. But then he was reminded of another day in the woods, the woods of Croyden Castle, and a sense of foreboding returned.

* * * *

During the first week of October 1938 German troops occupied the Sudetenland of Czechoslovakia – about one-third of the country's territory, including some of its richest assets – in accordance with the Munich Agreements between Adolf Hitler, Neville Chamberlain of Great Britain, Eduardo Daladier of France and Benito Mussolini of Italy. "Greater Germany," in the words of Hitler, now promised sovereignty to the remainder of Czechoslovakia.

That same week, Johann Richter began the second month of his Wehrmacht training outside Mainz, thankful that so far at least, his father's dire predictions of another world war had not come true.

The camp was bleak, Spartan and self-contained, surrounded by forest. Though he generally disliked it, Johann was doing well amidst the smell of boot leather, sweating bodies, gun oil and disinfectant. He was tall, sturdy, athletic and intelligent, and found himself automatically putting his abilities to good use whenever the opportunity presented itself. Besides the camp's physical and military training, cadets were fed a diet of propaganda as systematically as their meals. All the anti-British, Jewish, Russian, Slavic, anti-French and anti-Polish diatribes made little impression on Johann. Only the accusation of mass murder against the Soviet regime of Joseph Stalin had any ring of truth to it.

Stress was placed on the Wehrmacht's version of the Fuhrerprincep, an obedience to superiors and an awareness of strength over everyone else. The primacy of rank was tempered however. A directive straight from Hitler had decreed that, contrary to the last war, in which Hitler served as a corporal, officers would no longer play at being royalty, with enlisted men as their servants. There was to be true brotherhood and comradeship among all ranks in the Nazi Wehrmacht. So said the Fuhrer, whose word was now law.

Feeling secure in his skepticism of the entire process, Johann let himself be carried with the tide of instruction. He gave himself over to making no important decisions during his stay and deferred any concerns about the morality of what he was being prepared for. Meanwhile he reveled in a sense of immediate accomplishment – that he was the fastest man on the obstacle course, one of the best athletes in camp, was ranked as the top marksman and among the top ten in academic performance. He even allowed himself a modicum of satisfaction when his efforts were praised by ranking officers, in spite of his awareness that a craving for such reward was an important element of what camp life was designed to instill in the psyche of a junior officer in the making.

Though he resided only on the fringes of camp camaraderie, when it came time to choose leaders from the ranks, Johann was selected as one of only two cadet brigade commanders, an honor he had thought he would scorn. Surprisingly, he felt proud as he pinned on the extra set of gleaming bars that automatically won him new respect from his comrades. He took on the added duties of his new rank with enthusiasm. His routine, however, did not change much. Days, he continued to exercise, compete, listen, question, learn the arcane ins and outs of military life and its attendant disciplines, indulge a ravenous appetite, read and study training manuals.

Nights, he continued to sleep the sleep of the dead. He dreamed once of Christine Johns. The dream made him excited and unhappy at the same time. When he awoke from it, he did so to a heavy feeling of loss and carried the emptiness around with him for weeks before it finally wore off.

In early March 1939, six months after it had begun, Johann's Wehrmacht training drew to a close on a stepped-up schedule.

Something was in the air. With unexpected suddenness he was yanked from the camp and sent to an Abwehr facility near Berlin.

He had learned the rudiments of intelligence and counterintelligence with the Wehrmacht, but here he studied a much-expanded curriculum of spycraft. Here he also received specific intelligence information on England and an extra dose of indoctrination to inoculate him against enemy propaganda.

Finally, he was given instructions about his own intelligence-gathering mission.

Meanwhile Hitler moved to occupy the remainder of Czechoslovakia in a lightning-fast strike. Parts of the defeated nation were parceled out to Hungary and Poland, both of which had grabbed Czech territory after Germany's annexation of the Sudetenland. The Spanish Civil War finally came to a victorious conclusion for the Fascists of Generalissimo Francisco Franco, and Spain promptly clasped hands with Germany, Japan and Italy in adhering to an Anti-Comintern Pact aimed at containing Communism. Johann went home to Orienbad a newly commissioned Wehrmacht officer assigned to the Abwehr. His father had summoned him for one final pep talk before he was to leave for England.

On 31 March 1939, Great Britain, with Chamberlain finally forced to take a stand, joined France in guaranteeing the borders of Poland against any foreign aggressor. On 22 May, Mussolini signed the "Pact of Steel" cementing Italy's military alliance with Germany.

In his London flat, Johann Richter read in the *Times* that England was preparing to sign a formal treaty of mutual military assistance with Poland. This time his father's predictions were about to come true.

CHAPTER IX

"**Y**our wife. I have a message from her." Father Hidalgo produced an envelope from the folds of his robe and handed it to Johann Richter.

"Thank you Father. Once again, you bring to me what little hope I have left." Which was not an exaggeration, Richter thought. The Catholic priest had been his only immediate source of hope since he had been tossed into prison. Along with Frederico, and more recently his lawyer Hiram Benevides, Father Hidalgo had been his sole bridge to the outside world. Though he'd had some contact with this priest before his imprisonment, the irony did not escape him that God in some form had returned to his life in this seemingly godforsaken place. Nor that the return had been cloaked in the garb of the Roman Catholic Church. Erich Borchers – and Claus von Stauffenberg, for that matter – would have approved.

After a brief conversation about how he had received the letter, Father Hidalgo stood to take his leave. "I leave you alone with her," he said with a small chuckle. "A man does not want to share his wife with another man. Even with a priest."

Father Hidalgo rang the bell for a guard. Frederico was not on duty today. None of the others ever said much. Richter accompanied the priest to the door of the roomy cell. He felt at times as if he were a medieval king, captured and held for ransom in a castle keep. Perhaps in the mountains of Italy. Somewhere that could be hot one day and bitter cold the next. Without the lifeline of Father Hidalgo, he might have been believing such delusions by now.

When the priest had left, his footsteps echoing in tandem with the guard's down the long corridor of stone, Richter stood at a sunlit window striped by vertical bars and inspected the envelope. He turned it over.

Held it up to the light. It did not appear to have been tampered with. That was because it had arrived via Father Hidalgo, the only man in here he could fully trust.

But could he trust the letter? The priest had said a young man had brought it to him. The man had said very little; only that Elena Stein had instructed him to deliver this note to the priest who served the prison. He knew nothing else about the young man, Father Hidalgo said. Only that he was tall, like Richter, and appeared to be American or European.

Something similar had happened once before. A man named Terry Harper had managed to contact him, and Richter had agreed to meet him in La Negra to keep him from getting any closer. Harper had turned out to be an old acquaintance, a man who'd had ties to British Intelligence. Now he was a writer, interested in Richter's story, he said, and he had been quite convincing. Richter had bought him off by telling him part of his story, some of it true, some of it not so true. This was several years ago. Harper had left, seemingly satisfied, but Richter had always expected to hear from him again someday.

Now who was this new one, and how had he found Elena? Richter asked himself. He even felt a tiny stab of jealousy, though he trusted Elena implicitly. Inside these walls he felt completely helpless toward his family. He could not protect them, and it was torturing him. What would happen to them if he were sentenced to a long prison term? Or executed?

He was allowed to phone his wife once a week, on Sundays. She had to make a special trip in to Riberalta to receive the call. Sometimes it did not go through. When it did, they were allowed only ten minutes. Just enough time for him to absorb the pain of their separation. He had never sent her a letter, for fear of alerting the wrong parties to her whereabouts, and he had never received a letter from her before. Nervous and eager, he opened the envelope. The two pages inside were covered on both sides with a familiar scrawl that tugged at his heart.

My dearest Johann, I send this to you by way of Michael Cohen. He somehow find me out here. He is a good man, I think. One who can be trusted. He is a prisoner at Dachau during the war. Richter's feelings toward the young man shifted slightly, though he wondered if this piece of information were true. How could Elena know that? Why had this Cohen sought her out? He tried to set aside his concerns, as he warmed to the familiar cadences of his wife's speech. *I tell him a little about you and me. I hope that is okay. I miss you. So very much, my lover.* Richter smiled. Elena always used "lover" for "love" when she spoke in English, and it usually came out sounding better than if she'd said it correctly. *Tomas miss you too. Even Teresa. I can tell.*

I ask you again, may I come to La Negra? I want to be where you are. I am feeling too far from you here, and can not concentrate on anything. I do not want to come against your wishes, but I must come soon. I must. I bring the children with me. Perhaps you can see them.

Our outdoors family, they miss you too. Garcia the goat is a little slow, but it is only the heat maybe. Sacha, I think, is pregnant. Soon we may have a new baby horse to care for. The jeep is broken, but with help from R- I am able to get into Riberalta once a week. I am trying to be there Sunday for your call.

I am glad you are feeling better. Is there anything you are needing that I can get for you?

You ask me before if all is well. It is, except that you are not here with us. If anything happens R- is looking after us, so please do not worry. Just take good care of yourself. We pray to see you soon, and we will, I am sure of it.

My loving to you always, Elena

Richter held the letter at his side and stared through the iron bars. The mention of R-, which meant "Rivera," a guerrilla fighter who operated up by Riberalta, was a code device he and Elena had agreed upon a long time ago. Rivera was a friend. Her reference to him meant stay optimistic, help was on the way. From what quarter, he could not imagine. She had helped get him out of prison once before, but this time was different. This time the stakes were immeasurably higher. The coded message didn't comfort him. It made him worry about her even more.

The sky today was a perfect blue, so crystal clear the colors seemed magnified, but he hardly noticed. His thoughts were torn between a simple longing for his family and the fear they could be in danger. Bringing them to La Negra might increase the risk. But where they were now, out on the farm, reminded him all too clearly of Eberbach at the outbreak of war. A safe haven supposedly so far off the beaten path the Nazis would never bother with it.

This time the Nazis were only one of his worries. His few remaining contacts in the German underground had not been able to tell him immediately after his capture whether British MI6 had played a part in it.

Prison security had clamped down since then and he had heard nothing more from his contacts.

For once, he could have used Odessa, the super-secret organization set up by the SS to clear escape routes from Germany in 1945. But he was on his own. The two men he knew to be in Odessa did not trust him. They suspected, perhaps even knew, that he and his father had been involved in the plots against Hitler. Most of Odessa were die-hard believers. Some said the group was led by "Gestapo Muller," Hitler's much-feared secret police chief who was supposed to have died when the Russians took Berlin. There were even rumors Hitler himself was still alive and somewhere nearby. This was nonsense, Richter knew, but the Fuhrer was still Odessa's god. He had kept Elena carefully isolated from them. The last thing he wanted was for her to get mixed up in all that. He prayed that was not the help she was seeking.

These thoughts triggered a flood of memories.

He and Elena had fled occupied France, via Lisbon, before Odessa had become a going concern. They had been among the early German arrivals in Argentina, but their numbers would grow quickly as the war played itself out in 1945. In Buenos Aires, Richter had briefly tried the import-export business in partnership with two former Wehrmacht officers. It was black market trade, mostly, but had appeared to be the accepted way of doing business, greased by routine bribes.

When his background became more widely known, however, especially his connection to those who had sought Hitler's ouster, the local expatriate German community had turned on him. His two partners had attempted to frame him, and Elena had been forced to sell virtually everything they owned to buy his way out of prison. By the time he was released, his old war wound where he had been shot in the side by Yvonne Duchamps was bothering him again. It was only now, as Elena nursed him back to health a second time, that their relationship had become an intimate one. By then, they had been through so much together he no longer saw her as a child, or someone his only role was to protect. The next step, when it finally happened, had seemed a natural one.

Six months later they had managed to scrape together sufficient resources to leave Buenos Aires. They lived in a couple of different places in Argentina, then worked another farm in closer to La Negra before they finally found the place out beyond Riberalta where they thought no one would ever find them.

Once they were settled in there, he and Elena had gotten married. She kept the name "Stein" to honor her family. Tomas had arrived. Then Teresa. They had made their own little world. Their neighbors had gradually accepted them. The guerrilla fighters who sporadically gave the government fits had sniffed around for a while until they too had finally seemed to accept them. The best known, Rivera, had befriended them over the past few years. They had thrived in their new home. All in all, Richter had felt more content than he would ever have imagined possible given the cataclysmic upheavals of the preceding decade. Until they had found him.

Even now, he was not certain who "they" were. They had identified themselves as members of Israel's Shin Bet intelligence branch, but from the very start he'd had his doubts. Where had they picked up his trail? He had remembered Terry Harper and wondered if he'd played a role, inadvertently or otherwise. When first captured, he had been sure MI6 was somehow involved. But when they turned him over to the local authorities rather than kill him, he had changed his mind. If MI6 hadn't been there at the start, however, he knew they were here by now.

The British Secret Intelligence Service, MI6, had been part of a deal with the devil his father had engineered for him at the start of the war. It was Britain's overseas intelligence wing, their equivalent of Canaris' Abwehr and eventually of Heydrich's dreaded SD. His father's old friend Lord Neville Johns, an MI6 section chief, had quite willingly eased Richter's way into the outer fringes of British Intelligence early in the war.

They had kept him at least one step removed from anything important, had relegated him to dealing with men like Anders Hardy, who would become his control officer at MI6. Men whose job was to use him but also keep him in the dark. Appropriately, perhaps, Hardy had been the man he had trusted least in the whole setup. Aside from an abrasive personality and an overbearing class consciousness of the most virulent Oxbridge variety, Hardy had offered up a personal complication as well. He was a former lover of Christine Johns' and had suspected from the start something was going on between Christine and Richter. When he'd eventually confirmed it, it had infuriated him.

Since his discovery and capture up above Riberalta, it had occurred to Richter more than once that MI6 would probably have been happier if no one had ever found him. Certainly they would try to see to it that he never returned to England for trial. He knew something they would prefer to leave buried. Two somethings, in fact. His lawyer Benevides wanted him to testify on his own behalf in the extradition hearing. So far he had resisted out of fear for his family. MI6 would have difficulty getting to him in here, but they could get to him that way. Through his family. And they would not be at all shy to do it.

They were an unblushing bunch, especially when it came to keeping things under wraps and protecting themselves. Or, as was likely in this case, themselves and some very important people.

Now this Michael Cohen character had stepped into the picture and thrown one more mystery into the mix. "A good man," Elena thought. One who could be trusted, she said. Richter was not so sure. Had this guy really come out of Dachau, or was he connected to the British? Or both? Richter had been burned once before by a well-camouflaged undercover agent of the most unlikely kind.

Whatever, if British Intelligence had somehow missed Elena and the children earlier, they wouldn't anymore, whether Cohen was MI6 or not. Now they would find some way to put the squeeze on. The idea of a man like Anders Hardy – whom Richter had long suspected of playing a role in Christine Johns' death – getting hold of his family made Richter feel sick at the pit of his stomach. He was reluctant to have them leave the farm for La Negra. It felt like trading an amorphous risk for a very real one.

He could think of no way out. Save maybe escape, an idea he had begun to toy with. But even if he made it, what then?

Richter took one more look out across the eye-level panorama of hilltop and sky, then turned away to reread the letter he still held in his hands.

What then, indeed? he thought, as he began to read again, *My dearest Johann. . .*

CHAPTER X

Monday morning in court. The proceedings had been delayed several days because of some unexplained indisposition of the judge. Cohen had used the time to recover from his jaunt up into the jungle, which had drained him.

John Weaver had met him eagerly this morning, all ears. Cohen did not want to tell him about Elena Stein, but felt an obligation to say something. Without Weaver he might never have heard of her at all. Besides, to be too coy about it would arouse suspicions. The man was a reporter, after all.

"So she really exists?" Weaver said.

"She does." He tried to sound as neutral as possible.

"And she has two children?"

"That's right."

"Richter's?"

"Yes, I believe so." Cohen's responses sounded sluggish, even to his own ears. Along with the intentional attempt to keep Weaver's curiosity to a minimum, he still hadn't entirely shaken the lethargy he had felt since his return from Riberalta. The visit had shaken him up more than he wanted to admit.

"What's their place like, where they live?"

"A cabin, sort of. They built it themselves apparently." He wasn't going to be more specific. His main promise to the assistant in the prosecutor's office had been not to reveal Elena Stein's whereabouts, something Weaver already seemed to know something about, however.

"Is she European, like we'd heard?" Weaver's interest sounded to Cohen somehow more personal than professional.

"She's German."

"Pretty?"

Cohen raised his eyebrows. He didn't like being interrogated, nor did he want to expose Elena Stein. He already felt guilty for saying as much as he had.

He needed some way to dampen Weaver's curiosity. "Quite honestly, she didn't have much to say," he lied. "I doubt Richter lets her in on much."

Weaver shook his head. "So she really exists," he murmured. "Who'da thunk it?"

Court had started late today. Perhaps to give the media time to settle in. John Weaver and Cohen had now been joined by much more than just the BBC. Over the weekend, as word had gone out the case might not last as long as some had thought, the competition had begun converging on La Negra. Now there were several newsreel outfits – including Fox MovieTone News, famous for its worldwide coverage – as well as perhaps a dozen print reporters from various nations. Members of the prosecutor's team had dressed for the occasion and were demonstrating an added formality in their courtroom demeanor today.

When Clay Johns was called to the witness stand, he was met by a barrage of flashbulbs popping out a staccato beat. The judge banged his gavel. He looked none the worse for whatever his "indisposition" had been. "This is not a circus," he said. "The next photographer who uses his camera in the courtroom will be banned for the duration."

As Clay Johns seated himself at the front of the courtroom, he stared for a moment directly at Johann Richter. The look he passed to his old friend appeared sympathetic and encouraging. From the seating area for witnesses at the front of the courtroom, Anne Wheldon Johns fixed her husband with a baleful glare.

The ubiquitous white man with the beard, Cohen noticed, was again seated near the rear of the room, on the far side. Though it was a little tricky, Cohen turned at intervals during the testimony and began to sketch the man.

Under a proviso of the rather loose proceedings, the defense was being allowed to lead with this witness. Richter's lawyer Mr. Benevides arose to open the questioning. Despite his expanded audience today, he looked as rumpled and distracted as ever. Studying his notes with perhaps an exaggerated slowness, he asked the witness to begin at the beginning.

"We first met at the Whitby School, near St. Albans, in January of 1933. We were roommates there for the next, ah, I suppose nearly four years." Clay Johns' voice was a low, clipped British monotone. Deliberate, as if he had rehearsed and taped it and were now playing it back at a slightly slower than normal speed.

After the first quick look, Clay Johns kept his eyes averted from Richter but Cohen continued to wonder if he were a reluctant witness. Cohen kept his own eyes on the defendant as much as possible. For the first time, Richter appeared uneasy in a way that might be interpreted as a sign of guilt, repeatedly stroking the scar on his face, his features frozen into a vaguely distracted look.

"After we both graduated from Whitby in '36," Clay Johns said, "I didn't see Johann again for another three years, until the summer of 1939. And when I did see him again it was a bit of a shock. We had corresponded, but he had never mentioned he might be returning to England."

The witness' use of "Johann" in reference to Richter seemed a definite nod in favor of the defendant, Cohen thought.

"Please give us the details, Mr. Johns, of your initial reunion with the defendant in 1939," Mr. Benevides said softly.

"I was still up at Oxford then, trying to rush my studies and graduate before war broke out. We all knew it was coming. I didn't quite make it." As he spoke, Johns looked out toward where the morning sun slanted into the room, as if communing more with himself than with Mr. Benevides or the court.

"In any case," he continued, "I was studying in my rooms at St. John's one afternoon, in June, I think it was, and Johann simply appeared at the door. I really could hardly believe my eyes. I stood up, we shook hands. We both stood there for a moment gawking at one another. For one thing, he had this scar, this dueling scar, below one eye. He had written me about it once, I believe, but I'd entirely forgotten about it at the time. It was really rather impressive.

"It was Johann, I think, who finally suggested we sit down. Then without batting an eyelash he announced that war was on the way, that England and Germany would shortly have at it. 'Within two or three months, certainly no more than that,' is what he said. He spoke quite assuredly about Hitler's determination to have this war. I was hardly shocked, of course, by this prediction. Much less so, I should say, than I was by Johann's mere presence at Oxford that morning. I was quite pleased, really, that he was back. He seemed much matured somehow since we had last been together.

"He then asked me, rather bluntly I thought, if I could assure him the confidentiality of our conversation. I replied that of course I could. I could hardly imagine what was coming next."

Johns looked to Mr. Benevides as if for guidance. Receiving none, he plunged ahead. "He wasted no time getting to the point. He said German Intelligence had sent him to England. As a spy. This, I confess, did jolt me a bit. In particular, he said, he was supposed to be using me and my family to establish himself in London before the war started, so that he might be of use to the Abwehr, their intelligence branch, once the fighting was underway. This jolted me rather more. He quickly added, however, it was his father who had maneuvered him into this posting to England, and that his father was interested, to the contrary of spying, in keeping a reliable line of communication open to our intelligence people and the government in London.

"Johann assured me there was a sizable group of dissident officers within the German military establishment. These men, he said, were so strongly opposed to Hitler's policies they had been prepared the year before, during the German planning for the invasion of Czecho-slovakia, to attempt a coup d'etat against the Nazis. That is, until dear Mr. Chamberlain, our prime minister, and the others had made the invasion unnecessary with their concessions at Munich. His father, he said, had contacts inside this group of German officers and wanted to be able, using Johann as his 'go-between,' so to speak, to act as liaison between these men and England.

"I was, I must confess, more than a little skeptical about the whole thing. I asked him what he thought I could possibly do for him. He said he needed me to 'sponsor' him with my father, said Lord Neville could be of incalculable value to him in meeting the right people in government. Perhaps in British Intelligence as well.

"He asked me if I might help. I told him that of course I would try. We were still friends, after all was said and done."

As he paced the courtroom, Mr. Benevides appeared content with Clay Johns' testimony to this point. Cohen wondered if he were setting something up.

"And just what did you do for Johann Richter?" the lawyer asked.

"I spoke with my father, who had a good many connections in government," Johns said. "He said Karl von Richter had contacted him about Johann. Actually I believe Johann had told me that already. In any case, my father had always been terribly fond of Johann and took rather a personal interest in this idea Germany might be ripe for a military coup.

"Over the next few months, he enabled Johann to speak to any number of influential men. He must have introduced him to half the membership of White's and St. James's. Unfortunately, most of them were more concerned at the time with securing the Soviet Union as an active ally than they were about trying to foment any major internal upheavals in Germany. They considered Johann naïve, my father once told me.

"Then, of course, Hitler attacked Poland, and that was that. Once the war began, no one of consequence would even listen to Johann anymore, would they. It wasn't surprising. British pride was puffed up in the early going, along with overoptimism. No need to resort to subterfuge to defeat Hitler, we thought. Then again, it may have strained credulity a bit, I suppose, to think the army just then overrunning Poland in triumph was an army that was going to turn on its leader, regardless of what we did."

"What happened to Mr. Richter once war broke out?" Mr. Benevides continued to pace, pausing only to ask his question.

"As Lord Neville once said of him, 'He is a Whitby man, after all,'" Johns said with the trace of a grin. "Perhaps the one positive result of Johann's London activities, and of the connections my father had made for him, was that when war started he was not interned or expelled as were most of the German nationals then in England. He was in effect given special dispensation. He was still classified an enemy alien, technically, but he remained able to move about on his own quite freely, particularly in the unrestricted areas."

Johns, Cohen noticed, now kept his eyes straight ahead as he gave his answers.

"In addition, he was eventually assigned a task that was quite sensitive, security-wise. From time to time he was asked to interrogate German POWs or German nationals suspected of spying or sabotage. Great care was always taken to protect his identity in these interviews. MI5, our counterintelligence branch, had very few authentic German nationals it thought it could trust for such duty, particularly at the start of the war. So when they thought they'd found one, they would jump to recruit him and go out of their way to protect him. Johann was only loaned out to MI5, however. He was controlled by the Secret Intelligence Service, MI6."

"How is it you are privy to all this?" Mr. Benevides asked.

"I had. . . 'acquaintances' in the intelligence service, shall we say. And before I deployed with the Royal Marines, I still saw Johann on occasion and he confided in me."

As the energetic little defense lawyer strode back to his table to check some notes, Cohen shuddered at what might come next. He was chilled by all the talk of British Intelligence. The Americans had been first to enter Dachau as the Third Reich crumbled, but it had been the British who were his true liberators, quite literally bringing him back to life. When they found him, he had weighed barely a hundred pounds and had little will to live, thinking Rachel was dead. He was in their records as an American citizen, and they had treated him accordingly. Once he was out of immediate danger they'd shipped him to a London hospital, where the medical staff took him on as a special case. They had healed him as much through kindness and understanding as through any medical skills. Bonding with them had become a part of the healing process.

The British had saved him, and in the end had recruited him. By the summer of 1946, when he had his feet back under him a bit, they had begun testing him – his loyalties, his aptitudes – then begun training him. They had started slowly and had gradually intensified the regimen as he returned to good health.

For many months Cohen had not known, or really cared, what their plans for him were. He had understood it had something to do with intelligence work, that was all.

Then one day he was taken north of London to Bletchley Park, the hub of British Intelligence, and ushered into the presence of Sir Stewart Menzies himself. The legendary head of MI6 was a persuasive man. As he explained it to Cohen, MI6 needed a man inside Haganah, the Jews' core organization in Palestine, to monitor what they were up to. He was not being asked to betray anyone, Menzies assured him. The British had plenty of connections on the Arab side, he said. They just wanted to balance things out. Sooner or later the Arabs would overwhelm the Jews, who already had their backs against the wall. England didn't want to see another wholesale slaughter of Jews, after what had just happened in Europe.

"But you of course know better about all that than I, old boy," he told Cohen with a convincing note of empathy. "We just don't want it to happen again. And of course, too, we don't want that part of the world destabilized, do we, so old Joe Stalin can stick his big clumsy Russian paw in the door. Old Joe has his paw in too many doors already. We need to slam a few on him."

There was something ironic, and more than a little sinister, about all this for Cohen. At Dachau, Rachel had dreamed of Zion, a Palestine the Jews could call their own. An Israel. It had been her life belt, had kept her from going under. For Cohen, it had been America, his mother's native land, that had been the dream. The land of the free, where everybody was equal and nobody starved. Where fruit could be plucked from trees and the streets were paved with opportunity. Where the Yankees played baseball.

Now it appeared he would be the one headed for Palestine, if not to fight for Zion then at least to play a role. He wasn't sure what he would be doing, but for now he trusted England's good intentions.

It had taken another six months of preparation and delays before Cohen was routed to the Middle East via a Displaced Persons camp in the British sector of occupied Germany. He remained in the camp for two more months to build his cover. Finally, in March of 1948, he had been placed on a transport ship, a nondescript old tub ferrying "illegal" immigrants into Palestine.

He arrived just as the British were leaving, preparing to give up their thirty-one years of sovereignty over the area for good. That meant they needed a man inside Haganah even more, his control officer had told him shortly before his departure from Germany.

With that thought, Cohen was abruptly jostled back to the present by an emphatic exhortation from Mr. Benevides to Clay Johns, still on the stand, to "Go on, please."

"Johann had no trouble passing security checks at the start of the war," the witness said, evidently continuing an observation Cohen had missed during his brief flashback to MI6 and Palestine. "He told the investigators exactly what he was supposed to be doing in England. Spying. Rather ironic.

"For a while, I believe, there was even talk of sending him back into Germany as a double agent, but Johann was not interested in that idea. He had his own agenda, and was performing his interrogation duties, so far as I know, only half-heartedly. He was still in contact with the Abwehr and his father, and had to be very careful not to jeopardize his father's position with Hitler's inner circle. The key to understanding Johann's actions, certainly in the early stages of the war, was his father. Johann had always, even at Whitby, shown intense loyalty toward his father. He would have done anything, wouldn't he, to protect him. Bloody well anything. He tried so hard to make useful contacts for his father, he eventually came to be considered, in certain Whitehall circles at any rate, as rather an aberrant character. A little out of whack with reality."

"Did you think, at the time, that your good friend Johann Richter was 'out of whack with reality,' as you have put it?" Mr. Benevides asked.

The question reminded Cohen of Terry Harper's assertion that Richter was convinced he had somehow killed Adolf Hitler. Cohen tried to focus in better. He still felt distracted by memories of MI6 and Palestine, which seemed to be sparking thoughts of Elena Stein as well.

"No. Not at all. I trusted Johann. I believed in him." Clay Johns finally looked at Richter again. Richter returned the stare a moment, then lowered his eyes.

"Were you yourself, Mr. Johns, connected in any way, at any time, with any branch of British Intelligence?"

The witness chuckled. "God forbid. No. Not officially anyway."

Mr. Benevides approached the witness stand and turned up the intensity a notch. "I must ask you to be more specific then," he said, "concerning how you know so much about Mr. Richter's relations with British Intelligence."

Clay Johns appeared unruffled at what sounded to be an implied accusation. "As I said, Johann himself confided some of this to me. But most of it I knew from, ah, as I've said, 'other' sources."

"Your father, Lord Neville Johns, was he in the service of British Intelligence?"

The witness paused, but only for a second. "Yes he was," he said.

"In what capacity?"

"He was in MI6. A head of station."

The revelation was hardly surprising, Cohen thought. He could not recall Sir Neville's name from his own very carefully controlled stint with MI6.

"MI6 is normally in charge of England's foreign intelligence operations, its overseas espionage," Mr. Benevides said. "Is that correct?"

"Exactly," Johns said. "My father, I should point out, was terribly discreet. He told me a few things about Johann before Johann disappeared – back into Germany, as it turns out – in the middle of the war. But most of what I am telling you now I didn't know until well after Johann was gone and the need to keep it secret was no longer imperative."

"I see." Richter's lawyer wandered back over to the defense table and shuffled some more papers.

The judge took this opportunity to interrupt the proceedings. "Since it is nearly noon already, Mr. Benevides, I believe we will recess for the meal hour, if you have no objections."

"No objections, your Honor. If it please the court, the defense will rest with this witness now, but will reserve the right to cross-examine him later."

"Very well. Court will reconvene at two p.m." The judge pounded his gavel, stood up and left. In a general shuffling, Cohen, Weaver and the rest of the nearly packed courtroom swiftly followed suit.

"Consummations"

Déjà vu was what Johann Richter felt as he cantered his mare over the summer-green fields of Croyden Castle early on an August afternoon in 1939.

The sun beat down pleasantly warm, but the air itself was brisk. In spite of the beauty of the day, Richter had not been able to completely distract his thoughts from the discussions he had been holding with government officials in London for nearly two months now. Despite his connections with Neville Johns and despite his own father's important position inside Germany, his argument that the Nazis could be defeated from within appeared to inspire nothing but skepticism from the British. Unless it was outright contempt. Hitler had broken the Munich accords with his occupation of Czechoslovakia and his new demands for Danzig and the Polish Corridor, but many of the aristocratic and influential Cliveden Set and their allies were still clamoring to appease him in hopes of avoiding war at any cost.

His meetings with British officials to date, it seemed to him, had been virtually useless. He had been running an obstacle course of bureaucracy. The denizens of Whitehall were unresponsive, and he was becoming frustrated. He knew time was growing short. It was already late August, and Hitler would have to attack Poland soon, or not at all, this year. His job here, he knew, would likely become well-nigh impossible after that.

He forced himself back into the present. He had let the mare slow to a walk. A heavier breeze was beginning to blow from the east. Croyden Castle was as enchanting as ever. Very little, he thought, had changed here during his three years away. The grounds looked the same. The house staff was the same. The typically subdued but sincere family greeting he had received upon his arrival the day before had seemed hardly different from the ones he'd so often received here in years gone by.

Lord Neville and Lady Eleanor appeared not to have aged at all. With Clay still up at Oxford, Richter had dined with the two of them and Samantha and Elliot the night before in the cavernous dining hall he remembered so well. At the dinner table, Samantha, now eleven, had displayed intelligence and a quick wit, while the five-year-old Elliot had seemed to Richter just a bit stiff for his age. He was going to be a handsome young man like his older brother, but was put together on a thinner frame. Plans were already in the works to have him prep at Whitby.

Richter's hosts had steered the previous evening's dinner conversation very politely, and very carefully, around the one thing on everyone's mind – What would Hitler do next? And would it be something that would force Britain and France, perhaps even the Soviets, to declare war on Germany? It seemed impossible that after a mere twenty-five years the same questions were once again being pondered, the same dire consequences deemed inevitable.

The conversation had quickly turned to the extravagant soirée to be hosted at Croyden Castle the following evening. A large gathering of family friends and notables would be weekending here to attend the event. Richter had wondered aloud which of his old friends he could expect to see. Eleanor Johns had named a few. She also said that Clay, Christine, and Anne Wheldon were all due in sometime tomorrow afternoon. Christine, it appeared, was now keeping a flat in London and working full-time as a photographer's model, an enterprise not fully approved at table. Fashion work mostly, Lady Eleanor avowed. Anne Wheldon was up at Cambridge.

A branch sideswiped Richter's shoulder. His horse was taking a familiar path into the woods. Half-consciously, he gave the mare her head and left their destination up to chance. As they ambled deeper into the trees, sunlight slanted through the branches, at times a bright and warming burst, at times a chilling hint filtered from above.

After an indeterminate stretch of time, he suddenly awoke to surroundings that seemed familiar. He stopped and looked around for verification but found nothing specific. The feeling persisted, however, as he rode on. It made him vaguely uneasy, but had a pull he could not resist. After several more minutes, he was sure he knew where he was and took up the reins again, guiding his mount toward the sounds of bubbling water.

When they reached a quick-running stream, he was confused at first. This was not the place he remembered, but memory told him it should have been. He let the mare sip from the brook, reined her in and headed upstream. The water broadened and deepened as the forest closed in around its edges, a tunnel of dark green. He began to wonder where he was going. Another few minutes upstream a hole had been blown in the tunnel. Here, the sky beamed down on a small clearing dominated by a huge boulder that loomed above a dark pool just off the edge of the stream.

For a moment he was mesmerized by the enchanting tableau. All that was missing, thought Richter, was Anne Wheldon and her friend Emily. Feeling oddly excited, he dismounted and let his horse wander free. He sat down on the rock and stared at the pool, idly tossing a few pebbles into the still water and watching the quickly expanding wavelets ripple and disappear. The memories this started to dredge up still had the power to kick up turbulence in his gut.

"Welcome back."

Richter, heart stuck in his throat, swiveled toward the female voice.

"I've been following you," she said. "If you hadn't been so bloody preoccupied, you would have heard me."

He was still too startled to say anything.

"Mind if I join you?"

"No, of course not." Regaining a bit of his composure, he looked back down at the water as if searching for the rest of it. He had not been alone with a woman for many months, much less a woman the likes of Christine Johns.

She left her horse untethered and sat beside him on the sun-drenched rock. Richter could not take his eyes off her. As with everything else at Croyden Castle, she seemed barely changed at all from three years ago, though she had filled out a bit. And there was something about her face, in her eyes, that he quickly decided made her even more appealing. A new maturity, perhaps. He had heard she quit smoking.

"Why did you come back Richter; you a Nazi spy or something?" she teased.

He laughed, his heart finally beating out a reasonably even cadence again. This was the Christine Johns he remembered. The one with the rapier wit that cut at the same time it kidded. Richter had been feeling apprehensive over their impending reunion. Now he laughed again, partly in relief and partly in amazement at how close her joke touched to reality.

"How did you know?" he said. "But of course I am a spy for the *Vaterland*. With orders to rape, pillage and plunder wherever I go."

Christine, still smiling, let her eyes go more serious. "Where did you get this?" she said, running her fingertips along the dueling scar below his right eye.

"A sword. I dropped my guard." He touched her hand where it rested on his face. "It taught me a valuable lesson."

"What was that?"

"Never drop my guard."

Her eyes searched his, as if looking for a signal. "Do you remember three years ago?" she said. "That day on the hill near St. Albans?"

"Yes, I remember." He felt a need for caution, as he sensed the humor suddenly leaving the conversation. His mouth was dry. He wondered if she were going to tease him or abuse him with the unpleasant memory of their last encounter, a memory that still hurt for the sense of loss it gave him.

"You get one more chance," she said. The smile was gone.

"One more chance?" Richter had been ready to defend himself – with anger, if necessary – but Christine had thrown him instead into confusion. Now it was her turn to laugh. That rich, almost baritone laugh he remembered so well. "Ah, yesss. . . the past three years have done wonders for your sense of humor, *mein Herr*." Her words were mocking. He sensed a slightly hysterical edge to them.

"Come on, you idiot. One more chance. Right now. It's the only way we'll ever be friends again, you know."

Richter was dumbstruck. He could not think of an adequate response.

Christine turned her back to him. "Unbutton me," she commanded.

Something seemed wrong. It was all too sudden, too unbelievable. But Richter, caught up by the incredible offer to regain something he thought he'd lost forever, was not going to let doubts stand in his way this time. Awkwardly, he fumbled with the top button on the row that ran down the spine of her blouse.

As he worked, she asked nonchalantly, "Will you be at the party tonight?"

"Yes," he said. He had somehow reached the bottom button.

"Good, it will be such fun," she said. "You seem to inspire me." The blouse dropped away from her body, and she wasn't wearing anything beneath it. Richter cupped a loose breast with his left hand. Christine turned to him and laughed again. "Brrrrr. . . Your hands are cold, Richter," she said, the familiar hard look settling back into her eyes. Richter, with the slightly unnerving sensation he had lived this scene before, squeezed her taut nipple until she gave a small cry, then pushed her back down against the hard, warm rock.

* * * *

The party was centered in the main ballroom. Sparkling tinsel fluttered everywhere in the muted lighting. A small orchestra played from a stage that dominated one wall of the huge room. The dance floor was ringed by a hundred tables of partygoers in formal gowns and tuxedoes. There was a sprinkling of military uniforms. Richter had not left the woods until late in the afternoon. The festivities were already well underway by the time he arrived.

The first to spot him was Clay Johns, whom Richter had so far seen only once at Oxford and once in London since his return to England. His old friend's hairline was receding prematurely and he was a little heavier than three years before, but he still cut a handsome figure. His new bulk made him seem all the more commanding, Richter thought.

Clay took him eagerly in tow and began introducing him to other guests – and with a confidential smile, to the young women in particular. "My friend is a bit starved for female companionship," Clay told one gathering. "He has spent the past three years at Heidelberg.

Studying, he says." The pair of them stirred up excitement wherever they went, leaving a trail of eager gossip about the evening's hosts and their adopted German "cousin," as Clay sometimes introduced him. Their movement provided a shifting focal point for the party as they whisked from table to table, standing, sitting, talking, laughing, then moving on to the next group.

They weren't the only focal point of the evening however. With a twinkle in his eye, Clay led Richter into a small crowd gathered around two people, a small immaculately dressed man and a stunning woman.

"Johann, I'd like you to meet Mr. Beaton, Cecil Beaton, the photographer," Clay said, not hesitating to interrupt the conversation of a middle-aged dowager who was addressing the gentleman in question. "Mr. Beaton has photographed Christine."

"How'd'you do," the man said to Richter.

"I'm an admirer of your work," Richter replied. Beaton simply smiled his acknowledgment.

"And this," Clay said portentously, "is Miss Greta Garbo. The most beautiful woman in the world." He grinned like the cat that had just swallowed the canary.

"Puleeze, Mr. Johns. Do not exaggerate," said Garbo, extending a slender hand to Richter. Her voice could have melted butter, and certainly melted Richter's defenses. He had heard all about her, of course, but had seen only one of her movies. "Camille." For weeks after, he had found himself fantasizing he was Robert Taylor, with this exquisite woman dying in his arms. Now, he tried to hold a smile on his face to soften the sharp edge he knew the dueling scar gave his features.

He and Clay joined in the small talk for a few minutes, Richter having no idea what was being discussed and caring not a whit. Only Clay's insistent tug on his jacket sleeve finally tore him away from the world's most famous movie star.

"Snap out of it, dear boy. You look like a bloody Cheshire cat," Clay said. "She is best left to the cinema, from what I hear."

Before Richter could ask for an explanation of this remark, Clay had dragged him into another gathering and was introducing him to a tallish man with thinning hair and owlish glasses. "Ambassador Kennedy, this is a good friend of mine from Germany, Johann von Richter."

Richter had little time to wonder if Clay were including the "von" to tweak him, as the ambassador immediately introduced them to a rail thin, boyish-looking young man at his side. "I'd like you both to meet my son, Jack," he said in an upper crust accent that sounded to Richter as if he were putting it on. "Jack has just returned from Germany."

"Pleased to meet you," said Jack, with a smile that lit up his handsome face.

Richter was already quite familiar with Joseph P. Kennedy, by reputation. His pro-German stance as United States Ambassador to Britain had been an important linchpin for Chamberlain's policy of appeasing Hitler. It had won Kennedy the label of a defeatist before any war had actually broken out, and had put him in league with the acclaimed American aviator Charles Lindbergh and innovative auto maker Henry Ford as, at the very least, an indirect supporter of the Nazi regime.

Watching him now, chatting amiably in this small group, Richter saw only a rather friendly fellow with sharp eyes and a touch of ego in his pronouncements.

Left at the periphery of this discussion while Clay and others bantered with the ambassador, Richter was jarred awake by an abrupt, pointedly blunt question from the man's son.

"What do you think your country will do next?" said Jack Kennedy. His tone was genuinely curious. There was no hint of aggression in it.

"Only one man could possibly answer that question," Richter said.

"Hitler?"

"That's right."

"Do you know him?"

"My father does. I've seen him only once, ever. Going by in a motorcade."

"He seems a bit like the Wizard of Oz, at least at a distance," Richter's youthful interlocutor said, referring to a recently released Judy Garland movie.

"Maybe," Richter smiled. "But his power is real."

"So what do you think England and France should do?"

Richter was taken with the young man's candor and obvious interest. "They should've taken a stand a long time ago," he said, hoping this Jack Kennedy fellow would be discreet about what he was being told. "There's not much they can do now." There was in fact something they could do. It was why he had been sent to England. But Richter couldn't explain that here. Ambassador Kennedy, he was quite certain, had been informed of the high-level Wehrmacht opposition to Hitler's war plans.

"Could the United States broker an agreement, do you think?"

Richter looked more carefully at the young American. He seemed a mere boy, but carried himself with confidence and sounded like someone twice his age. "I believe the idea has been proposed, but Chamberlain's government was not receptive," he said. "They're nervous here about alienating Hitler and Mussolini."

"Too nervous, you think."

"Too nervous about everything."

Jack Kennedy smiled. "Have you met Garbo yet?" he said.

"Yes, I just had that pleasure."

"Even better than in her films, don't you think?" There was an almost puppyish eagerness in Kennedy's voice, but also a tinge of adolescent insinuation.

"Without question." Richter couldn't help but like the young man. He was about to ask Kennedy his thoughts on the current international predicament, when Clay grabbed him by the arm, excused them, and guided him over to a relatively quiet corner by the main fireplace.

Clay pointed out a man standing at the edge of the crowded room, alone with his champagne.

"I want to introduce you to him," he said to Richter. "Partly for your own protection. The man can be dangerous, so watch what you say to him. He's a part of the MI6 apparatus. All very hush-hush secret service. Still quite junior, but in his case it hardly matters. He is a schemer, a plotter, and bloody well-connected. A power to be reckoned with inside MI6. Something like your Heydrich, I should say."

Richter doubted Clay knew enough about Heydrich to know whether anyone could match his evil wiles, but he got his friend's point nonetheless. The man didn't look their way as they approached, but Richter had the sense he knew right where they were and what they were up to.

"Anders, old chap, I have someone here I want you to meet. The two of you may share a common interest." Clay was applying his best comradely tones. Johann could hear him straining at it just a bit. He wondered if the other fellow could.

"Johann, this is Left-tenant Anders Hardy. Anders – Johann Richter, an old school chum of mine from Whitby."

Richter was jolted by the name. He had heard it before. Years ago, in connection with Christine. Her visit to Malta, and afterwards. This was the man she had supposedly been seeing back when she had been teasing and deflecting Richter's interest.

"You are German," Hardy said.

"Yes, in fact, I am." Richter tried to smile off the rather rude opener.

"Lord Neville must have the only 'house German' in all England." Hardy's return smile was cold as ice.

Richter was not entirely certain what the remark meant, only that it was no compliment.

"Bugger yourself, Anders," Clay said. "You do talk the most infernal rot sometimes."

"Thanks awfully." Hardy's smile grew a little wider.

"Johann is on our side. I believe he has some information of importance, in fact, for a chap in your line of work, but this is neither the time nor the place to discuss it."

"Actually, I have caught wind of Mr. Richter's mission already. Lord Neville has passed him around quite liberally."

Hardy was a decidedly unattractive man, Richter thought. This in spite of a personal appearance – medium height, dark hair slicked back, dapper in a perfectly cut tuxedo – that was striking in the slightly effete way common among upper-class Englishmen.

Clay began to launch into another approach, but Hardy's attention was so obviously drawn elsewhere he interrupted himself to look back over his shoulder.

Anne Wheldon and Christine Johns were making their way through the crowd, both young women dazzling with their hair piled high to show off white shoulders and heirloom jewelry. Christine,

Richter noticed with a spark of pleasure, was slightly sunburned from her afternoon on the rock. He thought Anne's beauty tonight a bit too brittle for his taste, but Christine's sparkled like a perfect diamond.

Hardy, he noticed, was staring at her with a look of admiration that mirrored his own.

"Ah, Clay," she said. "You have two of my favorite gentlemen here."

Hardy managed a smile that appeared almost genuine. He beamed at Christine. Richter tried to assess her response. "Welcome back to the farm, Anders," she said. "It's been awhile." Christine, it was readily apparent, had been drinking.

"Too long, my dear. But there is a war on, you know. Or soon will be."

"Is there? It's no excuse, regardless. Though I must say" – and here she turned to Richter – "I always give Anders some leeway because he, the dear boy, weaned me from the wiles of Turkish tobacco, even if he was a bit bloody harsh about it."

Richter didn't like the obvious rapport Hardy still had with Christine. Was she a part of their "common interest"?

"I stand rebuked." Hardy gave her a mock bow. He started to say something to Anne Wheldon, whom he seemed to know as well, but a Royal Navy officer approached and interrupted. He whispered something to Hardy.

"I must excuse myself. It's that damned war again," Hardy said. "You haven't seen Kim tonight, have you old boy?" he said to Clay Johns.

"Not yet," Clay said.

Hardy performed another half-bow for the women, who seemed to enjoy the display. "Later this evening, I trust."

Richter wondered what he meant by that. A jealous anger stabbed at him.

"If we may, as well," Clay said. "Anne and I need to discuss something for just a moment. Please excuse us."

They moved a table length away for privacy, and talked quietly between themselves. Richter and Christine were left alone.

She leaned over to him. He could smell the liquor on her breath. Before he could say anything about Hardy, she threw him off balance. "Well, *mein Herr*," she whispered rather loudly, "did you enjoy fucking an Englishwoman this afternoon?"

Richter, startled and embarrassed, didn't know whether to take her seriously. Was she joking? He glanced around to see if anyone had overheard her and decided, fortunately, that no one had. "You certainly have little sense of propriety, Love," he said. "Why not just get up and announce it to the world?"

Christine's eyes suddenly caught fire. "What a smashing idea!" She turned and strode toward the stage as fast as was possible in her long flowing dress. Richter, following at her heels, caught up to her just as she mounted the first few steps to the raised platform. He grabbed her by the arm, a sudden rage stiffening his body. His fingers darkened her skin as he hissed, "What are you doing?!"

Christine's eyes were still wild. "What do you think I'm doing? I'm going to end my days of hypocrisy! Tell the world of my evil ways, my utter and hopeless immorality! I shall throw myself at their feet. Deliver myself into their unstained hands and beg for mercy." Putting a hand to her brow in a parody of anguish, she mocked the angry expression on Richter's face. "Ah, cruel fate! What hast thou done to me?"

He had no idea whether she would go through with this charade. Still holding her by the arm, he tried to coax her back down the steps. "Come on, Christine," he said, trying to sound calm and reasonable. "Let's go."

"Is everything all right, you two?" Neville Johns had mounted the stage from the opposite side and surprised Richter and Christine both with his question. Christine recovered first, addressing her father in the tone of respect she reserved only for him. "Yes, Father. Everything is fine. We're just fooling around." Lord Neville gave his daughter a stern look – unusually stern, it seemed to Richter – as if he were communicating a specific message to her, one meant distinctly for her and not for Richter. "Splendid," he said. "Now how about letting your brother and I borrow the stage for a few minutes, there's a good girl. Then you two can put on whatever show it was you had in mind."

"Certainly, Father. Please do. I'm sure they'll enjoy your 'show' much more than they would have ours, anyway." Christine's jabbing undertone of mock formality, Richter felt certain, was being picked up by Neville Johns.

"Thank you, my dear."

Christine finally descended the bottom steps as Anne Wheldon and Clay joined Lord Neville up on the stage. They were accompanied by a handsome young man new to Richter.

"Who is that?" he said.

"That, if you must know, is Harold 'Kim' Philby," Christine huffed. "A friend of Anne's and Clay's. A correspondent for the *Times*."

"The man your friend Hardy was looking for?"

"The very same."

The orchestra, at a signal from the elder Johns, brought its number to a close. Lord Neville stepped up to the mid-stage microphone, which the conductor had been using periodically for announcements. He turned and smiled encouragement to the young couple on the stage beside him, then addressed the microphone, "Could I please have your attention? Please. . . Ladies and Gentlemen, your attention for just a moment, please."

The crowd quickly stilled and assumed an air of polite expectancy. Richter suddenly realized what was coming. He looked at Christine and had the feeling that she did not.

"Thank you very much," Lord Neville continued. "This will take only a moment. I am a very proud man tonight, and I want to share the source of my happiness with all of you. I would like to propose a toast." He paused while the servants made quick, prearranged rounds with trays of champagne. Then he lifted his own glass toward the towering ceiling of the great hall, his gesture copied by every guest who had a glass in hand. "A toast to the engagement of my son, Claiborne Johns, to Miss Anne Wheldon of York. A toast!"

Glasses were raised, tilted, emptied, all around the huge room. There was a smattering of applause from those with two free hands, and a flurried round of Hear! Hear! from the rest. Up on the stage, Kim Philby flashed a million-dollar smile, hugged Anne Wheldon and shook Clay's hand. As Neville Johns left the microphone to personally congratulate his son and future daughter-in-law, the party crowd erupted back into a low buzz of conjecture.

The news had come as a genuine surprise to most. It had not been expected for at least another year or more. There was general agreement the deteriorating world situation had speeded up the event. Richter himself felt – curiously enough, he realized – little emotional reaction. There was his knowledge of Anne Wheldon's secret sexuality, and a pinprick of guilt over his having kept it a secret from Clay. But all of that had happened more than six years ago. For all he knew, Anne's fling with her friend had been nothing more than an adolescent experiment. All he felt, at the moment, was the vaguely unhappy sense that whatever chance he might've had of becoming as close to Clay as before was now likely gone.

Standing beside Christine during the announcement, Richter had been lost in his own thoughts and had failed to notice her reaction. When he finally looked at her, he detected behind her thin smile a hint of vulnerability. But there was an edge to it as well. The unlikely mix of emotions was in her eyes. On impulse, he touched her on the shoulder and kissed her cheek. She abruptly excused herself and left the room.

Neither of them had noticed the household's elderly, dignified-looking butler walk up onto the stage and whisper something into his employer's ear. Lord Neville's expression turned instantly grim. He asked the butler a few questions. Apparently satisfied with the answers, he nodded to the man and addressed the microphone once again. Behind him, the orchestra, which had begun playing a soft slow dance tune, came to a jumbled halt in the middle of it, leaving half the guests stranded cheek-to-cheek out on the dance floor.

"Ladies and gentlemen–" Lord Neville's solemn concern was heavily evident. The crowd went silent almost immediately this time. A line of well-wishers waiting to talk with Clay Johns and Anne Wheldon stopped and listened. "Ladies and gentlemen, please excuse the interruption, but I have just learned something of the utmost importance, something I feel it my duty to pass on to you without delay. . . Ladies and gentlemen, dear guests. Hitler and Stalin have signed a nonaggression pact. Hitler has sealed off his Eastern Front."

There was a moment of complete and utter silence. Then suddenly, all at once, like the bursting of a dam, the din of excited babble was total. Neville Johns tapped on the reverberating microphone to regain the room's attention. "I've one more thing to say while I'm up here." He waited for the noise to die down. "As most of you know, I am not overly given to fits of sentimentality. . ." He looked down at his champagne glass, then quickly back up again. "But, by God, if Hitler dares to attack England or France, dares to force our hand, then we shall oblige him. We shall crush him. And Germany as well, this time!"

A spontaneous cheer arose from the assembled guests. The orchestra, falteringly at first, then picking up their harmony and finally, like a burst of pride, their volume, took a few broken bars of "God Save the King" and built them up into a wave of emotion that flooded the great hall. Lord Neville, as if on cue, lifted his empty glass toward the ceiling, then hurled it to the floor of the stage where it splintered gloriously into a thousand tiny fragments. The gesture was immediately picked up and copied by everyone who had access to a glass, and explosions of breaking crystal erupted throughout the ballroom. Richter caught sight of Cecil Beaton and Greta Garbo grinning at one another, then tossing their own glasses into the air, champagne raining all around them. He looked for Ambassador Kennedy and his son but couldn't spot them.

The only person in the room besides himself who did not seem a part of the celebration was Kim Philby, still up on stage and looking quietly stunned. As if he had lost a loved one.

In front of the stage, Richter stood alone, an island adrift in a sea of self-righteousness, a dark chill of premonition making him shiver. The orgy of breaking glass, the mass, malevolent mood in the room, reminded him uncomfortably of the Nazis and their penchant for this kind of hysteria. His more immediate thoughts were of his father, his family. Of Erich Borchers and Claus von Stauffenberg. All were in jeopardy. The world was in jeopardy. He wondered if there were any hope left for mankind anywhere.

In the general melee, he didn't notice Anders Hardy, standing just a few steps behind him, sipping nonchalantly from his own glass. The man had a smile, not so much on his face as in his eyes, which were locked intently on Richter. Then he too, though somewhat casually, tossed his glass up against the wall and watched it shatter, its splinters showering a floor already covered in the broken glass of a people finally ready for war.

"Nelson's Dive Bombers"

The hillside flat Johann Richter had taken in London upon his return to that city in June 1939 was in the Chelsea section, on the sixth floor, high enough to command a view of the back of Buckingham Palace and one corner of St. James's Park across the tops of the trees. From the opposite windows he could see Battersea Park across the Thames. To someone standing on the threshold of the flat, "cluttered English comfortable" might come to mind.

It seemed to him at the time as good a place as any, probably better than most, from which to ride out this inevitable war that was on the way, this war he had no belief in and no stomach for. But he also felt alone and isolated. When the fighting broke out, he would be neither on one side nor the other. His Wehrmacht indoctrination notwithstanding, he did not believe in Hitler's quest for a "new order." And yet the old order of the British Empire seemed not much better. His basic loyalties favored Germany, but Hitler himself was such anathema to him his loyalties were split.

He made up his mind the things most important to him now would be those he could relate to most personally – his immediate surroundings, his family, his friends and himself. The pigeons of St. James's Park and Trafalgar Square, he decided, shared his feelings in that regard. He often watched these birds in idle fascination. They inhabited their territory with an utter disdain for the metallic monsters and pale two-legged creatures they shared it with. They dropped like dive bombers from Nelson's brow to accept from the earth whatever was offered. In his isolation and frustration, he sometimes wished he could emulate their seeming focus and detachment.

So far his mission here – in spite of help from Neville Johns and Clay – had been a complete and abject failure. Other Germans who were trying to avoid war had been warning British officials to take a tougher stand as well, and were having no more success than he. Only the out-of-office Winston Churchill, who had met with Goerdeler and von Schlabrendorff among others, appeared to take these warnings seriously.

He knew from his father that Hitler's recent "Pact of Steel" with Mussolini included assurances no war would start before 1943, at the earliest. Mussolini did not feel prepared for a general war yet, and if left to his own devices probably never would. He also knew by now, however, that Mussolini's squeamishness, much less words on a piece of paper, was not going to stop Hitler if he felt strong enough to plunge ahead.

And plunge ahead he did, Mussolini be damned.

Hitler's September 1 invasion of Poland and the declaration of war trade-offs that followed two days later between Richter's host and native countries made him automatically an enemy alien in England. Though the War Office, in a rather Byzantine move, declared only certain areas of the nation restricted to enemy aliens, it was obvious to him his position was in jeopardy. Once again, as promised, Neville Johns came to the rescue. He accepted personal responsibility for Richter, and Lord Neville's status inside MI6 made that appear an acceptable security risk. For now at least Richter would remain free to move around. Under surveillance, he assumed.

Another small bit of good news was that on September 3, the day England declared war on Germany, Neville Chamberlain appointed Churchill to the post of First Lord of the Admiralty, a position he had held some twenty-five years earlier at the start of the Great War. The hope was that the Germans who opposed Hitler had now gained a more sympathetic ear in the halls of power.

In December of that year, 1939, Clay Johns married Anne Wheldon. The ceremony was lavish, considering the general austerity prevailing as the nation girded itself for battle. To accommodate the Johns, and in particular Lord Neville's war-related distractions, the wedding was held not in York but at the country estate of close friends of the Wheldon family's in Wallingford, near Henley-on-Thames. Richter attended with mixed emotions. He still thought the bride a poor choice of partner for his best friend.

His consolation was the presence of Christine Johns, with whom he had been carrying on a four-month affair already given to precipitous ups and downs. After their first time together in the woods of Croyden Castle, they'd repeated the performance there several times. Later they met in Christine's London flat, but never in Richter's, which he felt certain was being watched. The nation's war fever was adding to their own.

At the wedding in Wallingford on a dreary, rainy Saturday they managed to find an empty upstairs boudoir in the hosts' manor house, a huge Edwardian showpiece. The period four-poster there fit their purposes nicely. It helped them both forget what they each, in their separate ways, considered the travesty of Clay marrying Anne Wheldon.

Six months later, Clay Johns had earned his commission and was on his way to Malta. He was with a detachment of Royal Marines being committed to battle in hopes of keeping the Central Mediterranean sea lanes closed to the Germans. His new bride returned to her classes at Cambridge.

By the start of 1940 Richter was growing restless. He was not doing much of anything constructive, he thought. The British were no longer even pretending to listen to him. In the meantime, several messages he had received through intermediaries from his father discouraged any realistic hopes for an overthrow of Hitler, at least for the time being. With Poland in his pocket, **the part Stalin hadn't grabbed,** the Fuhrer was too much the man of the hour. An attempted coup now could ignite civil war in Germany, Karl von Richter said. He told his son he hoped perhaps Hitler's "sanity" might ultimately prevail and allow him to bring the war to a quick conclusion.

His father's vacillating position churned up old doubts. Richter tried to tell himself the General was simply being a realist, and would take action against Hitler when the right time arrived.

Meanwhile his own position remained in limbo. During the "phony war" of that winter he was of little use to the British it seemed. For the Germans, technically, he was supposed to be spying for the Abwehr. But as promised, his father and his father's friends, including Lord Neville, had seen to it from the start he would be covered for on that score.

On April 9, German troops invaded Denmark and Norway and support for the Chamberlain government began to crumble. By the time the Wehrmacht launched a seemingly unstoppable blitzkrieg into Holland, Belgium and Luxembourg on May 10, a weary Chamberlain was ready to step aside as prime minister and an eager Churchill was ready to take his place. The change had no impact on Richter's role on the sidelines however. He still had nothing to do, really, but sit back and wait for something to break.

In June 1940, France broke and Stalin started collecting on his secret pact with Hitler, occupying Latvia, Estonia, parts of Romania, Finland and Lithuania. Interspersed with the hail of bombs that began to fall on England was a Luftwaffe airman or two, survivors of lost battles with the Royal Air Force or British ground fire. This set of circumstances led to Richter receiving his first and only official wartime assignment from his host country.

One morning in early August, as the Blitz intensified along with rumors of an imminent invasion, he was rung up by a man who announced himself as an undersecretary of something-or-other at the Foreign Office. The man directed him to report immediately to an office near Waterloo Station in Southwark. On arrival, he entered a building of dull gray stone, a kind of above-ground dungeon. Churchill's war rooms, he had heard, were buried beneath King Charles Street not far from here.

He was promptly ushered into a large, dingy office. Books and papers were scattered about on a conference table and a cluttered desk. A dull light from a row of tall but nearly opaque windows suffused the room. An officer stood with his back to him, looking out one of these windows. When he turned, it startled Richter. The man was Anders Hardy.

"We meet again, Mr. Richter."

From the way Hardy said it, Richter assumed this was no coincidence. Hardy gave him no further greeting. Made no move to shake his hand.

"Left-tenant," Richter said.

"It's 'captain' now, old boy."

Richter nodded his congratulations.

"So. How is our mutual friend?" Hardy said.

Richter assumed he must be talking about Clay, but he was not inclined at this point to give the man an inch. "Who is that?" he said.

"Christine Johns."

Something about the way Hardy said it warned Richter a message was intended.

"You do know her, do you not," Hardy said when Richter didn't reply.

He remembered quite clearly Hardy had seen them together at Clay's engagement party, though that seemed a lifetime ago now.

Stifling the urge to say something sarcastic, he said, "I went to school with her brother at Whitby." Instinct warned him to be cautious with this man.

"That would be Clay." Hardy spoke as if he were born to command, and was only temporarily inconvenienced by this rather shabby posting far beneath his station.

"Yes, that would be." Richter could hear himself reacting to the man's air of arrogant officiousness.

"Ahh, Christine," said Hardy, refusing to abandon his agenda. "A difficult girl, that. So mercurial – But what a beauty," he added, trying on a man-to-man tone. "And now that the bombs are dropping, the women in this town are getting rather loose with their favors. Have you noticed, Richter? Your Fuhrer is doing us at least that favor."

Richter didn't respond. Was Hardy trying to say he knew Christine better than Richter might realize? The thought was not a pleasant one.

Hardy stared at him a moment, as if weighing another jab. "Quite," he finally said, and broke off the stare, wandering over toward the grimy windows. "Do sit down, Richter. This will take a bit."

Remaining by the windows, Hardy said British interrogators were encountering difficulties when they interviewed downed German airmen. No doubt the flyboys could provide useful information, but so far most of them were balking, he said. They did not want to talk to Englishmen, even to ones who spoke flawless German.

"And that, you see, is where you come in, my good man." Hardy examined his fingernails a moment. "You are roaming free, as it were, at the pleasure of His Majesty's government. More to the point, perhaps, at the pleasure of this office. You could just as well be digging anti-tank trenches down along the Thames right now." Hardy shot Richter a glance to drive home his point. "I am aware that you have several of those proverbial 'friends in high places,' not the least of whom is of course our erstwhile host Lord Neville Johns, father of the fair maid we were just discussing." Hardy now inspected the ceiling, as if perhaps in search of such high places. "That however does not worry me, does it," he said, "as I took the precaution of clearing this meeting with him in advance.

"Lord Neville thinks the world of you," Hardy said. "But not all of us, to put it bluntly, Richter, completely trust you. We think you are rather too good to be true, as they say." Hardy's tone, his haughty manner, took Richter back to his worst days at Whitby, when he had felt isolated and looked-down-upon. But a part of him appreciated that for the first time in all his months of dealing with British bureaucrats, he was probably hearing the truth. Or at least something close to it. Intrigue was layered so thickly everywhere these days, one could never be certain.

Hardy began pacing as he continued his lecture. "We are familiar of course with your professed aims, that you're here seeking support for a 'potential' military putsch against Hitler. That's all well and good – if it really is your mission. I suppose you think it gives you the moral high ground."

The Englishman allowed himself a sardonic smile. "Oh, we know there is opposition to Hitler," he said, "and that some of it resides in the Wehrmacht. But it's hardly trustworthy, now is it. In the end, your generals couldn't quite bring themselves to do it, could they? Knock Hitler on the head and stop the war before it really got started. Too many successes in the field, perhaps? Too tempting to keep the victories rolling, the careers intact."

In spite of his irritation, Richter was captured by Hardy's monologue. His words had the ring of truth. It was ten times the response he had received from anyone else, and this time he hadn't even brought the subject up.

"So, Richter, can we count on you?" Hardy now stood behind the desk – the proper place, perhaps he thought, to deliver his official interrogatory.

"For what, exactly?"

"To apply your native charm to interrogating some of these German flyboys. Under deep cover, of course. None of them will know anything about you. We'll make quite certain of that beforehand."

"Do I have a choice?"

Hardy laughed – a dry cracking sound. "Well, there you have it. I suppose you don't."

"Then I suppose I'll do it."

"Spare me the enthusiasm, old boy. Personally, I am skeptical this is going to work out. But you're to be given your chance, aren't you. You will be working under tight surveillance. I assure you, you won't be given enough leeway to do any real harm, should you intend any. Just enough to hang yourself, perhaps." Hardy laughed again. "I will function as your control officer," he said. "I, and only I, will be your contact with the Foreign Office. Is that understood?"

"Control officer" seemed an odd turn of phrase for a Foreign Office man, Richter thought. Clay had said Hardy was some kind of operative in British Intelligence. He hardly seemed the Foreign Office type. Through Lord Neville, Richter had already worked a bit with MI6, trying to gain their confidence while helping them as little as possible. But he knew better than to say anything to Hardy. He held his tongue. By now he was well-practiced at censoring himself.

He left the interview with Anders Hardy feeling angry and discouraged. The man personified the lack of moral center Richter had feared when he had joined the Abwehr. He was starting to feel the inevitable poison of espionage seeping into his own blood stream.

Bomb damage down near the Thames in this part of London was considerable. The Luftwaffe was turning large sections of the city into rubble. Picking his way through the debris, Richter was overcome by shame. He was ashamed of Germany. He was ashamed of himself. But he was also uncomfortable with the role he was playing with the British and their intelligence organizations. Where did his loyalties belong? Where should they belong?

His thoughts were cut short by the sudden wail of air raid sirens. When the Blitz had first begun, he had often stayed topside and watched as the German bombers dropped their deadly cargo. At first he couldn't help himself, he had silently rooted for the bombers. But that soon changed. By now he'd seen far too much random death and destruction. As with everyone else, the air raids were starting to make him jumpy. He felt a mix of fear and irritableness as he hurried through a tube station and down an entrance to the Underground.

Down below, he crowded onto the station platform with hundreds of others, many of whom had the usual assortment of blankets and other minor comforts they kept at the ready these days. He marveled at the discipline of even the small children. There was a sense of power in the way these people pulled together and offered each other care and assistance. But did they have any idea of the kind of power that was massing against them across the channel? Hardy said the British government preferred to leave Hitler alone, let him lead the Nazis to defeat. But what would happen if he led them to victory?

After less than half an hour, the all-clear blew. A false alarm evidently.

On the way back to his flat he stopped by Trafalgar Square. He still liked to watch the pigeons there. Nelson's dive bombers, blissfully unaware of the cataclysmic events going on all around them. Had Horatio Nelson, First Lord of the Admiralty, the hero of Trafalgar, had to deal with bureaucratic fools and conniving spies when he was trying to defeat Napoleon? How had the British ever managed to conquer a quarter of the entire globe?

Richter watched the pigeons, who continued doing what they were doing, appearing full of purpose. He wished he felt the same about his own role in this war.

CHAPTER XI

"What do you think of this guy?" John Weaver was leaning over, confiding in Cohen. He was talking about Clay Johns, who had informally wandered up and retaken his seat on the witness stand while the last stragglers filed back into the courtroom from lunch.

"I don't know," Cohen said. "What do you think of him?"

"I don't trust him," Weaver said.

"Why not?"

"The way he talks about his father, about British Intelligence. The connections. What was going on. Just listen. Something's screwy."

Something was screwy all right, Cohen thought, as the judge entered the courtroom and the spectators rose. But it wasn't just Clay Johns. Cohen's only coherent impression of the morning's testimony was that Mr. Benevides was a better lawyer than he had expected him to be.

"Does this look familiar?" He handed his just-completed sketch of the bearded man to Weaver. The man seemed to have disappeared from the courtroom, but Cohen thought he'd captured a pretty good likeness.

"Not bad," Weaver said. "You definitely have a talent. I've seen him around."

"I drew him because I thought he might have been following me the other night."

"It's that kind of place. I always feel like somebody's following me down here."

"Be seated," the judge said.

Clay Johns was resworn in.

Once again Raoul Zamora, the prosecutor, handed over the questioning to Sir Anthony Wilde, who stood and delivered a short recapitulation of the morning's testimony, right up to the start of the war. "Perhaps it would be most useful," Sir Anthony said, "simply to have Mr. Johns continue with his story. Possessing the whole picture will help us make sense of things. Such as motive." As before, Sir Anthony had a way of phrasing even the mundane in a way that loaded it with unspoken meaning. In this case, that there was indeed a motive for Johann Richter to have killed Christine Johns. "Please continue, Mr. Johns," he said.

Looking slightly pained but resigned, the witness sat back and stared out toward the ceiling at the back of the room as he picked up his story.

"Two weeks after the invasion of Poland, and our declaration of war against Hitler," he said, "I enlisted in the Royal Marines. In December 1939, Anne – Anne Wheldon and I – were married, and shortly thereafter I was sent to Southampton for training. From there I went to Malta, and then to Egypt.

"I was corresponding with my family at the time. With Anne, principally, of course. I believe it was she who first told me that a relationship appeared to be forming between Johann and my sister, Christine. They had spent quite a lot of time together at Croyden Castle before I left England, and I'd already, in fact, thought Christine might be coming to have quite a genuine affection for him. But I was still rather surprised by the news."

Johns ventured a quick look toward the defendant. "Christine was, umm. . . Well, it's difficult to describe. Men found her irresistible. They followed her around like hounds after a fox, but usually kept their distance after she had nipped at them a few times. Which she invariably did."

As advised, Cohen had pricked up his ears trying to decipher the testimony. There was in fact an undercurrent of something beneath the surface, he thought. Perhaps something being withheld. He glanced at John Weaver, whose grin said *I told you so.*

"How did a Mr. Anders Hardy fit into the picture at this time?" Sir Anthony asked Johns.

"I really couldn't say," he replied. "Anders had been much taken with Christine at one time. Somewhat obsessed, actually. But Christine, when she made her decision about a person, was like ice, wasn't she. Ice that never melted. She'd made it quite clear that whatever had transpired between herself and Hardy was over and done with. That she wanted nothing more to do with him. To be perfectly honest, I assumed Johann would meet a similar fate one day. But with Anders Hardy, it was just as well, I felt. I knew the man at Oxford. He was a bit of a blighter, I had always thought. Accomplished but distant. Even a little sinister. Ran with the socialist crowd, though he wound up with British Intelligence eventually. In any case, he was rarely mentioned in Anne's letters to me in Egypt."

"So this Anders Hardy was out of the picture, so to speak, with your sister by that time?"

"That certainly appeared to be the case, yes," Clay Johns said. "Though I daresay with Christine apparently warming up to Johann, I wondered about Anders from time to time, simply because he was such a difficult fellow. But I was in Egypt. For any such goings on in England, you must understand, I had only Anne's side of it, as Christine and I never corresponded. Anders Hardy was not my main concern at the time. There was something about the letters I was receiving from Anne. Some quality, I can't explain it. They were really quite cold, I suppose, almost angry. I asked her several times by return post if anything were wrong, but she never responded to my questions on the matter. It disturbed me a good deal.

"I was also corresponding with Johann during my stays in Malta and Egypt, and his letters too, I thought, had a rather strange ring to them. It seemed almost as if he were trying to warn me of something. The last thing I heard from either of them was that Anne was planning to move into London to do volunteer nursing work.

"In March of 1941, I was transferred to Greece. Less than two months later I was captured – of all places, near the pass at Thermopylae – just before the Germans finished off the entire Ionian Peninsula.

"At first we weren't treated too badly. German officers in the field had a decent attitude toward their prisoners, really. But after about a month in detention camp in Greece, we were shipped out to Germany in railway cars packed tighter than boxcars full of cattle on their way to slaughter. We were given nothing to eat; very little to drink. Many of the men died in transit. The rest of us lived through a hell on earth locked up inside those boxcars for nearly four days. The stench of death and excrement was unbelievable. One of my best friends simply cracked up. By the time we arrived at our prison camp – 'Camp Kraut,' we called it – somewhere outside Dresden, he was no longer coherent. He was taken out to be 'interrogated,' and that was the last we ever saw of him."

"Did the Germans ever mention the defendant while you were in that place," Sir Anthony asked.

A rather leading question, Cohen thought. He wondered if the response had been scripted in advance.

"The Germans interrogated all of us," Johns said. "I myself was never physically tortured, other than by long hours of belligerent questioning, though I knew of others who were."

Sir Anthony waited, looking a little impatient. The witness appeared determined to tell the story his own way.

"I did receive a bit of a jolt, however, at my very first interrogation," he continued. "My inquisitor was a young SS officer. Enthusiastic, but a little over-eager, I thought. Of medium rank. He sat at a desk, which I stood before. I gave him my name, rank and serial number. His assistant handed him a file that, as I had not been interrogated before, I was rather stupefied to see my name on. He glanced through it briefly. Suddenly he stopped and stared at me, and practically shouted, 'Do you know a man named Johann Richter?!'

"I was caught completely off guard. I didn't know what to answer for fear of jeopardizing Johann or his family in some way. 'We know about MI6, we know about this man Richter,' he said, to make me think twice about lying, I presume. I finally told him a chap named Johann Richter had been my roommate at boarding school years ago, but that I had last seen him in 1936 and had no idea what had become of him. It was rather obvious the man did not believe me. In a most unlikely and quite gentlemanly fashion, however, he didn't press the point.

"But this bringing up of Johann's name in such context, whatever the reason for it, set off a rather odd chain reaction in me. I must have relived that scene with the SS officer a thousand times, worrying over that one question he had put to me, how he had put it, how he had reacted to my answer and to his initial discovery of Johann's name in my file. He'd certainly reacted with surprise. But then, it seemed to me, he had purposefully composed himself and rather abruptly discontinued our interview."

"What did you make of all that?" Sir Anthony inquired.

"At the start it was simply a puzzle I used to occupy myself," Johns said. "In the back of my mind, I knew, I was quite certain, Johann was trustworthy. But I let my thoughts begin to toy with the idea that he really *was* a German spy. I thought of it as a mental exercise, a game to fight off the boredom. I mucked about in my memories to fit his behavior, his words, into a sinister mold. I recalled the uneasiness I'd felt over the letters I received from him while stationed at Malta and Egypt. And over

the ones from Anne as well. Somehow the two things began to fit together in my mind, and my worries took a new tack. Thinking about
Anne's letters, trying to remember them word for word, I recalled allu-
sions to Johann, references that now sounded to me suspicious. I relived
scenes and conversations with both of them in England, and saw these in
an entirely new light.

"Eventually I concluded Anne and Johann were having an affair.
I was mortified when I thought of the things I had confided to the two
of them, particularly to Johann. This was no longer a game. As the
months passed, my suspicions escalated. They gradually created a
logic of their own. Rather than considering them a plaything, I now
tried to suppress these thoughts as consistently as I conjured them up.
There were times the whole thing seemed ridiculous to me, a ghastly
creation I had made up to torture myself with. But in the more difficult
stretches it undoubtedly helped keep me going, helped me stay alive.
It gave me a reason—"

"What reason was that, Mr. Johns?" Sir Anthony interrupted.

Clay Johns hesitated a moment, his eyes once again coming to rest
on Richter. "Revenge," he said. "At times I was possessed by the idea. I
harbored terrible fantasies of returning home to have it out with Johann.
And with Anne too, I suppose."

Johns averted his eyes from Richter. "My best friend and my wife,"
he tacked on with a distracted air.

Cohen noted how quiet the courtroom had become. Only a few
coughs, backed by the constant hummingbird whir of the movie cameras,
were audible.

The testimony had a subplot that intrigued Cohen as much as the unfolding story of Clay Johns. It was in the silent interaction between the
witness and Richter and between the witness and his wife. More empathy
appeared to be flowing between the former two than the latter pair, Cohen thought. Anne Johns had sat throughout the testimony with a hard
look on her face, her stare locked onto her husband, an obvious tension
building.

After a moment's silence, Sir Anthony coaxed the witness back to his
story. "Go on, Mr. Johns. Please go on." Clay Johns, continuing to look
away from Richter, picked up as if he had never paused. "Much later,
sometime in the late spring or early summer of 1943, I believe, long after
I had last been interrogated by the SS, I was startled to be roused early

from my bunk one dreary night. Two guards led me through rain to the main administration building of the camp, then through a long maze of hallways and down into a little cubicle, somewhere in the cellar I believe.

"A bare light bulb lit this room. There was a wooden table with one chair in front of it. I was told to sit in the chair and stay there, then was left alone. I was wet and cold, in a state of extreme agitation. I could not imagine what they wanted of me this time. My mind was spinning round and round and going nowhere. The glare of the light bulb was giving me a headache. Suddenly an officer stomped into the room, shaking the rain from his black overcoat. The light blinded me. I couldn't see his face.

"He stood there and inspected me, or at least so I imagined. All I could see was the black overcoat and the rain dripping off it. He leaned back against the table, lit a cigarette and offered it to me. I took a long hard drag and tried to get a grip on myself.

"The officer, a rather high-ranking SS man – a standartenfuhrer, I believe – was waiting, giving me a moment. Another unlikely gentleman in that hellhole, it seemed.

"Then out of the blue, in impeccable English, he said, 'How would you like to go home?'

"I looked up at him. He had moved in front of the light bulb, so I could see him now. He had a young face, with deep lines cutting across it. Though I could see no dueling scar, he could almost be Johann, I thought. He was tall and had a similar look about the eyes.

"I remember his next words exactly. 'You are a lucky man,' he said. 'A trade has been arranged. This is an unusual thing.'

"'What do you mean?' I said.

"He said, 'You have powerful friends, evidently. We are exchanging you for an Abwehr man.'

"It seemed I was being given the chance to return to England. God works in mysterious ways, I thought."

While the witness paused, apparently chewing on this thought, Cohen found himself contemplating the mysterious ways of God. "Mysterious" was not the right word, he concluded.

"And then what happened?" Sir Anthony prompted.

"Two days later," Johns said, "I was taken from the camp, given a new set of clothes, fed a decent meal and put on an aeroplane. Bound for where, I hadn't the foggiest notion. The plane, as it turned out, took me to Paris. From there I was slipped across the border into Vichy France,

Spain and then Portugal, always under guard by the SS, who wore civilian clothes once we crossed into Spain.

"These fellows, the four of them, all spoke some English and they loosened up a bit more with each border we crossed. One of them told me he'd heard that General von Richter, Johann's father, had arranged for this prisoner exchange. The General had something of the reputation of a maverick on the German General Staff, according to my traveling companions.

"In Lisbon, in a rather elaborate ceremony, my SS guards delivered me to officials at the British Embassy and departed with their Abwehr man in exchange. I was among my own countrymen again – embassy stuffed shirts, to be sure, but no less a welcome sight. I was home free. Or almost.

"It was another several weeks before I was able to fly to England. By that time, our intelligence and Foreign Office people had debriefed me and the embassy meals had fattened me up a bit. I was flown to an RAF field near Bedford. To my amazement, the first to greet me at the field were Anne and Christine. They had twisted Father's arm to let them be there."

"When did you first see Mr. Richter again?" Sir Anthony said.

"Not until the weekend my sister was killed." Clay Johns sounded wistful. He looked distracted again.

"Would you describe to us what happened that weekend, please."

Johns stared blankly at his questioner.

"Mr. Johns?"

The witness snapped out of his trance. "I, ah, had been home, at Croyden Castle, only a few weeks," he began. "The Royal Marines had granted me sixty days convalescent leave. I believe one of the reasons everyone was invited that weekend was to welcome me back. Back from the dead, as it were." Here, Johns flashed an easy grin. It showed a glimmer, Cohen thought, of the self-confident young aristocrat he once had been.

"There was a rumor afloat that the P.M., Mr. Churchill, was to be there. Father set me straight about that, but said I was not to discuss it with anyone. Our houseguest was apparently a 'double' for the prime minister, some sort of variety artist, I believe."

"An actor, you mean."

"Yes. He was to be at Croyden Castle as a decoy while the prime minister attended an important conference somewhere. I am sure he was to be kept mostly under wraps, but I was curious to meet him. Unfortunately, I was rather under the weather that weekend. My temperature was well over a hundred. I was experiencing periodic sweats, my first episodes of flashback. Sometimes to the battlefield, but more often to my POW days. It was not pleasant. Bad enough that my wife was sleeping elsewhere for the time being."

"Do you still, Mr. Johns, suffer such flashbacks?"

"I do. But much less frequently now. They are. . . " He trailed off, lost in thought.

"What then, Mr. Johns? What happened next that weekend at Croyden Castle?"

"I was quite low that Friday evening, so I didn't come down to dinner. Johann did, however, come up to visit with me just before."

"And what did Mr. Richter have to say to you?"

"He welcomed me home, basically. Told me he and Lord Neville, my father, had worked with General von Richter, through intermediaries of course, to obtain my release. The first I'd heard of that, I daresay."

"How did he seem to you that night?"

"Johann? He seemed a bit preoccupied. I expected him to ask me more questions, but he asked very few. He did make some joke about how glad I must be to be back among women again. Maybe he was being ironic, but if he was, I thankfully failed to pick up on it. And perhaps I was being wretchedly ungrateful, but I was having this little problem, you see, of not exploding in his face. It was probably only because I was so weak with fever that I didn't. My old prison camp obsessions about him and Anne had resurfaced on my return to England. To see him in the flesh made it even worse."

"Was anything said about any of this that night?"

"Between myself and Johann? No. Not in so many words. But I treated him rather shabbily because of it. That has caused me some distress. Thinking back on it, I've often regretted that my last conversation with him was so full of ill will because, oddly enough, a part of me was glad to see him. In some ways, he was still an old friend I'd missed. Not to mention that he and his father were largely responsible for my freedom. Perhaps even for my being alive."

"And later that night?"

"After Johann left, I was brought up my dinner. I ate what I could, read for a bit and tried to get some sleep. But I was too restless. Perhaps I nodded off, because I heard a noise outside my window and when I glanced at the clock it was past two a.m. I was still a little shaky, but I got out of bed and went over to the windows. My room was in a corner. It looked out over the back lawns and, off to the right, the pool.

"There was ample moonlight that night to see quite well, but at first I saw nothing out of the ordinary. Then suddenly out from a hedgerow bursts a man in bathing costume. It was Johann, I was quite certain. He dived into the pool without a splash. A passing cloud darkened the picture momentarily and I could hardly see the pool. I heard a laugh. Distinctly a woman's laugh. I was dumbstruck. It was as if my nightmare had come alive and I was being forced to watch my best friend and my wife cavorting together before my eyes. Mixed with the fever, I can't begin to describe the state this put me in. I kept my eyes riveted on the pool, though I could still barely make it out.

"I heard someone get out of the water. There was whispering. I had nearly made up my mind to grab my service revolver and put an end to things – which things, exactly, I'm not entirely certain – when the moon suddenly came clear again and I could see what was happening. Johann was reaching down to help the woman out of the pool. As she popped up out of the water and into his arms, I was hit by two things at once. First, that she was au naturel, which was somewhat startling, to say the least, on the immediate grounds of Croyden Castle. And second, whoever she was, she was not, thank God, my wife."

"Who was she, Mr. Johns?" With his tone, Sir Anthony did not trouble to disguise that he already knew.

"My sister. Christine."

Cohen, as attentive as the rest of the courtroom, focused intently on the witness, trying to determine his state of mind. Could *he* have had anything to do with his sister's death?

"And what effect did this have on you?" Sir Anthony said.

"I was surprised. And tremendously relieved. She and Johann disappeared straightaway, and with them went my nightmare. Or so I thought. I'd no idea, of course, that it was all about to end so quickly."

"What did you do next, Mr. Johns?" Sir Anthony appeared now to be brimming with good will, confident he had made his point – the connection between Richter and the victim on the night of the murder.

"I went back to bed, feeling almost well now. For a while I fell in and out of sleep. Once, I thought I heard Johann and Christine out by the pool again. It seemed to me they'd been there a long time, but it was difficult to assess how much time had actually gone by.

"Eventually I fell into a deeper sleep, and slept until I was awakened by a scream. One horrible scream. That was all. I lay there in bed, resolved to get up and investigate if I heard anything more, but for a long while there was nothing more. It wasn't until at least fifteen or twenty minutes later that a general hubbub in the hallway outside my door finally got me up and out of bed to see what was happening."

"And?"

"A servant said my sister had been attacked. I wasn't very mobile, but I managed my way down to her room, where everyone was gathered, and found a dreadful scene. She was already dead."

"And Richter?"

"Johann was gone. He could be found nowhere, said Anders Hardy, who had taken charge of things. Hardy had been invited for the weekend. I believe he'd arrived sometime late that evening."

"And where had Mr. Richter gone?"

"We didn't know it for at least another month or two, or at least I didn't, but he had somehow found his way back into Germany, where he rejoined the German army and eventually commanded a post in occupied France."

"He had been recalled to Germany, had he not?"

"Objection, your Honor." Mr. Benevides rose to make his point. "Calls for speculation."

"Sustained."

"At any rate," Sir Anthony said, "if he were returning to Germany, and had indeed planned to leave that very night, he would not have wanted anyone to know. Even a lover. Especially–"

"Objection!"

"I withdraw the question, your Honor."

Sir Anthony put his head down, preparing, it seemed to Cohen, his coup de grâce. "And the conclusions, Mr. Johns, of those present? About how your sister had died?"

Mr. Benevides started to stand, then apparently thought better of it and stayed put.

"Right from the start," Johns said, "there was little doubt she'd been murdered. Her throat had been slit. Everyone assumed Johann had done it. Later, when Scotland Yard became involved, including at the inquest, the assumption was always the same."

"Did you agree with that assumption?"

Here, Clay Johns stared again at the defendant. "I couldn't believe it. Part of me didn't *want* to believe it. But on the other hand, I suppose I did want to. The part of me that had been poisoned against Johann for so long wanted to believe he was guilty. And I didn't know what else to think. Who else could have done it?"

"Maybe he should look in the mirror," Weaver leaned over and whispered, a bit loudly. Cohen had almost forgotten he was there.

Richter stared back at the witness impassively. There was no clue in his eyes either way, Cohen thought.

Sir Anthony pressed on. "How did you feel, Mr. Johns, after the murder of your sister?"

Again Mr. Benevides appeared to be restraining himself, but made no objection.

"I felt sad about Christine," Johns said. "But quite truthfully, I was numbed more than anything else. I believe I had simply been through too much too recently, seen too much death and despair, to properly grieve for Christine. And the idea of her having been killed by Johann was in the same realm for me as my prison camp nightmares of the home front, about my wife and Johann. It wasn't real and it wasn't unreal. I tried to make my peace with it."

If Johns were lying, Cohen thought, he was doing a good job of it.

"But that night was a watershed of some sort for me," the witness continued, on his own tack now. "I've tried to make my own peace with a lot of things since then. After the war, I entered the transport business with my father. He was in a motorcar crash two years ago, and is still in a coma. My mother and my younger sister Samantha died in the crash. I've tried to carry on. I stood for the House of Commons last year but was defeated, quite soundly. I have no children. . ."

As Johns trailed off, Sir Anthony returned to the prosector's table, seemingly done with the witness. About to take a seat, he suddenly straightened and fired off one last shot. "When you returned from that POW camp, what did your wife reply, Mr. Johns," he said, "when you confronted her with your suspicions about Richter, that they'd had an affair?"

"Nothing," Johns said. He looked a little chagrinned. "I never asked her about it, actually. Somehow it never seemed right, after Christine's murder."

Sir Anthony was plainly disappointed. Evidently he had been fishing in the dark, Cohen thought. It seemed an odd question, from the prosecutor's side of things. It struck something decidedly less than a high note on which to conclude his questioning. Sir Anthony paused, as if considering this, then gave in.

"No more questions, your Honor."

"Some friend he is," Weaver said, nodding toward the witness. *"Et tu, Brute?"*

"You don't seem to think too much of the gentleman," Cohen said.

"I think the 'gentleman' has his apron strings tied too tight. I'll be interested to see what his wife has to say about things. Bet she doesn't pussyfoot around."

On cross-examination, Mr. Benevides wasted no time stepping into the void left by Sir Anthony's final unverified implication.

"Mr. Johns," he said, "your testimony implies the defendant might have killed your sister for reasons of military expediency. To cover his tracks, as it were. Or that perhaps he killed her over – what should we term it? – some kind of unrequited love, or fit of jealousy. Is that not correct?"

"Objection!" Sir Anthony rose from his chair. "Requires speculation from the witness."

"Sustained."

Mr. Benevides, having set the stage, merely continued. "But if we're looking for the latter sort of motive, or perhaps either sort, wasn't there an even better candidate present that night?" Before the prosecutor or Sir Anthony had time to react, Mr. Benevides waved a hand for them to remain seated and came up with a more specific question for the witness. "I believe you said earlier that Anders Hardy was 'obsessed' with your sister. Was he not a former lover of hers?"

"To the best of my knowledge, yes, he was," Johns said.

"And wasn't Mr. Hardy the defendant's control officer for British Intelligence?"

"That I couldn't tell you. As I've said, he was an MI6 operative. I knew that from early on. But that's all I knew."

"Do you think, Mr. Johns, that Anders Hardy, that night in June of 1943, still had an interest in your sister?" As he asked this question, Mr.

Benevides stared pointedly in the direction of Anne Johns, as if implying she might have a stake in the answer.

"Objection. Speculative."

"I withdraw the question, your Honor. Mr. Johns, were you aware that your sister was thought to have attempted suicide the year before she was killed?" The lawyer's eyes remained on Anne Johns.

"I knew about that, yes. But not much. I was a prisoner of war at the time it happened."

"Did you know it was your wife who found your sister unconscious on the floor, her wrists slit open by a kitchen knife? Your wife who rang up an ambulance and police?"

Now Johns himself looked out toward his wife. "I had heard that, yes," he said.

"Did you find that at all odd?"

"What do you mean?"

"That it was your wife who found your sister in that state."

The witness hesitated. "No, not particularly," he said with caution.

"Whose scream was it that awakened you that night? The night your sister was killed." Mr. Benevides continued to stare at the woman he was talking about. Her head was turned from where Cohen sat. He couldn't see her reaction.

"Anne had screamed. I found that out later."

"So your wife was first on the scene again?"

"Yes. I suppose she was."

Finally, with an exaggerated deliberateness, Mr. Benevides unglued his eyes from Anne Johns. "No more questions," he said.

Cohen felt led to the edge of a precipice and abandoned there. He was not alone. What had been the point of these last several questions, he wondered. Was Benevides trying to imply Johns' wife had played a role in the death of his sister? Or even killed her?

Appearing equally puzzled, Clay Johns left the witness box. As he passed by, John Weaver leaned over and whispered to Cohen, "I still don't trust the guy."

Cohen could only nod his head and shrug. *Who knows?* he thought.

CHAPTER XII

It was Anne Johns' turn to testify. As she took the witness stand, she appeared quite purposefully to avert her eyes from the defendant's table. She wore a look that stopped just short of being a scowl. It struck Cohen as being a permanent feature of her expression.

Responding to Sir Anthony's initial, rather general, question, she stated firmly, "I first met Johann Richter" – pronouncing Richter's name with evident disdain – "in 1933, when we both happened to visit Croyden Castle at the same time." She seemed about to add something, then to think better of it. "I saw him a number of times more," she went on, "between then and 1936, almost always at the Whitby School in St. Albans, where I visited Clay occasionally. After that, he left England for a couple of years, to attend school at Heidelberg, I believe, and did not return, so far as I am aware, until sometime in 1939.

"The first time I saw him after his return was at a house party Clay's parents gave at Croyden Castle on the twenty-third of August of that year. I remember the exact date because it was the night my husband and I announced our engagement. It was also the day the Hitler-Stalin pact was signed. I don't really remember much about Johann Richter that night at the party, other than his spending most of his time with Clay's sister Christine."

"And the next time you saw the defendant?"

"In December, at the wedding," she said, "Clay's and mine. After that, during the first few years of the war, I saw him on only a small number of chance occasions. Though I did hear quite a lot about him."

Anne Johns, Cohen noticed, had still not once looked at Richter, who was taking her story in with a quietly attentive, almost amused, look on his face. Clay Johns, on the other hand, appeared to be more focused on Johann Richter, and presumably on his old friend's reactions, than he was on his own wife's testimony. He was probably familiar by now with whatever she had to say on the subject, Cohen thought.

"Clay had joined the Royal Marines right at the start of the war and was sent to Malta, then later to Egypt, as you have already heard from him," she continued. "I had dropped out of Cambridge just before we were married. But when Clay was sent so far away, I decided to reenroll, and began university again in the fall of 1940.

"Those were, of course, trying times in England. When I'd first decided to go back to school, the Nazis had by then dropped only a few bombs on us. By the time I actually returned to Cambridge, France had been overrun and we were caught up in the middle of the Blitz. I did not drop out again right then only because both Clay's parents and my own thought it better that I remain outside of London for the time being.

"So there I was, in this traditional, pastoral setting, my husband fighting a war a thousand miles away, aeroplanes flying overhead every now and then – as if to remind us that the war did indeed exist – and Dr. Anthony-Smythe, my Latin tutor, taking me to task if I could not conjugate *'amor'* or some such nonsense properly. I felt, as it were, totally useless and quite guilty.

"At the end of classes in the spring of 1941, I dropped out of Cambridge again and moved into London. I did various types of volunteer work there, mostly in nursing. And it was in London that I occasionally, but only very occasionally, really, bumped into Johann Richter. I saw Christine much more often. She was modeling and doing film work. For the war effort, of course. I even roomed with her for a short time, in Chelsea. After I moved to another flat, we still saw each other at least two or three times a week, I should say–"

"Could you move ahead to the summer of 1943, please, Mrs. Johns?" prompted Sir Anthony, eager perhaps, thought Cohen, to move on to more rehearsed territory.

"Certainly," she switched gears smoothly. There was no way to tell if she were irritated by the interruption, Cohen reflected, because she looked perpetually irritated. "In June of 1943," she said, "my parents decided to come down from York and spend a week's holiday with my in-laws, Lord Neville and Lady Eleanor. By that time, you understand, I had been in London for more than two years, and Clay had only recently returned from being a prisoner of war. While he recuperated at Croyden Castle, I commuted from London. On this particular visit, I joined my parents there on about the twelfth of June, I believe.

"Christine Johns and Johann Richter arrived from London, separately, a day or two later. There were, as my husband has said, rumors that Mr. Churchill might come up as well. He was an old acquaintance of Lord Neville's. Several other family friends had been invited. Including Anders Hardy, but he was not expected to make it. Anders never could be depended upon for social engagements. His government job was all very hush-hush, which was often rather convenient for him."

"What happened on the night of the murder, Mrs. Johns?"

"The evening Christine and Richter arrived, after dinner, we, the three of us, took a stroll. To be honest, I had felt rather bored until Christine arrived. Clay was quite sick in bed with a virus of some sort, and I felt restless I suppose.

"It was a gorgeous night. The moon was out; the air was fresh, almost balmy, though Christine had a bit of a chill. We walked the back roads, through pastures and woodlots, talking up the latest London gossip. Discussing the war, of course. Mostly impersonal things. Christine and Richter were more friendly and easy with one another than I had ever seen them before. This disturbed me because I had never cared for him. He could be quite gracious, in his way, but I always thought it hid a cold streak.

"Henley-on-Thames was like another world that night. So peaceful and quiet. As if the war did not exist. We stopped by an inn with a pub, a tiny place out on one of the old post roads, and had a few drinks. Quite a few. We drank rum toddies and made toasts to ourselves, the holiday – the RAF, of course – whatever we could think of. Richter, I remember, was just as effusive about our successes against the Luftwaffe as Christine and I were. That did seem a bit odd to me, but then I was one who had never quite trusted him in the first place.

"By the time we left the pub, at close to midnight, we were all of us a jot tipsy. Christine most of all, I should say. Richter had one of us on each arm, and Christine, as I remember it, was resting her head on his shoulder and acting quite the little fool over him. As I said, I had never seen them like this with one another before. It's difficult to describe. They were always kind of nasty to one another, nasty and personal, but seemed rather to enjoy themselves at it. That night, though, there was something else. I really can't explain it. I thought perhaps they were having me on, acting so keen on one another.

"Directly upon our return to Croyden Castle, I excused myself and went up to my room. I left the two of them sharing a nightcap in the library. My room adjoined Clay's. We had agreed on separate sleeping arrangements while he was sick.

"I undressed and got into bed, but had difficulty falling asleep. I was worried about Christine. I was fond of my sister-in-law. She and I, by then, had become quite close.

"Finally I drifted off. I awoke with a start, however, a short while later. Something felt queer. There was a small private hallway, with two water closets off it, that connected my room with Christine's. When I couldn't stand it any longer, I got up, threw on a robe, entered this hallway and went to her door.

"At first I thought I heard voices, but then decided I was imagining things. The hallway was pitch black. I opened the door just a crack and looked in. Her room was dark, but there was moonlight from the windows. I couldn't actually see her, but I thought she must have gone to bed. She had been drinking, as I have said, quite heavily. I could smell alcohol in the room. I walked over and stood beside her bed a moment. Before I left, I just wanted to be sure she was all right. I reached out to touch her. The moment I did, I was grabbed by the wrist and violently jerked into the bed. By Johann Richter."

Anne Johns punctuated the melodramatic scene she had just painted with a defiant glance at her husband. Cohen wondered if she were exacting some sort of personal revenge with her testimony. If she were, Clay Johns appeared to be taking it all pretty passively, as did Johann Richter, in whose direction the witness had yet to look since taking the stand.

"I panicked," she said. "I had never been so completely startled and terrified in my life. He pulled me close. He stunk of alcohol. I had on nothing but a flimsy nightshirt, which he simply tore right off me." Her voice had dropped now to nearly a whisper. "At that moment, I believe I may have hated myself, my own helplessness, as much as I hated him."

Sir Anthony smiled at Richter. "You were raped then, Mrs. Johns, by Johann Richter, is that correct?"

"Objection," piped up Mr. Benevides. "The witness has neither said she was raped nor by whom. That is not up to the prosecution to conclude."

"I shall withdraw the question," Sir Anthony replied.

"For the record, defense objection is sustained," the judge said. "Strike the question from the record."

Anne Johns answered it anyway. "Yes, I was raped," she said, before anyone could stop her. Staring directly at the defendant for the first time, she looked more smug than angry.

"Strike that from the record," said the judge. "Mrs. Johns, please listen to me in future."

She gave the judge a look of disdain. Meanwhile Sir Anthony appeared to be waiting for something more from her. "I realize this is difficult for you," he prompted, "but could you be more specific about what happened?"

"Is this line of questioning entirely necessary?" the judge said.

"If you will, your Honor, this testimony leads directly to who killed, who murdered, Christine Johns."

"Proceed then. But to a purpose, please."

"Thank you, your Honor."

"I don't remember much about it," said Anne Johns – returning to her script, thought Cohen – "I was in some sort of shock, I suppose. When it was over, I got up, picked my nightshirt up from the floor, and left. I went back to my room and went right to sleep. Still in shock, I am certain. But when I awoke later in the night, it was different. Very different. It took me awhile to decide who I wanted to kill more. Johann Richter or myself. Unfortunately, by the time I finally decided on Richter, it was too late. He was gone."

"How was that Mrs. Johns? What happened?" Again, Sir Anthony had his eyes on Richter, as if on guard against a sudden attack by the alleged murderer.

"After I was awake again, it must have been three or four in the morning, I heard odd noises coming from Christine's room. I heard a voice; just barely, but I was reasonably certain it was Christine's. I don't know. . . I certainly did not want to go back in there, except perhaps with a gun to shoot Richter. But I had to do something, didn't I.

"In any case, I found myself standing back out in the hallway outside Christine's room, listening. I had a letter opener, I believe it was, in my hand, which I suppose was pretty ludicrous. There was light shining through the crack beneath the door. The noises had stopped. At first I could hear nothing but my own heartbeat, but after a minute or two I heard a low moaning sound, as if someone were having a nightmare, or was in pain. That gave me courage enough to open the door a crack and look inside."

"And?"

"I don't know exactly what happened after that. I screamed, I believe. Then I blacked out. I suppose I fainted."

Anne Johns looked down toward the courtroom floor. In convincing fashion, she appeared on the verge of tears, breathing from the diaphragm in short gulps.

"Go on please, Mrs. Johns. What had you seen in that room?" Sir Anthony's sense of urgency was undercut by what seemed a tone of genuine sympathy. Between the two of them, it was effective testimony, Cohen thought.

Anne Johns continued to stare at the floor. "I had seen Christine. Lying on her bed in a pool of blood."

"She was dead?"

"Yes. Or dying. Her throat had been slit, they told me later."

"She didn't say anything to you before she died, then?"

"No."

"And Johann Richter?"

"As I said, he was gone. Scotland Yard was put on the case. They never found him. He simply disappeared. I myself saw him again for the first time just last week. Right here."

Michael Cohen and John Weaver stared at each other. Weaver grinned and shook his head in amazement. One more wild story. Cohen realized he was starting to like this guy.

"Was there any further evidence of violence at the murder scene?" Sir Anthony asked.

"They found that she had been raped. There was semen–"

"Objection. Hearsay."

"Sustained. Strike that answer from the record."

Sir Anthony smiled, just slightly. He had made his point, Cohen thought. Even an experienced trial judge couldn't entirely erase this kind of subliminal information, improperly introduced or not.

"Thank you very much, Mrs. Johns. You have been most helpful," he said. "Your Honor, reserving the right to recall this witness, we have no further questions at this time." As Sir Anthony took his seat, he smiled at Richter again. The gesture could have been anything from a polite formality to a discreet display of gloating, from where Cohen sat.

Mr. Benevides stood and, in his deliberate manner, prepared to address the witness. The judge, however, abruptly intervened and told him to save his breath. Court would reconvene at ten o'clock tomorrow morning. He stepped down from the bench as if in a hurry. "Maybe it's a bladder problem," Weaver said.

Cohen turned down Weaver's invitation to dinner. He needed to be alone with his thoughts for a while. "Maybe tomorrow," he said, excusing himself and exiting the courtroom almost as quickly as the judge.

CHAPTER XIII

Michael Cohen wandered up into the hills above La Negra. He felt depressed. Whatever he had hoped to get out of being here seemed to be eluding him. Instead, a potential flood of forlorn memories, pushed along by the troubling revelations of Elena Stein, was lapping over the top of the dam he had long ago constructed to hold them in check.

It was cold. As he walked an ancient path curling up past a cemetery with the dead stacked in multistoried vaults above the ground, the simple act of breathing was difficult. His gimpy leg, at least, seemed to hurt less at this altitude.

The hill he was climbing was steep and grassy, without trees. Finally, near the top, he found a small clump of bushes where he could sit protected from the cold wind and still receive the sun's filtered late-afternoon warmth. A huge canopy of billowing gray clouds, anchored by a ring of sharp white mountain peaks, closed him into himself. He wished he had a bottle of bourbon with him, a taste for Kentucky mash being one American predilection he had allowed himself to acquire since moving to New York.

It occurred to him he had not written one word since he had arrived in La Negra. Brilliant. But then again what could he write about? He had no idea what was really going on down here. He wasn't even sure whose side he was on anymore. That was a quandary he had never expected to face.

Jack Ames, his editor at *World Horizons*, had made it all seem so simple. *"You're going to La Negra? You have an obsession with Nazis? Great. So go. But write about it for us. Be obsessive. Go nuts. Win us a Pulitzer."* Said Jack.

Cohen looked around at the spectacular peaks and valleys; the huge expanse of lake, forbidding now in the darkening afternoon light. It was no wonder the locals believed all creation had begun here. The incredible vista encouraged a perspective of universals, of abiding nature and human striving, the existence of higher forces. The landscape in parts of Palestine had affected him in similar fashion. But he had seen too much of universals at work in the world to look to them for redemption at this point. It hardly seemed to matter whether they were good or evil. Whether they were kindness, bravery and sacrifice – or greed, cruelty and indifference. In the end they always led, all of them it seemed, to the same death and destruction and meaninglessness.

If only his father had listened to the warnings. If only his father had been willing to start all over again. He would have been a poor man, but a free one. And he would still be alive, along with his family. Cohen's mother, a transplanted American, had never been comfortable in Germany and had begun to hate it after Adolf Hitler took power. She had pleaded with his father countless times to get them out. They'd had the resources to do it. We must protect the children, she had said – Michael, his younger sister Nicolette and baby brother Jeremiah. Let the Nazis have Germany. They could go to America and start over again.

But to his father that had sounded like cowardice. He was a German Jew, a hardworking man and a proud veteran of the World War who had met his future American wife when he'd been a prisoner of war in 1918. After a stint in a POW camp in Georgia, he had been assigned to work on her family's potato farm in Maine, helping with the harvest. Shortly after their marriage they'd moved to New York City, where Cohen's father found work in the textile industry. Less than a year after his first son's birth, his wife pregnant with a second child, he had returned alone to a defeated Germany and had begun a highly lucrative business career based in Ulm. It was a time of intense economic hardship for most, but he did not intend to apologize to anyone for his success, he said. Anti-Semitism was not confined to Germany. He had seen it in America too. Germany's would die down soon, he promised his wife and children when they had eventually joined him there.

But it only got worse. When things got really bad in '38, with *Kristallnacht* and an expansion of the Nuremberg racial laws that stripped Jews of their basic rights as citizens, his father had finally tried to get them out of the country. By then it was too late. In hopes of keeping her safe, Nicolette was sent to relatives in Dresden, an uncle whose wife was a Christian, shortly after the war began. That family, including Nicolette, disappeared two months later. *Nacht und Nebel.* Desperate now, Cohen's father attempted to smuggle the rest of the family out via Switzerland and Portugal, but they were stopped at the Swiss border and were lucky not to be arrested or shot on the spot.

Soon after that, as it became obvious their time was about to come, they went underground, paying a willing acquaintance, an Aryan, to let them hide in an old abandoned barn in the country. No kitchen, no bathroom. But also few neighbors and backed up against a large forest, so a good place to hide.

Cohen was in his early teens then, and with his brother Jeremiah still barely more than a baby, he was lonely for companionship. His parents allowed him to roam the forest out behind their new home. They warned him to stay in the woods and to let no one, absolutely no one, see him. He obeyed this rule for nearly two years, until one day he'd come upon a girl sitting by herself in a pasture beside the woods, her back against an apple tree, reading.

From the edge of the tree line, he studied her. She was blond and very pretty. Near his own age. He hesitated, but eventually, afraid she would leave, he stepped out of the woods and pretended to be walking by. As he neared her, she looked up from her book. She was even prettier than he had thought. "Hello," he said.

"Good afternoon," she returned.

"A beautiful day to be reading out of doors."

"Yes."

"What are you reading? If I may ask." He nearly blushed. He was unpracticed at making small talk with the opposite sex.

"Thomas Mann. *Buddenbrooks*," she said.

"That's a good book. Do you like it?"

"I don't know. I've only just begun reading it."

"Do you come here often?"

"Yes. Sometimes. I live near here. Our farm is just over there," she pointed. She acted a little shy, but didn't appear to be nervous. "And you? Where are you from?" she asked.

He was not prepared for this. He stammered out the name of his village near Ulm, then anxiously tried to determine whether he had compromised anything.

"That's a long way from here," she said.

"We have a house in the country," he said. It was not entirely a lie. They hadn't gone to their country house because too many people there knew who they were and what they were.

She looked puzzled. As if she knew of no such place in the vicinity. She stared at him, thinking.

Her eyes suddenly brightened. "You are a Jew, aren't you."

He fought down panic. The instinct to lie came and went. It was Yom Kippur. His empty stomach was a reminder. "Yes," he said proudly, "I am a Jew."

"I won't tell," she said, and he believed her. "My name is Gudrun. Come, sit down. Please."

As he sat, a large formation of American bombers glided by far overhead, barely visible in the summer haze. Heading northeast, probably to Berlin. He and Gudrun looked up, but said nothing.

They had spent the rest of the afternoon talking of many things. They agreed to meet there again the next day. When Cohen had returned to his parents, he knew he should tell them, but he did not. If the girl told on him, they could all be sent to the camps. But he trusted her. That night he prayed to God his trust was well placed.

Cohen shook his head and took a few deep breaths of cold air. He did not want to remember further. He felt depressed enough already. In lieu of thinking, he concentrated on his surroundings. The cemetery was growing darker, but the mountain peaks that hemmed in the horizon on all sides still sparkled like jagged diamonds. The row of high-rises down along the lake to his right stood out like the teeth of a giant saw.

His thoughts lingering in the past, he reflected on the number of compartments that past was split into. He wasn't that old in years, but his life, or his memory of it, was so broken into separate chambers that at times he felt like an old man.

Finally tugging himself back into the present, he reviewed the latest courtroom revelations about Johann Richter. The bottom line, he thought, was that not much had really been revealed yet.

He doubted much would be, either, unless they put Richter himself on the stand, something John Weaver was firmly convinced they would never do. In which case any clarity would likely have to wait until Richter was extradited and put on trial in Europe. And that would be a circus. Whatever came to light there would be drowned out by self-serving ideological fanfare from a dozen different directions – the "loyal" French, the French Resistance, closet supporters of Vichy, neo-Nazis, the Communists. Richter's guilt or innocence would become a minor skirmish on an expanded battlefield.

It seemed odd, but so far the most convincing picture he had of Richter was still the one that had been painted by Terry Harper. That portrait had been more sympathetic, closer to Elena Stein's, than the one being drawn each day in court down here. Which was hardly surprising since it drew primarily on Richter's own recollections and point of view. Nonetheless, it had more the ring of truth than anything Cohen had yet encountered in La Negra.

He was experiencing a growing sense of unease. He didn't like the feeling he was starting to get when he contemplated Richter and his likely fate. As a human being, the man remained largely an enigma, a hazy life that made no sense. Richter himself meant little to him. He was a symbol. A hated symbol. The uneasiness, he supposed, must come from the man's ties to Elena Stein. To bring Richter down, was to bring her down too.

He had been trying to stifle any thought of Elena Stein. It put him too close to his memories of Rachel. When he did think of her, it made him uncomfortable in the way it did when he occasionally daydreamed about Maria Zamora, Rachel's best friend. Maria had been a ray of hope in an otherwise bleak landscape, and had become a good friend during his time in Israel. He hadn't seen her since he had left there nearly four years ago, but she was still alive the last he knew. She triggered memories he would prefer to leave buried. Now Elena Stein was doing the same.

He shook his head to clear it.

Behind the clouds, the final rays of sun were nearly extinguished now. The lights of La Negra filled the earthen bowl below the cemetery. Cohen awoke from his reverie and looked around at this unfathomable new world. The wispy edges of a low cloud began to swirl around him, near enough to touch. In the misty cold, the ring of dimly outlined mountains glimmered more softly now. And in spite of his resolve he was swept by a sudden urge to talk to Elena Stein.

* * * *

Back at the Miranda, Cohen phoned the man in Riberalta Elena had said would take messages for her. He gave the man the Miranda's number, said he could be reached the next day at noon, and would be waiting for her call. The man's English was passable. Cohen hoped he understood.

For a while he tried to read, but felt too restless. He put on a jacket and left the hotel. Outside, he bumped into the young bellhop he had not seen since his arrival.

"Did you find my little present for you?" the boy said.

"I did. Thank you."

"Would you like some more?"

Cohen hesitated, then decided he did want some more. "Yes. I'll pay you this time."

"Gracias. Come with me, please."

As they walked through narrow streets and back alleyways, the boy made small talk and Cohen asked him his name.

"Cisco Rojas, Señor." He said it as if he were proud of it.

They stopped by a door in an adobe wall that had no windows. Cisco Rojas opened it and beckoned Cohen to enter.

A low hallway, barely lit, led to an open courtyard, also barely lit, where silhouetted figures flitted here and there in the dark.

"Wait here, Señor. I will be only a minute."

While he waited, Cohen took in his surroundings as best he could and concluded he was in a bordello of some sort. Or that sex for money was at least a part of what was going on around him. The building's nondescript exterior had given no hint of the bustling commerce inside its walls.

True to his word, Cisco Rojas returned with dispatch. He handed Cohen a small bag, presumably of coca leaves. He had already named a price. Cohen gave him that amount, plus a little more. "For the free sample," he said.

The boy smiled at his good fortune. "Gracias."

They returned outside and Cisco Rojas guided him back to where they had started.

"Thank you," Cohen said, and headed off to nowhere in particular, chewing on a coca leaf. As he walked, he realized his mind had slipped a gear, was spinning in neutral. It didn't worry him too much.

This was something it did periodically, something it had been prone to do ever since. . . since whenever.

He kept walking. He had learned it was the best antidote. His leg was a little numb, but it didn't hurt. He had the sensation once or twice that he was being followed, but chalked it up to the coca and the paranoia that seemed an almost normal part of La Negra after dark.

He wandered into what appeared to be a red light district. A more obvious one than Cisco Rojas' neighborhood. An advance team of small boys kept approaching him with offers. Partly to escape them, he ducked through swinging doors into a hole in the wall called the Prado Bar. It was a rickety tin-roofed affair that threatened to collapse in the next heavy wind. Inside, a couple of out of action ceiling fans hovered above a few broken down booths and a more respectable-looking teak-wood bar rimmed with wooden stools.

The only inhabitant of the place was the bartender, a short dark mestizo with gloomy eyes.

There was no bourbon, so Cohen ordered a beer. He drank deep and tried to relax.

He was on his second beer when he realized someone else had entered the bar and was standing at his shoulder. Cohen looked up. The man was of medium height, an American or European. Trim, good-looking. Dressed in an expensive suit and tie.

"You are Michael Cohen, I believe." The accent was Etonian British, the tone level and assured.

Cohen waited.

The man extended his hand. "Anders Hardy." Cohen shook the proffered offering, trying to match up his image of Anders Hardy with the man standing before him now.

"Could we?" With pronounced flair, as if perchance tea and crumpets awaited, Hardy motioned toward a dingy booth on the far side of the room. Once seated, he ordered tequila for both of them. Cohen ordered another beer for good measure.

"Cheers," Hardy said, raising his glass and downing half of it in one shot.

The two men sat in silence for a moment. Cohen's hatred of MI6 came flooding back. Along with the fear. These were the bastards in whose name he had betrayed Rachel and her dreams. How much did Hardy know about his past, he wondered. He found the man's stare unsettling. Hardy's cool gray eyes were intent, but not quite focused on anything, including on Cohen, who looked around and noticed the bartender had disappeared.

"This is rather a delicate matter, Mr. Cohen, but I'm afraid I must be blunt," Hardy opened. "You could be a valuable man for us down here, you know."

"How so?"

"Through your access to Richter. You are one of the few who possess it."

"I've never met the man."

"We have been watching you. We know where you've been. Who you've talked to."

Cohen felt a shiver run through him. It was an old nightmare. That MI6 would find him. Had they followed him out to Riberalta? Did they know about Elena Stein and her children?

"Who is 'we'?" he asked, assuming he knew the answer.

"We're a sort of 'private contractor' for MI6, you could say. Down here, though, we have our own agenda."

Cohen shuddered at the mere mention of his old employer. The "private contractor" part he hadn't expected.

Hardy grinned. "And yes, we do know about Israel. Your involvement with us there. Your defection to the Jews."

"I didn't 'defect' to anyone," Cohen retorted. "I just found out what you were up to, and left."

"It's all right," Hardy said, still with a smile. "I'm on your side, old boy. Our little organization doesn't always see eye to eye with the chaps in MI6, do we. We're not here to hunt you down. You're an *American*, after all."

This last had a facetious ring to it. Hardy said nothing more. His grin began to fade, but his eyes still reflected amusement.

"So why are you here?" Cohen finally rose to the bait.

"I can't give you the details, can I, old boy. I daresay you know how that goes. I can, however, tell you that we are quite willing to pay you a lot of money for a little help."

"Doing what?"

"Don't you want to know how much?"

"No. Doing what?"

"Passing on a little information. Bringing a little back."

"Why?"

Hardy paused, then recited what sounded to be a scripted piece: "Richter represents a bit of a problem for us. He is a loose end, shall we say. One of the many left lying about after the Second War. We almost had him in Argentina just after, but lost him. Quite obviously. This time, the Jews caught him and turned him over, amazingly enough. No offense Cohen, but I would've bet ten to one the Mossad or Shin Bet would've put the bloody bastard out of his misery, not turn him over. It would've been better for everybody. Now, we have to deal with him."

"What is this 'bit of a problem' you're talking about?"

Hardy inhaled audibly, as if offended by the lack of tact. *A show of poor breeding*, no doubt he was saying with the gesture, Cohen thought.

"Well, let's put it this way Cohen. We didn't exactly do much to encourage the Wehrmacht to revolt against Hitler. One could even say we discouraged it."

"You're talking about MI6."

"Some of us in MI6, yes. And we in fact used Johann Richter to that end."

"Why?"

"That's a fair question. Unfortunately I am not at liberty to answer, am I. It's a bit dodgy. Let's just say we were following orders."

"That's what the Germans said." Cohen was feeling an instinctive aversion to this man.

"Quite so." Hardy grinned insipidly. "But our orders didn't come from Hitler, and they didn't come from MI6. We like to feel our motives were of a slightly higher order. On a higher moral plane, if you will. Unfortunately, keeping Hitler alive prolonged the war and cost a lot more lives. And not just Jews."

"Whose orders?"

"Beg pardon?"

"Whose orders *were* you following?"

"Sorry. Can't tell you that. Let's just say it's a name you would recognize. And that might surprise you."

"So Richter is a danger to you. Is that what you're saying?"

"A potential embarrassment, shall we say. He knows a few other secrets as well."

Cohen thought to ask if Richter knew about Communist moles in MI6, but some instinct held him back. It occurred to him all the rest of this could be a diversion. "Why are you trying to extradite him then?" he said.

"It isn't as simple as that, is it. In our business, it seldom is. We are not trying to extradite him." The man held Cohen again with his alert but oddly unfocused eyes. "So, Cohen. I am authorized to offer you 10,000 pounds sterling. That's $25,000 in American dollars. A good deal more than you'll make from *World Horizons*, I daresay."

Hardy's delivery was so direct and matter-of-fact the message did not entirely register at first. "The money is not important," Cohen replied, once it sank in. That one more stranger knew who he was working for down here was a disturbing notion.

"A man of principle, eh. You've other motives then. Well, why not? Richter's guilty of enough crimes to justify that, I suppose." Hardy said this with just a hint of threat in his voice.

"Just what *is* he guilty of?" Cohen said. "I'm not really very clear on that."

The man finally focused on him with a cryptic stare. "I don't wonder, given how this so-called 'hearing' has gone so far. But for starters, he killed his lover, Christine Johns. We know that much beyond the proverbial shadow of a doubt."

"How do you know that?"

"My dear fellow, it's our business to know these things. His father, a German general, was among those plotting against Hitler. Richter had found out we had a plant – we had several, actually – with the group of plotters that would eventually perpetrate the 20 July attempt on Hitler's life. He was desperate to warn his father, but he knew we had infiltrated his contacts in England and he didn't want our plants in Germany to know he was on to them. His only alternative was to return to Germany himself."

Hardy shrugged. "He wanted to help his father. A natural desire, I suppose. He needed Christine's silence, because she's the one who had told him about our meddling in his father's plans. And Christine was never silent for long about anything. We knew that. He knew that."

"So you think he killed her to keep her quiet." Cohen remembered Hardy had been the woman's suitor too. *A bit of a blighter*, Clay Johns had called him on the witness stand. He wondered how much his version of events could be trusted.

"We know he killed her. From unimpeachable sources. He slit her throat."

Cohen blanched. The image brought back vivid memories. Of Dachau. Of his own father. Of what came after.

"Listen carefully to the rest of Anne Johns' testimony tomorrow," Hardy said. "That should give you some illumination on the subject."

Cohen's thoughts had lurched off track. He stared at the bar. The bartender had not returned.

"He also commanded an occupation garrison in France later on. You don't imagine, do you, that he made the going any easier for your people while he was there," Hardy said.

"Us Jews, you mean?" Cohen said, seeking traction back into the present.

"The Jews, and others." Hardy knew to tread carefully. "He murdered Christine. There is evidence he killed this Yvonne Duchamps. The man deserves whatever's coming to him."

"And what is that, exactly? What does he have coming to him?"

"I can't tell you that now, but you will know soon enough, I assure you. So what do you say, Cohen? If you like, we can send the 10,000 pounds to Israel. Should buy them a tank or two. MI6 won't appreciate it, but what the hell." Hardy eyed him intently. "Will you help us out?" Again, Cohen heard a hint of threat.

"I might," he said, surprising himself a bit with his answer. "I'll think about it." He did not trust Hardy. But anything that ran counter to MI6 had an appeal.

"Splendid! Absolutely splendid. You think it over. Time is getting short, but think it over. We need your help. No doubt you'll make the right decision." The steely gray eyes grew more intense. "And may I suggest, with all due respect, that you do."

"Make the right decision?"

"Bingo." The eyes spun back out of focus, as if controlled by dial. "We'll be in touch," he said.

With that, he slipped out of the booth and was gone before Cohen had barely blinked. The bartender, as if on cue, rematerialized out of nowhere, eyeing Cohen obliquely as he began returning freshly washed shot glasses to the shelves behind the bar.

"Do you know that man?" Cohen asked him, referring to the already departed Hardy.

"Señor?"

"Sabes esta hombre?"

"No, Señor. Lo siento." The bartender's voice was raspy, like a scratchy, overplayed record.

Cohen suddenly felt nervous. He downed the rest of his tequila and beat a hasty retreat, stepping outside into a heavy mist. He picked his pace up almost to a jog, blindly dodging the few late-nighters conducting business in the narrow alleyways. The air had grown even colder. Cohen heard one explosion, then another. It seemed much closer in tonight, and this time it sounded more like artillery than thunder. He took a deep breath but kept moving. After two or three seconds, a streak of lightning cracked the sky and he breathed a little easier.

He finally stopped in an unfamiliar doorway and leaned up against a wall to rest, his leg aching and his chest heaving in the cold, thin air. He felt disoriented, sweating and shivering at the same time. From the corner of his eye, he detected movement, a shadowy figure about two blocks down a deserted street. He could've sworn it was someone familiar to him. Not his previous shadow, but someone he knew. By the time he took a second look, the apparition was gone. Only his own breath, fogging up the chilled night air, stirred the silent darkness of La Negra.

CHAPTER XIV

Johann Richter lay on his prison cot, staring at the ceiling, at nothing. The day in court had sunk his depression deeper than ever. Now there not only seemed no escape from his predicament, now old wounds he had spent years trying to heal were being ripped open again.

Anne Johns' testimony would almost certainly be the more damaging, the way she was twisting things around with all her talk of "rape," but it was seeing Clay on the witness stand that had hit him hardest. He still thought of Clay as a friend. In some ways, the best friend he had ever had. Now that old friend was caught in the middle, with no way out that would not hurt Richter, and Richter could sense the pain of his dilemma.

Clay's story that he'd been tortured by thoughts something had happened between his wife and Richter – long before she could ever have accused him of rape – had been a revelation to Richter. But today's testimony had struck him in another way as well. Richter was already suspicious of Anne and what role she might have played the night Christine died. Now he wondered how much Clay knew about that night. And had Clay ever forgiven him for what happened to Christine? On the witness stand, he appeared still to be struggling with it. Richter suspected that Clay, however, like everyone else, hardly knew the real truth about either Anne or Christine.

The real truth. During the war nothing had seemed real, he thought. Everything had been relative. Relative to where you stood. . .

"A Red Twist"

Following his initial interview with Anders Hardy in 1940, Richter had spent the next few days being half briefed, half interrogated by a lineup of British military intelligence people, including one full colonel, an RAF officer. All of whom had known a surprising amount about his past.

After a week of this, he was outfitted in the uniform of an English army officer, without benefit of rank, and put to work interrogating captured German airmen in a small, bare, totally whitewashed room designed to isolate and disorient the POW, to make him more pliable. He refused any second-interrogator assistance in this task, a repugnant chore he would continue to perform, though less and less frequently, for the "Foreign Office" right up until his departure from England in June of 1943.

During that time, he was lucky enough to avoid the nightmare he often imagined of one day having to interrogate someone he knew. Doubtless this was in part because the British thought him a potential double agent and wished to maintain his credibility with the Abwehr. While downed airmen remained his specialty, he was on occasion put to use questioning German nationals suspected of undermining the Allied war effort in one way or another. In all his interrogations, he obtained as little and as useless information as he possibly could, while still trying to maintain a basic level of trust with the British.

Though his work was closely monitored, the British officials and intelligence analysts he worked with, most of whom were attached to the MI5 domestic intelligence branch, appeared to become reasonably comfortable around him as time went on. His social acceptability at any given moment, he noticed, appeared to fluctuate in inverse proportion to the current fortunes of the Third Reich.

Anne Johns moved into London and began to do volunteer nursing work. Shortly afterwards, Richter started receiving an almost constant stream of anxious letters from Clay, first from Malta, then later from Egypt. He was worried over whether his wife was remaining faithful to him. In several of his letters, Clay said he'd heard London had become a hotbed of random sex ever since the bombs had started dropping. The anxiety was perhaps exacerbated, Richter thought, by the fact that Clay himself had taken a navy nurse as his lover in Valletta, and that the woman had contrived to be transferred with him to Alexandria.

Clay wrote also that his in-laws, the Wheldons, seemed for some reason intent upon promoting closer ties between Anne and Christine. This development apparently upset him as well. Richter began to wonder just how much Clay knew of his wife's former, or perhaps not so former, extracurricular sex life.

In any case, in April of 1941, Clay Johns, who had been with the British rear guard at the Greek passes at Thermopylae, was listed as missing in action. When he heard the news, Richter felt sad and helpless. He did what little he could, got word to his father asking him to look into Clay's fate. He was in a funk for weeks trying to reconcile his role in the war with what had happened to his old friend. Anne Johns, on the other hand, seemed to accept the news with relative calm.

In the summer of 1941, the war itself took a dramatic turn. With the Balkans secured and with Rommel's tank battalions racing eastward across North Africa, Hitler unleashed his vaunted war machine on the Soviet Union in Operation Barbarossa, the most sweeping military offensive the world had ever seen. Within two months, his troops had laid siege to Leningrad and were driving toward Moscow, arriving virtually at the gates of the Kremlin by mid-November.

But as it had with Napoleon, nature intervened. As winter set in and caught an unprepared Wehrmacht without sufficient warm clothing or proper supplies, the Russians managed to stabilize the front near Moscow by the time the Japanese bombed Hawaii and brought the United States into the war.

Meanwhile, Karl Richter had determined that Clay Johns had survived the battle at Thermopylae and was now in a German prisoner of war camp near Dortmund. At the news, Lord Neville immediately began pulling whatever strings he could to arrange a prisoner exchange, and Richter pressured his father, as best he could with the erratic contact they now had, in hopes something could be done.

By 1942, developments on the war's scattered battlefields and in the diplomatic arena filled the British with hope of their own and reinvigorated their determination to take the war to the enemy. This drive showed itself in various ways at Richter's level of operations with the "Foreign Office." Early that year, long after Richter's first round of attempts to enlist British support for his father, newly minted Major Anders Hardy reopened the subject, asking, at times even pressing, him for more information on any Wehrmacht plans to oust Hitler. He said the British could help. In addition to logistical details, Hardy wanted names, which Richter steadfastly refused to give him without more evidence of interest from the top echelons of British command, as well as an okay from his father.

Richter was suspicious of this rather sudden awakening of interest from Hardy. His own inquiries into the matter, however, met a brick wall. His Abwehr contacts in England, who he could never be certain had not been compromised by British Intelligence, knew nothing about it, they said. And Neville Johns, the only Englishman he could talk to about it who might know something, was not saying anything either. Lord Neville would only theorize that perhaps with the Nazis finally staggering a bit, it might be more believable now that a coup d'état against Hitler could be mounted and succeed.

By early November of 1942 the tide had indeed begun to turn, though it was barely perceptible at the time. The British under General Bernard Law Montgomery began to drive Rommel's forces back at El Alamein, and combined British and American forces landed in French North Africa at Morocco and Algeria to

catch the Germans in a pincers movement. Hitler reacted by occupying the remainder of France he had left under Vichy control
in 1940.

In southern Russia, where the Wehrmacht had pushed all the
way to the Volga River, the German Sixth Army under Field Marshal Friedrich von Paulus, after months of street-to-street fighting
in frozen Stalingrad, surrendered its surviving 91,000 men. Included were 24 generals and von Paulus himself. Hitler, who had
ordered von Paulus and his army to fight to the death, was furious.

Later that same month, February 1943, Richter's regular
Abwehr contact passed along a message that he was to return to
Germany as soon as possible. He was ordered to report back to
his command headquarters in Berlin immediately upon his return. As far as he could ascertain, this order had not been sent by
his father. His contact with Karl Richter by this time was infre-
quent. For security reasons, any such contact had to be initiated
by the General. The order to return appeared to be straightforward regular-channel military orders. Perhaps he was being reassigned on the continent. Maybe it was something as simple as
that. In the end, however, he ignored the order. He knew it was a
risk, but his father, he decided, might still need him in London.

By the spring of 1943, Rommel's back was to the wall in Tunisia, the British and Americans were poised to win the battle for
North Africa, and the Allies, led by Roosevelt and Stalin, were
now calling for the "unconditional surrender" of the Axis nations.
The Allies could have had peace, and Hitler's head as well, it
seemed to Richter. But it was evident they preferred to obliterate
Germany.

As the battlefront news continued to worsen for the Wehrmacht, Richter began to change his mind about returning. The
end was not yet in sight, perhaps, but it was clearly on the way.
With Germany headed toward defeat and his father's position
growing ever more dangerous, he began to feel the pull of his
homeland again. He knew he had to go back.

First, however, he needed to do a few things.

Not knowing where else to turn, he turned to Christine. Swallowing his pride, he asked her to use her ties with Hardy to find out what he needed to know.

"How badly do you need this information?" Christine said, lying beside him in her bed one cold rainy spring day. "Shall I sleep with him? Is that what you want, darling?"

She was bantering with him, but with an edge that made him uneasy. He didn't want to know about her past with Anders Hardy. Or her present. He harbored suspicions that even now he was not Christine's only lover. Since it was too dangerous to meet at his flat, she controlled the timing of their rendezvous. Something in the way she handled it had always made him acutely aware that he was only a part, perhaps even a minor part, of her schedule. He had no clue about her other engagements, and he preferred not to investigate. But he knew Christine. Another man in her life would hardly have been a surprise.

Hardy had continued to pump him at every opportunity for information about the Wehrmacht's internal opposition to Hitler. He said if he knew more, he could pull the strings to win backing from Churchill and his ministers. When Richter had passed this information along, Karl Richter had authorized him to give Hardy a few names, real names, as a show of good faith. Richter, however, still didn't trust the man.

He needed to know what Hardy was up to. It was important. It could be crucial to his father, and to his father's increasingly perilous position with Hitler, as well as to the success of any future move against the Fuhrer.

"Do what you have to do," he told Christine, unable to reflect her wit in his reply. "I'm so flattered," she returned, her good humor deflated. "Flattered indeed."

She had nonetheless done as he asked. And what she brought back to Richter had confirmed his worst fears and dashed any ambivalence he might've had about returning to Germany.

MI6 and the Special Operations Executive branch, Hardy had told her, were on a roll. They had succeeded in dropping the three Czech loyalists into Prague to assassinate Reinhard Heydrich, who as head of the SD and overseer of the Gestapo was second in command only to Himmler in the SS.

Six days later, in random retaliation, the SS razed the village of Lidice, near Prague, to the ground. Its male inhabitants were shot, the women sent to concentration camps, and its children dispersed to foster homes. Thousands of Czechs were sent to the KZ at Mauthausen. This outcome could not have suited the British better, Hardy had bragged. The objective of alienating the Czechs and the Nazis forever had been fully achieved.

Now Hardy, Christine said, was playing point man for an MI6 initiative to infiltrate the clique of Wehrmacht officers who were plotting against Hitler. It sounded as if they were getting inside information on the plotters already, she said.

But the real news was that the British objective was not to kill Hitler. It was to protect him. This chilled Richter to the bone.

"Don't you want to know how I pried that out of Anders?" she teased him.

"No."

"You would be proud of me."

"I don't want to know. But thanks. You did a good job." He felt slightly sick.

"Lovely. You're ever so welcome, I'm sure."

"Why, though? Why would they want to protect Hitler?"

"Your attempt to recruit us Brits for your little plot to kill him was doomed from the start, my Sweet," Christine said. "At least with the intelligence boys. I'm afraid some of their key people, including our dear friend Anders, are Communists."

"Communists?"

"Well, he didn't come right out and say it, did he. Not exactly a career-enhancing move. But that's what it added up to. The bad boy was sounding quite the idealist the other night. Apparently he was first infected at Oxford. It was going around there, you know, during the '30s. Not so much as at Cambridge, but at Christchurch, in particular, it was in vogue. And then of course he spent time at Cambridge as well, where I'm sure his leanings were duly noted by fellow travelers. Years ago, I know he socialized with Kim Philby, one of that crowd.

"In any case, now he dreams of a socialist Europe once Hitler is gone. Not of deals with the German General Staff to put things back as they were. Stalin – Stalin the former seminary student –

is his god. And in spite of that 'no separate peace' agreement among the Allies last year, Stalin's great fear is that the U.S. and Britain will cut their own deal with Germany, particularly if Hitler is put out of the way."

"That's pretty bloody unlikely though, isn't it, from what I've seen."

"No matter. It's all in how you look at it, and Stalin evidently sees it that way."

Richter was stunned by Christine's revelations. At first he wondered if she might be lying. But instinct told him no, she was not, and her suppositions, if true, would answer a lot of questions about Hardy's past behavior. How much of this did Lord Neville know, he wondered.

"What does Stalin really want, do you suppose?" he said.

"He wants to grab as much of Europe as he can. To level Germany, and salt the earth it stood on. Rodger it up the bum, like Rome did to Carthage. He wants it destroyed, not resurrected as a potential ally for the West. He also wants the Nazis' secret 'wonder weapons,' and is targeting the capture of Berlin, in particular, for some kind of new bomb they're developing. And what Stalin wants, Anders Hardy will try to get for him. Rest assured. For now, he says, a live Hitler is their best bet to achieve what they're after."

Christine screwed up an ironic little smile. "It's amazing what a man will say, sometimes, when you press the right buttons."

"Spare me."

She looked at him as if to say, Well what did you expect? "He told me an odd little tidbit about Stalin, by the way. The big bad Communist apparently lives in mortal fear of being assassinated. By anyone and everyone. Anders says he employs 'doubles' to throw his would-be killers off the track."

"That's not surprising," Richter said. "I've heard the same of Churchill. It's not paranoia. It's a legitimate fear."

They stared at one another, each looking for a sign of recognition that might reaffirm their old relationship. Richter, for his part, was not ready to give up such hope, however forlorn.

"So what now?" Christine asked.

"I've got to get back into Germany, and I'm going to need your help." His return was doubly important now. He had to let his father know what the British were up to, and he needed to do it in person.

"I'll miss you." Christine sounded almost as if she meant it. She didn't look particularly surprised at his decision. She had probably known it was coming, he thought.

"You'll survive," he said, feeling a pang of remorse as he said it. But he also felt reasonably certain by now that she was seeing someone else. Someone other than Anders Hardy. Who it was, he had no idea. Had he known then, he often thought when he looked back on it, the anger that exploded later might have been dissipated in advance, and things might've happened differently. Very differently.

In the ensuing weeks, Christine dutifully helped him lay the groundwork for escaping England. She was the only one he could trust. Her contacts were better than his outside London. He could only hope they were trustworthy. With her help, he began to put together a convincing second identity, to gather travel papers, to figure out how to lose himself for forty-eight hours in a way that would not put British Intelligence or Scotland Yard immediately on his trail. When the time came, Christine promised she would help cover for him. She was, he had to admit, proving to be an invaluable ally.

Because of her importance to his plans, however, there would be a delay. It began on a beautiful morning toward the end of spring, 1943. Years later, lying on the hard cot of his cell in La Negra, thinking back, he would still have a crystal clear picture of Christine as she had been that morning. They were in the second-floor bedroom of her subleased Belgravia townhouse, not far from his own more modest flat in Chelsea, which they continued to avoid as too dangerous. They had made love barely awake. Reluctantly, he had pulled himself out of bed, showered, shaved and dressed. As he was about to leave, he paused by the bed. Christine was lying naked on her stomach, the bright sunlight reflecting off her blond hair and emphasizing the whiteness of her back and buttocks. London was noisily rebuilding itself outside the bedroom's large bay windows.

He sat on the bed and rolled her over onto her back. Her hair fell to the side, exposing her breasts. She was all softness and sleep smiling up at him, not even opening her eyes. Two familiar impulses assailed him as he looked down on her, two impulses that somehow connected. A desire to absorb her beauty and a desire to reject it. The feeling was so overwhelming he dared not even touch her.

While he was staring at her she opened her eyes, expressionless. Her faraway look unsettled him a moment. But then she closed her eyes again, smiled and said good-bye. He lifted the sheets up to her waist, ventured to brush the hair back from her face, and left. As he stepped out into the busy streets of London that morning, the day had already begun to lose its glory for him even before the sun slipped into hiding behind a gray cloud.

His day at work was like any of the hundreds of others he turned in in London during the first few years of the war. No interrogations were scheduled that day, and he spent most of it doing paperwork and exchanging bits of war news with office staff. He drank the weak war brew that passed for coffee, and listened to the BBC announce the expulsion of the Wehrmacht from several Russian villages and expound on the pounding the Ruhr Valley was taking from American day bombers and British night bombers. Huge firestorms were reportedly raging through Essen and Dortmund in the aftermath of the previous night's air raids.

Richter thought of Clay Johns, still a captive somewhere inside Germany despite their best efforts to win his release. Karl Richter's last communique on the subject had been encouraging, however. The Abwehr had identified an important agent captured by the British they might be willing to exchange Clay Johns for, he said. Johann, hoping soon to make his own escape, had replied that time was of the essence.

The constant bombing raids, the firestorms and incredible destruction in Germany also made him think about his father, and his mother and sisters. He tried to picture them as safe, somehow. Conflicting emotions ate away at him, as they did every day now. He wasn't sad to see the Nazis going down to defeat, but to be sitting idly by while Germany was being destroyed, its people decimated, was becoming each day more difficult for him. At times he would think of the American Civil War, which he had studied at Heidelberg, and see a parallel between himself and the Southerners who'd chosen to fight for the North against all personal and emotional reason. They must, he thought, have felt much the same as he did now.

He left the office early that afternoon. He wanted time to take in the fresh air on his walk home and to bathe, dress and have a drink before he met Christine for dinner at seven. Her birthday was approaching, and they had been saving up food-ration coupons so they could have a private celebration that night before she went home to Croyden Castle for a larger and more formal one the next day.

In spite of the unsettling emotions she still at times provoked in him, Richter had felt, ever since Christine had coaxed Anders Hardy into spilling some of his secrets, that their relationship, hers and Richter's, had enjoyed a renaissance. It might last only a brief Indian Summer, he knew, but Richter had actually begun to entertain the idea, however undefined, that they might yet have a future together awaiting them up ahead somewhere. After the war perhaps. It made a nice daydream, at any rate, as he walked home that afternoon.

The sky was still overcast, but the air was pleasantly warm. The walk to his flat took him past Christine's. As he neared her building, he realized something was out of order. A small crowd was gathered in front of her address. People were milling about a perimeter cordoned off by police vans and an ambulance.

Richter was put instantly on guard. There had been no air raid, so it had to be something else. It could be the older gent who lived in an adjoining flat. He was a quiet fellow, always tending his garden, but you never knew. Instinct told him that should it be Christine, should she be involved in anything – in what, he had no idea – then he, Richter, might be as well.

He circled around behind a row of bushes that lined a park across the street and stood where he could watch the entrance to her building as unobtrusively as possible. In short order, two women in white hospital uniforms emerged carrying a loaded stretcher and placed it in the rear of the ambulance.

From where he was observing, Richter could not identify the figure on the stretcher. A few seconds later, however, two bobbies and several other men emerged from the building with a woman who appeared to be badly shaken up. It was Anne Johns. The moment Richter saw her, he knew who had been on the stretcher.

As soon as he had retrieved his wits sufficiently, he sought out a phone box on the other side of the park and dialed Christine's number. A light rain had begun to fall. After an inordinate number of rings, someone finally picked up on the other end. There was another long pause before a man finally said, "Yes?" Richter asked him for Christine Johns. The man asked his name. Richter hung up the phone and rang up Lord Neville at Croyden Castle. He got Christine's mother, a very distraught Eleanor Johns answering her own phone, instead. She'd just heard about what happened herself and was on her way out of the house to come into London. She told him, in a surprisingly firm voice, that Christine had apparently slit her wrists with a kitchen knife, and that Anne Johns had found her already half dead. Lady Eleanor asked that he keep this information to himself.

On the one hand, Richter was relieved that he himself was not in some sort of hot water, that his escape to Germany hadn't been put in jeopardy, perhaps just delayed. On the other, he experienced a gut reaction to the idea that Christine had tried to kill herself, a reaction that made him so weak in the knees he had to make a conscious effort to maintain his footing. Lady Eleanor said Christine could still die. He asked her which hospital they had taken her to, returned the phone to its cradle and escaped the closeness of the tiny booth before it made him sick. The rain was a welcome balm. The strength of his reaction, once he'd begun to recover and could reflect on it, had somewhat surprised him.

It was two days before he was allowed to see Christine in the hospital. When he asked her why she had done it, she told him he could never possibly understand and said she wanted him to forget it ever happened. This response played on his suspicions. He didn't question her on why she'd been at home that day, when she had told him she would not be, but he asked her point-blank if Hardy or MI6 had been involved in what happened. She looked away and said no.

Despite her wishes, he brought the subject up several more times during the next few weeks, but always with the same negative results from Christine. Finally he gave up and dropped the matter, though not from his thoughts.

After a while Christine appeared to regain her old spirits, which were boosted by the news, delivered by Richter, that her brother Clay might soon be released from his POW camp. When she started complaining about the boiled cabbage and Brussels sprouts that had become staples of the Londoner's diet since the start of the war, Richter decided she must be getting better. After her release from hospital, he worried a bit that she was drinking more than she had before, but that was perhaps to be expected, he thought. That they were no longer meeting to have sex did not surprise him much either. He didn't make an issue of it. He was too preoccupied with his plans to escape.

* * * *

Richter's eyes remained glued to the crumbling stucco of the ceiling above his cot. Here in this prison in this obscure tucked-away corner of the world, he saw things from a different perspective. The old jealousy was gone. But even with Elena filling the void, there remained a feeling of attachment to Christine. The only important question that remained for him was who had killed her. Anders Hardy? Someone else in MI6? He had long suspected Hardy had tried to kill Christine that first time, at her London town house, and failed. Or perhaps had tried to warn her off by half killing her. Over the years, only one thing had become clear to him. She had not, he was convinced, tried to kill herself.

Christine had never told him whether she had informed her father of what she'd learned from Hardy about the Soviets' penetration of MI6, and he hadn't pushed the point after her brush with death. At times he had been tempted to tell Lord Neville himself, but there were too many risks. He would've had to acknowledge Christine's role. And for all he knew, Lord Neville knew all about it. Or could even have been involved, though he doubted it. If Hardy had indeed discovered the leak, he would have been capable of just about anything, either in revenge or to eliminate the danger. Or both.

Richter's dislike of Hardy, which had grown over the years with his suspicions about Christine's fate and about Hardy's indirect role in his father's death, was now crystallizing into true hatred as he worried about his family. It was not an emotion Richter liked to have; it was like a sickness in need of exorcism. But he felt a certain desperation about Elena and the children, and about his lack of ability to protect them, and the focus of his fears was Hardy.

If MI6, and particularly Hardy, were here in La Negra, how long would it be before they discovered the farm, and what would they do then?

Hardy's motivations might be an important clue. Seeing and listening to Marie and Clay, and Anne Johns, in court the past several days, and being forced to confront it all again on penalty of separation from his family and possible death, he had started putting some pieces of the puzzle together. A key piece, he now believed, was that Anders Hardy and his confederates were still protecting someone inside British Intelligence. A mole for the Soviets. Perhaps several. Well-placed double agents would be even more important now than during the war. Guy Burgess and Donald Maclean had not acted alone. When they fled to Moscow, they had almost certainly left someone behind. Hardy and his cohorts didn't want that someone discovered.

Their interest in him, he thought, must mean they suspected he knew who it was. Did he? After Christine had told him, during the war, about Soviet moles inside MI6, he'd kept his eyes and ears open but had not come up with much. Since then, he had learned little more. Kim Philby remained his only suspect. He had crossed paths with Philby several times during the war, and knew he was close to Hardy.

But Philby was also a friend of Clay's, and the archetype of the upper-class Englishman. Not NKVD material; as unlikely a Soviet mole as you could imagine, at least on the surface. Like Hardy, however, he had been an admirer of the Soviets, at least in the '30s. And Richter recalled a tidbit Christine had once told him about Hardy: that in his university days, he had been contacted by a Soviet agent scouting potential recruits. The agent had told him he would first have to distance himself from socialist groups, and from his leftist reputation on campus, if he were ever going to be of any use to the cause.

It was a difficult puzzle to put together without more information, a weary Richter thought. And even if he did manage to figure it out, the next big question would be, what could he do about it?

Night was closing in, and he was beset with a feeling of emptiness he had come to dread during his months in El Morro. The fears for his family heightened his sense of loneliness. He'd heard nothing from

Elena since the message delivered by the young man, Michael Cohen, who he still worried might be linked to British Intelligence. He had asked Father Hidalgo to ask around about this Cohen.

He stroked his scar, thinking. The chipped spot on the ceiling he had stared at for at least an hour seemed to have grown larger during that time. Perhaps, he thought, if he concentrated long enough and hard enough, a hole would eventually open up there and he could simply climb right through it.

In the descending darkness, it almost seemed possible. He would not give up. Not while he could still draw breath. Meanwhile, he had to do something about his family. Maybe it was time to bring them into La Negra.

After mulling it over for a while, he asked Frederico to send for Father Hidalgo.

CHAPTER XV

"Why did you not scream or cry out when you were being 'attacked,' as you say, by Mr. Richter?"

Mr. Benevides was addressing Anne Johns. It was early morning on Tuesday, and she was back on the witness stand.

"Objection! May I come up to the Bench your Honor?" Raoul Zamora took the lead this time for the prosecution. He was already halfway to the Bench by the time the judge gave his assent. Mr. Benevides promptly joined their huddle.

One explosion had already ripped through court this morning, leaving Zamora's confidence visibly shaken and his table-company considerably diminished. The Israelis and the French had pulled out. The Israelis had not even shown up. It was rumored they'd been unsuccessful in their efforts to link Johann Richter to Gerhardt Gruning or to any of the atrocities of the German occupation of St. Sentione.

The chief lawyer for the French delegation, in dropping his country's case against Richter, had told the court there was simply not enough evidence against him to justify his trial in France for the murder of Yvonne Duchamps. Or anyone else. Period.

He and his assistant had then walked out of the courtroom, leaving the British, once again, to carry on alone. Richter himself, Cohen noted, had not seemed particularly moved one way or the other by these apparently favorable developments for his defense. But the whole thing left Cohen a little shaken. He knew the Israelis, and how tenacious they were. If they couldn't make a case against Richter, or chose not to, then perhaps there was not one to be made.

On the other hand, Cohen, reflecting on his encounter with Anders Hardy, wondered whether British Intelligence might have had a hand in today's courtroom surprises. If they had that kind of power, though, why couldn't they have blunted their own country's case against Richter? They should've had all manner of strings to pull if their motives for keeping him out of a European courtroom were political.

He missed having John Weaver beside him to bat such questions around. Weaver had not shown up yet today.

As if to make up for the loss of the Israelis and French, the number of armed militiamen in the courtroom was perhaps double what it had been the day before. Growing too, Cohen noticed, were the number of media types watching over the proceedings. Determined to get some kind of start on his assignment for *World Horizons*, he was taking notes today when he wasn't scribbling little sketches he couldn't resist.

The huddle finally ended.

"The question stands," the judge declared, as Zamora, retaking his seat, displayed a sour face.

Mr. Benevides moved with his usual deliberateness as he approached the witness stand again. "Now then, Mrs. Johns," he said in his high, mild voice which held, Cohen thought, an exaggerated gentleness, "you will please forgive me if I continue with the prosecution's fascination in this unpleasantness just a bit longer. I assure you that I will be as brief as possible."

The diminutive defense counsel had stationed himself halfway between the witness stand and the courtroom audience, and when he spoke he seemed to address the entire room at the same time. It crossed Cohen's mind again as he watched that he should perhaps not underestimate Richter's pint-sized defender.

"Allow me to repeat the question," he said. "Why did you not scream or cry out, when you were being 'attacked,' as you say, by Mr. Richter?"

Though she'd had several extra minutes to think about the question, Anne Johns still paused before she delivered an answer. "Right after he first grabbed me," she said, "I did scream. Once. He threatened me, he warned me to keep quiet, but that wasn't the most important thing; I made myself stop as soon as I realized what was happening. I was not going to have my husband's entire household, and my own parents – and Winston Churchill, for all I knew at that point – find me naked in bed with this man, was I. Not under any circumstances. I think perhaps I was more fearful of discovery than he was."

"Forgive the indelicacy, please," Mr. Benevides said, "but were you ever examined after this alleged incident, medically?"

"What do you mean?"

"You say you were raped. Were you ever examined for semen?"

If the question bothered her, Anne Johns hid it well. "No, I was not," she answered.

"Why not?"

"I told you. I didn't want anyone to know."

"So there really is no evidence, other than your word, that you were raped?"

"I suppose not."

"And after this alleged rape, you returned to your room and promptly fell asleep. Isn't that what you testified?"

"Yes."

"Wasn't that room just a short hallway away from Christine's?"

"It was."

"How could you sleep with your 'rapist' practically next door?"

"I was in shock, I imagine. I believe I said that."

"But Mrs. Johns," Richter's lawyer said, "what was Mr. Richter doing in that room, in Christine Johns' room, in the first place? And where was Christine Johns?" Here, it seemed to Cohen, was another question the witness did not appear eager to answer. She took a long breath before she said, simply, "I don't know."

"Don't you? Your husband has testified he saw them out by the pool that night, on what appeared to him to be rather intimate terms."

Anne Johns looked away from the defense counsel. "I suppose he was there for Christine," she conceded. "He said she was in the bed across the room. I never had the chance to look and see if she really was."

"Then, in your statement to police back then, you say you left the room, returned sometime later that night, and saw Christine Johns with blood all over her. And then you 'blacked out,' I believe you said."

"Something like that. It was a long time ago."

"And what happened to you, may I ask, after this little fainting spell?"

"When I finally came around, I was back in my own bed." Anne Johns, as she spoke, continued to focus out beyond her questioner. "Lord Neville, Christine's father, was attending me. He told me Christine was dead."

"Anything else?"

"He asked me if I knew where Johann Richter was. Which I did not, of course."

"Did you tell him what had happened to you earlier that night?"

"No."

"Why not?"

She fastened a dagger stare on Benevides. "If you were a woman, sir, you would know. Barring that, I cannot hope to make you understand."

Mr. Benevides appeared about to challenge this, but changed direction instead.

"Was Neville Johns' word, then, all the evidence you had that Christine Johns was dead? Had been killed?"

Anne Johns gave the lawyer a look of total amazement. "What are you trying to say? Are you implying she wasn't killed? I saw her, there on the bed. I saw the blood. I attended her funeral. Her obituary was in the *Times*."

"Yes, quite," Mr. Benevides said. "But how can you be so certain, as you indeed appear to be, Mrs. Johns, that Johann Richter had something to do with her death?"

"Isn't it rather obvious?"

"That is, of course, merely your own conclusion," Richter's lawyer noted. "Again, then, how can you be so certain?"

"He disappeared. He was never seen again by any of us after that night. The autopsy proved Christine had been raped shortly before her death. He did it. It's quite obvious. Who else could have?"

"The autopsy concluded Christine Johns had had intercourse shortly before her death, Mrs. Johns, not that she had been raped."

"She was raped," Anne Johns shot back. Her voice had turned to ice, her features freezing along with it. She turned cold eyes on Mr. Benevides, then shot an accusatory glance straight at Johann Richter.

"And how do you know that, Mrs. Johns?" The level of skepticism in the defense lawyer's tone made it apparent, for the first time really, that he was growing impatient with the witness.

"I know she was raped," Anne Johns said now in a lower, softer voice, "because Christine would not have done that with him willingly."

"What makes you think that?"

"She was a lesbian."

The courtroom crowd suddenly seemed a living organism. Necks craned, heads swiveled to catch the reactions of the husband and the defendant. Clay Johns looked a bit embarrassed, Cohen thought, Johann Richter somewhat troubled, but neither man seemed particularly startled.

At that moment it occurred to Cohen the room was packed almost entirely with men. As he scanned the sea of male faces, he noticed for the first time that morning the bearded man in his customary spot at the rear of the courtroom.

The judge gaveled for a return to order.

Mr. Benevides, wearing a distracted look – perhaps to hide his own surprise, Cohen thought – meandered over to the defense table and shuffled through some papers. Suddenly he turned and began striding back toward the witness stand with a purposeful air.

"Mrs. Johns," he challenged, "how do you know that Christine Johns was, as you say, a lesbian? Your own husband has testified, hasn't he, that you wrote to him during the war saying you thought she was developing a relationship with Johann Richter."

For a brief moment, Cohen thought he caught a flicker of what must have been the younger Anne Wheldon Johns. Her features, for whatever reason, softened, and her eyes became distant with an unfocused thought. Her face transformed itself from its narrow severity into an unguarded slackness. The look was gone before he could define it any better, the eyes quickly going cold again, the voice sounding tightly controlled, as she said, "I just knew. I'm a woman. I knew. I don't know how she involved herself with a man like Richter. I've always thought it likely that British Intelligence put her up to it. That they were using her to keep an eye on him. I don't know. But it would perhaps explain why he killed her. From his point of view, I suppose, it could have seemed that she had betrayed him."

"So now you're saying she had slept with Mr. Richter before."

"Perhaps. But not willingly. Or at least not of her own accord. They both liked to ride, and sometimes rode together at Croyden Castle. He tried to seduce her while they were on one of these rides, Christine once told me. I never quite understood whether she had succumbed."

"So that night she could have done it again?"

"I don't know. Possibly."

"Putting aside the question of British Intelligence for the moment, Mrs. Johns – we'll return to that later," Mr. Benevides said, "did you ever confront Christine Johns with your knowledge of her sexual orientation?"

"No, of course not."

"But you were close friends at the time, isn't that correct?"

"Yes, we had become quite close in the early war years."

Anne Johns was getting angry again, but so far was managing to hold it in check, Cohen thought.

"Did your sister-in-law, to your knowledge, have any heterosexual, ah, leanings at all?" the doughty little lawyer persisted.

Anne Johns stared down at her dull suede shoes. "No, I don't think so. I never saw any evidence of it. At least not during the years I knew her best."

"Though she got along rather well with Johann Richter the night she was killed, I believe you said."

"Yes, but that wasn't necessarily sexual, was it."

A look traversed Mr. Benevides' face that indicated his skepticism. "You shared a flat in London with Christine Johns for some months, did you not?" he said.

"Yes. For about two months early in the war."

"Did she ever make any sexual advances toward you?"

"Of course not!" the witness shot back.

"I see. Thank you, Mrs. Johns, for accepting this unpleasant line of questioning so pleasantly," Mr. Benevides nodded. "Now, in your earlier background testimony," he went on, "you seem to have left out the years 1941 and 1942. What was happening then? For instance, with Christine Johns?"

Anne Johns appeared relieved to leave the question of Christine's sexuality behind. "Those two years," she said, "with ups and downs of course, I think were Christine's happiest. She was doing work she enjoyed. I believe she actually enjoyed the war, for that matter, with all the excitement and uncertainty. The freedom too, I suppose. In a strange way, of course, it was all quite intoxicating, wasn't it."

The witness looked away for a moment, and added wistfully, "Perhaps it's just as well she didn't survive those years."

"And what exactly," asked Mr. Benevides, "was Mr. Richter's status at that time? What was he doing, aside from allegedly pursuing the favors of Christine Johns?"

"As far as I know," Anne Johns answered, "he was doing some sort of secret work, as I've said, for the government. For British Intelligence, I'd been led to believe. All quite mysterious. And he was beginning to develop rather a reputation as a man about town. To be a German in London, of course, was quite unusual in and of itself in those days, wasn't it. Particularly one who hobnobbed with the smart set, as he did."

She looked over at the defendant, sternly, as if to somehow emphasize her point, or perhaps to undercut what she said next: "He was considered quite handsome, reputed to have a way with women. His life seemed exotic – rather glamorous, I suppose. He was known by a lot of people, a lot of the 'right' people, as they say. It was generally thought that he was one of 'them' who had had enough foresight to see the light and become one of 'us,' you see, before it had become too late to do so with the proper motivation still intact. Personally, I'd always had my doubts about that. Even before June of 1943."

"And personally, Mrs. Johns, have you yourself ever had any connections with British Intelligence?"

The witness paused for a split second before answering. "No. Of course not."

"You appear somewhat hesitant, Mrs. Johns. Did you have any connection at all? Official or otherwise?"

"I, um. . . I guess I can answer that, now that the war is long over. Very unofficially, I kept tabs on Richter for an old friend. A friend who happened to be in British Intelligence, yes."

"Did you keep tabs on anyone else?"

"I beg your pardon?"

"Did you also keep this friend of yours up to speed on what Christine Johns was doing?"

The question brought a studied reaction to Anne Johns' face. If she had been any less haughty, Cohen thought, she might even have been embarrassed. "Yes, I suppose so," she conceded. "Even more informally, though. I just mucked about a bit. He had more of a personal interest in Christine, really."

"And who was this friend?"

"Anders Hardy. A major at the time, I believe."

"How long had you known this man? This Major Hardy."

"Most of my life. Since I was a young girl."

"What kind of man was he?"

"I don't know. What do you mean by that?"

"Was he trustworthy? A patriot? An idealist? What was he like?"

"He came from a very good family."

"That's not exactly what I meant. What was he like? What did he believe in?"

"He was inquisitive. Liked to know everything. Very political. But he could keep secrets. He was a perfect man for MI6."

Cohen nodded in silent agreement.

"What were his politics, Mrs. Johns?"

"Objection, your Honor." Raoul Zamora was on his feet. "It is irrelevant, these questions."

"Your Honor, the politics of Anders Hardy is relevant," Mr. Benevides said. "We will show it bears on why he persecuted the defendant."

"Proceed. The witness may answer the question."

"Anders Hardy's politics, Mrs. Johns?"

"He abhorred the Nazis and their Fascism. He felt very strongly about it. It wasn't showy with him. But then that was his style, wasn't it."

"What form of government did he prefer, then?"

"What do you mean?"

"Did he prefer anarchy, democracy, what?"

"Well, democracy I presume."

"What were his thoughts on the Soviet Union?"

"He was an admirer of Stalin, if that's your point. When the economy was in the toilet in the '30s, lots of people were."

"Wasn't he perhaps even a little more than that, Mrs. Johns? Wasn't Anders Hardy a card-carrying Communist, as far back as the start of the war?"

"I wouldn't know about that. If he was, he would never have told me, would he. I was certainly not a Communist."

"Did he associate with Communists while he was at university, Mrs. Johns?"

Anne Johns looked perturbed. "I only know he was idealistic," she said in a condescending tone. "He was a little older than I. I didn't see much of him during his Oxford days, if you must know. When he came up to Cambridge for a short term of post-graduate work, we saw each other a bit. During that time, he seemed actually to have cut most of his ties to the left-wing crowd."

"Did that crowd include Guy Burgess and Donald Maclean?" Mr. Benevides said, invoking the names of the two former members of the British Foreign Office who had defected to the Soviet Union the year before.

The witness did not respond. "Come now, Mrs. Johns. Surely you know who Burgess and Maclean are. That they were Soviet spies in the Foreign Office."

"Of course I do."

"Well then, did Anders Hardy know them at Cambridge?"

"He might have. I don't know. Perhaps they were gone by then."

"And Christine Johns, did she know Hardy was a Communist?"

"I've no idea."

"An excellent motive for him to kill her if she did, don't you think?"

"Objection! Is drawing a conclusion," Zamora shouted out.

"Withdrawn," Mr. Benevides readily acquiesced.

Richter's lawyer had made his point, Cohen thought. Everything these days seemed to boil down to the East-West equation, the battle between Communism and the democracies with its attendant fear of nuclear Armageddon. And here it was again, muddying the waters of what had once seemed the relatively simple trial of a Nazi war criminal. Or rather, "extradition hearing," he corrected himself. But more and more, he realized, this was taking on the feel of a full-blown trial.

The defense counsel suddenly switched gears: "Hadn't this Anders Hardy had an affair with Christine Johns? A rather long-term affair?"

Anne Johns for the first time looked out toward her husband, who offered her, Cohen noticed, little sign of support. "I wouldn't know about that," she said.

"Why not? You were close to her, weren't you? I believe that's what you said."

"I was, yes. In some ways. In other ways she was a very private person."

Cohen gave her credit, if she were lying, for being an excellent actress.

"Anders was at one time Christine's supposed 'beau,' when she was quite young," the witness continued. "If she did have an affair with him, it would have been an adolescent fling. Nothing more."

"Why is that, Mrs. Johns?"

"As I've told you, men were not her primary interest. Not as an adult, anyway."

"Where is Anders Hardy today?" Mr. Benevides asked.

"I have no idea."

"Is he still with British Intelligence?"

"I haven't the foggiest notion. I haven't seen him in years."

"And where was he the night Christine Johns was murdered?"

The witness did more than pause this time. She closed her eyes and did not answer.

"Mrs. Johns?"

She opened her eyes.

"Where was Anders Hardy the night Christine Johns was murdered?"

"I can't say for sure."

"Why not?"

"I never actually saw him that night."

"Were you supposed to?"

"Well, no, but. . ."

"But what?"

"He was to be at Croyden Castle that weekend, as I understood it. Formally, he made some excuses, but that was just a cover. He knew – we knew – Richter was preparing to make a run for it. When we returned from the pub that night, I felt pretty certain Richter was about to make his move. So when I excused myself for bed, I scouted about for Anders, but never found him."

"What did British Intelligence intend to do about Richter?"

"I'm not sure what Anders had in mind. To stop him, I imagine."

"So you never actually saw Major Hardy that night?"

"No."

"But he was there, you believe."

"He was supposed to be. Others too, presumably."

"Other operatives of MI6?"

"Yes."

"What role did your father-in-law, Lord Neville Johns, play in all this?"

"None, that I'm aware of."

"You are aware, of course – your husband has already testified about it – that Lord Neville was a head of station in MI6 before, during, and after the war?"

"I had some idea, yes."

"Did you ever talk to him about it?"

"No."

"And you have no knowledge of his role in regard to Johann Richter during the war?"

"Just that he appeared to be supportive. For some reason, Lord Neville seemed to like him."

"You didn't know that Lord Neville was sponsoring him, in essence, in government circles?"

"Objection." Raoul Zamora was up again. "The defense is leading on the witness. And it's an improper question, in any case. A question of speculation."

"I withdraw the question," Mr. Benevides said.

He paused a beat. "And you say that you yourself never had sexual relations," he abruptly changed the subject, "of any kind, with Christine Johns."

"I have already answered that question. I'll not dignify it further." Anne Johns was clearly furious beneath a barely calm facade. Mr. Benevides looked over toward Johann Richter. Cohen thought he saw the defendant give his counsel a slight negative shake of the head. Benevides, with a rare, for him, show of perturbation, turned his stare straight onto Anne Johns, the high beams on. As if, thought Cohen, he were silently accusing her of being a liar.

The witness, with a steady look of her own, stared right back at him.

"You swear, under oath," the round little lawyer spat out, "that you played no role whatsoever in the death of Christine Johns?"

"No. None whatsoever," she returned, maintaining the steady gaze. "Though I would be quite happy to play a role in the death of her killer."

Mr. Benevides cocked an eyebrow. "I'll wager you would, Mrs. Johns. I'll wager you would. So you maintain you know nothing further about the matter."

"That is correct."

The witness and the lawyer locked mutually defiant stares for a moment more before Mr. Benevides suddenly wheeled and returned to his seat, only partially surrendering with, "Your Honor, I would like to reserve the right to recall this witness later."

"Granted." The judge looked at Raoul Zamora, who signaled he too had completed his questioning of the witness for now. Court was quickly adjourned for the day. Most of the journalists cleared the room first, in a headlong scramble for a good place in line at the city's only wire-service office a couple blocks up the street.

Cohen glanced at Richter. Richter was looking at Anne Johns who was looking at her husband who was looking at Richter, as if one of the cameras at the front of the courtroom were stopped on a single frame of film. Time hung suspended, events waiting to be edited into some kind of coherence. Nothing right now seemed clear-cut to Cohen. Least of all, guilt or innocence.

He found himself thinking about his discussion with Anders Hardy, and what Hardy had said about Richter. He still didn't trust it. He wondered when their next encounter would be. He was not looking forward to it.

"Now there's a woman you can trust." John Weaver was standing beside Cohen, who had been waiting for the clamor to die down before leaving his seat. "I've been listening for a while," Weaver said. "All that backstabbing kind of makes you wanta puke, doesn't it?"

Cohen smiled. "I wasn't quite that moved by it. But it did make me wonder a bit."

"Wonder? For chrissake. That was Mata Hari up there."

"I was thinking more along the lines of Alice in Wonderland. The Queen of Hearts maybe."

Now Weaver smiled. A man who liked to smile, Cohen thought as he stood up. It was contagious.

"So, mate. How about our dinner date? It's a little early, but what the hell. I'm buyin'."

The courtroom had finally cleared enough for them to make their way to an exit, where they stepped out into the cool afternoon sun.

"Crossroads"

Christine's injuries and hospitalization, from whatever cause, delayed only briefly her continuing efforts to help Richter in his plans to escape England. To all appearances, her willingness to help was still unwavering. Less than three months after her release from hospital they were finally ready to make the attempt.

It was June 1943, and Richter took leave to visit Croyden Castle. Clay Johns had returned from a German prisoner of war camp two weeks earlier, following a prisoner exchange, but Richter hadn't seen him yet. His eagerness for a reunion was tempered by the knowledge this could well be the last time they would ever see each other.

Though he still met Neville Johns on occasion in London, Richter had not visited at Croyden Castle for months. He arrived in the late afternoon in a rather somber mood. As London rebuilt, Germany was reportedly being reduced to rubble. The BBC earlier that day had broadcast a report of the bombing destruction of a factory district near Zossen, an area he knew to be only several miles from Orienbad. The radio report said the town of Zossen itself had been heavily bombed. No mention was made of the expansive Wehrmacht command headquarters located there, a place his father spent a good deal of time.

This matter was weighing on Richter's mind as he was very cordially received, as always, by Lord Neville and Lady Eleanor. Anne Johns and Christine were out riding when he arrived and were not expected back until dinner time.

Anne's parents had come down from York to spend the week at Croyden Castle, Lord Neville said. Anders Hardy, he said, had been invited as well, but unfortunately had been unable to make it. Richter felt relieved at the news. He needed no more members of MI6 present at a scene from which he was hoping to vanish. Particularly not Anders Hardy.

"And of course Clay is eager to see you," Lord Neville said. "We're having him tended to in his room for now, but the doctor says he'll soon be up and about enough to take some sun in the garden. You may go up directly."

As Richter took his leave to do just that, Lord Neville added, as if it were an afterthought, that the prime minister might also pay a visit to Croyden Castle this weekend.

"Churchill?" Richter said.

"Yes. He and I go back a long way," Lord Neville said.

Hiding his discomfiture over the news, Richter climbed a long sweeping stairway to a familiar room where he found Clay propped up on pillows, napping. Trying to forget about Churchill, he quietly drew up a chair beside the bed and studied his old friend. Clay's face was pale, the skin unhealthy-looking, his emaciated features giving his eyes a sunken look. His hair appeared to be newly trimmed. He was dressed in rather formal pajamas. Richter found himself beset by conflicting emotions. He felt the guilt of a German over Clay's condition, but some anger was mixed in. Irrational, he thought, to blame Clay for what was happening to Germany.

After about ten minutes, Clay opened his eyes. He stared intently at Richter, then looked away.

"Welcome back to the land of the living," Richter said, trying to affect a jovial tone. Clay's lack of response made him feel awkward.

"I'm glad you made it," he added after a brief silence. It sounded a bit lame, he thought.

"Are you?" The reply was devoid of emotion. He continued to look away.

"Of course I am." It wasn't hard to see something was wrong. "I'm sorry. It must have been pretty grim. It's odd, but I feel responsible somehow.

"Do you hate us all now?" Richter tacked on, venturing to put a hand on Clay's fragile-looking wrist where it lay on the bed.

Clay pulled his arm away, gently but firmly.

"I suppose I don't blame you," Richter said, knowing things were about to end between them and hating to see it end like this. "Was it really tough?"

Clay looked at him again. "The hardest part was thinking about home. And feeling as if I no longer mattered to anyone here." His voice sounded parched, dried out.

"You weren't forgotten. We talked about you ten times more than if you had been here, or been safe."

"Did you." He sounded skeptical.

"Your father did everything he possibly could to get you out. He took some risks. He had to go through my father to do it. In-directly, of course."

"How?"

"He went through me. He knew I was still in touch with my father."

Clay said nothing.

"Believe me, you were not forgotten. Not by any of us."

"And does that include Anne?"

"Of course."

"Be honest with me, Johann."

"Anne doesn't show her emotions as much as most. But she was concerned."

"Good show, old boy. But not very convincing."

"She was worried about you. We all were."

"And did she find solace, do you suppose, from all this worry? Someone to tell her troubles to, perhaps."

"What are you asking me? If Anne was faithful?"

"Well now, that's the rub, isn't it."

Richter made his answer as convincing as he could. "As far as I know, she was, yes."

Clay eyed him closely, then looked away again.

Richter decided now was not the time for small talk. "I'll be back later," he said, rising to leave.

At the door, he looked back. "Maybe you should ask Anne," he said. "She's the only one who can tell you for certain."

This earned him a cold stare as he left the room.

* * * *

That evening the entire Johns family, plus Richter and Anne Johns' parents, Lord Robert and Lady Vanessa Weldon, who held titles Richter had not caught in introductions, were at dinner. Everyone, that is, but Clay, who remained in his room. Samantha, on the verge of becoming a lovely young woman, seemed rather quiet and withdrawn for the moment. Young Elliot was present in an RAF cadet's uniform.

During pre-dinner cocktails, Christine, on condition that he keep it to himself, had set Richter straight about Churchill's visit, much to his relief. If anyone arrived, she told him, don't be alarmed. It would only be an actor playing Churchill, trying to draw attention away from the prime minister while he had important business to conduct outside England. His own travel plans, she said, should not be affected.

At dinner she and Anne Johns sat just across the table from him, laughing together, exchanging intimacies and generally enjoying themselves. Christine would send an occasional good-natured wink in his direction. It was good to see her looking so happy again, and yet, he reflected, it made him uncomfortable in an almost forgotten but oddly familiar way. She shouldn't be so happy on the eve of his departure, he thought.

The general mood at table was upbeat and convivial, with Lord Neville and Lady Eleanor positively glowing in the reflected light of Christine's return to apparent good health and humor. Her invalid brother upstairs was another matter. After a quick summary of Clay's return and how happy they were to have him back, the two hosts rather studiously, Richter thought, avoided the subject the rest of the evening.

Lord Neville announced rumors were flying in London that the Germans were preparing a new form of warfare, some kind of bombing that employed rockets on automatic pilot. "Hitler is not done yet," he said. "I saw our old friend Kim Philby this week. He has been looking into these weapons. They're enough to keep one awake at night, he said. I invited him to come out here with Anders, whom he sees from time to time. He said he couldn't make it this weekend. That they, ah, they. . ." Lord Neville trailed off, as if thinking twice about whatever he had intended to say. "Well, perhaps it's for the better, isn't it," he tacked on cryptically.

Richter wondered at his host's remarks, particularly about Philby, who had left the *Times* to join MI6 several years earlier. Lord Neville was famously tight-lipped about British Intelligence, even about matters only on the periphery of that shadow world. He had sounded a little gloomy the moment he had mentioned Philby. Did he suspect something about the man; about his allegiance perhaps? Perhaps even about Hardy. Richter still had no idea whether Christine had told her father what she'd learned from Hardy about the Soviets' leverage inside MI6.

After a brief silence, the dinner conversation quickly returned to more general topics. Right now the war news was almost uniformly good, and everyone at table agreed Britain was rebounding nicely from the Blitz, with some help from the colonies, both former and present. Particularly the U.S., to which Lord Neville, still a bit gloomy, offered a toast. Even Lord Robert and Lady Vanessa, a regal, handsome pair rather more stiff than their hosts, joined in a round of charitable remarks about the American troops, whose sometimes intrusive presence in England was both an irritation and a comfort.

At the conclusion of dinner, Richter suggested they all use the beautiful evening to advantage and stroll out to a tavern for a nightcap. Only Anne and Christine, however, were interested.

The evening air was cool, but pleasantly so. After a short walk, the three of them spent several hours drinking and conversing at a cozy inn. Christine was chain smoking. She had picked the habit back up after her release from hospital. The brand no longer mattered to her. All the talk of war, the successes of the American Army Air Corps and the RAF, depressed Richter. His own sarcasm on the subject, he was quite certain, would have been readily apparent to anyone who'd not already had a few drinks too many, as had both Anne and Christine.

Over the course of the evening, as they talked and drank, drank and talked – about the war, about Christine's friends in the fashion and film worlds, about anything and everything – Anne Johns gradually dropped out of the conversation, becoming oddly silent and almost a little sullen. That was fine with Richter. His attention was focused on Christine, and now she was focused more on him than on Anne. For a while he worried that she'd forgotten her role in his impending escape attempt, but by the time they left the inn he was feeling more comfortable with her again.

Upon their return to Croyden Castle, Anne abruptly took her leave, saying she was tired and needed to go to bed. Everyone else had apparently retired already. Everyone but young Elliot, at any rate, who appeared as soon as Anne Johns had disappeared down a hallway. "I'll have a Scotch whiskey, straight up," the boy said. Richter, who got on well with Elliot, scooped him high into the air. Elliot whooped in delight. "Bed time," said Christine, taking her brother by the hand and leading him off to his room. "Good evening, old boy," Elliot said over his shoulder as he was being led away.

Left to his own devices for a moment, Richter realized he was feeling the effects of the liquor he had been pouring down his throat. It was not unpleasant, and he wasn't drunk, but he reminded himself to keep his eye on the ball. He had serious work to do this weekend. He also realized he had missed his chance to visit Clay again, at least for tonight. Perhaps it was just as well, he told himself, but did not feel much consoled.

When she returned, Christine made herself and Richter each a Scotch and water and sat down on the staircase in the main hallway. She looked tousled and lovely, as she always seemed to when she was a little drunk. When she looked like that she also, for some reason, never failed to make him feel immensely sad.

He sat down beside her.

"So here we are," he said.

"Quite so. Here we are. Cheers." She lifted her glass.

"Cheers." They touched glasses and drank.

"Have you told your friends we're on our way?" he said.

"I have indeed. They are expecting us day after tomorrow. By tea time."

"The motor car will break down. That's our story?"

"That's our story."

"Sounds like a B-movie."

She laughed. "Good God. We *are* a B-movie, you and I, don't you think?"

"And how will you alibi for yourself, afterwards?"

"Afterwards, *mein Herr Kraut*, you are on your own. I'm blaming it all on you. 'He took my virginity and left without so much as a thank-you.' You, I assure you, will be the villain of our little movie."

"And are you going to let me at least earn a bit of that reputation," he said, nuzzling the nape of her neck.

"Ummm," she purred, closing her eyes. "There's a good chap."

When his ardor began to spread to other regions of her anatomy, she pulled back and gave him a coquettish smile. "Let's have a swim," she said.

* * * *

Back in her first-floor room after a whispering, laughing, caressing dip in the pool, au naturel, they made love for the first time since she had been released from hospital. In all likelihood, it was their swan song to whatever had once existed – perhaps still existed – between them, Richter thought reluctantly. The taste was bittersweet.

Christine, apparently released by the liquor and by his imminent departure, threw herself into the reunion with gusto. Without prompting, she threw a towel onto the bed, flopped onto her stomach and elevated her hips with a pillow, inviting him to take her that way, an invitation he accepted with alacrity. They both made animal noises of pleasure, Richter finally dropping away from her with a growl, finding himself once again, as he always did in bed, infatuated with this mercurial woman. The bed itself in this case, however, being uncomfortably narrow, Christine eventually climbed out of his arms to fall asleep, or perhaps pass out, in another twin bed across the room. He was fast asleep when she got up an hour later, threw on a robe and left the room.

Richter awoke sometime after that, still in the dark and still light-headed with drink, to a scraping sound at the hallway door to the bathrooms. With a start, he suddenly realized the compromising situation they could find themselves in. To his left, he saw a shadow breaking the moonlight that slanted across the room. The figure stopped just at the edge of the dim light, still unrecognizable, and dropped a robe from its shoulders, slowly, as if for effect. It was a woman. Christine must have gotten up to use the loo. Relief flowed through him.

The woman paused, then moved silently to the side of his bed, which was in darkness. Richter, playing along, rolled over to the far side of the bed, as if in sleep. She responded by pulling back the sheets and climbing in, very carefully not touching him.

Aroused and still half-drunk, he rolled back over to her and began sleepily fumbling his hands along her body. She stiffened and mumbled some words he couldn't quite pick up. Something was wrong.

"What is it?" he said.

"Let go of me!" she hissed. This time the words were quite distinct. And were spoken by Anne Johns.

Richter reacted instinctively. As he moved, she let out a sharp, short scream. He clamped a hand over her mouth. She tried to push away from him. Her hair was wet, her body damp. She wore a heavy perfume he was surprised had not alerted him earlier. His thoughts were hopelessly jumbled, his confusion total. All he could think to do, out of misplaced embarrassment, was to warn her in a whisper Christine was in the room and asleep in the other bed. Anne's possible motivation had not even entered his head yet.

For a moment they lay together as if lovers, he absorbing her heartbeat against his chest, she perhaps weighing her options. Only now did it come to him why she was there. Later, he would wonder why he'd been so stunned. But he had. And right behind the shock was rage. He took Anne's head in both his hands, one of them still clamped over her mouth, and twisted. Just enough to get her attention. A quick jerk of his wrists and it would have been over. Instead, he whispered he would kill her at the first sound, and took his hand away from her lips. In a blind fury, holding her around the waist and arms, he pushed her still-damp legs apart. She resisted at first, but then let her body go slack and just lay there. As if accepting retribution – or saving her energy for revenge.

As he started to mount her, though, the fury departed as suddenly as it had arrived. He stopped himself before he was inside her, and rolled off and away from her.

For an indeterminate length of time his mind went blank. Anne Johns must have gotten out of the room somehow while he was in this state. As he lay there, still stunned, he finally knew what he had to do. Or try to do. Any doubts abruptly disappeared.

He felt some anger toward Christine, but it wouldn't have stopped him from using her help. That, however, was out of the question. It was simply too dangerous now, with Anne Johns about to alert who-knew-whom. The preparations were already in place. It would be more difficult without Christine, but it could be done. Though he now had more doubts about her than ever, there was no choice. He'd simply have to trust her to cover for him, or at least not give him away. Maybe it was better this way, he thought.

Dressing quietly by moonlight, he managed to leave the room without waking Christine. Or so he assumed, realizing later that in his daze he had never even confirmed whether she was still in the bed across the room. Heading for the stables, he narrowly avoided a dark figure moving toward the house. The man was not hiding himself, but appeared to be moving as inconspicuously as possible across the lawn. There was something familiar about him, but Richter had no time to worry about it.

He commandeered a horse from the stables and spent most of the rest of that night riding back toward Epping, on the outskirts of London. There, before daybreak, and before he had really come out of his personal fog, he made contact with an Abwehr operative he was reasonably certain was not under surveillance by British Intelligence. This contact arranged for him to be smuggled by fish-van to Aldeburgh, a village on the east coast about 120 kilometers north of London. He was to rendezvous with a U-boat near there two days later. He put up, as a laborer on vacation, at an out-of-the-way little inn where he was eyed suspiciously by the housemistress for two miserable rainy nights and a day. He tried repeatedly to come to grips with what had just happened at Croyden Castle. Anne Johns was hardly a shocker, but Christine was, and he could not sort out his feelings about it. Had she cared for him at all? Ever? Or, he began to wonder, had she been keeping tabs on him for British Intelligence, maybe even feeding him misinformation. He refused to believe it, but the idea nagged at him.

Very early on the second morning, he paid his bill, tipped the housemistress as generously as being a laborer would permit, and made ready to leave. Just before he did, however, something caught his eye on the front page of a copy of the *Daily Express* that had apparently arrived late the day before.

He picked the newspaper up from the breakfast table and was confronted by photos of Christine and Neville Johns. The headlines fairly shouted out that Christine, "a well-known model and actress, eldest daughter of Lord Neville Johns, Earl of Darbyshire," had been murdered. She had suffered apparent knife wounds to the neck, the newspaper said.

Richter felt sucker-punched, desperate for air. Stumbling blindly along, he skimmed the story beneath the photos and found that he was the prime suspect in the case, that he was being sought for questioning by Scotland Yard. In a sidebar on the back pages there was even a photo of him. A very grainy one, thankfully. He looked up to find the housemistress eyeing him intently.

In a stupor, he left the inn and struck off walking north along the coastline above Aldeburgh. The rain had finally let up, but he didn't notice. Later, he was never able to fully reconstruct his thoughts during this hike. That they were painful and confused was all he could ever remember. That, and how depressed he felt.

Just before twilight, he found the cove he had been looking for. He picked out a sheltered spot on the cliffs that overlooked a narrow beach and the open ocean, and sat down to wait. Most of this rugged area was deserted, but here there must be a small settlement nearby, he decided. For an hour or more, though he saw no one, he could hear the voices of children playing somewhere down along the strip of beach.

His thoughts, such as they were, continued to dwell on Christine. He reviewed their relationship from beginning to end, in minute detail, dredging up everything he could remember, trying to bring her back, trying to untangle his emotions. His feelings toward her were not that simple, now even more than before. He had cared very much for her somewhere along the line, and that feeling had been rekindled the night she'd apparently died. But the final betrayal he suspected her of that night, and the nature of it, with Anne Johns, still preyed on him.

How had she died, and how much of it was his fault? He had worried about British Intelligence since the day he'd enlisted Christine to pry information from Anders Hardy. Assuming she had not been working for Hardy, she'd succeeded admirably, and MI6, in particular Hardy himself, was capable of anything in retaliation.

Hardy was a man Richter had never been comfortable with, never trusted. He knew too much about too many things. Including about Richter and Christine. The man had already hated him for being Christine's lover. Who knows what he thought about her. Richter knew he shouldn't have coaxed her into undermining Hardy's position. It had been far too dangerous. What had happened to her might well have been caused by it. He remembered the shadowy figure he had seen moving across the lawn at Croyden Castle, toward the house, and how familiar he'd looked. It could have been Hardy, but he wasn't certain.

He also considered Anne Johns suspect, but had trouble picturing her actually killing anybody. Much less her own lover. Or possibly it could've been Christine herself. She certainly could have seen, or heard, Anne Johns and him together that night. And if her entwined affairs with the two of them, Anne Johns and Richter, had been enough to drive her to try suicide before, as perhaps it had, how would she have reacted to watching her two lovers brought together in the same bed?

It tortured him, too, to wonder what Clay and his family must think of him now. Could they really believe he had killed Christine? He yearned to see them and tell them the truth. That he was innocent. Especially Clay.

But it was the manner of her death and who killed her that most consumed him. The question continued to nag at him as the sun departed and it grew cooler on the cliffs where he awaited the U-boat. The voices from the beach eventually faded and the evening winds grew even colder. Dressed only lightly, he started to have shivering spells. And doubts. In keeping his separate peace, he realized, he had become virtually useless to either side. He questioned whether the Kriegsmarine would bother to divert a U-boat to pick him up.

A thick depression crept steadily over his already dazed and confused spirits as a heavy coastal fog began to set in. The only ray of light he could see anywhere in his immediate future was the prospect of reunion with his family. He especially longed to see his father again, and to talk with him. Thinking about him was his only effective antidote to thinking about Christine.

The submarine surfaced shortly after two o'clock in the morning. Richter's first awareness of it came from the blinking light signal it aimed toward the cove. He had long since forgotten how to read signal codes. Knowing the U-boat would not stay surfaced in such dangerous waters very long, he scrambled down the thankfully moonlit hillside and out onto the light strip of sand. The water stretched out to sea in smooth swells that soon lost themselves in the fog.

He waited five, maybe ten minutes, for a rubberized dinghy to come. The submarine was too far away to see what was going on aboard it. Time ticked away. Richter could see short stretches of horizon through the fog. For a moment he thought – imagined? – he could see a warship, possibly a destroyer, silhouetted like a toy boat in the distant shrouded moonlight. There was still no dinghy in sight.

When the U-boat, which itself moved in and out of the fog, finally sent out another blinking light signal, he decided there must have been a mix-up somewhere. They seemed to be waiting for him. Again, Richter thought he could see what looked to be a destroyer, a sub killer, in the far distance, still tiny, but larger this time. Presumably British.

Making a decision, he stripped to his underwear and walked out into the icy water. There was a good chance, he knew as he dived in, that he was about to die. At the same instant, he realized he did not want to die, which in itself was a ray of hope. He prayed he could make it, and make it before the U-boat decided to dive.

He quickly cleared a small series of breakers and began pulling his way up and down the swells. He felt strong at first, but the sea began to tug at him, gently at first, then more insistently. He kept swimming. As his body tired and his mind began to argue the merits of giving up, Richter reached down and continued to push through the water. He swam for as long as he could. It seemed forever. At his last glimpse of the U-boat, it appeared to be diving, though he was too low in the water to be certain. He lost sight of it. He prayed again. As he neared where he thought it should be, his hopes sinking, he could feel the numbness in his limbs. He felt disoriented and lost, but oddly at peace. He remembered looking back over his shoulder at the dark cliffs of England just before he passed out.

When he awoke, the air was close, heavy, and hard to breathe. It was filled with the stench of diesel fuel and a constantly strobing, whirring and whining of shipboard machinery that made him feel nauseous and added to his disorientation. He had trouble focusing at first. A blurry figure approached and announced himself, in a voice that sounded unnaturally low and loud, to be the U-boat's captain. He seemed to be shouting at Richter that he had just received a "return message" from Richter's father. He addressed him as "Major," saying that his father was most gratified at the successful escape and had requested him to personally look after his son.

"I have already assured your father you will recover quite nicely, that you only took a little water up the nose." The man's tone softened a bit. "So please do not disappoint us. It would do my career no good at all to displease the General." He laughed, in what appeared to be genuine good spirits.

"You're going to have to brace yourself for the changes that have taken place in the Fatherland since you were last there, Major," the U-boat captain said. He was fading out of focus again, and Richter had to concentrate all his energy just to hear the words. "Things are a little rough in Berlin at the moment," the man seemed to be whispering now. "You will be flown directly there as soon as we reach the mainland. You are looking forward, I presume, to your return?"

Richter could not answer. He escaped back into darkness.

"Berlin Homecoming"

Richter was not flown directly to Berlin, as the U-boat captain had said he would be. When the submarine docked for repairs to the brass band accompaniment of "Deutschland uber Alles" some 300 kilometers northwest of Berlin at Kiel, he boarded an overloaded train for the trip to Germany's embattled capital.

He was accompanied by a young Wehrmacht lieutenant, who did not speak unless spoken to. The ride, through the outskirts of Hamburg and then down along the Elbe, was not as horrifying an experience as he'd been led to expect. This part of Germany, at least, had not yet been physically affected by the war to any great degree. His fellow passengers, however, seemed restrained and apprehensive. There was little conversation. It was as if they were all in some kind of entranced awe of the times they were living through and were bracing for the inevitable retribution to hit.

As for Richter, in spite of the unhappy times and his own troubled spirit, he actually felt a warm glow of homecoming beginning to build inside him.

In Berlin, there was extensive bomb damage similar to what he had seen in London two years before. It was terrible devastation, but confined largely to two blocks here, three or four blocks there. Much of the city still stood, and life went on around the wreckage. When asked about it, the young lieutenant said some of the better restaurants and places of entertainment had moved out of the city center and into more residential areas in the suburbs. Horchers had closed, the Neva Grill had closed. On the other hand, the Hotel Eden was managing to carry on behind a façade that had been bombed to rubble, and the Adlon and a few others continued to provide services, including fine dining, at something akin to a pre-war level. "If you like oysters and wild game, you've come to the right place," he said with a discreet smile. "They're not rationed. Not yet."

The Friedrichstrasse train station was packed with people, most of them in uniform. Johann blended in. He had been provided with the uniform of a Wehrmacht major. They were met at the station by his father's adjutant, a Colonel Otto Sprague. The lieutenant saluted Sprague and Richter crisply and disappeared into the crowd. Colonel Sprague informed Richter his father was still attached to the General Staff, which was presently with Hitler at his Wolfsschanze command headquarters at Rastenburg in East Prussia. He said the General was expected to return to Berlin sometime the following day on military business, as well as to pay his wife a visit. A rare visit, he added. And to greet his returning son, of course.

The Colonel wanted to escort him directly to Orienbad, but Richter, saying he was still dazed from his narrow escape, insisted he be allowed to spend a night in Berlin to collect his thoughts. At a hotel, rather than officers' quarters. Reluctantly, Sprague agreed. He offered Richter a cigarette, an American Lucky Strike. "Thanks, I don't smoke," Richter said. Sprague accepted a light from an enlisted man at the open door of a black limousine and drew a deep breath of smoke. He indicated Richter should enter, then climbed in beside him and gave directions to a second soldier serving as driver. They drove the short distance to a small hotel on a street just off the Kurfurstendamm, and Sprague made the necessary arrangements with the desk clerk. Richter declined an offer of dinner, and Sprague said he would pick him up for the drive to Orienbad at eight o'clock sharp the next morning.

His hotel room was furnished with a telephone the clerk made a point of telling him was in working order at the present time. Richter made some inquiries and eventually rang up a number at the War Office in the Bendlerblock that was answered by his old friend Erich Borchers, now an oberstleutnant, a lieutenant colonel, in the Wehrmacht's signal corps. Borchers sounded surprised and genuinely delighted to hear from him, and agreed to meet him at seven that evening in the coffee shop of Richter's hotel.

Lying on the bed fully clothed, Richter was unable to fight off thoughts of Christine any longer. As he reviewed, one by one, their most intimate moments together, he let any lingering anger dissipate and the sense of loss take control of him. Once again, he analyzed how she could have died and who her killer might be. Hardy and MI6 emerged as even stronger suspects than before.

He longed to sleep, but could not. Shortly after 6 p.m. he got up, splashed water on his face, shaved, straightened his uniform and went downstairs.

Sitting at a small bar nursing a schnapps, Richter wondered if his father had covered for him with the Abwehr, whose orders recalling him to Germany he'd ignored just four months earlier. He had no idea how much of a problem it might pose for him.

Sharply at seven, Borchers strode into the coffee shop. He looked commanding and fit. The starch of his officer's uniform matched the rest of his appearance. Richter wondered at once if his old comrade from Heidelberg had been co-opted by the Nazis.

"Come," Borchers said. "Let's take a walk before the bombs start flying."

Out on Wilhelmstrasse the early evening air was warm, almost balmy. There was a light breeze. The two young men strode with more apparent purpose than they possessed, catching up on their years apart. Even in uniform, Borchers said, it was wise these days to walk as if headed for something specific. "You missed the 'fun' part of the war, my friend," he said. "After the fall of France, when the wine flowed and a man in uniform was a hero to every woman in Berlin. Now. . ."

Richter didn't have time for small talk. They had walked only three or four blocks before he took a chance and hinted at what he had been trying to do in England for his father and the others.

Borchers picked up on it immediately. "Things are simmering beneath the surface everywhere here," he said. "The defeat at Stalingrad changed everything. People are disillusioned. Students in Munich have demonstrated against the Nazis. Several of them were put to death for it. Beheaded. There's an underground movement in the churches. Protestant and Catholic both. In Warsaw, even the Jews rebelled and caused a lot of disruption until they were slaughtered."

Richter couldn't tell for certain from his old friend's tone which side of the fence he was on.

"But it's the military situation, of course, that is worst of all," Borchers continued. "Hitler refused to pour troops into North Africa while Stalingrad was still hanging fire. When he did, it was too late. We lost most of them; nearly 100,000 in Tunisia last month. Good troops we could ill afford to lose. Not even the great Rommel could avert the disaster."

The slightly ironic twist Borchers applied to the word "great" surprised Richter. As a worthy opponent, Rommel was respected, if not revered, by many of the British.

"Since Stalingrad, the opposition to Hitler inside the Wehrmacht has grown," Borchers said. "Especially in the East, among officers on the front lines. Without this 'unconditional surrender' foolishness of the Allies, Hitler would probably have been overthrown, maybe even dead, by now. I say this to you as an old and trusted friend, Johann. I put my life in your hands simply by saying it."

Richter breathed a sigh of relief. Borchers did indeed appear to be lining up against the Nazis. He had to risk putting him to a firmer test, however. "I'm glad to hear where you stand, Erich," he said, praying he wasn't about to step into a trap. "Now that I am back, I'm hoping to be of some use to the opposition."

Borchers eyed him carefully. "Just be sure that you are discreet, my friend. Or we may both wind up over there." He nodded toward Gestapo headquarters across the street. "Their cellars are famed, and not for their fine wines.

"The Gestapo shares that building with the SS Directorate General of Security for the Reich, which – in case you've forgotten – includes the Party's own intelligence branch. Himmler ran the whole apparatus for a while, after Heydrich's demise, but handed it over to Kaltenbrunner a few months ago when his duties as head of the SS called."

Borchers looked toward the pavement and shook his head. "If it weren't so horrible," he said, "it could all be an absurd joke. Himmler's priesthood. The great SS. The Black Order. Order of the Death's Head. All the brainchild of a chicken farmer with notions about genetics. Did you know SS men are now expected to sire at least four children? If not with their wives, then with other women." Borchers laughed. "Aryan women are to consider it a great honor to mate with a member of the SS, no matter how lowly a specimen he might be. But of course it is racial treason to marry a Jew, whatever his accomplishments."

Borchers eyed Richter, this time with empathy. "In short," he said, "it's a bad state of affairs you have returned to. To say the least."

"In England, they think the elimination of Heydrich may have improved things, at least a little," Richter said.

Borchers laughed again. It was not a pleasant sound. "Ask the people of Lidice," he said. "Ask them if the elimination of Heydrich has improved things." Richter remembered what Christine had told him about the role of British Intelligence in Heydrich's assassination, and the subsequent liquidation of **Lidice** by the SS. "British arrogance," Borchers tacked on in disgust.

The comment made Richter uneasy. He said nothing in reply.

After they had walked another block or two, Borchers broke the silence, this time with a distracted air as if he were talking as much to himself as to Richter: "Things are getting worse, not better, for the powerless, as the war goes downhill. If the war is lost, the Nazis know they are too. Heydrich may be gone, may he rot in hell, but the SS and Gestapo are still on the job, and they seem bent on carrying out their programs while they have the chance. They are very serious about it. People have been interrogated over there" – he nodded again back down Wilhelmstrasse, toward the other side of the street – "simply for harboring Jews or other undesirables. It is strictly forbidden in any way to assist these 'U-boats,' as they are called. Their lives are submerged. To obtain papers or ration cards, they must steal them. Or forge them. Or they depend on their friends, whose lives are then put as much in danger as their own."

Borchers looked at Richter. "For extended interrogations, the kind many never return from," he said, "the Gestapo ships them out to a Konzentrationslager, generally the KZ at Sachsenhausen."

The beautiful night, the warm, heady air. It hardly seemed possible. Several blocks beyond Gestapo headquarters, Richter could see extensive bomb damage ahead.

"Not a pretty sight, eh?" Borchers said, eyeing him for a reaction. "But this kind of thing will be nothing compared to what's in store for us if something isn't done soon." Borchers' look grew more intense. "Johann, can I trust you?" Richter raised a questioning eyebrow in his old friend's direction. "I mean really trust you. I know this is a lot to throw at you all at once, so soon after your return, but–"

Richter cut him short. "You can trust me, Erich. Completely."

"All right. . . Do you remember Claus von Stauffenberg, the fellow I used to talk about at Heidelberg?"

"From Stuttgart. The student of Stefan George. Yes, I remember. I met him once."

"He too is an oberstleutnant now. Recently returned from North Africa minus an eye, a hand, and some fingers on the other hand. But he has a will of iron. Just two days ago I saw him again, in a hospital in Munich. He is about to be released."

Borchers glanced around, making sure their conversation was private. Crossing over into the Tiergarten and walking past the towering Siegessaule, a 200-foot column erected in honor of Germany's Nineteenth Century victories over Austria and France, they passed by the Grosser Stern Rotary, with its huge statues of former Chancellor Otto von Bismarck and Field Marshal Helmuth von Moltke, two of the principal architects of those victories.

"Stauffenberg convinced me," Borchers said, "that all the petty squabbling and foot-dragging of the opposition crowd is about to end." He looked around again. "I am not at present an active member of the opposition. Stauffenberg himself is only a recent recruit, and he wants me to join him. I'm already privy to a few of their maneuverings. Sympathetic officers are trying to get Stauffenberg assigned, perhaps as chief of staff, to Friedrich Olbricht, the general who is deputy to Fritz Fromm, commander in chief of the Reserve Army. Olbricht, I am quite certain, is anti-Hitler. Two days ago Stauffenberg implied to me that Erich Fellgiebel, the general in charge of communications at Hitler's Wolfsschanze headquarters in Rastenburg, is also with them. That may be–"

Suddenly a lone air raid siren began to wail. Within seconds, it was joined by a chorus of others.

"We're in luck," Borchers shouted over the din. "Let's give the Votivkirche a try. My passes should get us in."

They joined a multitude of Berliners streaming toward the Votivkirche, the city's largest bomb shelter, near the southwest corner of the Tiergarten. Popularly known as the "Zoobunker" because of its proximity to the Berlin Zoo, it housed a fully equipped field hospital and could shelter and feed 8,000 civilians and a regiment of troops during air raids. The huge fortress-like structure was topped by the Wehrmacht's heaviest anti-aircraft weapons. The SS was detailed to check papers at an entryway at the end of a descending approach ramp as wide as a section of autobahn.

Inside, Richter and Borchers ignored the area covered with people sitting or sleeping on the floor, and wandered off into back reaches of the huge poured concrete space that were surprisingly empty.

"Kind of like being buried alive," Richter observed.

"The Fuhrer's brave new world," Borchers said in apparent agreement.

"Perhaps I can arrange a meeting with Stauffenberg for you," Borchers said, as if there had been no interruption in their earlier conversation. "He could give you some orientation. And he is inspiring, I can assure you. Even more than when you met him before."

"Fine." Richter said nothing more for a moment. When he spoke again, his voice was heavy. "This is pretty depressing, Erich. What's going to happen to Germany?"

"I don't know, my friend. We are in deep trouble, is all I know."

As if to emphasize the point, bombs started dropping close enough that the sound of their muffled explosions penetrated the shelter's twelve-foot-thick slabs of reinforced concrete. Seconds later, the Zoobunker's 128mm flak guns opened up, shaking the massive structure with their thunder.

When the Armageddon-like cacophony finally died down, Richter spoke again. "The British, you know, are totally set against negotiating a peace with us, regardless of what happens to Hitler."

"They want only this ridiculous 'unconditional surrender'?" Borchers said.

"So they say."

"And the Americans?"

"Are worse, if anything. Roosevelt hates us."

"Then perhaps we are doomed. There will certainly be no mercy in the East. We showed none to the Russians. They will show none to us. Day by day, they are forcing us back in the Ukraine. We will soon have no bargaining chips left."

"That bad, eh? I was hoping Soviet successes were being over-blown by the British."

"Unfortunately, no. And that's all the more reason, I think, for you to talk with Stauffenberg. He believes it's still not too late to take action against Hitler. That there is hope. And he is a very convincing man."

"I hope he's right," Richter said.

The all-clear sounded ten minutes later. "A short raid," Borchers noted.

Returning to Wilhelmstrasse, they walked by Abwehr head-quarters, two nondescript townhouses along the dead-looking canal at Tirpitzufer.

Richter wondered again how much trouble he was in.

"Orienbad"

The next morning, Sprague arrived in a nondescript black sedan promptly at eight o'clock.

"You slept well, I trust," he said in greeting.

"Quite well," Richter returned. In fact, he had slept very little, troubled by dreams he remembered upon awaking only by the residue of terror they had left behind. Had he heard more air raid sirens? He wasn't sure.

Sprague lit up a Lucky Strike. He held it out in front of him and grinned. "Your father would not approve. He forbids his staff to smoke in his presence. He is stronger than the rest of us."

As they started to drive south through Berlin, Sprague mentioned the car's windows were bulletproof. He smiled at Richter when he said this, as if quite proud of the fact.

"You know, Goebbels might've put you on a platform spewing out propaganda, as a true German whose heroic escape from England should be an example to us all, if we hadn't managed to convince him your intelligence activities were too sensitive for that," Sprague said.

Richter had no response for this. Sprague seemed a good enough sort, but he made Richter uncomfortable. The Colonel kept a wary eye on him as Berlin flashed by the bulletproof windows. Here too, the destruction was not so bad, though he was to learn later the driver had been instructed to take the least-damaged route. Still, Berlin looked in no worse shape than London. Germany was far from done, he thought.

On the outskirts of the city, the Colonel suddenly knocked him from his reverie. "How is England holding up?" he asked. It was a pointed question. With, it seemed to Richter, a nervous edge to it.

Richter looked at him. "England is holding up quite nicely. With America in the war and Germany spending all its energy on Russia, England is probably in better shape than we are." He felt an odd resonance at identifying himself with Germany again. The Fatherland.

"And how is Germany holding up?" he asked Sprague.

The Colonel stared out his window at the untouched open countryside now rolling by. "As well as can be expected," he said. "But not well enough," he tacked on, glancing back at Richter, then quickly away again.

That was the end of their conversation.

The BBC's report on the bombing of Zossen had been greatly exaggerated. The town had taken a few hits, but had sustained no widespread damage. Sprague pointed out the Wehrmacht command headquarters had not been hit at all. They arrived at Orienbad itself shortly before 11 a.m. After four years of war, the place looked unchanged. Perhaps a little run-down. No one emerged from the house to greet them. Sprague ushered him inside with what seemed to Richter a proprietary air.

As he stepped into the front hallway, he was again struck by the sensation that everything was still in place, at least physically. A minor furniture rearrangement was the sole change that he could see. Only an indefinable feeling of quietude and vacancy felt different from the way he had always remembered it. But then he thought those feelings might be more his own than Orienbad's.

Sprague, less a stranger here it seemed than Richter, ascended the hall stairs. Richter listened as the Colonel's bootsteps marched a path across the upstairs hallway, then he returned to inspecting the house. Not surprisingly, perhaps, everything seemed slightly smaller than his memory had pictured it. Standing there, it was difficult for him to believe the events that now separated him from the young boy, the boy about to leave for school in England, who had stood in this same room not much more than ten years ago. He walked out onto the huge back porch that overlooked an open pasture and the woods beyond. For some reason, he found himself caught up in thoughts of Marie Renault.

He was awakened from memory by his mother's "Welcome home, Johann." They embraced and exchanged greetings and a few words, communicating as they always had, awkwardly. Otto Sprague had disappeared.

His mother's beauty had dimmed. She looked old and tired. Her light brown hair had turned gray, her face was heavily lined, and her once-commanding voice was now more a whisper, flat, nearly devoid of emotion. His own emotions at seeing her again were difficult to pin down. His feelings toward her seemed somehow absentminded, as if he had misplaced the real ones somewhere.

"I don't know much about your father," she said, answering her son's unspoken question. "He is rarely here anymore."

"When do you expect him?"

"I don't know. I never know these things in advance. He simply appears."

"Do you think he has something in mind for me?"

"Doesn't he always?" She said this with an unveiled sarcasm he had never heard her use in regard to the General before.

When Richter asked where his sisters were, though, she looked back at him with a sudden spark of life in her eyes. "Ellen has married a major general." She said this with a hint of pride. Not as pronounced, however, as Richter would've expected. "He has been recently posted to the Eastern Front."

Richter had already noticed that was how everyone referred to it. No matter that it covered thousands of miles and that this someone, this new brother-in-law of his, could be anywhere along it. It was always simply "the Eastern Front." There was an ominous ring to it.

"She is living at his family's estate in East Prussia," Frau Richter added, her animation already fading. "Just outside of Konigsberg. I am trying to talk her into coming home before the Russians get there, but she is stubborn, like your father. She says the Russians won't get there."

His mother hesitated, as if to say something more, but held her tongue.

"And Gretchen?" he asked.

She looked away. "Gretchen," she said, "was killed in an air raid late last year. In Berlin. Her body was never found."

This news disturbed Richter less than his own lack of reaction to it. He didn't feel much of anything. A small surge of compassion for his mother, was about it. He had not seen his younger sister for nearly five years. He was sad, yes, but sadder for himself, he thought, than for Gretchen, who seemed at this point more a symbol of something he had lost rather than a real person.

He wanted to change the subject.

"Is it lonely for you here?" he asked.

"The women of the neighborhood get together every day," she said in her near-whisper. "We sew things for the Wehrmacht. Some of our women have even gone to work in the factories this year. We have been lucky. There has been no bombing here. No blackouts or looting." She paused uneasily, perhaps wondering at his lack of response to the death of his sister. Her eyes closed briefly, in what Richter interpreted as a sign of resignation. He knew she was feeling pain. He felt some connection to it, but was unable to put the emotion into words for her, or show it.

She suggested he unpack before his father arrived. He told her he had nothing to unpack. They were running out of conversation. He looked out again at the fields behind the house. The sky was sharp blue, without a cloud.

He asked his mother if any of the old horses were still at Orienbad.

"Only Sacha," she replied. "She was so ancient the army had no use for her. It was not too difficult to keep your father from having her slaughtered, even for the war effort." She gave out a little laugh of uncharacteristic irony when she said this.

Amazed to learn Sacha had weathered the past four years, Richter excused himself and hurried out to the stables. The building was deteriorating badly from lack of maintenance. He found his old friend, alone and forlorn-looking, lying on the floor of one of the stalls. At first he thought she must be either dead or dying, but as he approached her and spoke to her, she suddenly came alive with unexpected energy. She stumbled to her feet and nuzzled her nose up against him.

As he hugged her, tears came to his eyes. He thought of Christine. He thought of Gretchen. More than any human being, perhaps even his father, Sacha was the past to him. They had wandered their youth away together, had come to know and love each other as well as man and animal might. Now, when Richter saw the old mare still remembered him, and as he thought of the sad state of both their lives, he wanted only to be twelve again and riding her under a blue summer sky like the one above them now. His dejection struck absolute bottom at the thought of that impossibility. For one brief moment he pictured himself going back into the house, opening the gun locker and taking out his father's old First War revolver, returning to the stables and shooting Sacha, then himself.

Once this wave of depression and self-pity rolled over him, he was left feeling empty but also strangely becalmed. Some time passed, he did not know how much, before he gradually became aware of a familiar voice dimly pricking at the back edges of his consciousness. At first it seemed one more dream from the past. But as the voice, which was calling out his name, grew louder and more insistent, Richter realized there was no awaking from this dream. He gave Sacha a quick last hug and obeyed his father's command.

* * * *

During the first part of the war, he had often wondered if his father would seem much changed when they finally met again. Now as he sat alone with him in the study of the Orienbad house, both of them drinking schnapps to toast their reunion, Johann could see he had aged a good deal. His face was etched with deeper creases than before, and his eye had a softer, sadder focus. His weary features made even the eye patch seem less severe.

But if the strain of war was showing, there was still no crack in his military bearing. Somehow Johann could never imagine the man being obsequious in anyone's presence, even Hitler's. His short-cropped hair was as thick as ever, though it had turned from iron gray to snow white in the four years since they had last seen one another. It reminded Johann of von Hindenburg.

His father's commanding voice had not changed, but his manner toward Johann had altered. Somewhat favorably, Johann thought. The touch of arrogance the General had once affected was gone. He seemed more human. His concern for Johann's welfare, in particular, seemed more real and less self-serving than it ever had before. Perhaps, he thought, his father was seeing changes in him as well and was responding to them.

At the start his father did not ask him a single question about England. The General seemed already to know and accept the fact that Germany's old enemy was in better health and spirits than the Fatherland.

As their small talk began to wind down, Johann ventured to ask how the war was going. Really going. He said he'd never been sure how much of what he was hearing in England had been propaganda. And the evidence he had seen so far in Germany had been inconclusive at best.

Karl Richter shook his massive head. He gave out a little snort of derision, then launched into a diatribe Johann had a feeling he had probably recited many times before, his voice low, in dead earnest.

"In Russia, all the years and heartaches that went into rebuilding the army from the ruins of the First War are being thrown away by a military stupidity unmatched in modern warfare. Since Stalingrad, all those years of effort are 'paying off' by delaying the inevitable and ensuring the end of the war will also be the end of Germany.

"We are capable of holding out one more year," he said in a hard, calm tone, "maybe even two, with Guderian, Speer, myself and a few others doing what we can to offset Hitler's mad schemes. But the General Staff is breaking in two – into Hitler's camp, those who owe him everything and are still fanatically loyal to him, and ours, those of us whose first loyalty is to the Wehrmacht and to Germany.

"It's insane," Karl Richter said. "Hitler never should have attacked Russia and never should have declared war on the U.S." He looked pensive for a moment, then stared straight at Johann, sharply, as if taking stock. "You must tell no one, not a single soul, what I am telling you now." His voice was just as sharp. "That is understood?"

"Of course," Johann said, a little shaken by the unexpected outburst. He wondered if Erich Borchers and Claus von Stauffenberg were considered a part of this anti-Hitler camp, but resisted asking his father. He felt a sudden need to return to something more personal.

"Am I going to have problems for not returning sooner, when the Abwehr ordered me back?" he asked.

"Ordered you back to Germany?"

"Yes."

"How long ago?"

"About four months."

"I know of no such orders." Karl Richter's eye took on a darker cast. "I will look into the matter.

"If you ignored the Abwehr," his father asked, "why did you leave England, then?"

"I had learned something I thought I should bring back to you. Something that couldn't be sent through regular channels. The British have infiltrated the group of Wehrmacht officers who want to. . . change the government." Even here, in his own home, Johann felt nervous speaking aloud against Hitler or including his father's name among the conspirators. "They may even be getting word to Keitel or Jodl about these officers."

"To what purpose?"

"I have been told British Intelligence, or at least MI6, is riddled with Communists. That Stalin wants Hitler alive and putting up a fight long enough for the Soviet armies to reach Germany before any peace agreement is worked out. He doesn't want a new government here that could ask for a separate peace. He wants as much of Europe as he can grab. And he wants Germany's secret weapons."

If this news surprised Karl Richter, he did not show it. "Do you have the names of these infiltrators?" he asked.

"Two."

"Good. There are probably more. But this is good. Perhaps we can flush the others from hiding. How did you find out?"

"Lord Neville's daughter, Christine."

"How did she know?"

"One of their operatives over there, a key one, was once her lover."

"Why was she willing to tell you?"

Johann looked at his father, wondering if perhaps the General did not entirely trust his own son.

"I'm not questioning your sincerity, Johann, but I must know how reliable this information is. The British are past masters at planting false information."

"She told me, because *we* were lovers."

Karl Richter raised his eyebrows and almost smiled. "That, however, hardly guarantees her reliability," he said.

"What guarantees her reliability," Johann countered, "is that she was killed for telling me. I believe she was, anyway." It made him feel a traitor to Christine's memory, speaking so dispassionately about her death.

"Killed how?"

"I'm not sure. It happened the night I left Croyden Castle, to escape England. The newspapers said she was murdered. Her passing such sensitive information to me seems the most likely reason, to my mind."

"The British don't know who killed her?"

"They think I did it."

His father eyed him intently. "But you didn't," he said.

"I did not."

This answer appeared to satisfy the General.

The two men sat for a moment in silence. His father's earlier diatribe, his evident despair, as analytical as it had sounded, now emboldened Johann to ask about something that had been weighing on him. "I have heard the SS has been turning the KZs into death camps. Is that true?"

Karl Richter did not flinch. His reply sounded almost matter-of-fact. "There will be war crimes enough to go around. More than enough," he said. "I toured a labor camp in the East, early in the war. It was not a pleasant place. But given the way the war was being fought, it could have been worse.

"Now, everything is different. At Wannsee last year the Nazis formalized their plans, not to subjugate or expel, but to exterminate, Europe's Jews. For the most part, they're being killed in those camps to the east by thugs of the Totenkopfverbande, the SS 'Death's Head' units. In the field, the killings are carried out by SS Einsatzgruppen. The Wehrmacht is not involved."

"Hitler has approved this?" Johann knew Himmler and some of the others were capable of anything. But he surprised himself now, as he realized that even he had his doubts Hitler – the man who once wanted to be a priest – would sink to such depths.

"He was not at Wannsee. But one way or another, everything comes from the Fuhrer," Karl Richter said. "Hitler vowed he would change the world, and he has kept his promise. Even if he loses, the world will never be the same."

His father's next words, aimed into thin air rather than at Johann, seemed cold and bloodless, drained of all emotion save a depressing note of resignation and fatigue: "Hitler's determination to eradicate the Jews – and others, but first and foremost the Jews – is the single most important reason we're losing the war. It has deprived the Wehrmacht and the civilian sector of key manpower, and it has ensured that the conquered peoples – particularly in the East, where it's being pushed the hardest – will continue to resist rather than join us." The

General raised his hands in mock surrender, and shrugged. "God is sending us a message," he said. "We will all need absolution before this is over."

Johann didn't know what to say. He needed time to absorb things. Before he could even begin the process, however, his father was focusing in on him with all the considerable intensity at his command. "Johann, time is short. Allow me to get right to the point. There appear to be only two ways for Germany to go right now – total destruction, with division and occupation, or a negotiated peace settlement of some sort, salvaging what we can. And there is only one way to have a negotiated peace. Hitler must be gotten rid of, and quickly. The Allies say they will accept only unconditional surrender from us, but things would look different to them with Hitler gone."

He studied Johann carefully before picking up the thread of his argument again. "There are civilians – Goerdeler, Gisevius, von Moltke and others – in the movement to oust Hitler, but it's the Wehrmacht that will ultimately have to do the dirty work," he said. "We have each sworn an oath of loyalty to the Fuhrer. It will be treason, but to save Germany it must be done. And we must move before Canaris is sacked. Certain officers of the Abwehr, with his support, have been actively helping us. But Canaris has stuck his neck out so many times it could be cut off at any moment. Himmler and Schellenberg are on to him, and they will persuade Hitler soon enough."

The General continued to inspect his son, assessing the impact of his message. Apparently satisfied, he pushed on. "There have already been several attempts to end the Fuhrer's life initiated from inside the Wehrmacht and the Abwehr. When he visited Army Group Center Headquarters in Smolensk in March, Henning von Tresckow – you remember him? – and Fabian von Schlabrendorff, his adjutant, planted two brandy bottles containing plastic explosives aboard Hitler's plane before it took off for Rastenburg. It had to be very powerful, because the plane is equipped with a section designed to break away and parachute Hitler safely to earth in the event of a problem. As it turned out, the bomb had a faulty detonator and did not go off. Schlabrendorff actually had to fly to Rastenburg and retrieve the bottles under some pretext.

"Hitler should have been dead by now. Several times over. He has the lives of a cat." Karl Richter shook his head and laughed dryly, as if at the absurdity of painting Hitler in feline terms. "There is not going to be any popular uprising against our Fuhrer. Only we in the military are strong enough to get rid of him. We have always had the power–"

"But not always the will," Johann said without thinking.

The General stared at him, a rare look of surprise on his face. "But not always the will," he repeated, glancing out a window of the study.

He paused, as if dwelling on the thought. "We must, however, confront the here and now," he finally said. "A new coup d'etat has already been planned. Right now such an attempt has probably no better than half a chance for success, even if the Fuhrer were dead. No chance at all with him alive. And killing Hitler is going to be at best a very risky business. Perhaps suicide for whoever attempts it."

He looked back at Johann, grim-faced. "How is your marksmanship these days?" he said.

"Rusty."

"Start practicing. With no little difficulty, I have persuaded the Abwehr not to assign you to the Eastern Front. You will be going to Paris instead.

"We need you," he continued, his tone lacking the emotion that should have been there. "We need you to help us kill Hitler."

Oddly enough, Johann thought, he felt no surprise, though he suddenly felt more estranged from his father than he could ever remember. "I thought you just said I would be in Paris," he said.

His father unexpectedly smiled at this. "You will be," he said, deadly serious. "And so will the Fuhrer. Just as soon as we can talk him into making the trip."

CHAPTER XVI

It was odd how the time of day meant so little to a prisoner. Particularly when you were alone, Richter thought. It was very late, three or four in the morning, but he could not sleep. He stood at the barred windows, through which a chilling breeze gusted, and stared at the night sky above La Negra. The moon was nearly full. His overheated thoughts competed for attention. Several important decisions had been made tonight, and for the first time since his capture he saw a glimmer of hope. It was only a glimmer, to be sure, but it was more than he'd had to hold onto in a long time.

Earlier in the evening, Father Hidalgo had told him there was an escape plot brewing on the outside. That he was its target. His immediate reaction had been one of suspicion – the word was that it was part of some kind of intelligence game and would be risky – but the priest had had enough details in hand to make him think it might actually provide a way out. With a lot of "ifs" attached.

More definite, and just as important, was the news his family was now on its way into La Negra. In spite of his fears for their safety, the thought of having them close by gave Richter a great sense of relief. Somehow it felt more like he could protect them here. True, he had allies at home, Rivera and his men up around Riberalta. But he had a few here as well. And here he could at least keep tabs on what was going on.

He still had some doubts, however, about this Michael Cohen that Elena had met and sounded as though she trusted. He had asked Father Hidalgo to find out what he could about the young man. The priest had reported back that he could discover little other than Cohen was supposedly a writer working for an American magazine. And that he was acquainted with a John Weaver, who claimed to work for the *Baltimore Sun*, a well-known newspaper in the U.S. Father Hidalgo's street sources had placed this Weaver several times in the company of a man believed to be an intelligence operative for either the Americans or the British.

It was not a report to quell Richter's suspicions about Cohen, or his fears that British Intelligence might try to get to him through his wife and children. It sharpened his skepticism, too, about the alleged plan to break him out of prison.

It was just such concerns that had led him to decide earlier that day, in counsel with Mr. Benevides, to request extradition as soon as possible to England. For now, anyway, it seemed the most effective way to distance Elena and the children from danger. The change in venue should help to shield them, even should they accompany him to London. Yes, it would give MI6 the jitters he might wake sleeping dogs, but in case the escape didn't pan out it was worth the gamble. The reins of authority in La Negra were too loosely held to ensure anybody's ultimate safety here, on any grounds. And MI6 was here by now. Of that much he was certain.

On other matters, he was not so sure of his ground. Anne Johns swore she had not been involved in Christine's murder, but Richter had his doubts. He had little doubt, however, Anders Hardy had been involved. Though he couldn't prove it, he was more certain of it than ever now. Hardy had not actually wielded the knife, perhaps, but somehow, Richter was convinced, the man had played a role. And Hardy too was in La Negra. He could sense it.

Searching the stars, he spotted a constellation that as he watched, gradually metamorphosed into an image of Claus von Stauffenberg. It was no surprise. It was an apparition he had become accustomed to. For years, it had come to him unbidden and unexpected, with the power to interrupt all other thought. The magnificent von Stauffenberg he had so briefly met at Heidelberg. The horribly wounded Stauffenberg, maimed in the last days of fighting in North Africa, and later, making his heroic, pathetic attempt to kill Hitler. And coming so close. Thwarted only because of incidental events beyond his control.

Otherwise, it would all have been so different. He knew it was simply a chance happening, Hitler surviving the blast, but a part of him believed it was more than that. It had not been in the stars, he decided, that Stauffenberg should kill Hitler. His motivations had been too noble. It took a touch of the Devil, a motive like revenge, to kill the Devil. He remembered similar thoughts, from shortly following his own. . .

It had been the hope of meeting again with Stauffenberg – whose stay in a Munich hospital had been extended – that had prompted him to see Borchers a second time after he'd met with his father at Orienbad in the summer of 1943. It had proved impossible, which was disappointing, but Richter had told his old friend to keep him in mind if Stauffenberg and his friends ever needed help.

In the meantime he told Borchers about his posting to Paris, but kept to himself most of what his father had told him about the plots against Hitler. It was not that he didn't trust Borchers. He simply didn't know enough about what was going on to let anyone in on it.

As always, this train of thought trailed off into thoughts of his own depressing role, the unintended treachery that had led to so many deaths and contributed to Germany's final demise. He had betrayed his own father and failed his homeland. He had not meant to. But there it was. Whatever his intentions, those had been the results. The weight of this guilt was lifted only when Elena and the children were near.

There was another, more intimate, guilt he also continued to shoulder. It started with Christine, and the way in which he was convinced she had met her fate. With Anne Johns' courtroom testimony, he had wondered briefly where Christine's loyalties had lain. But ultimately – whatever her ties to MI6, whatever her sexual orientation and true feelings for him – he remained convinced she had been on his side. As the key to his wartime escape back into Germany, he had used her to that end with little compunction. Without his pressuring her to cajole information from Hardy – seduce him for it, if necessary – the man would never have gone after her. Any urge he felt to avenge Christine by going after Hardy was undercut by a sense of his own complicity in her death.

And as it often did, thinking about what happened to Christine made him think of Muriel. Two women from more different backgrounds he could not imagine. One had had the world at her beck and call; the other had been a Jewess in the clutches of the SS. One he had once loved; the other he had encountered only briefly at a concentration camp. And yet in his mind, in the way he remembered them, and what happened to them, there was an intrinsic link. A key part of that link was the undiminished guilt they both still, nearly ten years later, evoked in him.

He took a coca leaf from a drawer of the small table beside his cot and chewed on it, still watching the heavens. The stars here seemed so much nearer than in the skies up near Riberalta. By now he was used to the placement of these southern constellations, so different from how they patterned the sky above European soil. Most nights they offered comfort, lent him perspective. But on this night his mood only darkened as he contemplated them and tried to work out an equation that would balance motive and intent with failure and guilt.

"Kaisenher"

Before Richter left for Paris, he had a duty to perform. With the help of Otto Sprague, and through his father's liaison office in the Bendlerblock, he gained access to a huge load of POW and concentration camp records, including some reluctantly handed over by the SS. In two full days of scouring the lists for names of people he knew, he came up with only one. Elena Stein.

Seeing her name on a list thousands of names long gave him a queasy feeling. It seemed unreal, but set everything else off in stark relief, a floodlight of reality: the KZs, the war, Germany's sins. Even Christine's death.

If Elena Stein were still alive, she was in the concentration camp at Kaisenher, a satellite of Dachau northwest of Munich. Special passes were required to visit there, but Richter found being the son of General Karl von Richter was sufficient leverage to produce such a pass.

The General was against his son visiting the camp. It could jeopardize his usefulness in any action against Hitler, Karl Richter said. Only when Richter explained who Elena Stein was, and promised she would be his only rescue mission, did his father give way. Richter insisted on making the trip alone. He did not want to risk compromising the General's position any more than necessary. And regardless, he thought he could better accomplish what he needed to alone. After his father and Otto Sprague left Orienbad to return to Rastenburg, Richter departed early the following morning for Kaisenher at the wheel of the General's prized old Daimler-Benz.

The drive was magnificent. The towns and villages here appeared to have resisted posting signs declaring themselves *Judenrein*, free of Jews, a practice popular in other parts of Germany. Deep inside the towering firs of the Black Forest, it was difficult to believe a world war was raging anywhere. For a short while, Richter was almost able to forget the past four years and pretend he was in some dream world where all was right with the universe. Just south of Ingolstadt, he took a narrow branch road southwest toward Augsburg. Kaisenher had been built to handle the overflow from Dachau, but was sited at a discreet distance to the west.

Passing through the village of Ulm – home town to Field Marshal Erwin Rommel, as well as to Hans and Sophie Scholl, two of the student leaders beheaded four months earlier for fomenting unrest at the University of Munich – he was given polite if somewhat unenthusiastic directions to the camp. Ulm was the birthplace of Albert Einstein, one of the many Jews and intellectuals compelled to flee Germany as the Nazis prepared to take power ten years ago. Richter wondered whether his uniform was a plus or a minus here.

Two miles out of town, he drove into a stand of ancient forest that twenty minutes later gave way to a large clearing and a sign – *Arbeitslager*, work camp – that introduced Kaisenher and its depressing vista. After passing nothing but trees for miles, suddenly there were none. Only nondescript buildings surrounded by seeming miles of concertina wire. It was as if all color had been drained from the place. Everything was a dull black and white. It felt ten degrees hotter than it had in the woods.

At the checkpoint, Richter presented his pass to an SS sergeant, a man of perhaps sixty sweating profusely and in need of a shave. The guard inspected the pass carefully. It appeared visitors from Berlin were not common here. Displaying a deference that could've been mistaken for disdain, the man told Richter in a thick Bavarian accent to wait while he rang up the commandant.

The camp commandant arrived ten minutes later on foot. Sturmbannfuhrer Heinrich Mueller was young, about Richter's age. His rank, the SS equivalent of Richter's, was low for the commander of a KZ, probably because Kaisenher was a relatively small camp.

"I know a Mueller family in Berlin," Richter said, trying to break the ice.

"My family name is 'Muller,'" the man countered. "My mother, after my prick of a father deserted us when I was nine, started spelling it 'Mueller.' When she died, I stuck with her version."

The angry response was a jolt. As was the name. The same name as the mysterious Heinrich Muller – "Gestapo Muller" – who headed up the Nazis' dreaded secret police. Could they be related? Richter didn't ask.

Even the possibility, however, blunted the edge Richter had assumed he would have with a father on the Wehrmacht's General Staff. It might be better to approach this man as an equal, he thought. Make use of their shared lack of rank. Both of them were still junior enough to commiserate about it.

"What can I do for you, Major?" Mueller was a bit stiff. Defensive, Richter thought. The man thinks he is being inspected. Checked up on. *Put him at ease.*

"I am here to ask a favor. A rather private one." Richter looked pointedly at the several camp guards present.

Mueller took the hint. "We will go to my quarters."

As they walked across the compound, the guards trailed along keeping an eye on Richter. He wondered how much Kaisenher resembled the camp his father had once toured. The place looked like an army post. An incredibly bleak one. The long low barracks were lined up in parallel rows baking in the sun, surrounded by virtually no landscaping, nothing that lived. No trees, no flowers, no bushes. No grass. As they walked, their boots scraped across the gravel, reminiscent of marching troops. Richter could see one, perhaps two, larger buildings beyond several tiers of barracks, tall stacks belching a dirty smoke that quickly blended with the gray skies above them. The larger buildings appeared to be just beyond the perimeter of the main compound.

Mueller saw him looking. "Our factories," he said. "This is a labor camp, you understand. Mostly Jews. The Final Solution takes only small steps here."

Mueller spoke of a "final solution" as if this were now some kind of official policy category. Richter was not certain exactly what it meant, but he had a pretty good idea. He felt himself at the edge of a deep abyss that hid an unimaginably ugly world.

Conversation had already hit a lull. "How is Speer doing as head of war production?" he said, trying to sound genuinely curious. Albert Speer, Hitler's favorite architect, had replaced Fritz Todt as Reich Minister for Armaments and War Production after Todt died in a plane crash.

"Speer is very good. More effective than Todt. He has successfully increased production of virtually everything. Some say his need for free labor has undercut the programs that produce more direct results, but there is a price, after all, for everything."

Mueller smiled a wan smile. A veritable martyr to the cause. Richter held himself in check. He was going to have to swallow whatever this guy dished up if he wanted to get Elena Stein out of here.

"What do you produce in your factories?"

"Ball bearings. Other small metal parts. Primarily for tanks. Our Panzer divisions, the Tigers in particular, depend on our replacement parts." Mueller's voice was flat. Richter detected no hint of pride.

"My quarters." Mueller pointed ahead to an old homestead, perhaps a former farmhouse. It was the only structure in the compound Richter had seen so far that appeared not to have been built expressly for the camp. It had apparently been moved here from somewhere else. Plunked down crudely on top of a makeshift foundation. In spite of its age, it looked as impermanent as the rest of the camp. Set just inside the perimeter of barbed wire, the house did have a few stunted shrubs around it and a short stone walkway leading up to the front door.

"We moved my quarters, as well as the guards', in closer a few months ago because the Allies don't bomb the KZs themselves," Mueller said. "The camps appear to be off-limits for them. Our factories, too, are protected by this."

Without any apparent orders, the guards posted themselves around the perimeter of the house as Richter and his host stepped inside.

Indoors, the blast from a bevy of ceiling and floor fans made it feel considerably cooler. The furnishings in the main living area were sparse and unimpressive, with the exception of an ornate mahogany liquor cabinet that Mueller headed for directly.

"Drink, Major?" he inquired.

"Do you have gin?"

"I have everything."

"A gin with tonic water, then. Thank you."

"Where did you get your dueling scar?" Mueller asked as he made Richter's drink and poured a straight whiskey for himself.

"Heidelberg."

"The Reichsfuhrer has one he received at university in Munich. Smaller than yours, but he is quite proud of it."

Richter detected a note of scorn in this comment. Whether it was aimed at him or at Heinrich Himmler, he was uncertain.

Mueller handed him his drink and raised his own glass. "The Fuhrer," he said.

Richter raised his glass and drank. The Fuhrer be damned, he thought.

"So, Richter. How are our English friends? You must have some extraordinary stories to tell. Please. Sit down."

So Mueller knew about him. He supposed his applying for the pass to visit Kaisenher had alerted the SS. If Mueller knew about England, he must know who Richter's father was. If so, the knowledge didn't appear to faze him.

"I have a few stories," Richter said, taking an uncomfortable chair. "But I can't tell them. I haven't been debriefed by the Abwehr yet."

"Of course. We all know how efficient the Abwehr is." Mueller gave a slight smile. There had long been the suspicion, among the SS and others, that the Abwehr was not sufficiently enthusiastic about Hitler's agenda. Little did they know, thought Richter.

"Well Richter," Mueller said, changing gears, "you have missed some exciting years for Germany while you were off on your little holiday in England. We are reaching for a new destiny, a new order, on the continent of Europe." There seemed no real conviction behind Mueller's words. It was more as if he were reciting a speech he had learned somewhere. Perhaps someone had drummed it into him during SS training at Bad Toelz, Richter thought.

"We'll have to win this war before there is going to be any 'new destiny,'" he countered.

"Ah, but that's where you are wrong, my friend. Another drink?" Richter shook his head, no. Mueller poured himself a second whiskey. "We are not waiting," he said, testing his new drink. "We are forging a new order right now. In the middle of war."

"A war we're in danger of losing."

Mueller raised an eyebrow. "The war, my dear fellow, is being won. The war against the Jews. By this time next year, or perhaps the following, Europe's Jews will be no more. Gone forever. Kaput. The Fuhrer has ordered it."

Richter strained to hear a note of irony, but detected none.

"Ten years ago, Theodor Eicke turned Dachau into a model KZ. Now they stretch from France to the Ukraine and provide the Reich with much of its needs."

"I thought you didn't approve of using the Jews for labor, Sturmbannfuhrer."

Mueller stared at him, as if contradiction were not a familiar form of speech to him. "It's not the most efficient means to the desired end, I believe is what I said, Major. I do, however, appreciate the need. As well as some of the system's finer points. At Sachsenhausen, for instance, there are skilled prisoners who forge documents. They even counterfeit money. Mostly to pay spies, as I understand it. Prisoners can also be useful in scientific and medical studies. Women, I am told, are given special treatment in this regard, especially at Ravensbruck." Mueller gave this last comment a confidential man-to-man tone, apparently seeking to include Richter as one who would understand such things.

Richter cringed. Was this what was left of the German cause? It was like the underside of a rotted log in the woods, all worms and maggots.

He braced himself, knowing he was going to have to pull all the right strings to manipulate this man, and knowing too that the camp commander's ignorant prejudices would not make the task any easier. It was like trying to make a deal with the Devil.

But he couldn't resist one question that carried some risk. "I could not help but notice, Sturmbannfuher, that you share a name, or used to, with the head of the Gestapo. Is that just coincidence?"

For the first time, Mueller flashed what seemed a genuine smile. "Why? Would it worry you if it weren't?"

"No, not particularly." Richter waited a beat. When it appeared no specific answer was on the way, he held up his empty glass with an inquiring look.

"Another gin and tonic? Of course. A proper English drink," said Mueller, an amused glint in his eye. He got up and poured himself another whiskey while he was at it.

"To killing the Jews," Mueller said this time before he drank. Richter put the glass to his lips but did not drink. He worried Mueller might notice, but his host was distracted by a ringing telephone.

After a short exchange with someone on the other end of the line, Mueller said to Richter, "You're just in time for a new shipment, Major. Shall we go greet them?"

Noting his guest's hesitation, he added, "This shouldn't take long. As soon as we're done, we will return here and discuss whatever it is you need."

Richter got up, reluctantly, wondering what horrors might be in store.

"A Preview of Hell"

Richter followed Mueller silently back across the compound, to one of the uniform rows of low buildings just inside the front gate. A long line of women stood outside the first structure. Mueller led him through a side door.

Up some steps, a guard stood in an empty room, staring through a slit-window at something. "Take a look, Richter," Mueller said. "See what you've been missing."

The guard stepped aside to give him room. Through the strip of glass was a long narrow room with showerheads dotting the ceiling. The line of women was moving into this room. They were naked now. There must be a changing room at the far side, thought Richter, embarrassed to be staring down at the spectacle.

Mueller joined him at the window. "See any keepers?" he said. "Most of them are too dirty to touch, but there are exceptions. Among the non-Jews, of course." The final observation sounded sardonic, but Richter could not believe Mueller was either that sophisticated or that subversive.

He was gripped by a sudden apprehension. "What are they doing in this room?" he said.

Mueller grinned. "Delousing. We like to get them used to showering together. Sometimes it's the little things that break the pride. And one day we may be allowed to do more than clean them up." He did not elaborate. Richter did not need him to.

"Their men are across the way, doing the same thing. We keep them segregated here."

"Where are the children?"

"Not here." Mueller tapped the edge of the window. "This, by the way, is one-way glass. They can't see you."

The showers suddenly came on. Even through the thick walls, Richter could hear screams. He forced himself to watch. Some women were crying, some were on their knees or even lying down. Most sunk back toward the walls, huddled together trying to avoid the shower spray, but the showers were designed to hit everything in the room. There was no escape. The women shut their eyes. Some held their noses. Had Mueller lied to him? What was going on here?

After about a minute, the showers were turned off. The screaming died down. The women opened their eyes and looked around. Some laughed out loud. Others, including some of the stoical ones of before, cried. A door opened at the far end of the room and an SS man ordered them out.

"Come on," Mueller said. "Inspection time."

Richter could not shake the image of the showers. Had Elena had to go through that? She was so young, but that wouldn't have protected her. For the first time, really, he began to doubt she was still alive.

They entered an adjacent room where the women were being herded through another line, at the head of which each was being given a cursory inspection and passed along. "Dr. Roarke," Mueller said. "Unfortunately he's our only medical man right now. He is overworked."

Richter could see that much from the inspections, which lasted an average of twenty to thirty seconds. Dr. Roarke gave each woman a quick once-over, peered briefly into each orifice – mouth, nose, eyes, ears, vagina and anus – and passed her on. Occasionally, mostly with the older women, the examination was even quicker, and in each of these cases the woman was led away in a different direction from the others.

"Why are some of them being sent over there?" Richter said, pointing.

Mueller looked at him as if it were none of his business. "Medical reasons," he said, switching on an insincere grin. "They need something looked at more carefully."

This answer made sense. It was the older, less healthy-looking women who were being sent off from the others. But still, Richter felt a nagging doubt.

Women kept emerging from the showers in what seemed an endless stream. Many of them tried to cover their nakedness with hands and arms, but Richter had already become numbed to it. There was too much nakedness and too much suffering to absorb all at once. He felt no sexual arousal whatsoever, and was relieved that he did not. Mostly he felt embarrassed and ashamed.

Suddenly, Mueller stepped over to the line. Richter automatically followed him. Mueller addressed a young woman with long black hair which she had arranged to conceal her breasts. Her hands were over her sex. She had huge dark eyes.

"Your name?" he said.

The woman's reply was barely a whisper. "Muriel," she said.

"And where are you from, Muriel?" Mueller was making a distinct effort to be polite, Richter thought. As if he were addressing this naked, frightened woman in line outside a restaurant on the Unter den Linden.

"Arnsruhe. In Bavaria," she answered, her beautiful eyes downcast.

"Don't be frightened, Muriel," Mueller said in a calming tone. "You may find life here not so bad as you think." He touched her on the shoulder. Surprisingly to Richter, she did not flinch.

Mueller took a guard aside and pointed the woman out to him. Then he showed Richter into another room. Here, the women who had passed medical inspection were having their heads shaved by four matrons wielding their scissors and electric razors as roughly as if they were shearing sheep. In another line, some of the women were ordered to lie down on a table while another matron shaved their pubic hair. Mueller noticed Richter staring. "That is only for Jews," he said.

"We use the hair," Mueller said. There were piles of it where the four matrons were hard at work. "It makes good stuffing material for items for which we are short of rubber or cotton."

Mueller indicated to Richter it was time to go. He led the way back through the first room, where the woman named Muriel was about to be inspected. As he stepped outside, Richter glanced back at the young woman. Dr. Roarke was inspecting her mouth, but she had her eyes on Richter, full of a pleading he suspected held little hope.

Outside, the flat summer air now seemed cooler, almost soothing, in contrast to the stifling barracks. As they walked back across the compound, Richter took a chance and asked Mueller what he had told the guard.

"I told him to clean her up and bring her to my quarters. I need a new housekeeper and cook." Mueller glanced at Richter. "And, because he is new here, I told him to keep his hands off her."

"How do you know she can cook?"

Mueller grinned. "Really, Richter. Does it matter if she can cook?"

In spite of Mueller's earlier remark against fraternizing with Jews, Muriel was almost certainly a Jewess, Richter thought. He had pegged the commandant as a standard-issue Nazi Jew hater, but even if he wasn't, it amazed him an SS officer would so openly flaunt the racial laws prohibiting sexual contact between Aryans and Jews. He was not about to say anything, however, that might jeopardize the girl or his own mission here.

Back at Mueller's quarters, they settled in with another round of drinks. "All right, Richter. What is it you need from me?" Mueller said – somewhat impatiently, Richter thought.

"There's a young woman listed on your manifest. Her name is Elena Stein. From near Eberbach. I would like her released into my custody." To Mueller, this must sound no different from his own prospective dalliance with Muriel, he supposed.

Mueller appeared caught off guard. This was evidently not the request he had been expecting. He inspected Richter with a calculating look. "This is of course a highly irregular request. Why do you want her released?"

What he's really wondering, Richter thought, was, Why didn't you simply have your father ask the SS to release her? "She's an old acquaintance from my university days," he said. The truth, or at least a portion of it.

Mueller grinned conspiratorially. "A Jew professor's daughter, perhaps?"

"Not exactly." Richter wanted to give out as few details as possible.

Mueller fell silent a moment. Considering the angles. Then, brightening visibly, he said, "I have an idea, Richter. Are you a gambling man?"

"Only when I have to be."

"Are you any good with firearms?"

Richter felt a chill at what Mueller might be up to. "That depends on what kind of firearms we're talking about," he said.

"Let's say rifles. A little marksmanship contest."

"For what?"

"Assuming I have your young woman here, she will be the prize. Winner takes all. You win, you get her."

"And if I lose?"

"You lose, you shoot her."

"I didn't come all this way to shoot her," said Richter, trying to play Mueller's game without losing his composure.

"That's the only way I will release her." This time when Mueller grinned, Richter could see his skull outlined beneath the taut skin.

There was a knock at the door. Mueller answered it, asking first who it was and putting a hand automatically on the holstered sidearm hanging from a wall hook beside the entryway. Richter couldn't hear the answer, but when the door was opened it revealed Dr. Roarke, a guard beside him. Roarke beckoned to someone behind him, and Muriel emerged from the shadows looking touchingly vulnerable in a long loose, pale white dress. Her hair had not been shaved. It was piled up on her head and held in place with a plain white clasp. She was barefoot. Younger than Richter had first thought. Maybe fifteen or sixteen.

Mueller took her immediately in tow. For the first time, Richter realized his host was at least a little drunk. "A lovely sight. A lovely sight, isn't she, gentlemen?" Mueller said. "Almost another Rachel Stern, eh, doctor." Putting an arm around her shoulder, he took her off to one side and spoke to her confidentially in a low voice, to all appearances genuinely interested in her. Once again, Richter was surprised by the girl's apparent lack of fear. She listened intently to Mueller without saying a word in reply. Eventually, he led her off into the kitchen.

When they were gone, Richter asked Roarke, "'Rachel Stern?' There have been others?" Roarke gave him an appraising look, then spoke with an accent Richter could not place. "This is not the first, no," he said, "but she's one of the healthiest specimens I've ever seen here. She must have been living in the countryside. Somewhere where the food supply is still plentiful."

Richter's impulse was to ask about Rachel Stern, but he held his tongue. Maybe Muriel's arrival would take Mueller's mind off the "contest" he had proposed. Richter made a quick decision to pry whatever information he could from Roarke, who seemed at least on the surface more human than Mueller. "Doctor," he said, "do you know a young woman in the camp named Elena Stein? A girl, really. Only a teenager." He looked toward the kitchen. "Like this one."

Roarke, in the process of lighting a cigarette, gave him a suspicious look. "Why, may I ask, do you want to know?"

Before Richter could answer, a beaming Mueller was back in the room. "Muriel's first test," he said. "She will fix us a little something to eat. Roarke, you are just in time. Richter and I were about to engage in a little shooting wager."

Roarke stared at Mueller. He said nothing. As if he understood what the wager would be, or knew not to ask.

Richter decided he had nothing to lose. There had been something in Roarke's response that made him think Elena might still be alive. In spite of his lack of recent practice, Richter thought he could out-shoot anyone who wasn't a competition-level sharpshooter. If he won this bet, he won Elena's freedom. If he lost, he would refuse to shoot her. Perhaps he'd be able to buy her from Mueller. Bargain for her, somehow. Or as a last resort, there was always his father to call on, though that option had its own set of risks.

Mueller ducked into another room and returned with a 7.92mm bolt-action Mannlicher, a vintage rifle probably thirty or forty years old, but in fine condition by outward appearances. He was smiling. He acted as though he had made this sort of wager before. "You realize if you win, Richter, I could be putting my neck in a noose by letting your Jewess go."

He looked around, as if counting noses. "I trust Dr. Roarke implicitly, or he would not be here," he said. "Roarke here, by the way, is an American. Born and bred."

"From just outside Chicago," Roarke said with a touch of pride, tapping ashes into a glass he cradled in his lap. "Oak Park. I grew up with the writer Hemingway. My parents were German, of course."

"Hemingway is a favorite of mine. A fine writer," Richter said. "I hear he's hunting U-boats off Cuba."

"Always the dreamer," Roarke smiled.

"I've never been to America," Richter said, wondering how this mild-looking man had ever wound up at Kaisenher. He looked to be in his forties, of medium height and build, balding in back. Totally unprepossessing.

"You must go some day. It's an incredible country. So different from Europe."

"Maybe after the war," Richter said.

Mueller laughed. "Our Dr. Roarke has a touch of what ails Himmler's doctor, the Finn, Kersten, who is forever wheedling Jewish lives out of the Reichsfuhrer. There are some who say Himmler pays him in spared lives. Dr. Roarke has a similar soft streak. Perhaps it's an American trait."

"My countrymen are proving to be hard fighters though, are they not, mein Sturmbannfuhrer?" Roarke smiled, apparently confident he could say such a thing in safety.

Mueller glared at him, but sounded more playful than threatening as he replied, "They haven't tried to land in France yet. They know what awaits them there. The Russians are the only fighters we have to worry about.

"Come. Let's step outside," he said to Richter. Roarke stubbed out his cigarette and followed along behind them. Somewhat reluctantly, it appeared to Richter.

They walked out beyond the SS guards, who seemed to take little notice of them. Nearly a hundred meters away, closely supervised prisoners were clearing away a large pile of rocks and other debris. They were using their bare hands, a couple of wheelbarrows and little else.

"We will see who can bring down a Jew in the fewest shots," Mueller said. "Whoever does, wins."

"I prefer to shoot at an inanimate object," Richter countered.

"Ah, my friend. You miss the point. Only one part of the contest is marksmanship. The other part is the target. Whether your aim remains steady with a live target in your sights."

Richter scanned the gray sky, looking for a way out. The heat seemed even more oppressive than before. Sweat trickled from beneath his uniform hat brim. He rubbed his forehead with the back of his hand to wipe the moisture away from his eyes, and gently stroked his scar in contemplation.

"In that case, I have a counterproposal," he said. "One that includes a live target."

"Yes. I'm listening."

"Let the bet ride on one shot. I will knock that sentry down without killing him, or even wounding him." Richter pointed to a sentry standing in a guard tower about the same distance as the prisoners at the rock pile. "If I fail, you win the bet."

Mueller laughed. "You really do love the Jews, don't you," he said. "But I accept your bet. I don't believe you can do it. Not in one shot."

He handed the rifle to Richter. "Good luck. You're going to need it."

Richter wondered if his own expression looked as doubtful about the possibilities as Roarke's did. He examined the Mannlicher slowly and carefully, trying to get a feel for it. The weapon was similar to a bolt-action Mauser he had practiced with as a child at Orienbad. A modified sniper's model with one round in the chamber. He had at least a fifty-fifty chance at doing what he'd said he would do with it, he thought.

"Your play," Mueller prompted. "But do not kill my guard. There will be consequences if you do."

Mueller might well have him shot on the spot if he killed the sentry, Richter suddenly realized.

He raised the rifle to his shoulder and whispered a quick prayer to himself. The gunsight looked true, but to try it out was really the only way to know for sure, and he had no practice round to test it.

Mueller was eyeing him carefully, enjoying the game. "One shot," he reminded.

Richter held his breath and gave himself a countdown to steady his aim.

He squeezed the trigger.

The Mannlicher kicked against his shoulder, its retort quickly swallowed up by the wide open spaces and nearby forest. Nothing else happened. The sentry spun around a moment, as if puzzled.

"You lose," Mueller said, his glee undisguised.

"Herr Commandant," Roarke pointed toward the sentry tower. The guard had suddenly slumped against the railing, his helmet tumbling toward the ground, where it landed against a large rock with a sharp clanging sound.

"Get me that helmet," Mueller shouted to the nearest SS man.

Richter said a silent prayer of thanks as the helmet was being retrieved.

Mueller grabbed it from the guard and inspected it. He shook his head and handed the helmet to Roarke.

"Nice shot," Roarke said, holding the headgear up so Richter could see the crease his bullet had made in it.

Richter looked back at the sentry, who was standing now, rubbing his head, his weapon nowhere in sight.

"Let's go back in," Mueller said. His voice was like ice.

As they reentered the house Mueller again went straight for the bar and began mixing a drink, but this time did not offer Richter one.

He took a long swig of whiskey before he spoke. "That was an impressive shot, Richter. But you still lost the bet."

"I knocked him down. I didn't kill him. That's what I said I would do."

"You didn't knock him down. He was against the railing, holding onto it. He wasn't down."

"That's a technicality," Richter said, frustrated and starting to let his anger show. "I took you to be a man of honor. I won the bet."

"No you didn't. You lost. Get your pistol ready."

Richter locked stares with Mueller. The man was truly evil, he thought. Maybe he should have used the bullet on him. His hopes for freeing Elena Stein ebbed. *There must be another way* kept ringing in his ears.

"I'm not going to shoot her," he said.

"Then I guess I'll have to," Mueller said. "Dr. Roarke, are you familiar with a – what was it, Richter? – Elena something? Stein, I believe you said."

Richter watched as a look passed between the two men. Roarke appeared confused, as if the rules of the game had suddenly been altered. Richter hoped this was a signal Mueller was only toying with him. That he was bluffing about shooting her.

"Yes. I believe so," Roarke said in carefully measured reply. "If she's who I think she is, shooting would probably be a relief for her." The words, thought Richter, held a mild tone of rebuke.

"Well then, bring her–" The sound of something breaking in the kitchen interrupted Mueller. He sprang up and rushed toward it. Roarke and Richter followed.

Muriel was on the floor. At first Richter thought she had fainted. But then he saw the large red stain spreading across her white dress, at the abdomen. A long wooden-handled kitchen knife stained red was on the floor beside her amid shards of a broken plate.

Mueller put his hand on where the blood appeared to be flowing from, as if he could stop the bleeding. Roarke kneeled down beside him and felt the girl's neck for a pulse. "She's dead," he said. "Or will be in a few seconds."

"Whoever left that knife in here will pay," Mueller said. He meant it, Richter thought. This man who presided over death every day appeared genuinely shaken by this one. Richter supposed he had been looking forward to an adventure with the girl. Maybe she'd even reached some small corner of humanity that remained in him. She had stabbed herself in the stomach, an incredibly painful way to die.

Richter was hit with his own set of emotions, and wondered that his reaction was so much stronger than it had been to the death of his younger sister in the rubble of Berlin. His sadness extended far beyond this poor victim on Mueller's kitchen floor. "I'm sorry," he said – to the girl, more than to Mueller.

Mueller stared up at him with an oddly detached look in his eyes. His words were ice cold, completely sober. They bore a welcome message. "I've changed my mind," he said. "Take your damned woman. Just don't tell anybody you got her from me."

Then he tacked on a curious postscript. "She may have lost some of her charm by now," he said. "Don't blame me. I didn't know she was somebody's sweetheart."

"To me she was only a Jew," Mueller said.

CHAPTER XVII

Cohen was caught unawares by the turn of events on Thursday morning. Richter did not appear in court. Benevides, alone at the defense table, arose and announced his client, Mr. Johann von Richter – the "von" added this once presumably out of deference to court documents – was petitioning the court that he be extradited for trial in England. The lawyer then read a short prepared statement he said was written by Richter.

Raoul Zamora, seated among the remnants of his own troops, let his eyes show pure delight at this latest development. That was to be expected, Cohen thought. He wondered, however, at the lack of reaction from the prosecutor's three remaining advisors. Particularly Sir Anthony Wilde, who Richter had become accustomed to trying to read when he was looking for the prosecution team's state of mind. Now Wilde, normally an open book, was as poker-faced as the other two as they shuffled papers and whispered among themselves with no sign of recognition for what was happening around them.

The bearded man didn't appear to be in the courtroom today. Neither did John Weaver, who Cohen once again kind of missed. The rest of the media was there, making up for any lack of excitement at the prosecutor's table. Their palpable anticipation of more action, however, was cut short by the judge, who abruptly adjourned the proceedings so he could deliberate on Richter's motion. "We will reconvene at two p.m.," he said, and rapped his gavel in dismissal.

It was warmer than usual outside. The sky was cloudy but bright, the mid-morning streets of La Negra nearly deserted. Cohen, for once drawing an easy breath and feeling no pain in his leg, walked along at a smart pace trying to get his thoughts together. He started toward the lake, but halfway there darker clouds began to roll in from the mountains and obscured the sun. A few drops of rain fell. He turned back and headed, in no real hurry now and with no premeditation, toward the prison.

Standing outside the old fortress, thinking about the prisoner inside its walls, Cohen could still not draw a true bead on the man. He had to be guilty of something, but so far in court no one had really pinned a specific crime on him. Cohen had gotten little feel for Richter watching him react to testimony. Whatever his emotions, he masked them well. And whatever his connections to Heinrich Mueller and Kaisenher, so far they seemed blameless, even commendable.

There was no way they would let him go now, Cohen thought, no matter what the evidence. The judge would have to extradite him. Hell, Richter himself was asking to be extradited. But why? Cohen thought about Anders Hardy. The memory was unsettling. Did Richter understand the British were out to get him?

He also wondered about Elena Stein. She had not returned his call.

Rain still threatened, but for some reason his spirits lifted as he reluctantly turned away and headed for Miguel's, where he had eaten with Weaver. Things were happening. The afternoon held promise. He might yet, he thought, even salvage something for his magazine assignment. In any case, he was hungry. He felt alive. It was a feeling he had not always possessed since he'd lost Rachel, and he treasured the moments it came to him.

* * * *

"I would like to make a few observations about this hearing before I announce my decision." The lilting, almost lyrical quality of the judge's deep-throated Spanish accent gave his words an added power. The courtroom this afternoon was more packed than Cohen had ever seen it, and silent with anticipation. Johann Richter was back. So was John Weaver, but Cohen had arrived too late to sit anywhere near him. Opting for his drawing materials over a notepad for the moment, he looked around for a likely subject.

"The evidence," the judge began, "presented against Johann Richter during this hearing has been almost entirely circumstantial. The case against him in the death of Yvonne Duchamps has been dropped. The case the prosecution has presented against him in the death of Christine

Johns is marred by evidence so obscured by the passage of time as to make most of it unacceptable before any reasonable court of law. The chief prosecutor, in private chambers, has outlined to me additional evidence he considers pertinent, but it's all of a similar nature, obscure and unsubstantiated. The link between Mr. Richter and his perpetration of, or direct involvement in, any specific indictable crime, remains to be seen. And it certainly remains to be proven.

"Furthermore, the question of the defendant's entire role in the Second World War, it seems to me, has only been clouded by these proceedings. The often confusing and even contradictory evidence as to just what his role actually was, leads this court nowhere but to the conclusion that Mr. Richter was indeed an officer in the German army's Abwehr intelligence branch – in itself perhaps something of a negative distinction, but certainly no crime. In several instances, at least, Mr. Richter appears to have acted as honorably as possible, given the circumstances under which he was operating at the time. It is said that for those who opposed Hitler inside Germany, a sense of fate and God's will was all-important when they were laying their lives on the line. Mr. Richter's actions, for the most part, appear to have been consistent with this guiding ideal."

The judge paused for a sip of something from a glass he always kept beside him. Cohen, who had just crumpled up a clumsy sketch of Raoul Zamora, now began one of the man who presided over the courtroom. He was beginning to think Richter might be let off the hook after all, regardless of the request for extradition, and wondered if the British had somehow maneuvered for just such a result.

"I, for one," the judge said, "would like to see some of the mystery cleared up." He cast a look at Richter that seemed to say this was his last chance to speak up.

"Unfortunately, Mr. Richter has chosen neither to testify nor to make any statement of explanation to us. He has decided only to request extradition. That is of course his prerogative. But it leaves me with little choice. After consultation with both Mr. Zamora and Mr. Benevides, and with some regret on my part, I am hereby ordering the extradition of Johann von Richter to Great Britain, there to stand trial for the murder of Miss Christine Johns. Mr. Richter's subsequent disposition, as soon as arrangements can be made, will be entirely in the hands of that country. Perhaps his trial there will serve to illuminate some of the darkness we have been left with here. Personally, I hope so. I am taking this action, let it be noted, at the direct request of Mr. Richter himself, as expressed to me by his counsel."

The judge looked around the courtroom expectantly, as if he were an auctioneer waiting for a final bid. When he heard none, he rapped his gavel. "This hearing is adjourned."

The announcement was lost in a general clamor the judge did not try to quiet. He stood and departed the room. Flashbulbs popped, as if in celebration. Spectators stood and milled aimlessly about. A low hum, the chorus of muted voices, rose to the vaulted ceiling and hovered there.

Cohen had barely finished an outline of the judge's face. The outcome of the hearing, though not unexpected, felt to him somehow too sudden, as if it had dropped out of the sky from nowhere. As confused in his reactions as everyone else, he watched Clay Johns, in court without his wife today, hurry out with an unhappy look on his face. Raoul Zamora, seemingly well pleased with his unearned victory, paced up and down the length of his table shaking hands with the remaining members of his staff and anyone else available and willing.

On the far side of the room, Johann Richter held Mr. Benevides by the elbow. It looked, it seemed to Cohen, as if he were trying to cheer his lawyer up. The defendant himself appeared in better spirits than Cohen could ever recall having seen him in before. Perhaps it was his relief at closing out this phase of the ordeal.

Richter was not immediately whisked away, as he usually was. The cameras, microphones and reporters began to converge on him, but he waved them away. To Cohen's amazement, they did not persist, and actually backed off to a respectful distance. A few noisy shots from the small army of flash cameras present, and a couple of throwaway questions ignored by the prisoner, marked their only protest.

Marie Renault, who had been sitting beside Clay Johns at the front of the courtroom, now pushed her way through the press cordon and approached Richter with a tentative air. The flashbulbs let go a salvo of miniature explosions. Cohen could see Richter smile and say something to her. Over the general din, he couldn't hear what Richter was saying, but whatever it was, it seemed to put the woman more at ease. She even smiled briefly. Cohen watched them hug and exchange a few more words before Marie Renault turned and walked away.

Richter leaned over and whispered something privately to one of his guards, each of whom was heavily armed. This man then addressed another armed mestizo planted protectively in similar fashion on Richter's other side. At a signal, their little entourage – one guard in front of Richter, one behind, and several at the sides – began a slow procession back down the courtroom aisle, parting the international press corps as it went.

On his own way out of the courtroom, Cohen was accosted by John Weaver.

"How about a drink?" Weaver said. "Nothing like a good war crimes trial to work up a thirst."

It was early, but Weaver had proved a pleasant dinner companion the night before and right now a drink sounded like a good idea. Cohen wondered how the man was going to make deadline for the *Baltimore Sun* tonight, but he wasn't about to sweat it if Weaver wasn't going to.

* * * *

Through saloon doors, they entered a place called La Cucaracha – The Cockroach – chosen by Weaver, who said he loved the name. They took a small table by the wall. Weaver reached inside the pocket of his suit jacket, produced a rolled up London tabloid and handed it to Cohen.

"For a laugh," he said.

Cohen unfolded the paper to an enormous front page headline that trumpeted, *J'Accuse!* The subhead read, "Daughter-in-law of Earl of Darbyshire claims Nazi is a murderer." The dateline was La Negra, and the story was a lurid rendition of Anne Johns' most recent testimony.

"Great stuff, huh," Weaver said, lighting up a Camel. "Shades of Emile Zola defending Dreyfus. Wouldn't it be a kick if we could all write like that?"

Cohen smiled. He had a fleeting thought about his lapsed assignment for *World Horizons*, but quickly banished it, along with the prick of guilt that came with it. He would get to it, he told himself. Soon. Very soon.

"Actually, they've got some pretty good background details," Weaver said, pointing to the paper. "If you read between the lines, it's obvious somebody must be leaking to them."

British Intelligence came most immediately to mind for Cohen. This place reminded him of the Prado Bar, and had already given him some gloomy thoughts on whether Anders Hardy would contact him again.

They started off with shots of tequila, toasting everything from the completion of the hearing to the joys of good, honest journalism. After about an hour of this, Weaver was totally, absolutely drunk, in Cohen's opinion – an opinion strongly held but weakly focused, his attention span having shrunk to no more than several seconds at a pop. Drunk, that's what Weaver was. Cohen himself, of course, was well under control. He suspected, still, in the back of his mind, there had been an ulterior motive lurking behind the American's inviting him here, though for the moment what that could possibly be eluded him. It occurred to him that for the amount of time they'd spent together, Weaver had asked him surprisingly little of a personal nature. The man was a reporter, after all. Where was his curiosity?

Something else that still eluded him was a believable reason Weaver had sent him out after Elena Stein. Even if he *was* slightly tipsy, Cohen wasn't buying the explanation that Weaver was too over-the-hill or too lazy to go find her himself. But nothing else appeared to make sense either. In fact, he thought in a flash of slightly sodden illumination, very little about John Weaver made much sense.

"You know, maybe the Nazis were right about a few things after all," Weaver suddenly piped up between quaffs of the local brew he had switched to from the tequila. "Look at Korea, Eastern Europe, the Mideast. Indochina. Look at the friggin' barrel the Commies have got us over now. Hitler wanted to get rid of old Joe Stalin. Maybe we shoulda let'im."

Weaver raised his glass. "To the–" He stared at Cohen. "No, the Nazis were still bastards. Screw them too. Here's to Churchill and FDR. Our boys." To this, Cohen was only too happy to drink. In return, he toasted Eisenhower and MacArthur for his new American compatriot, kicking off a new round of drinking to the health of familiar names from the war against the Fascists.

Eventually, the range of their praise broadened and they were in the middle of yet another toast, this one to the fine courtroom performance of Mr. Benevides regardless of the cause he was arguing, when John Weaver suddenly broke off in mid-sentence, his inebriated camaraderie evaporating into thin air.

Cohen swiveled slightly. Standing beside him was the bearded man.

CHAPTER XVIII

"Good evening, Mr. Cohen. Permit me to introduce myself. My name is Leland Powell. I would like to talk to you for a moment, if I might."

Cohen looked at John Weaver. "It's all right," Weaver said. "I know Mr. Powell. Why don't we go over to a booth. It's more private."

Cohen felt completely sober by the time they were seated in the booth. Leland Powell sat across from Cohen and Weaver. He was tall and dressed rather formally for the surroundings. The neat, close-cropped Edwardian beard gave him a look of authority.

"I suppose you're wondering what in bloody blazes this is all about," said Powell with a gentle, almost soft smile. The accent was Oxbridge.

"You might say that." Cohen was in fact wondering why John Weaver had never told him about this man, even after being told by Cohen he thought he was being followed by a white man with a beard. And after seeing his sketch of the man.

A waitress interrupted and took their order for drinks. Powell ordered a beer. Cohen was tempted, but he followed Weaver's lead and asked for coffee.

"I'm told you are a writer, Mr. Cohen," Powell said when she was gone. "I must ask you to keep everything I tell you confidential. You cannot write about it for *World Horizons*. Or anyone else. That is clearly understood, is it?"

"I'll keep your secrets." Cohen wasn't entirely sure he wanted to hear them. "That's assuming I don't come by them some other way," he said.

"Splendid. There's a good chap. Perhaps I'd better start, then, by introducing you more properly to Mr. Weaver here, if I may." Powell held his hand out in Weaver's direction. "John Weaver, of the American Central Intelligence Agency."

Cohen turned to Weaver, who smiled a bit sheepishly. "I hope you don't mind, Cohen. I'm afraid I'm not a brother journalist, after all." Weaver no longer sounded drunk.

Cohen was not sure how he felt about this information. Vaguely betrayed, was the best he could come up with.

"And I am with the British Secret Intelligence Service," Powell said. "MI6."

Cohen felt the same chill at this pronouncement that Anders Hardy had produced in him two days ago. It brought back Rachel. The guilt. Worries about Elena Stein. It was a good bet these men knew as much about him and his past as Hardy did. Maybe more. He decided to make a clean breast of it before they forced him to confess anything that might be dangerous to him, or to somebody else.

He took a deep breath and tried to clear his mind. "I'm familiar with it. I worked for you once, in Israel."

"Yes, we know, old chap," Powell said. "We wondered if you would own up to it."

"Why is that?" Cohen said, deciding he might as well shoot the works, find out just how much they did know and where he stood with them.

"You left there rather abruptly, didn't you. There were some who wondered why."

"I didn't like what you were doing in Israel," Cohen echoed what he had told Hardy. "So yes, I left."

"Without contacting your control officer," Powell said. "Very poor spycraft, Cohen."

"Spycraft be damned. You were sabotaging the Israelis."

"Well, that's beside the point now, isn't it old boy. But so is this discussion. What you did in Israel is a thing of the past. We're willing to leave it there. We have more immediate concerns here in La Negra, don't we."

"Which are. . ."

"We're here," Powell said, "because we have reason to believe the Soviets have penetrated British Intelligence. We should jolly well be shouting 'rape,' we have been buggered so thoroughly, if the evidence is to be believed. And it goes way back, back before Richter's connection to our organization during the war."

Powell gave Cohen a significant look. A punchline was on the way.

"We think, in fact, Richter might hold the key that would allow us to uncover our moles. We'd like to get him back to England. Or at least to somewhere safe. Somewhere we can control. He's in danger here."

"What kind of danger?"

"There are several former intelligence agents here in La Negra. Rogue elements, if you will. Bad eggs no longer in our basket but still causing trouble. We believe they're here to protect their colleagues who are still in service. Our moles."

"How can they do that?"

"By killing Richter," Powell said without a hint of emotion. "Weaver here was assigned to keep tabs on you to keep from giving this bunch any hint that we might be on to them. That we know they're in La Negra, and what they're up to. They would expect CIA to be mucking about down here."

"Have you ever heard the name 'Anders Hardy'?" Weaver abruptly threw at him.

Cohen wondered if he were being tested. If so, he was about to deliver a failing answer. "No," he lied. "Not that I recall."

"A rather small, rather dapper man, very proper British speech?" Powell said. "He might be using another name. Bloody well should be, anyhow."

Cohen shook his head, no.

"We now believe that during the war, Anders Hardy was the leader of a clique inside MI6 operating hand in glove with the Abwehr, the German secret service. It's not that they sabotaged our war effort. We don't believe they did. Not directly, at any rate. What these people did, strange as it may seem, was to do everything they could to ensure Hitler stayed alive. Particularly later in the war."

Hardy had told him something similar, he remembered. But not the part about the Abwehr. "I thought the fellow who ran the Abwehr," he said, "was supposed to be a closet anti-Nazi. How could your people have protected Hitler through him?"

"Very good, Cohen. Quite on the mark. Admiral Canaris, the man of whom you speak, was not however the only powerful man inside the Abwehr. Others were not so sympathetic to the anti-Hitler movement that was gaining support among the officer class. These others were the ones our fellows, our renegades, worked through. Between them, they eventually succeeded in ousting Canaris altogether."

"And why, pray tell, did anybody in MI6 want to protect Hitler?"

Hardy had not answered this question, had said they were simply following orders.

"We're not entirely certain. Perhaps that was not their ultimate objective. It was the effect, though, wasn't it, when they continually undercut the German brass who were trying to get rid of Hitler. They went so far as to filter information on the plots against him back to the SS and Gestapo through the German legation in Switzerland, to make it look more credible."

Powell's eyes searched for the waitress, who had yet to deliver their drinks. Not finding her, he looked at Cohen as if asking whether he had any questions.

When none were forthcoming, Powell dropped a piece of the puzzle that seemed to fit. "For what it's worth," he said, "we believe they were taking their cue from Moscow. In itself, that perhaps wouldn't matter so much, but we now believe our renegades, most of them, are still in place and helping the Soviets steal our most sensitive weapons secrets."

"It's something more than just 'believe,'" Weaver interjected pointedly. "We pretty much *know*."

Powell frowned but did not disagree. "Recent events, unfortunately, have borne that out. We are now virtually certain there was a 'third man,' someone highly placed on our side, who tipped off Burgess and MacLean just before they went to ground in Russia last year. You remember that unfortunate episode? Two chaps in our Foreign Office who turned out to have been Communists since their Cambridge days in the '30s."

Cohen nodded.

"This third man was at first thought to be Anders Hardy, who was forced to resign shortly after the defections of Burgess and MacLean. But then, I regret to say, an old school chum of mine, Kim Philby, came under suspicion and was also forced to leave MI6. Ending, I daresay, a brilliant career. But it hasn't solved the problem. Whatever the truth of the accusations against either of these two gentlemen, we now know" – he gave a nod to John Weaver – "there are other Soviet moles in our organization."

"The CIA, though, thinks Hardy and Philby are key figures in all this. Maybe *the* key figures," Weaver said, sounding almost sarcastic.

"We don't necessarily disagree, do we," Powell said a bit peevishly. "Our American friends think we dropped the ball on this one. We're fully aware Hardy and Philby knew each other socially at one point. They had plenty of opportunity. We just haven't been able to prove anything yet."

Powell took a deep breath. "The Americans aren't the only ones stirred up about all this. MI5, our domestic intelligence branch, is all over us about it as well. Two years ago, we uncovered Klaus Fuchs' work for the Soviets during the Manhattan Project at Los Alamos—"

"*Finally,*" Weaver noted dryly. "Meanwhile, we give the Rosenbergs the electric chair for compromising our nuclear weapons program, while our English friends here sentence Klaus Fuchs to fourteen easy-time years in prison for doing the same."

"There's more housecleaning still to be done, obviously," Powell said with a touch of exasperation, "but without Fuchs, you wouldn't have the Rosenbergs. Or Harry Gold or David Greenglass."

Before Weaver could respond, Cohen switched the subject back to something that still puzzled him. "Why would Stalin, of all people, have wanted Hitler protected?" he said, wondering if Stalin were the unnamed man behind the anonymous orders Hardy had said he'd recognize. He was wracking his brain to remember what Terry Harper had said about this Kim Philby who Powell had just mentioned.

"Stalin was once an admirer of Hitler's," Powell said. "The invasion of Russia was a slap in the face. A lover's rejection, if you will. Like they say, never underestimate the wrath of a psychopathic mass murderer scorned," the MI6 man smiled. "But now he's being driven by tactical reasons." The smile dimmed. "Once he knew the war was won, what Stalin feared most was a separate peace, one directed against him between Germany and the West. The man is certifiably paranoid, but this idea was not so far-fetched. Plenty of German officers – including Johann Richter's father – were hoping to make just such an accommodation with the Western Allies. If Hitler had died in '43 or '44, it might've happened. We know Stalin vetoed plans by his own people to assassinate *der Fuhrer*. Hitler was Stalin's best insurance against a separate peace."

"On the other hand," Weaver grinned, "maybe Stalin just wanted to capture him alive and put him in the Moscow Zoo."

"And these moles?" Cohen said. "Richter can help you find them, you think."

"Anders Hardy ran Johann Richter for MI6 during the war," Powell said. "We believe he recruited Christine Johns to keep an eye on Richter for him. Instead, she told Richter what Hardy was up to. Richter knows who has been naughty, or not so nice. We're not certain how much he knows, but it should be plenty, with the connections he had to British Intelligence and to his father, who was a major conspirator against Hitler. He may have the goods on Hardy. Perhaps even on Kim Philby and the rest." Powell looked to Weaver for support. Weaver nodded his confirmation.

"So what exactly is your role in all this?" Cohen said.

"Philby, to the best of our knowledge, is on the sidelines for now. But Anders Hardy is here in La Negra. I am here, or rather *we* are here, in an official capacity, to keep an eye on him and his crew. This is complicated somewhat because they have powerful allies in government now, our government, some of whom were involved in all this during the war and prefer not to see it come to light."

Powell paused, all hint of good humor leaving his eyes. "That said," he added, "*un*officially I am here to pay a debt to Christine Johns. It's time for our Mr. Hardy to take a fall. A bloody big one."

"You knew Christine Johns, then," Cohen said.

"Yes. Quite well."

Cohen and Powell stared at one another.

"Quite well," Powell repeated.

Cohen got the message. "I thought Richter was supposed to have killed her," he said.

"He didn't."

"How do you know that?"

"Would you really like to know?"

"Yes. I would."

"John, would you do the honors? Out in the black sedan with embassy plates, on the far side of the plaza."

Weaver got up and left the bar. Cohen and Powell small-talked about La Negra until he returned a few minutes later. He brought with him a handsome young man in his late teens or early twenties. Powell got up and let the newcomer slide to the inside of the booth, directly across from Cohen. Weaver took his former seat at Cohen's side.

Powell made the introductions.

"Mr. Cohen, this is Elliot Johns. Elliot, Michael Cohen." They shook hands across the table. Elliot Johns said nothing. He looked a little nervous. His eyes periodically sought out the table top.

"Elliot was there, the night his sister was murdered," Weaver said. "He—"

The waitress finally returned with Powell's beer and the two coffees.

"One more coffee, please," Powell said, without consulting Elliot Johns. "Pronto. Gracias."

"He saw some things," Weaver picked back up when the waitress was gone.

"Like everyone else," Powell said, "I assumed Richter had done it. Then this young man came forward."

"I decided it was now or never, when I heard about Richter's trial," Elliot Johns said in the same clipped, upper-class tones of his brother Clay, his rendition undercut by a voice even softer than Powell's. He sounded younger than he looked.

"There's a good lad. Why don't you just tell Mr. Cohen the whole story," Powell said.

The young man looked up at Cohen, as if inquiring whether he wanted to hear it.

"I would appreciate it," Cohen said.

"Well," he began, staring again at the table top as he spoke, "it was hot that night, and I was having trouble sleeping. I thought I could hear someone out by the pool, so I got up and wandered outside, where there was a breeze and a full moon. I could see out past the tennis courts, the pool, the hedgerows, pretty well all the way out to where the woodlands began.

"I thought I heard whispering, so I crept out to the hedgerow that blocked the pool off from the house and snuck into a little hideaway I had built for myself inside the bushes." He looked again at Cohen. "I was only nine years old at the time, now wasn't I," he said, apparently feeling a need to explain. "When I peeked out from behind the leaves, I could tell someone was in the pool. At first I couldn't see them, but then they whispered again and I could make out two heads together at the far end, near the diving board.

"I pretended I was a spy, and they were Nazi generals making plans to invade England. I was to report to Churchill directly. The PM was an old friend of father's. Nothing happened for a while, but I knew I had to bide my time. Spies do that sort of thing, you know." With no sign of irony, Johns stopped to put cream and sugar in the coffee that had just been placed in front of him. For all Cohen's skepticism about the evening's proceedings, it was difficult for him to believe Clay John's young brother could be making this story up.

"Finally," Johns continued, "one of them climbed out of the pool and onto the diving platform, where I could see her against the moonlight. It was my sister Christine. She was stark naked. I was, fair to say, fascinated. She dived in cleanly. She was an expert diver, a wonderful athlete. Then the other one got up to dive. Sans bathing costume as well. It took me a few seconds to realize who she was. My brother's wife; my 'Aunt Anne' I called her back then."

"Anne Johns, you mean."

"Yes."

"So in her testimony she was lying," Cohen said.

"You mean about her and Christine."

"Yes. Among other things."

Elliot Johns looked at Powell, who shrugged his okay. "She made some major omissions, is perhaps the fairest way to put it."

"Go on with your story," Powell prompted.

"By the time Anne stepped up on that platform and dived in, I was one bloody confused little spy. Nine is a bit young to understand such things. When I saw them kiss, though, I knew enough to understand something slightly improper was going on. That I could not simply run out and join them for a bathe.

"Eventually they got out of the pool, toweled off, put nightgowns on and ran back up to the house. I was frightfully put about by the whole thing, so I lay back to mull it over and promptly fell asleep." Elliot Johns grinned. "Must have missed nap time that day.

"I was awakened by someone else coming from the house. A man. Half-asleep, I thought at first it was my brother Clay, which surprised me because he was recuperating at the time and rarely left his room. But it was Johann Richter, I quickly realized. I liked Richter. No one really talked about it, but it was understood he'd helped get Clay out of his prisoner of war camp in Germany. And he had always been very good with me and Samantha, who were much younger than everyone else generally attending these weekend affairs. But something told me not to approach him now. So I stayed hidden and watched. He had a small bag slung over his shoulder and moved toward the woods, where he disappeared.

"I headed back for the house. It was still night. When I passed the door to Christine's room upstairs it was ajar I noticed. I stood down the hallway for a bit and considered investigating. I still had to report to Churchill, now didn't I.

"Suddenly a man came out of her room. I ducked into an alcove. Luckily the hallway was dimly lit. The man walked right by me. He was making a low, guttural sound, as if he were talking to himself in Sanskrit or something–"

"Did you recognize him?"

"Yes. Anders Hardy. Who wasn't supposed to be there. He had been invited for the weekend, but had sent his regrets – or so everyone had been told. He was carrying something in his right hand, which was on his far side from me. I couldn't be certain, but afterward I thought it could have been a knife. I might be biased about that, however. Someone reminded me, several years later, she heard Hardy had once threatened Christine with a knife. I may have known that even when I was nine. That night at Croyden Castle I wanted to follow him, but spy or no spy I was too frightened. I had never liked Hardy. He used to weekend with us rather often. He was terrifically keen on Christine. The little scene I had just witnessed out by the pool would have unhinged him.

"I wasn't sure what else I should do – having no idea at that point, obviously, what had happened to my sister. Hardy had closed the door to Christine's room behind him when he left. I went back to my own room, where of course I was not able to sleep a wink. Eventually there was a scream, and all the commotion, when they found her.

"I never told anyone what I had seen. Not about Hardy. Or about Richter, either. Not until just recently, at any rate. Not even Samantha, who was my closest confidant back then."

"How about your brother?" Cohen said.

"I shied away in particular from telling Clay. There was no way around it, that I could see, to tell it and not also tell him about Aunt Anne and Christine. And it wasn't just a one-night thing between the two of them, was it.

"Two years ago my father, just before his accident, told me about Christine having pumped Anders Hardy for information for Richter, and about Hardy's rage at her when he found out, shortly before she was killed. He said Hardy's not showing up at Croyden Castle the weekend Christine was murdered was an MI6 ruse. He was there, my father said. Which of course I knew. And he was there – apparently my sister-in-law confirmed this in her testimony – because he thought Richter was about to bolt."

"By this time," Powell broke in, "Hardy knew Christine had, from his point of view, sold out. That she was helping Richter, not him. And presumably, that she was a danger to him now."

"Which, as you might guess, came from Anne Johns, our little Queen of Intrigue," Weaver said.

"That's correct," Powell said. "As you presumably heard in court, Hardy had recruited her to keep an eye on Christine and Richter, especially Christine, once he started suspecting something was up. My bet is he tagged Christine because she was being too nice to him after Richter asked her to squeeze him for information. It wasn't her usual style. Not with any man. But especially not with Hardy, with whom she had some history."

"And now of course it's apparent the two women had a sexual connection as well," Weaver said. "Which simply muddies the water that much more."

Cohen looked at Powell, who could not entirely hide a pained expression.

"A ménage à trois of spies," Elliot Johns chipped in.

"It was a strange war," Weaver said. "I imagine you don't have to be told that, Cohen."

No, he did not need to be told that. "So Anne Johns," he said, "she knew Anders Hardy, and she knew something about his relationship with Christine, obviously. Did she know back then he was a potential threat to her, to Christine – or later, that he may have killed her?"

"Frankly, that bloody well remains a mystery," Powell said.

"Before the accident," Elliot Johns said, "Father said he harbored suspicions about Hardy, that he might somehow have been involved in Christine's death. My father's contacts were very good. He had heard stories, he said. He even thought Hardy might've gone over to the Nazis. When of course it was to the Reds, as we now know.

"I don't know why I didn't tell Father what I knew then, but for some reason I did not. Guilt, perhaps, for having kept it a secret so long. I've been waiting a long time to let it out."

"Why didn't you testify?" Cohen asked.

The young man deferred to Powell, who said, "We can't tip our hand to Hardy. Not yet. We want them all. Or as many of them as we can lure into the net."

Cohen let that sink in. "And you think Anders Hardy still wants to kill Richter."

"He wants to keep him out of Europe – out of England, as it stands now – at all costs," Powell said. "They're a rough lot. If they have to kill him to do it, I'm sure they'll try."

Cohen turned to Weaver. "What's the CIA doing here?"

"If MI6 has been compromised by the Commies, then we have too," Weaver said. "Burgess, Maclean and Philby all spent time assigned to Washington. Hardy was there briefly as well. They may've passed atomic secrets to the Soviets. We'd like to help our British friends down here, and ourselves as well. We'd like to get hold of Richter, protect him, keep him out of the limelight and away from Hardy. Make everybody happy. Even these difficult bastards," he nodded at Powell with a shallow grin.

"Reasonably happy, old boy. Reasonably happy," Powell amended.

"So you want Richter to tell you about Hardy and his friends, and their fellow moles, is that it?" Cohen said.

"He's money in the bank, we think," Weaver said. "What he knows could be immensely important."

"He in effect has only two choices, now that he's to be extradited," Powell added. "Us, or being killed. We believe we're the better choice. We can offer him sanctuary for his family as well."

No one spoke for a moment. Cohen looked around the room, at nothing, not even attempting to organize his jumbled thoughts. With night falling now, the mists were so thick they had begun to invade the interior of the bar with a light haze.

"So, Cohen," Powell broke the ice, "can we count on you, if we need you?"

"Need me for what?"

"We're going to have to have more access to Richter at some point. Through something other than official channels. We've managed to get word in to him about our intentions to help him. About giving him a quid pro quo for his assistance. But we may need somebody who has contact with Hardy, as well. To put it bluntly, old boy, you are rather uniquely placed to meet those needs."

So they knew about that too, Cohen thought. Knew he had lied about never having heard of Hardy. They knew about that. They knew about Israel. What the hell didn't they know? The trip out to Riberalta and Elena Stein came to mind, the same concern he'd had with Hardy. Of course they knew. Weaver had sent him out there. Had his stay in Dachau figured into their calculations?

He wondered if they knew he had received the same pitch from Hardy, with cold hard cash included. In case they didn't, he decided not to advertise it yet. "I don't know why you think I have access to Richter," he said with a sense of déjà vu. "I've never said 'boo' to the man."

"Trust us," Powell said. "You and Richter are destined to meet. And when you do, we want to have you on our side."

"Now that Richter's extradition has been ordered, time is short," Weaver joined in. "Hardy and his pals will have to move quickly now."

"You may jolly well be upset with MI6, I can understand that," Powell said. "But this is important. You're in a position to help your new country." He eyed Cohen with a tight-lipped little smile. "What do you say, old boy?"

He wanted to say, "Quit calling me 'old boy.'" It was irritating. The man must think he held the ultimate trump card, knowing about Cohen's defection from MI6 in Israel. To his credit, he wasn't being heavy-handed about it. He was more subtle than Anders Hardy. Perhaps a little more human, as well.

"I'd say I need to think it over," Cohen replied. "I'd say I don't know which end is up right now."

Weaver laughed. It echoed through the thin haze of the empty bar.

"Take your time," Powell said. "We shouldn't need your services for at least another twelve hours." The smile broadened into a grin, but he did not appear to be joking.

Cohen glanced automatically at his watch. Were these guys any more legitimate than Anders Hardy? He had some thinking to do.

"Excuse me," he said. "I need some fresh air."

Weaver stepped aside and let him out of the booth.

"It was a pleasure to meet you, Mr. Cohen," Elliot Johns said. No one else said a word as Cohen walked out of the bar, but he felt their eyes on his back.

Outside, the night air was heavy but he breathed a little easier.

CHAPTER XIX

It was nearly midnight. Cohen walked back toward the Miranda alone. He needed to sift his thoughts. All the alcohol he had poured down his throat earlier in the evening had no effect on him now. It was a cool night, almost cold. Silent. No rumblings in the distance. No nothing. The air was still a veil of mist and only the main streets were lit. On the side streets, he navigated by the glow of a hazy moon.

He wasn't sure what bothered him most about his encounter in the bar, the stories that painted Johann Richter in a more positive light or the revelation that John Weaver worked for the Central Intelligence Agency. He still couldn't shake the bad feeling that being told about Weaver's subterfuge had given him. He could not believe he had been so gullible.

On the other hand, he did understand the stakes were high. If it were true Richter could help unmask Soviet moles in British Intelligence, he was worth his weight in gold. To both sides. The idea that Stalin might somehow have been protecting Hitler during the later stages of the war was still hard to absorb. But stranger things had happened. And Hitler had indeed been doing much of the heavy lifting for his fellow mass murderer to the East during those years, including killing off most of Europe's Jews. Powell had struck that chord with resonance. As much as he hated and distrusted MI6, it might be satisfying, Cohen thought, to help the U.S. in its battle with Stalin, in whatever small way he could.

Cohen took a deep breath. He had plenty of hate to go around. There were times he could still not believe all that had happened during the war, and afterwards in Israel. Could not accept it. Times when it all seemed an impossible nightmare.

He shook his head to try to clear it. Better to deal with the here and now. And right now he was facing something of a quandary, he thought.

The specifics were still a mystery, but between Leland Powell and Anders Hardy, it appeared he was being offered a choice of somehow either helping Richter, or of sealing his fate. He really didn't want to do either. Not yet, anyhow. In spite of Terry Harper's relatively benign portrait of the man, Cohen had arrived in La Negra with thoughts more akin to Hardy's point of view, that Richter was a man who likely deserved whatever he was about to get. And he continued to lean that way despite the growing evidence Richter might have tried to kill Hitler at some point, or might've at least tried to help – and the disappointing lack of evidence so far that he'd had any contact whatsoever with Rachel at Kaisenher.

On the other hand, Hardy had not been entirely convincing in his rendition of Richter's crimes, particularly the picture he had painted of the murder of Christine Johns.

But the story Cohen had just heard from Powell and Weaver, backed up by Elliot Johns, was a bit much to swallow all at once, as well. This was from MI6. It occurred to him he was perhaps being granted only a temporary reprieve for having bolted from MI6 in Israel. They must know by now that he had helped the Israelis more than he'd helped them. Were they simply waiting to assess his usefulness before they lowered the boom on him?

Whatever the truth, and whatever their motives, this latter group appeared to be on the verge of trying to help Richter escape, which made Cohen uneasy on several levels. He realized, however, that when he thought of the option Anders Hardy offered, to sabotage Richter, probably help get him killed, it depressed him.

In short, he had no idea where he stood right now.

As he emerged from a murky side street onto a main thoroughfare, he was reminded of walking to the prison his first afternoon in La Negra. It came to him again just how far he had wandered from his assignment for *WoHo*, the mechanics of which – in spite of occasional bursts of optimism – seemed to concern him less each day.

By the time he reached the Miranda the fog had begun to lift. Through wispy clouds, he could see the outline of Lake Tocqual in the distance. Outside the main entrance, he was met by Cisco Rojas.

"Hello, my friend, how are you tonight?" the boy said. He appeared to be agitated. Cohen wondered if he were a little drunk. Or maybe was sampling too much of his own product.

"My friend, mi amigo, I should be telling to you something."

"What is that?"

"I should be telling to you something," the boy repeated. "I should–" He looked over Cohen's shoulder nervously. Cohen turned, but saw nothing out of the ordinary.

"I am sorry, my friend. I am sorry." Cisco Rojas began to move away with an odd shuffling movement, as if he had been injured.

"Be careful, mi amigo," he said, as he moved off into the shadows.

Cohen felt disquieted by the encounter. Inside, there was no one in the lobby. Not even a desk clerk. Suddenly feeling a touch of paranoia, he skipped the recently repaired elevator and instead warily climbed the dimly lit stairs to his rooms.

When he opened the door, he was surprised to find a lamp burning in the outer room. He entered quietly, keeping his back to the wall. He keyed his senses to pick up anything suspicious. His alertness, however, did not stop him from giving a slight jump as an apparition suddenly filled the doorway to the second room.

"I am hoping it is okay, Mr. Cohen," Elena Stein said. "You are the only person here I can trust. I tell the man downstairs I am your wife. I am sorry. I can think of nothing else to say to him."

"That's all right," Cohen returned, still slightly off balance.

"Can we go outside for now?" – she indicated the balcony – "I try to get the children to sleep."

"Your children are here?"

"*Our* children, I tell the man downstairs, I'm afraid," she said sheepishly. Cohen wondered if the smile she gave him was meant to be hopeful or facetious. Was she as innocent as she seemed? He was glad she was here, but he was having trouble getting a fix on the Elena Stein he thought he had met before.

"Well, I guess we had better step outside then," he said, sliding the balcony door open for her. "The children, you know, my dear," he smiled, trying to match her mood.

"We leave it open a little, please?" she said. "So I can listen for them."

"Of course."

They stepped outside into the sharp, scented night air, even colder now. The moon had found a hole in the mists and was shining brightly. Its soft glow, suffused by the surrounding haze, gave La Negra a deceptively peaceful feel, Cohen thought. But it also emphasized the harshness of Lake Tocqual, from which its light was partially blocked by the dark row of towering peaks that spiked the western horizon. He was struck again by the row of high-rises along the shore, how forbidding and out of place they seemed here. A bolt of lightning flickered silently behind the distant mountains.

Cohen and Elena Stein leaned against the stucco balustrade of the balcony. He waited for her to break the silence.

"I am sorry I do not return your call," she said. "I am afraid of Johann maybe changing his mind about our coming to La Negra. I do not want to give him the chance. I go to the prison tonight, but they do not let me see him."

"He is going to be extradited. Sent to England. They're probably being extra careful with him now."

"Why? Why to England?"

"He requested it. Today in court. The judge granted his request."

"I see."

Here was one person, at least, Cohen thought, who truly believed in Richter's innocence. Regardless of his own doubts, he found himself wanting to ease her burden. "The war, I guess, will never end for some of us," he said. "That's just the way it is."

"Yes, the war. . ." She stared out over La Negra. The mists were starting to close in again, slowly pulling a curtain across the mountains and the lake. Elena looked at Cohen as if she were lost in a dream. She took his hand and turned it palm up as she had done the first time they met. Very lightly, she ran her fingertips over the numbers etched across his forearm.

"Since we first meet, I think of this many times," she said. "How does it happen? What leads you to Dachau?"

Cohen felt a sudden sadness enveloping him. When he looked at Elena, he sometimes fancied, as he once had with Rachel Stern, that he could see the image of his own soul reflected in her eyes. Now was one of those times.

It was a subject he did not talk about. Tried not to think about. Now a virtual stranger was asking him. But not really a stranger. While some survivors wanted nothing more to do with others who had been through the camps, Cohen felt an automatic kinship. To him, Elena Stein was family. A member of the only family he had left. His fate seemed tied to hers. If she survived, then somehow he would too.

"We were betrayed," he said.

He had no desire to continue, but patiently, expectantly, she led him on. More than her words, it was in her eyes. She had told him her story. Now she needed to hear his.

"I fell in love, I guess you could say. I was very young at the time. . . We had escaped our village, and were hiding out on a farm south of Augsburg. I met this girl – perhaps appropriately on Yom Kippur – 'Gudrun.' She was very pretty. Also very young. She loved books. She loved especially the classics about medieval knights with damsels in distress and dragons to slay. The Nazis were an abstraction for her. She had no real connection to them. Not even to the war, really. Her father had died in the '30s. She and her mother lived with relatives, she said."

Cohen felt a rush of cold air across his face. The wind was picking up. It felt good. "We began to meet, every other day or so, and go for walks in the woods. My parents suspected, I think, but they didn't stop us. For me, Gudrun and the world she inhabited were like a fairy tale. Being with her made me feel tucked-away and safe. . . Then one day, she and I became lovers. The first time for both of us. She told her mother. It was just something she needed to do; she couldn't keep it to herself. It wasn't malicious. She told me about it. She said it would be all right, because she had not told her mother we were Jews. But before the week was out, the woman had evidently decided we must be Jews and had reported us. Gudrun tried to warn me, but it was too late."

"You are sent to Dachau."

"Yes. The SS gave my mother two chances to live. One when we were first picked up, the other at the camp. She wasn't Jewish and had the papers from a *sippenforscher* to prove it. But she refused to leave us, in spite of my father's urgings." The memory hit Cohen in the gut as hard as if it had happened an hour ago.

He took a deep breath. "At Dachau, my father and I were quickly separated from my mother and my brother Jeremiah. Jeremiah was only five years old. We never saw them again. Like you and your mother."

Elena's eyes stayed locked on his, without a flicker. "What ever happen to the girl, Gudrun?"

"I never knew."

"And do you forgive her, for telling?"

"There was never anything to forgive. I still remember the look in her eyes when she told me what had happened with her mother. She loved me, I believe. It was only a young girl's love, perhaps, but that's how I remember it."

"And your father?" Elena Stein asked gently.

"We managed to be put in the same barracks, so we could communicate. We had nothing. He had used all the money and valuables he'd brought with him, trying to save my mother and brother–" Cohen broke off, as another silent bolt of lightning split the horizon. Coupled with the moon and the mountains, it painted an otherworldly image in its brief, flickering glow.

"My father was a strong man. He wasn't frightened by the camp; not for himself anyway. But he became bitter. It tormented him, I think, that he hadn't heeded the warnings and saved his family. He and several others decided to fight their way out. They had some kind of plan, and several hidden weapons. If they made it, they would form a partisan group and come back for the rest of us, he said. He forbade me to join them because their chances of escape were so poor.

"He believed my mother and brother were dead. My sister Nicolette too, most likely. She had disappeared with relatives who were rounded up earlier. Though he had given up on none of them. Before he left, my father told me that if he didn't make it, it was up to me to stay alive for the sake of our family.

"He didn't make it. He and the others were killed in the escape attempt, every single one of them. Their heads were cut off and placed on stakes around the camp, until they rotted so badly even the guards couldn't stand it. When they picked gravediggers – it was just a common hole for what little was left of the bodies, but someone had to dig it – I volunteered. We tried to bury them with dignity. A jeweler from Dusseldorf who knew the Talmud said some words over them. . . My mother and brother were dead. Now my father."

Cohen looked directly at Elena Stein. His stare cut right through her. "I stayed alive for them," he said. "To avenge them."

She said nothing. There was no need to speak. She understood in a way no one else could. Michael Cohen was the only fellow survivor of the camps she had ever met. She sensed he had the same survivor's guilt that plagued her. Her feelings toward him were a confusing mix of empathy, protectiveness, and an attraction tinged with sex but really, she thought, more like a sister's love for a brother. And behind all this was the nagging worry he might somehow pose a threat to Johann.

Then Cohen, flooded by unleashed memories, tried a long shot. He asked Elena if she had ever heard of a "Rachel Stern" at Kaisenher.

To his surprise – in an almost unbelievable alignment of stars – she said she had. A girl, really, like herself at the time. Her predecessor in the commandant's bed, this part no surprise to Cohen. She had never met Rachel Stern, she said, but the commandant, Heinrich Mueller, had talked about her, usually after bouts of heavy drinking. Elena did not measure up to her, he would say. "'She is not like you,' he says. 'Not at all like you.'" Rachel Stern, it seemed, was a strong-willed young woman from a moneyed Berlin family, accustomed to privilege, used to being catered to – though at Kaisenher she had learned a thing or two about her true station in life, Mueller had told Elena. He regretted having to give her up, he said, but had sensed a growing despair in her that he judged could become a danger. A danger to herself – "'Or to anyone sleeping beside her,' he laughs.

"I am convince this woman, this girl I never meet," Elena said, "eventually finds a way to kill him, and I think Mueller believes this too. So he sends her to Dachau. At least he doesn't kill her. That's what I always tell myself."

"She couldn't do it," Cohen said. "She couldn't bring herself to kill him."

"You know Rachel Stern?" Elena asked him.

Cohen hesitated, gave her a long look, then took the plunge. "Yes," he said. "At Dachau." And proceeded to tell her about Rachel. He felt a need to tell her. He hadn't had a confidant like this since Rachel herself. "She is why I am here," he said.

He told Elena everything, more than he had ever told anyone. After the final painful twist, she grew quiet. He thought she had tears in her eyes but could not be certain. The night haze was thickening again. Staring into it, Cohen couldn't shake the feeling of being watched, but he saw no one down below. It made little sense that Leland Powell might still be keeping an eye on him.

His reverie was abruptly interrupted by a distant explosion erupting from somewhere out in the dark void, as if Lake Tocqual were rumbling up a complaint from its depths. There was no lightning.

"That seems to be a common occurrence here," Cohen said, thankful for the distraction.

"You mean the dynamite?"

"The what?"

"The dynamite. That is dynamite. The rebels blow it up."

"What are they blowing up?"

"It is only to remind us, I think, that they are out there still."

They stood on the balcony a little longer, not looking at each other. Cohen shivered in the cold night air but Elena Stein appeared unaffected.

"Tomorrow, I try to visit Johann again," she said. "I must get up early to buy some things for him."

She took her leave. Cohen followed her inside. There was a double bed in each of the two rooms. Elena said good night and went into the other room, where Tomas slept in the bed, with Teresa on a smaller mattress laid on the floor.

Cohen felt a thousand conflicting emotions. He did not think he could sleep. He returned to the balcony and stared back out into the mists. There was still no one on the streets below, which were barely visible now. He heard another distant clap of thunder. Or dynamite. It reminded him of the war. Ultimately, everything reminded him of war. The war in Europe and the fighting in Palestine were one long war to him. Even sleep, with its lurking nightmares, would not have offered a reliable escape tonight.

For the next few hours, he sat out on the balcony wrapped in a blanket, chewing on coca leaves and washing them down with tequila. Looking for clarity he did not find. He kept thinking of his recurring dream with the woman stretched face-down across a metal drum, being whipped by an SS officer. He'd always assumed she must be Rachel.

The SS man had to be Heinrich Mueller. But now he'd dreamed it twice with a second man on the scene, one who seemed almost to be protecting her. Who was that supposed to be?

His mind drifted. He thought about Cisco Rojas and how oddly he had acted tonight. At one point, he thought he might have seen him for an instant on the street below, but he couldn't be sure. He still wondered if he were being followed. Or Elena Stein, perhaps.

Cohen tried to make sense of his meeting with Powell and Weaver and Elliot Johns, but made scant headway. He tried to get a better grip on Anders Hardy, but found little to work with on the subject. The man's message about Richter might be right, but something seemed wrong with the messenger himself. There were the alleged Communist ties; the implication he might have killed Christine Johns. But even if you could ignore those things, there remained something inherently untrustworthy about him, it seemed to Cohen. Untrustworthy and dangerous.

He thought he might finally be getting a handle on why John Weaver had sent him out to find Elena Stein. As a fellow survivor of the camps, he probably appeared to have the perfect "in" with her, and thus with Johann Richter. And British Intelligence and the CIA, he was sure, had no compunction about using every bit of leverage they could find. Maybe they thought Elena's background would help win him over to Richter's side, make him a more useful pawn in their maneuverings.

Shortly before dawn he ran out of tequila. In a haze of his own making, he stepped quietly into the room where Elena and her children were sleeping – his goal to retrieve a second bottle he'd been prudent enough to purchase the day before.

She was in bed, fast asleep, with Tomas beside her and Teresa on the mattress on the floor. Cohen found the bottle of tequila, then stood in the dark staring at Elena Stein, mesmerized. She was peaceful. She was beautiful, in the same way Rachel had been beautiful. And she had survived Kaisenher. In his mind, he still couldn't match her up with Richter. But in some small way he envied her – her family; even her attachment to Richter, however flawed it might be.

Back out on the balcony, after another few sharp, comforting shots of tequila, his thoughts of Elena and Rachel turned to thoughts of Palestine. Specifically, to his arrival there after the war in Europe as a newly minted British Intelligence agent. Not a true agent, exactly. More an inside listening post for the British.

The transit of the Mediterranean aboard a merchant vessel of uncertain vintage and dubious seaworthiness had been uncomfortable, but a cakewalk compared to Dachau. And Cohen, at least, had not had to worry that the British would stop the ship and return its passengers to Germany, as they had done with so many others. His presence ensured this ship would be allowed to go through.

Disembarking at the moonlit harbor of Haifa, Cohen was lifted by an almost tropical blend of perfumed air and a fragrance of pines he would later learn came from nearby Mount Carmel. He felt an unexpected affinity with the place the moment he set foot on its soil. Whether this was because it had been home to his forebears, or simply because of the desert balm, he was not sure.

Aboard ship, he, along with all the men and several of the women of a certain age, had been briefed and informally inducted into Haganah, fighters for Israel. The British mandate over the area, in effect since they drove out the Ottoman Turks in 1917, was due to expire in one more month. Fighting had already broken out between Jews and Arabs over who would control the region, or who would control what parts of it. A homeland for the Jews was at stake, they had been told aboard ship, and every pair of hands was needed for the historic and daunting task ahead.

Cohen was promptly trucked to a kibbutz outside Haifa that doubled as a military training camp. The Haganah were a motley crew, he soon discovered. They included Jews from all over, mostly various parts of Europe, most of them touched in some way by the Holocaust, and many of them speaking no common language, save for Hebrew, and even that was not universal.

There were others as well, including a few Englishmen. Among the training leaders was one "Major Hawkins," a ramrod-straight retired British Army regular who now felt compelled to choose sides according to the dictates of his conscience. Cohen liked the more informal regimen and indoctrination here better than his stint with the British, and he soon discovered a dogged determination among members of Haganah. This spirit could take the Jews a long way, he thought. It would have to, given the uneven battle that loomed.

After three weeks, he boarded another lorry and was driven to Tel Aviv with maybe a hundred other new Haganah recruits. He had been out of touch with the British since he'd boarded the refugee ship at Marseilles. Contact would have to be reestablished soon, he knew.

Following the relative quiet of the kibbutz, Tel Aviv was a wall of noise – cars, construction, honking, yelling and, not least of all, air-raid sirens. The first few sirens produced no air raids, but just as Cohen's skepticism began to kick in, another round of warning blasts sounded and six Egyptian fighters screamed in low and strafed a path of destruction through downtown, adding to the general turmoil and costing several lives.

It didn't take long for MI6 to find him in Tel Aviv. They had nothing new to tell him. Just to keep his eyes and ears open about Haganah and what it was up to. And to stay in touch.

Less than ten minutes after meeting with his control officer, Cohen was accosted on a busy street corner. "Shalom, old friend," a familiar voice called out. To his immense surprise and relief, it was the jeweler from Dusseldorf he had known at Dachau, a presence that evoked insistent memories of his father.

"My eyes are still not so strong," the man said, adjusting a pair of wire-rimmed bifocals, "but now I have my glasses again, and I knew it must be you."

Over a cup of strong Turkish coffee, he and his old acquaintance talked. The jeweler had arrived aboard the infamous *Exodus*, the Jewish refugee ship piloted and commanded by young Haganah fighters that the British had intercepted off the coast of Palestine, eventually returning its more than 4,000 refugees to Displaced Persons camps in Germany, to the drumbeat of worldwide disapproval. The jeweler, along with two others, had contrived to escape while the ship was still at anchor off the Promised Land. One of his two companions had drowned. The jeweler and his fellow survivor were trying to make themselves useful to Haganah.

As Cohen was about to take his leave, the man dropped a bombshell. "You have seen your lady friend from Dachau, no?" he said.

Cohen stared at him blankly.

"Your lady friend. Rachel Stern. I knew about her. We all did."

Cohen was dumbstruck. "She's alive?"

"Of course she is alive. A very brave young woman. She is with Irgun, our most ferocious fighters. Usually in Jerusalem, from what I understand. But right now she is here, recuperating."

This was a second shock. To the British, Irgun was the terrorist wing of the Jewish freedom fighters, responsible for a string of atrocities and civilian deaths.

"Recuperating?" he said, still amazed she might be alive.

"She was shot by a sniper with the Arab Legion, the only fighters we fear. They have Jerusalem under siege."

"Where is she?" Cohen asked.

"In hospital. I can take you there, if you like."

"Yes," he said. "Please take me there."

Cohen's thoughts of the past suddenly began to unravel. Sitting on the floor of the balcony, still wrapped in a blanket, he lifted his eyes to the night sky of La Negra. It was spitting an occasional raindrop. Worse, it was spinning. As it picked up speed, he thought he would be sick. The tequila and coca were finally starting to get to him.

For a brief spell – he did not know how long – he could remember nothing. By the time he fell into his own bed and into a cloudy slumber, Rachel was lost once again to the mists of time. He dreamed of other things. Other troubling things. He dreamed he saw Adolf Hitler, alive, frozen in time, sitting in the witness stand of the La Negra courtroom and testifying against Johann Richter. Richter, the bloodied end of a huge meathook protruding from his gut, dangled in midair before the judge. The meathook was attached to the courtroom's ceiling by piano wires. In his tormented sleep, Cohen knew the wires were piano wires because he himself was playing a funeral dirge on them.

Sometime in the night, he was awakened by Tomas crying out in his sleep, a cry of fear. He longed to waken and comfort the young boy, but resisted the impulse. This night, he thought, was darker than Tomas' dreams could ever possibly be.

"Peaceful Interlude"

In Paris, while he awaited further instructions from his father, Johann Richter more or less settled into a work routine. He had been posted to an obscure administrative position in an Abwehr field office on the Right Bank. The office was charged with interrogating captured British, American and other infiltrators who had been working with the French Resistance.

Before reporting to Paris, he had arranged for Elena Stein to be escorted to Orienbad. He told his mother that Elena, who he had renamed "Helga Schumann" for the occasion, was an Austrian being sought by Vienna Nazis because of her father's political involvement with Dollfuss and von Schuschnigg. He told her he had known "Helga's" family during his stay at Heidelberg, and that they had been especially kind to him while he was a student there. Somewhat to his surprise, his mother had quite willingly, almost eagerly, welcomed Elena, as well as her own role as the emaciated girl's keeper and protector. Gerta Richter's ardor for the Nazis had dimmed, it appeared, at least to the point where her instinctive feelings about the repayment of a family debt outweighed any obligation she may have felt to the state.

In Paris, Richter was not invited to participate in the interrogations his office was charged with carrying out. His days were spent bending over reams of paperwork, in a mindless routine that at least comforted him in its relative harmlessness. The records he handled were on mundane matters only – primarily supply, logistics and transport – which was likely an index of the level of trust he was held in by his immediate superiors, he thought.

He was something of a loner among his fellow officers, in part because he did not know who he could trust, and in part because they did not entirely trust him. They were suspicious of his years in England, and leery, even more, of who his father was. Richter was not surprised. With the war going poorly, the Abwehr's often fractious officer corps had become a den of intrigue, with no one ever entirely sure who was on whose side.

Meanwhile he did as his father had ordered. In his off hours, he practiced his marksmanship with both pistol and rifle.

* * * *

Paris was a virtual oasis of peace in the summer of 1943. There was sporadic action from the Resistance and often deadly reprisals from the Germans, but it still barely dented daily life three years after the Wehrmacht had first marched in. The occupiers' persecution was focused on specific groups – Jews, Communists, Freemasons, Gypsies, homosexuals. For most others, life went on. Though most of its population had remained or returned after the Germans had arrived in 1940, the city at times felt oddly deserted now. German officers, many of them sucked into the vortex of the Eastern Front, were not as likely to vacation in Paris with their wives anymore. There was a citywide curfew along with a long list of other occupation restrictions, and the lack of private automobiles, forced from the streets because of constant fuel shortages, added to the effect.

Day-to-day existence, while peaceful, was difficult for many. Factories had shut down because fuel and raw materials were no longer available. Jobs were hard to come by. Food was rationed and in short supply. A black market flourished, but was impossibly expensive for most of those with empty bellies. Escapism was the order of the day. Movies, opera, theater and concerts were all hugely popular for those who could afford them.

There were still intellectuals in the city, but little intellectual life. A surprising number of well-known writers such as Jean Paul Sartre and Simone de Beauvoir, artists such as Pablo Picasso, actors and others had opted to stay when the conquerors had arrived. They held widely varying views, however, of the Germans. While Maurice

Chevalier sang and bantered on Radio Paris, a prime outlet for Nazi propaganda, Sartre sought recruits for his Resistance group, Socialisme et Liberte. Political collaborators were abundant. Marcel Deat, editor of *L'Oeuvre* and head of the pro-Nazi Rassemblement Nationale Populaire, founded a unit of French volunteers the Germans deployed against the Russians on the Eastern Front.

By the summer of 1943, the city had been stripped of anything that was of immediate use to Germany, plus a good deal of historic artwork. Allied bombing in the suburbs and beyond had leveled some key industrial areas, but the old city center was still largely undamaged and still enchanting, with swastika displays and most other evidence of the occupation limited primarily to the more prominent arrondissements. Richter had not visited the city since a brief vacation stay in 1936. He had forgotten its heart-rending beauty.

His new living quarters were on the third floor of an old hotel on the Left Bank, with front rooms that overlooked a crowded tree-lined avenue of small shops and restaurants, including a *boulangerie* he grew to love. After work, he sometimes went out into the country, to a small French stable that still operated, and rode. When he didn't have the time for that, he took long evening strolls, in spite of the blackout darkened streets, always alone. This practice ran counter to occupation regulations designed to keep solitary German soldiers off the streets of Paris, particularly at night. They were encouraged to travel in groups. There were plenty of stories of what could happen, and at times had in fact happened – most recently to a Japanese navy officer, whose mangled body was found in a back alley – to those with the temerity to walk about in uniform unescorted.

Wandering around, Richter could sense the hatred from each French passerby, no matter how seemingly cordial or polite. He carried a pack of Gauloises – the brand he had tried during a brief flirtation with smoking at Heidelberg, prohibitively expensive for most Parisians on the black market – in case he ever got the opportunity to offer one, but he rarely did. On the other hand he was never molested, or even felt threatened. And as far as he was concerned, his prospects in the streets could hardly be any more grim than his prospects in general.

These long walks taught him to love Paris. He marveled at the magnificent boulevards, the Louvre, the Eiffel Tower, the Arc de Triomphe. When he visited the chapel of the Hotel des Invalides, he couldn't help but wonder if Hitler ever thought about his only visit here three years earlier, when he had stood above the earthly remains of Napoleon just one year before he too would risk everything against the Russians.

But it was the smaller shopping and residential streets of the Quartier Latin directly south of his hotel that truly infatuated him. As he walked the avenues and side streets between the boulevards Montparnasse and St. Germain, or around the Sorbonne and the Palais du Luxembourg or along the Seine, he fervently hoped the SS or Wehrmacht would not, in a fit of impotent rage, destroy the city when they were forced to evacuate it. Here was a monument to beauty, he thought, both man's and nature's, that had never been equaled elsewhere. To destroy it would be a crime against humanity as vile as destroying that humanity itself.

On these walks, his loneliness often translated into thoughts of Christine. It had yet to entirely sink in that she was gone. A part of him still wondered if it had all been some kind of ruse by British Intelligence to flush him out. But he had heard nothing to back that up since he'd fled England. If she had indeed been murdered, he thought, then he dreamed of avenging her one day. In his more grounded moments, on the other hand, he couldn't imagine a postwar life that included revenge or much of anything beyond peaceful pursuits and a feeling of relief.

He began to feel hopeful the war might be nearing a conclusion. The latest news for Germany was uniformly discouraging, on fronts stretching from Sicily to the Ukraine. Including the home front. In July, Allied bombing raids virtually destroyed Hamburg. Rumors of German secret weapons provided the only optimistic note. In the Abwehr, it was general knowledge that rockets and jet aircraft were being rushed into production and would soon return the initiative to the Reich. This news was seen as good or bad, depending on your point of view. To Richter, the silver lining was that the launch pads for the rockets were said to be primarily in France and the Low Countries. Here perhaps was one last opportunity to lure Hitler to Paris, or somewhere nearby.

His father in fact was trying to do just that, but Hitler as usual was proving balky. Displaying the instinct that had already kept him alive beyond all odds, he continually changed and delayed plans to visit coastal defenses and other installations in the West. At one point, specific logistics had been worked out and advance men dispatched for a trip that would include Paris in early August, but Hitler canceled the day before he was to depart. No reason was ever given. No reason was required. He was the Fuhrer.

Karl Richter, who had told Johann he would meet with him in Paris before Hitler's planned arrival there, scratched those plans when Hitler canceled his visit. The assassination attempt, it began to seem, might have to take place elsewhere. Meanwhile, however, his father successfully neutralized what he perceived to be an attempt to undermine his position on the General Staff. Namely, the orders that had recalled Johann from England. Issued by the SS or Gestapo rather than the Abwehr, they had been aimed somehow at uncovering the plot against Hitler, the General suspected. Perhaps Johann was to have been taken into custody without his father's knowledge, said the General, who warned Johann he could still be in danger. He added he had no idea what had derailed, or perhaps only delayed, the plans behind these orders, and cautioned Johann to remain vigilant.

After the August cancellation of Hitler's plans to visit Paris, Richter heard nothing more from his father for months. He tried several times to make discreet contact, but was unsuccessful each time. He was in touch intermittently with Erich Borchers, but there was no safe way to communicate with him about the maneuverings against Hitler. Then in mid-December, Richter received a set of orders that thoroughly surprised and perplexed him. Effective 1 January 1944, he was to relieve the commander of the SS garrison at St. Sentione, a small French agricultural and industrial city nestled among foothills where the Jura and Vosges ranges come together about 280 kilometers southeast of Paris.

The orders were issued by the Wehrmacht rather than the Abwehr, whose power was on the wane. The assignment had nothing to do with intelligence work. And since it represented another totally unexpected demonstration of trust in him, he assumed his father must have pulled some strings. In any case, it was an odd assignment for him, he thought. He felt as if he were being sucked inexorably into an abyss of unknown depth, with little control over matters.

The SS unit was being withdrawn from St. Sentione to be transferred to the Eastern Front, Richter assumed. Members of the Abwehr and other specialized branches were increasingly being called on to plug holes in backwater posts whose regular garrison troops were now desperately needed elsewhere. In St. Sentione, Richter was to command a small second-line Wehrmacht unit. In the same set of orders, he was given the rank of oberstleutnant, or lieutenant colonel, as a regular officer in the Wehrmacht, one more unexpected and unearned promotion that bore his father's fingerprints. Also effective on 1 January 1944.

Happy New Year, he thought.

He regretted having to leave Paris. He began to worry about what kinds of decisions he might be called upon to make as the commander of an occupation force. Though he had no reservations about his opposition to the Third Reich, sidestepping its power remained an extremely delicate maneuver, particularly from inside the military. He did not want any blood on his hands, or any more on his conscience, except perhaps Adolf Hitler's.

Late in December, during his last days in Paris, he finally received word from his father that they were to meet in Berlin on 12 January. This improved his spirits a little. He only hoped he could hold himself together until then.

* * * *

Richter had not been with a woman since the night Christine died. For the most part, he had not felt the need. He didn't join his fellow officers in their regular trips to the bordellos of Paris, reinforcing an already standoffish reputation among that cliquish crowd. The label of "prude" did not generally bother him, and on the whole, in fact, even suited his purposes. But on New Year's Eve, with an unanticipated two-day postponement of his new orders in hand, he finally did succumb to loneliness, as well as perhaps to the fine French burgundy he had been drinking most of the day. He agreed to help usher in 1944 at the fourth, and – with Italy surrendering to the Allies and Russian troops now nearing the prewar borders of Poland – presumably the last, annual Wehrmacht officers ball of Paris.

He arrived late, enjoying a leisurely walk down the Champs de Elysees. The huge ballroom at the Hotel Abelard was draped with giant swastikas and a band was trying to keep the mood upbeat with lively tunes. Fraternization between German soldiers and the females of Paris, particularly teenagers and women in their early twenties, had grown common by now. A recent estimate published by the Paris Immigration Services held that eighty-five thousand illegitimate children had been born out of such alliances. But it didn't take Richter long to realize most of the women in attendance tonight represented a different sort of hangers-on, the dregs of Paris who knew they were either going to sink or swim with the Germans. It perhaps added to the manic spirit of the occasion that by this time every one of them had to know her lifeboat had sprung a leak. The liquor was flowing, and decorum, with active encouragement from the Wehrmacht's finest, was rapidly deteriorating.

By the time Richter retrieved his coat, still an hour before midnight, several women were dancing around with the fronts of their dresses hanging open. Two or three of the younger officers, in total disregard of the senior officers present, had begun shedding various parts of their own uniforms. The Third Reich, Richter decided, was headed the way of the Roman Empire, only a hell of a lot faster.

As he was about to depart, his eye caught a startlingly familiar face. He watched, fascinated, as Marie Renault checked her coat, walked into the ballroom, took only a moment or two to see what was happening, then started to leave. He had not seen her in nearly ten years; had assumed she had left the city. Waving two drunken junior officers aside, he stepped into her path just before she reached the front hallway. She didn't recognize him at first. The surroundings for their reunion were perhaps too bizarre, the circumstances too incredible. She seemed embarrassed and a bit flustered when she finally recognized him, but readily accepted an invitation to join him for a walk.

Once Marie was bundled up again, they stepped outside into a fresh-falling snow. It was a beautiful night. As they walked and talked, they gradually grew more comfortable with one another. The memories she brought back made him feel at once both happy and sad. They stepped briefly into a *brasserie*, but it felt too public and she asked Richter to walk her home.

At her flat, it was so cold they kept their coats on and talked until dawn. He asked Marie to follow him to St. Sentione; he needed someone there he could trust. Though clearly apprehensive, she said she would. She would join him, they decided, as soon as he was settled in and felt he had his bearings about the place, and about what he was supposed to be doing there.

They embraced, somewhat awkwardly. As he stepped back out into the snow, he could not imagine what the New Year would bring, but felt a little better about the prospects.

* * * *

Arriving in St. Sentione two days later, Richter was not long in learning the crude etiquette of Nazi occupation life, introduced as he was to it by SS Standartenfuhrer Gerhardt Gruning, who had earned comparisons to Klaus Barbie, the so-called "Butcher of Lyon."

Gruning, it turned out, had heard of Richter as well. "Welcome to St. Sentione, Oberstleutnant. We have heard of your daring exploits in England," was the caustic greeting he received on the morning of 3 January when he first reported to Gruning's office.

The man reminded Richter of Heinrich Mueller, the commandant of Kaisenher, only he was more trim, more in control of himself. Gruning did not offer his hand or rise to greet his successor. Speaking slowly and distinctly, as if trying to spear him with each syllable, he bluntly implied Richter was riding his father's coattails safely through the war. Richter immediately found himself disliking the man even more than his predisposition had prepared him to.

"Since you have only two days in which to transfer command to me, I suggest you get on with it," Richter said.

"You have much to learn, Richter," Gruning retorted sharply. "A Wehrmacht oberstleutnant does not 'suggest' anything to an SS standartenfuhrer."

"In that case, Standartenfuhrer, I am 'ordering' you to get on with the business at hand. If you choose not to do so, I will have you expelled from St. Sentione."

Gruning was struck momentarily speechless by Richter's temerity, but was essentially helpless to do anything about it, as Richter had technically been in command of the St. Sentione post since 12 a.m. that morning. He knew, too, that if it came down to a dogfight, Richter had his father's leverage to back him up.

He tried looking Richter sternly in the eye. When that failed to produce results, he acquiesced to what could not for the moment be helped.

"I will show you around," he finally said, his voice still gruff but without its former bite.

The two men stepped out into winter sunshine that was quickly pecking holes in the ground's thin blanket of snow. Richter told Gruning he wanted only a tour of the troop compound; that he would prefer to look St. Sentione itself over without him along. Gruning gave him a smoldering glance, but said nothing.

In spite of his barely controlled anger toward Richter, Gruning was unguarded enough to let his contempt for St. Sentione and its inhabitants boil over into his tour of the compound. Perhaps it was to impress the newcomer. Or perhaps it was an obsession for him, like the searches he reputedly conducted for adolescent French girls to share his bed. Seemingly with no awareness that his grim world was about to die and that his own fate hung in the balance, Gruning spoke quite candidly, almost proudly, of the reprisals in human life he had been responsible for at one time or another. As Gruning talked on, Richter realized that had it not been for his father and the plot to kill Hitler, he could never have carried his charade as a German officer beyond this point.

He said his final farewell to Gruning, who was headed for the Eastern Front, on the parade grounds the next afternoon.

"I certainly hope, Standartenfuhrer, that a Russian bullet does not damage that fine Aryan skull of yours. I fully expect to see it hanging in the Reichsmuseum someday as an example to us all. Heil Hitler."

He knew he was making a dangerous enemy, but what did it matter? Right then, life to Richter seemed rather a tenuous affair, regardless. He had no way of knowing that less than ten years later, while he himself was being tried for extradition in La Negra for alleged war crimes, Gerhardt Gruning would be alive and well and prospering just two borders away. Only a few hundred miles from where Richter and Elena Stein had spent the past eight years, Gruning would be reading news accounts of the extradition hearing, savoring what he assumed to be the last laugh.

At their parting in St. Sentione, Richter's satisfaction in deflating Gruning was small. It was dwarfed by his ever-growing awareness of just how deeply Germany was being sucked into a bog of inhumanity. He felt its tug, and knew drastic action would be required to escape the undertow.

The emptiness he felt made his need for Marie all the greater. He resolved to get her to St. Sentione as soon as he could.

Karl Richter, for no given reason, canceled their meeting that had been scheduled for 12 January in Berlin. He said he would contact Johann again soon to set up another rendezvous. Talking with him by open military phone hookup, Johann felt helpless and totally out of touch with his father and his father's intentions. The General sounded distracted. Choosing his words carefully, Johann asked him if he didn't think it would soon be too late to do any good by going ahead with their plans. His father said in all probability that point had been passed some time ago, and abruptly ended the conversation.

When Johann Richter took over the St. Sentione garrison, he tried to the best of his ability to ease the townspeople's plight. There was no more torture; he had all political prisoners released from confinement; he dropped, as much as possible, restrictions on civilian movement and made an effort to help the city's sick and hungry. As the military district was continually short of food, doctors and medical supplies, however, this latter effort did not amount to much. He instructed his men to think of themselves as local gendarmes, rather than as occupying soldiers – another not entirely successful measure, as a combination of civilian distrust and unrest and disciplinary problems among his own men continued to provoke constant trouble.

When Berlin began increasing the pressure to export Jews from France to the KZs, he ignored it, reasoning that the influence that had gotten him posted to the job would help him keep it, regardless of what he did. That included protecting the well-known American writer and patron of the arts Gertrude Stein and her female partner, after he discovered they were living in the nearby village of Culoz.

At the start of February, Marie Renault arrived and Richter secured two rooms for her on the top floor of a small inn on the northern edge of town. She displaced no one. Her rooms had not been occupied for more than a year. They were large, but dirty and bare. Marie immediately set about the task of cleaning and refurbishing them as best she could, given the scarcities of the times.

The inn was built into the side of a steep hill, and the top floor, the fourth, offered a good overview of the entire town. On a clear day the Wehrmacht troop compound, all the way across the river-edged valley, could be made out by a sharp pair of eyes from Marie's windows. Richter visited her two or three times a week. He didn't feel ready to resume an intimate relationship, but he craved Marie's companionship. They went riding together at least once a week and had long talks about the war, themselves and the past. A few times they even ventured discussion of the future, though only in general terms. And they talked about St. Sentione. Marie gave him a number of ideas, several of which he was able to put into effect, for easing the restrictions and hardships of occupation.

Perhaps most important of all, she was sympathetic and understanding on the subject of Christine Johns. She believed him when he said he hadn't killed her. She understood his feelings about it and did not push him on the romantic front.

One thing he did not share with her. He never hinted anything about the plot to kill Hitler, or of his own potential involvement in it. He told her the target practice he sometimes indulged in on their rides together was simply a distraction for his mental health. While he knew Marie would never consciously do him harm, she had hated the General when she had been the family's governess. He wanted to take no risk of endangering his father or the others any more than he already had.

In late March, Hitler sent the Wehrmacht in to occupy his wavering ally Hungary. The Third Reich was coming apart at the seams, though it was difficult to see that from northern France. St. Sentione was experiencing a relatively mild winter. A little snow would come and go, come and go again, teasing of better weather and paralleling Richter's own fits and starts of frustrated impatience. Now, after the lull of Paris life, he felt a growing restlessness over the stalled assassination plans. He was becoming increasingly nervous and high-strung as he once again awaited word from his father.

When he first met Yvonne Duchamps, it was nearly spring.

"Yvonne Duchamps"

The new plan for a coup d'état was code-named Valkyrie, for the beautiful maidens of Teutonic myth who chose who would die in battle and who was worthy to ascend to Valhalla. The Wagnerian connection provided a touch of irony for the planners. Valkyrie was to be broadcast throughout Germany and the occupied territories by the Berlin-based commander of the German Reserve Army, General Friedrich Fromm, as soon as he had confirmation Hitler had been killed.

Disguised as a precaution against unrest among slave laborers or possible rioting on the home front, the Valkyrie orders would alert selected units of the army to occupy designated areas and direct military commanders to assume control over all civilian authorities. Additional orders were prepared with the aim of enabling a new government to bring effective military force against any elements of the SS, SD, Gestapo or Nazi Party that resisted the takeover. The goal was to neutralize Himmler, Goering and others at the top of the Nazi hierarchy after Hitler's death.

The plot's leaders felt that with Hitler dead they would have enough support among Wehrmacht senior officers, colonels and above, to allow them to use the army to consolidate their power. It was generally agreed that, following a successful coup, military rule should give way to civilian within three months. Ending the war on the most favorable terms possible was to be the new government's highest priority foreign policy objective.

Little of this information was conveyed to Richter during 1943 or the first half of 1944. His father was not maintaining any regular contact with him, and Richter was too much a latecomer to have been brought into any of the inner circles of conspirators. In Paris, though there were officers all around him plotting against Hitler, Richter had remained isolated. This was only partly by choice, and it caused him some occasional bitterness. His father had led him to believe he was to have an important and likely dangerous role, perhaps the central role, in the attempt on Hitler's life, and Richter did not appreciate what seemed to him a lack of support for what lay ahead.

And it was the key to everything, he knew. Hitler had to be killed before anything else the plotters wanted to do could work.

His anxiety continued to grow throughout the early months of 1944 in St. Sentione as Hitler finally sacked Admiral Wilhelm Canaris, the mysterious head of the Abwehr, as his Chief of Military Intelligence, and replaced him with Ernst Kaltenbrunner. Canaris had long been suspected of sympathy with the military's anti-Nazi faction. The good news was that he was not arrested. Instead, he was shuffled off to some make-work job in the Wehrmacht's economics section.

Not long after the ouster of Canaris, Richter received a welcome visit from Erich Borchers.

"Things in Berlin will explode soon, one way or another," Borchers told him. "I'm worried that our plans, even in the event of a successful assassination, may be too disorganized to control. In particular, I have little faith in Fritz Fromm backing us up with the Reserve Army. He may have to be removed."

"Is there anything I can do to help?" Richter asked, standing on the tarmac at the St. Sentione airport, where they talked during a brief layover on Borcher's staff junket to inspect the so-called "Atlantic Wall" defense preparations at Dunkirk and Calais.

Borchers looked surprised. "From what I hear," he said, "you are still a leading candidate to pull the trigger. If so, my very good friend, may God be with you."

Richter asked about Elena Stein. Borchers had been looking in on her at Orienbad from time to time at his request.

"She looks much better. Your mother is doing her best to fatten her up. She fusses over her. They seem to have become friends."

"Is she in good spirits?"

Borchers answered the question with a skeptical look. "She's trying to come to terms with what she has been through," he said. "I'm not sure that's possible."

Twenty minutes later, as he reboarded his Junkers JU 88 for the flight to Normandy, Borchers repeated the hope that God would watch over his friend in the fateful days ahead.

Meanwhile, Richter felt as if he were building toward some sort of explosion of his own. A combination of what he might be called upon to do, the uncertainty, and his isolation from any decision-making about it, was eating away at him.

But then during the last week of April Marie Renault introduced him to someone with whom, it struck him, he might be able to share what was on his mind. On only the third or fourth occasion he had ever laid eyes on Yvonne Duchamps, about two weeks after Marie had first introduced them, he told this virtual stranger of his intention to kill Hitler.

"You must be joking," she said.

"It's not a joke."

"You're mad. You're a German army officer."

"Many of us are prepared to do it. Particularly army officers."

"I don't believe you."

"Perhaps not, but my fate is now in your hands," he said, deciding, after a pause, he'd better add, "As much as yours is in mine."

Yvonne Duchamps was a very lovely young woman. There was a hard, intense look about her deep blue eyes. She was tall, brunette, statuesque but slender, and attracted Richter in much the same way Christine Johns had, with her quick wit and intelligence as much as her beauty. There was for him, in fact, a nagging familiarity about her, as if they had met before, but he chalked it up to her resemblance to Christine.

Yvonne was English, with a French husband she said was a prisoner of war somewhere inside Germany. She had their one child, a girl of three, with her in St. Sentione. To Richter, Yvonne seemed the perfect confidant. And that was soon borne out. Once she got over the idea he might be using her husband's predicament to coerce her into sex, she shared her political and philosophical views quite openly with him.

Richter began to see her at least as often as he saw Marie Renault. In a short time, his visits to Yvonne's place, an overstuffed three rooms on the inn floor just below Marie's quarters, fell into an almost domestic routine. While Yvonne washed dishes or performed some other household chore, Richter would feed and amuse the little girl, Giselle, a miniature of her mother with the same soft brown hair and big blue eyes. He loved the role of surrogate father. It gave him a sense of peace, however fleeting, he hadn't felt in years.

On a typical evening, the fun would come to a ritualistic, much-protested conclusion with Yvonne's motherly bedtime intervention. After which she and Richter would talk – as he and Marie still did as well – sometimes long into the night.

They discussed all manner of things. Yvonne Duchamps was a compelling woman. Before the war, just as Anne Wheldon Johns had, she had studied at Cambridge, where she'd acquired a solid grounding in history and zoology.

"When were you at Whitby?" she asked one night. She had poured them both some wine and was smoking a Dunhill, a brand favored by Anne Johns, a secret smoker who went to great lengths to hide her habit, for which Christine had often teased her.

Richter looked at her. "How did you know I was at Whitby?"

"Marie told me. Don't sound so suspicious." She blew a smooth stream of smoke from her lips. "I visited a boy there several times. During 1935 or '36, I believe it was."

"What was his name?"

"I hate to admit it, but really I can't seem to remember. A rather horrid boy, anyway."

He wondered if her visits to Whitby during his last year there perhaps explained the gnawing feeling that he had met her, or at least seen her, somewhere before.

Such small talk as this was relatively rare in their conversations. For the most part, they avoided personal topics. Each was nearly as protective of the other's privacy as they were of their own. They both kept a safe distance.

With one exception. Yvonne had eventually accepted Richter's sincerity about the plot to kill Hitler. Once he had convinced her he was just one member of a much broader conspiracy, she seemed quite willing, even quite eager on occasion, to discuss it.

"Have you thought about what you'll do if you try to kill him and don't succeed?" she asked one night after Giselle had been put to bed.

"I probably won't have to worry about it," he laughed. "The SS or Gestapo will see to that."

She was impatient with this answer. "I mean it. You need to have a plan."

"That's just it. I don't know yet how they plan to carry out the assassination. I don't even know for certain my own role. It's impossible to figure out what comes after that, until I know what 'that' is. Right now I am only at the edge of things."

"But you could work on an escape route. Something you could use just in case."

"Perhaps," he conceded. Such talk only depressed him, though. If the attempt failed, and Hitler lived, the war would go on forever. Until Germany was nothing but rubble. That much was about all that was clear.

As he did with Marie, Richter sometimes took Yvonne out riding with him. Both women were accomplished on horseback. Marie, who rode together with them occasionally at first, suspected from the start, he thought, that Yvonne and he had begun sleeping together. Which they had not. Though he and Marie were no longer lovers, the idea he might be with another woman appeared to trouble her. It showed on her face when the three of them were together. She distrusted Yvonne Duchamps; said she thought she was using him. Richter chalked it up to jealousy.

Yvonne, for her part, appeared to be purposefully backing away from her friendship with Marie. They spent less and less time together. Somewhat guiltily, Richter confessed to himself he felt relieved by this. He was feeling, he supposed, the tension of having shared his secret with one woman and not with the other, and he had at least a small fear Yvonne might be capable of confiding it to Marie.

After the first month or so they stopped meeting as a threesome altogether. Richter began the habit of visiting either one or the other of them, never both, when he dropped by the inn. His friendship with Marie grew more strained, and after a while they rarely mentioned Yvonne Duchamps when they were together.

* * * *

On 4 June 1944, Richter's father finally paid him a visit. Giving him only a few hours notice, the General flew into St. Sentione in the late afternoon. The two men sat in Richter's private quarters at the troop compound, sharing a bottle of Bordeaux claret while they talked.

The strain, he thought, was showing on his father. His haggard look matched the tired, distracted tone of his voice.

"Do you know Dr. Goebbels is making a film about Kolberg," Karl Richter laughed sarcastically. "He is commandeering huge numbers of men, horses and material, not to mention diverting rail traffic, for this purpose. It will be better than 'Gone with the Wind,' he says. And it will inspire the German people to beat back the invaders, as they did when they fought Napoleon at **the Siege** of Kolberg. The man doesn't even know his history. Yes, the good citizens of Kolberg **and their allies** defended the city heroically, but in the end Napoleon simply outflanked them, defeating the Russians at Friedland and forcing Prussia to sign the Treaty of Tilsit."

That, plus a few cursory personal questions, was the extent of their small talk. Still looking distracted and not always maintaining eye contact, the General plowed right in. "I want to thank you, Johann, for telling us about the two Abwehr officers working for British Intelligence. We were able to neutralize them. Without drawing too much suspicion, I believe.

"Unfortunately," he said, "that did not save Canaris' skin. And the loss of Canaris is crucial. He wasn't actively involved with us, but while he headed up the Abwehr we had a ready camouflage for our operations against Hitler. That is now gone. Canaris himself remains in great danger. Something must be done. Very soon. Everyone short of Hitler and a few fanatics around him recognizes that. Even Himmler is supposedly sending out peace feelers to the West."

He paused – gathering reserves, it appeared to Richter, as if under orders to launch an offensive he no longer believed in.

Abruptly turning to his son, he launched it. "We have chosen the man to kill Hitler," he said. The words sent shivers through Richter.

"His name is Claus von Stauffenberg, a Wehrmacht colonel."

Richter was suddenly aware of his own ragged breathing. From relief or disappointment, he wasn't sure. He had not been chosen. It was Erich Borchers' old Stuttgart acquaintance instead.

"I wanted not only to tell you this," his father said, "but also to express in person our – particularly my own – appreciation and respect for your willingness to have taken on this role yourself."

Richter had the sudden thought perhaps his father had been protecting him all along. That he'd never intended for him to pull the trigger; had kept him isolated and on the fringes of the plot to that purpose. But he quickly dismissed the idea. Karl Richter was a moral absolutist. Once he decided on a course of action based on his convictions, he would risk anything to carry it out. Even a son.

"Stauffenberg is not the ideal man for the task," the General continued. "He was wounded in North Africa. Lost an eye and an arm. But he has a strong will and the necessary access to the Fuhrer, and the deed must be done soon."

Richter already knew about Stauffenberg's wounds. He flashed back to the healthy, vital young Stauffenberg he had met briefly at Heidelberg and felt a stab of guilt. "Isn't there something I can do?" he said. "I will do whatever you need."

The General stared at him, then did something out of character. Patted his son's knee. "I know you would," he said. "You still have a role. I'm getting to that." He took another sip of claret.

"The new plan is called 'Valkyrie,'" he said. This was the first Richter had ever heard of it. "Transmission of that word over the military nets will mean Hitler has been killed. All German forces will be alerted. When you receive the Valkyrie signal here, you will mobilize your garrison and have your men transported to Paris as quickly as possible. You will transfer control of your troops there to the military governor general, von Stülpnagel, and help him secure Paris for the new government. The SS, of course, will provide your principal resistance.

"This, I assure you Johann, is the most helpful thing you can do for us."

This time Richter was definitely disappointed. He wanted to do something more than merely deliver troops, but he could tell the plans were set and knew better than to try to change them.

"If the coup is successful, what then?" he asked, masking his disappointment.

"We hope," the General replied, "to hold the Eastern Front while we negotiate a peace with the British and Americans. The success of Valkyrie depends heavily on our overthrowing Hitler before the Allies gain a foothold in the West. And it will not be long now before they try an attack on France."

Richter remembered Borchers' recent words of warning about the planned coup d'état. "And if we fail?" he said.

"If we fail," his father said with a wan smile, "this war could be the end of everything. Once Hitler's back is truly against the wall, there is no predicting what he might do. Our scientists are working on a new kind of bomb. A single bomb that could be delivered by rocket and destroy an entire city. When it's ready, Hitler will use it. And if that takes too long, we already have huge stockpiles of Sarin, a new nerve gas far more powerful than the poisons that killed so many in the last war. There is talk that the Fuhrer, who was temporarily blinded, nearly killed, by nerve gas himself in 1918, has refused to use Sarin. But with Hitler you can never be certain."

The chill returned to Richter's bones. The stakes seemed to be getting forever higher.

"And if we fail," his father continued, "you will be in grave personal danger, and I will likely no longer be in a position to help you. You'll be on your own. If you're planning to attempt an escape, it would be best to arrange it now, beforehand, as best you can." This echoed, somewhat ironically Richter thought, what Yvonne Duchamps had been telling him. "But be careful not to tip your hand," the General added. "Whatever you do, do not compromise Valkyrie. It is the best chance left for all of us. And for Germany."

That was the substance of their meeting. It was with continued mixed emotions over his own sudden reprieve – probably more relief than guilt; feelings which would, however, reverse themselves over time – that Richter prepared to bid his father goodbye.

He wondered if they would ever meet again. The General's air of fatalism had given his words a tone of finality that day. Even while he had discussed the plot to kill Hitler and overthrow the Nazis, he hadn't sounded entirely convinced it could succeed.

Richter hoped his father had been buoyed at least a little by their talk. He made an effort, however clumsy, as the General readied his departure, to communicate his support and pride, and how much he cared about him. His father's only response was a sad smile that Richter read as acknowledgment.

Karl Richter's final words to his son before he left early that evening were, "Well, in any event, we should soon know, one way or the other," accompanied by a determinedly optimistic grin and a firm handshake.

Two days later, on 6 June 1944, the Allies would land at Normandy.

CHAPTER XX

Elena Stein was gone by the time Michael Cohen awoke from a restless sleep. She left a note that she had taken Teresa with her, but asked if Cohen would please look after Tomas until she returned. She promised to be back no later than noon.

As Cohen sat on the side of the bed, still groggy, he looked up and found he was not alone. Tomas was standing at the door between the two rooms. He was looking Cohen over carefully, just as he had done when they first met. Without his mother, the small boy seemed lost in this strange place. Cohen suddenly wanted to make contact with him, comfort him if he could.

He had not had much experience with children. When he invited Tomas into the room the boy didn't move. Watching him, Cohen was flooded with unwelcome memories of his own childhood and how vulnerable he had felt.

"Where is my mother?" the boy voiced in plaintive demand.

"Come here, and I'll tell you," Cohen said. This time Tomas hesitantly approached the bed and leaned over it, looking up at Cohen.

"Your mother is visiting your father. She will be back very soon." Even to his own ear, the words sounded patronizing, tailored to a little boy who understood only simple concepts. He had never liked this kind of speech from adults when he was a child. He resolved to be more straightforward with Tomas.

"Where is Papa? When will he come back?" The words were heartrending to Cohen, but the young boy betrayed little emotion.

"I don't know." How to be straightforward about this? Cohen felt an indefinable guilt descend onto his shoulders. It made no sense, but that did not appear to matter. His gloom fed off shadows from the past.

He could see his baby brother Jeremiah, the look he had given Cohen when they were separated at Dachau. "I don't know," he repeated.

"Why did those men have to take him away? He never does anything bad," Tomas stated firmly.

Before Cohen could formulate a reply, Elena Stein walked into the room. He had the feeling she'd been standing in the doorway watching them. She looked down at her son. "No, he does not, Tomas," she said, giving Cohen a grateful smile. Tomas pushed off from the bed and ran to her. She scooped him up into her arms and carried him to the doorway. "One moment," she said to Cohen, and closed the door behind her.

By the time she returned, he had dressed and was standing by the sliding glass doors to the balcony, looking out at a foggy La Negra.

"Did you get in to see him this time?" Cohen said.

"Yes, for a short time." She seemed distracted. "I am not allowed into his cell." Her stare was focused somewhere out the glass doors. "He is so thin now. . ." She let out a whimsical little laugh. "I tell Johann about you. He is very curious about you."

Odd, he thought, but this last sounded almost coquettish. Was he imagining that? "In what way?" he said.

"He says you are here to write about him. For a magazine. He wants to be sure we are safe with you, the children and me. So I tell him about Dachau." Now she appeared slightly uneasy. "He tells me something about the way the numbers on prisoners are made at Dachau. It is different from other camps. May I? Johann ask me to look."

Cohen was taken aback. He seemed to have awakened to a topsy-turvy world. Were *they* safe with *him*?

"I am sorry to ask." Elena looked troubled, but nonetheless determined to put him to the test. No coquettishness now.

Cohen held out his right arm. It was starting to feel like a ritual. Like a lightning bolt, a sudden, searing memory of the steel-tipped stylus shooting the indelible ink beneath his skin flashed through him for the first time in years. The pain had lasted for weeks, but he had been lucky. No infection, and the swelling had been minor. The common belief among prisoners at Dachau was that being branded this way meant you were more valuable to camp operations, thus more likely to survive. Cohen had never believed it.

Awaiting Elena's verdict, he felt the twinge of an old remorse, but it was too complicated to fathom in this new light.

She let go of his arm. "Thank you," she said, apparently satisfied.

He said nothing, just wondered if anything were really worth it anymore. Muted echoes floated up from the city below. He had the urge for a drink.

"Johann, he wants me to meet with a priest tomorrow," Elena said, sounding a bit hurried, as if wanting to leave this little episode behind as quickly as possible. "A priest I know. Father Hidalgo. He visits me once at Riberalta to bring news from Johann."

"Do you know why? Why he wants you to meet him."

"No. But I must go. It is important. Can you watch Tomas a little while more, tomorrow?"

Cohen murmured his assent, absentmindedly.

"Thank you. Now I make him, both of you, some lunch." She got up and returned to the other room. He stared at the wall for a few minutes before he stepped out onto the balcony for some fresh air.

* * * *

That night Cohen managed to do his drinking without interruption. No one popped up at the bar to recruit him and he was left alone to ruminate and draw his own conclusions. Unfortunately, nothing much added up before his internal gears started slipping on tequila. The streets were still cold, still misty, as he limped back to the Miranda at 1 a.m. thanking God that Leland Powell's twelve-hour deadline had evidently been extended.

Up in his rooms, the inside door was closed. Elena Stein and her children appeared to have gone to bed. Not surprising, given the hour, but Cohen found himself disappointed he had missed her. In spite of the slight discomfort he felt around her, there was a connection, he thought. There was the obvious one, of course, the camps. But it went beyond that, at least for him. She drew him to her in a way no one since Rachel had. He had no idea what he could do about that, or whether the feeling was reciprocated, but he knew one thing. It made him feel more alive.

She had left a note on his bed – *Dear Michael, I am thanking you so much, for everything. You are a good man. Lovingly, Elena Stein.*

Cohen rolled that "lovingly" around in his mind. His mood soared. He stripped off his clothes and climbed into bed, tired and wary but feeling more hopeful than he had in years, and promptly fell asleep.

He awoke bathed in sweat, with Elena at his side in flickering candlelight, wearing a look of concern. "You are having a nightmare," she said.

"Sorry." His heart was still pounding in his ears. He remembered Tomas from the night before. How he had left him alone with his nightmare.

"I have such dreams too," she said. "I dream of old friends. Most of them dead." Her eyes were focused miles away. He wondered what she was seeing. What she was seeing was Erhardt, her savior at Kaisenher, and Mueller, the camp commandant. What Mueller had done to Erhardt. If she didn't fight it with every fiber of her being, she could be pulled back there in an instant, she knew.

"I was dreaming about my family," said Cohen, propped on his elbows now and noting Elena's prim cotton nightdress.

She looked away. She felt the undertow of something dangerous, a riptide she wasn't sure she could resist. "I do not dream about my family," she said. "Ever."

"Maybe that's for the best. It is. . . difficult."

"No. I miss them. But I cannot bear to remember them. My dreams seem to know this. Even my nightmares."

"You have a family of your own now," Cohen said, in spite of his doubts about Richter.

"It is why I survive. Without them, I am nothing." She felt suddenly very tired.

"I, uh–" Cohen had been about to say, "I envy you," but it didn't sound right.

"We are *your* family now. All of us," Elena said, her face only inches from his.

He wasn't sure exactly what she meant by "we". It mattered little, however. What mattered was that she was here, and the lift it gave him. "Thank you," he said, feeling inadequate to the moment.

"I am thinking since last night about your Rachel," she said, "about the terrible thing that has happen between you. It is hard to believe, maybe, but I understand. I want you to know that. That I understand, and that you must put it behind you and go on. It is not easy, but there is no other way."

She kissed him on the forehead. Intoxicated, both literally and figuratively, he reached up and kissed her on the lips. A wild mix of feelings – spawned by Richter as well as Elena, he knew – surged through him. Passion, lust and a kind of love was mixed with something that bordered on revenge. He held the kiss an extra beat, imagining he could detect a response. She paused what seemed an extra beat herself, then broke away and stood up.

"Good night," she whispered, disappearing with the candlelight.

Cohen lay still, staring into the darkness. This time it was no dream. This had been Elena Stein in the flesh, and this time it was not going to be so easy to dismiss. In spite of his confused emotions, she existed on her own for him now, not just as an extension of his memories of Rachel Stern or his thoughts about Johann Richter.

Sleep did not return to him that night. He continued to stare into the void until sunlight began to streak the walls.

* * * *

In the morning, Elena Stein fixed everyone breakfast. She politely declined Cohen's offer to accompany her to her rendezvous with the priest. He warned her to be careful, but she just smiled as she left with Teresa strapped against her chest in the local fashion.

When they were done eating, he took Tomas for a walk. The fog had only partially lifted. The city was still enshrouded, but the sun at least suffused the shroud with light and a modicum of warmth. People went about their business with a solemn air. Street vendors said nothing to hawk their wares. They merely waited patiently for customers. In spite of all the international publicity Richter's case had generated, Cohen and Tomas passed no other *norteamericanos* or European types on their walk.

For no particular reason, Cohen led them up into the cemetery he had visited the day before, up past the little village of tombs and mausoleums, up to where the vegetation petered out. He sat down, feeling the lack of sleep in his bones. The small boy sat beside him. Neither had said a word since they left the Miranda.

Tomas suddenly interrupted Cohen's thoughts. "Why do you walk funny?" he asked.

Cohen snorted. "You think I walk funny, eh?"

"Yes. You limp."

"That I do. That I do. It's kind of a long story."

Tomas moved on. "Where do you live?" he said.

"In the United States," Cohen replied. "A city called New York." It came to him suddenly how much he liked New York, with its anonymous streets and larger than life feel. As restless as he sometimes felt, it would take a major jolt, he thought, to make him leave the City.

"Is your family there?"

"No."

"Where are they?"

"They're dead."

"All of them?"

Cohen shook his head, involuntarily. "Yes," he said.

The boy appeared puzzled by this information.

"Where is your wife?" he asked finally.

"I'm not married."

"Do you have friends where you live?"

"A few." A very few, he thought. He supposed that was one reason it had been so easy for John Weaver to befriend him. Where was Weaver, anyway?

"Do you have friends?" he asked Tomas.

"A few," the boy mimicked.

Cohen smiled. "Good. It's good to have friends," he said, and patted the boy's shoulder awkwardly. He felt oddly comforted sitting there on the cloudy hillside with the small boy by his side. Surrounded by the dead. Tomas was perhaps about to face at least a part of what Cohen had endured as a child, and it made Cohen feel a bond with him, a need to protect him. He found himself hoping the boy would survive somehow with some of his innocence still intact. "Good," he repeated.

Staring absently at a nearby burial vault, Cohen's mind wandered to a miscellaneous assertion, one of many in the collection of notes Terry Harper had left behind. He claimed the Russians, when they had taken Berlin in May of 1945, had dug up the charred remains of Adolf Hitler and his new bride Eva Braun, identified them, and eventually reburied them in an unmarked grave in Magdeburg a hundred kilometers from the ruined capital city. The hope, he said, was that no one would ever find them there. Harper named his "highly reliable source" for all this as a Soviet defector who had been thoroughly vetted by British Intelligence.

If true, it was a major revelation. The Soviets after the war had said virtually nothing to the Western Allies about the fate of Hitler. Stalin had in fact encouraged rumors the Fuhrer was still alive.

Cohen took a deep breath. Such was the power of Hitler, he thought, that even those who had vanquished him were fearful he might somehow return, like a brush fire smoldering beneath the forest floor.

He understood the feeling.

As they continued to sit and look out over La Negra and the clouds, Cohen trying not to worry about Elena Stein, the view again reminded him of Israel. He remembered something a survivor of the death camps had once said to him, in an attempt at ironic consolation – *After all, it was Adolf Hitler, was it not, who made Israel possible?* This thought took him back to his tequila haze of night before last, to one more set of memories he had long kept repressed.

Only hours after their reunion in Tel Aviv, as requested, the jeweler from Dusseldorf had taken him to a makeshift military hospital on the northern outskirts of town, a small tent city of the wounded. A petite, very businesslike nurse led them to an empty bunk.

"Now where did she go this time?" the nurse said in surprisingly good-natured exasperation. "Ever since she's been on the mend, she's been our most difficult patient, bar none."

"Are you by any chance looking for me?"

Cohen nearly wrenched his neck turning to see the woman he thought he had lost forever. He barely recognized the figure who now stood before him on a pair of crutches. Her once-emaciated frame had filled out into full womanly form, and it made her always beautiful face even more beautiful.

"Mi-chi-ael?" She had a way of stretching the second syllable of his name into a Biblical sound. His heart melted as they stood eyeing each other mutely. Before there was time for awkwardness to set in, another woman appeared by Rachel's side, of similar size and build, but blond rather than dark.

"Who are your friends?" this newcomer asked Rachel, who promptly awoke from her trance and introduced the two men to Maria

Zamora. "Maria is from Spain," she said, with a note of both tenderness and friendly amusement. "She has come here all on her own, to fight for our independence."

"I am a Jew. I belong here like everyone else," Maria Zamora said, responding in kind, seriously, but with a smile.

Cohen had the same reaction he'd had aboard ship, a feeling of pride that the world's Jews had finally found a common cause. Something to rally around. He felt a stab of shame he couldn't join them, at least not for now.

Maria Zamora and the jeweler soon took their leave, and the two reunited lovers sat on the cot and talked about the lives they had led since they were last together. She'd been saved by the Americans, she said. They had nursed her back from the brink of death, just as the British had done for Cohen.

"I was still a little weak when I came here," she said. "But now I am fine, except for this little hole in my leg."

She lifted the bandage on her right thigh. He winced at the size of her wound. "Luckily, the bullet went right through," she said cheerily. "It was a clean wound."

As they talked, it was as if they were different people from the two lost souls who had met so briefly but intensely at Dachau. His feelings had not changed, however. He felt the same way about her he had felt back then.

"You know, I thought you were dead too," she said. "I tried to find you, but I couldn't."

Cohen was not surprised. The British, once they recruited him, had erased all evidence of him from Displaced Persons rosters. When they put him back in a DP camp for cover later, they didn't want anyone asking any compromising questions.

They talked for nearly an hour. Standing up to take his leave, he felt awkward. He realized they had not hugged, had not touched at all. Not knowing what else to do, he kissed her on the cheek.

"Come back again. Please," she said.

Over the next few months, while he trained with Haganah and she continued to recuperate, they saw each other about once a week. Little by little, Rachel convinced him the British viewed Irgun as a terrorist organization only because it was effective, a notion that gave him minor comfort in light of the danger she was in fighting for the unit. When she moved from crutches to a cane, they drove a borrowed car out to the beaches north of Tel Aviv to breathe the fresh sea air and stare at the waves. Finding themselves alone there late one afternoon in a small protected cove, they became lovers again, making careful, tender love that did not strain Rachel's nearly healed wound.

"I have to tell you something," she said to him a few days later. "I, ah, did not escape from Heinrich Mueller without paying a price. I lied to you because I felt ashamed. I was forced, but that's no excuse." It dawned on Cohen what was coming. He could feel it in the pit of his stomach. "He raped me," she said, "then he kept me around to satisfy his needs. Thankfully he was too drunk most of the time to bother. Most nights, he just fell asleep and snored.

"I could have killed him while he slept," she said. Cohen had the feeling this was a proposition she had weighed many times since her ordeal at Kaisenher. "I'm not sure how, but I could have done it. But I was in a mental fog. And very young. I chose to live. I'm sorry."

"Don't apologize," he said. "Never apologize for that." He meant it, but he also felt sick down deep inside, as if Heinrich Mueller still had a hold on their lives. He wished *he* could've killed the man. "Never," he repeated with as much conviction as he could muster.

That day, they did not make love. Over the next few weeks and months, they did their best to work around Rachel's revelation. As they renewed their intimacy, they tried to find a new version of their old relationship. Meanwhile Cohen kept up a periodic communication with his control officer. As the siege of Jerusalem neared a climax, his contact – who he knew only as "Jack," as in Union Jack – directed him to seek an assignment there. It would be invaluable to the British to have an inside source of information on the scene, he said. Cohen had qualms. He was beginning to comprehend the depth of British opposition to the founding of a Jewish state. They assured him, however, he would not be selling anybody out, that he was only being asked to report his observations to help guide British policy at a difficult time.

Cohen got the assignment. He dreaded saying good-bye to Rachel, but was given a last-minute reprieve. As he started to tell her, she surprised him with news that she was about to return to Jerusalem herself.

The announcement elated and upset Cohen both. While they could now hopefully continue seeing one another, they would not be fighting side by side. The more radical Irgun, often at odds with Haganah, was too small and too tight-knit an outfit for Cohen's purposes. Haganah, on the other hand, was bigger, looser, and needed every able body it could muster in Jerusalem.

All went reasonably well at first. They went in on the same convoy, via the "Burma Road" that Haganah had built through stretches of open desert to avoid Arab Legion strongholds along the more traditional route. In Jerusalem, however, chaos reigned. On arrival, Rachel left to report in with Irgun, which was spearheading the fighting there. She was gone for two days. When she returned, it was with disturbing news. The British were expected to evacuate the next day, and Rachel was to join an Irgun raid on "The Fort," a former British stronghold near Zion Gate at the Old City wall. The Old City remained in the hands of the Arab Legion. The fate of all Jerusalem hung in the balance, she said.

Cohen already knew the British had a secret protocol with the Arab Legion about The Fort. As they pulled out, they were to hand it over to the Arabs and leave them in control of as much of the city as possible. Irgun would be stepping into a virtual trap.

He and Rachel were holed up that night in a small abandoned hut that had been home to an Arab family before most of the Arabs had fled into the Old City or left Jerusalem altogether. Cohen wanted desperately to protect her. "Your fighters will be slaughtered if they try to take The Fort tomorrow," he said. "You must try to stop them. And, at all costs, don't join them if they do attack."

She gave him a curious look. "How do you know this?"

The British would consider this treason, he knew, if they ever found out, but he had to stop her. "I know what the British are planning," he said. "I know they have arranged for the Arab Legion to take over The Fort."

"How? How do you know these things?" Her look was growing darker.

"Because I am working for them," he said, knowing he was risking something as important as life itself with his confession. Rachel.

"You are what?!"

"I'm working for them. I report to the British."

Her features went totally blank, as if she were cutting off all communication with him. "Then I must tell my people," she said, but not to him.

With a sinking heart, he pleaded one more time. "Whatever you do," he said. "Do not join the raid on The Fort. Promise me that much."

She gave him a final look – one that had perhaps a flicker of sorrow in it, he thought – and left, promising nothing. He agonized all night about whether to go after her, but knew it would do no good.

He would never see her again. She was killed during the raid the next morning, by a sniper's bullet. "She died bravely," Maria Zamora told him. "She took incredible risks to help us breach the outer walls." Cohen tortured himself with the possibility she might have courted death because of him. This one he couldn't blame on Hitler. This death was on his head, and his alone.

The raid was successful, in spite of the British agreement with the Arabs. Cohen tried to console himself Rachel had died for a purpose, and that maybe his information had helped the Irgun assault. It did not work. He knew he should have gone after her, should have joined the raid and died by her side. And he knew this thought would never leave him, would torment him forever.

In a state of shock and mourning, he waited for the ax to fall. It could fall from Irgun, or from the British. It did not matter to him. He was sure he was about to die, and didn't care. He welcomed the notion of oblivion.

But nothing happened. It soon became evident that whatever else she'd done, Rachel had not told anyone about his connection with the British. He was not going to be killed, at least not right now and not by Irgun or by British Intelligence. Now all he had to do was find a new reason to live.

He found it by helping Irgun and Haganah whenever he could. Rachel had died for the creation of a Jewish homeland. If the same fate was in store for him, so be it. He took a chance and offered his undercover services to Haganah. They accepted, with few questions asked. The Jewish freedom fighters were in no position to be picky at this point. He became, in effect, a double agent, giving Haganah a clearer idea of British plans to help the Arabs take over Palestine.

On 14 May 1948, David Ben-Gurion announced the founding of the nation of Israel, an independent Jewish state carved from centuries of tragedy and loss, and rejoiced over all the more because of it. By the end of May, most of the fighting and jockeying for position be-tween Jews and Arabs was over and the Jews found themselves in possession of a fledgling nation-state. Though still small, it was larger than anyone had anticipated given the seeming military realities of only a few months earlier.

In his search for something to keep him afloat, Cohen had ac-cepted the friendship of Maria Zamora, who continued her work with Irgun seemingly oblivious that Cohen had once been a British plant. Maria had not been in the death camps during the war, a fact that per-haps enhanced her level of trust in others, Cohen thought. Her father and brothers had fought against Franco in the Spanish Civil War, and the family had been forced to flee after his victory. Her fiancé had died fighting Hitler. She was tough, a good fighter for Irgun, with a vulnerability that showed through now and then. Cohen felt drawn to her, but was definitely not ready for another woman.

Without Rachel, Israel came to seem bleak and gray, a gaggle of bickering factions beating as much on each other as on the enemy. At the same time, Cohen's position there was increasingly fraught with danger. He knew he couldn't play this game forever. The British, he sensed, might already be on to him. That they had saved him from death for this assignment was no guarantee they would not, in the end, kill him for not carrying it out.

His dreams, such as they were, had begun to focus again on an earlier fantasy of refuge. America. He resolved that as soon as he could do it without arousing too much suspicion, he would attempt to emigrate, escape back to a homeland that now seemed as exotic and out of reach as a barely remembered dream. In America, he thought, perhaps he could find a new reason for going on.

He confided in Maria Zamora and briefly considered inviting her to come along. The half-hearted impulse, however, never made it into words. She promised to keep his secret. Maybe one day he would re-turn to Israel, she added with a wistful smile that held out little such hope.

One more surprise was in store for him. The day he left, Maria, in her farewell, said, "There is something I should tell you." He waited, with no idea what was coming. "Rachel. She uh. . . She was going to have a baby. Your baby."

"She what?!"

"If she had lived. She was carrying your child. She was quite sure she was pregnant."

This was the final blow. It had sent Cohen into a chasm of despair he still fought every day. Time had dulled the heartache, but nothing, he suspected, would ever entirely erase it. Even Elena Stein, a virtual stranger, had been moved to something resembling tears when he had hesitatingly – he had never discussed it with anyone before – told her about it two nights ago.

He stared out at the clouds, letting the all too familiar pain wash over him, inviting it to do its worst, to hurt enough to earn him some redemption.

Cohen felt a tug on his sleeve.

He awoke as if from another world. "It's getting cold," Tomas said, looking up at him with soulful eyes.

"Yes, it is," he agreed, suddenly feeling the cold as he reawoke to the hillside of tombs and vistas above La Negra. "Time to go then," he said.

The small boy put his hand in Cohen's as they got up and walked back down the hill and into the city again.

*   *   *   *

In the Miranda lobby, the desk clerk stopped Cohen. "Señor," he said, "a priest is here to see you. He is in your room."

Everyone else seemed to have access to his quarters here, Cohen thought. So why not a priest? On his way up the stairs, however, his melancholy mood gave way to a growing tension. Why a priest? Wasn't Elena supposed to be meeting with a priest?

The door was already open. A priest indeed was sitting in the easy chair, staring at him intently as he entered feeling like a guest in his own rooms.

"Señor Cohen?" the priest said, rising from the chair. "Good. Thank God you are here. And Tomas, how are you, my son?"

"Hello, Father," the boy responded, smiling and making the sign of the cross.

"Very good, Tomas." The priest patted him on the shoulder as he closed the door to the hallway and said to Cohen, "Perhaps we could speak. . ." – He gestured around the room as if at invisible hazards, then indicated the balcony – "Just in case."

"I'll join you in a minute," Cohen said. He took Tomas by the hand and led him into the other room. He lifted the boy onto the bed and ruffled his hair. Tomas smiled a little uncertainly. "Stay in here, please," Cohen said. "Just for a few minutes." He squeezed the boy's shoulder gently, then shut the door behind him.

"I am Father Felipe Hidalgo," the priest said, out on the balcony. He was short and trim, with an intelligent face. Cohen thought perhaps he had seen him in the courtroom once. "I serve the prison here. I give counsel to Herr Richter; I know his wife and family."

Cohen waited for the punch line.

It arrived quickly. "I am here because she has been kidnapped," Father Hidalgo said. "She and her baby."

"Say that again?" Cohen could not believe his ears.

"She has been kidnapped."

"Elena Stein?" Cohen felt the mirage of last night evaporate. Any lingering fatigue vanished along with it.

"Yes. With her baby," Father Hidalgo repeated.

What the hell for, was all Cohen could think. He had a vague unsettling notion, however, that he should know. Should perhaps even have expected it.

"Are you sure?" he said.

"It happened while she was with me. They came into the church and took them away. I could not stop them."

"What do they want?"

"They want you to deliver a message to Herr Richter. They will be watching, they said, to be sure I do not return to the prison to deliver it myself."

"Who are these people?"

"I don't know. Europeans. Englishmen, I believe. One of them said you would know who they were."

It had to be Anders Hardy. Cohen wondered if it had been Hardy who had followed Elena earlier. He felt a cold anger rising.

"Where's this message?" He was expecting to be handed an envelope or a piece of paper.

"They gave me only a verbal message. And this." Father Hidalgo held out a simple gold ring. "Her wedding band. They said they would send along something else later – 'something more painful to extract'

– if you need more convincing. The message is quite simple. If Herr Richter wants his wife and daughter to live, he must, as they put it, 'do the world a favor and eliminate himself.' Kill himself, in other words."

Cohen inspected the ring. There was an inscription inside the band. He couldn't make it out. A pair of interlocking initials maybe.

"The man who appeared to be their leader said you would understand the necessity of this, why this should be," Father Hidalgo said. "'He is a survivor. He won't let another survivor die,' he said, speaking about you. 'And Cohen knows this is only justice, in any case,' he said."

Cohen took a deep breath, and for the first time in a while was aware of the oxygen-starved air. He vowed he would find a way to free Elena Stein. No matter what it took.

"Not a pleasant message to deliver, as you can see. My advice is don't do it. Whatever Herr Richter has done, he could not have committed the crimes of which he is accused. I am confident of that. I am here only because I gave God's Word that I would pass this along to you. And my advice to Herr Richter, which I hope you will add if you decide you must deliver this message, is to ignore it."

The priest tacked on an opaque postscript: "Either way, if you see him, be sure, I beg you, to tell him there is still hope in his deliverance. Soon. This is important."

Cohen looked out across the hazy rooftops. A few things, at least, were starting to come clear. And perhaps there was some kind of poetic justice at work that he was caught up in the middle of it all.

"What are you thinking?" Father Hidalgo interrupted his reverie.

He was weighing the pluses and minuses. Elena Stein and Teresa, and Tomas as well, on one side. On the other, a Wehrmacht officer accused of murder. After last night, it was no contest.

"I guess there's not much choice," he finally said. After all the delays and foot-dragging, it was time to face off with Johann Richter.

CHAPTER XXI

It was night before Cohen was able to gain entrance to the prison. The priest had arranged it, and had agreed to look after Tomas while Cohen was gone.

A heavyset guard backed by two men carrying carbines at the ready met him inside a side gate reserved for prisoners and their visitors. Father Hidalgo had told Cohen not to let Frederico – he had described the heavyset man – extort any money from him, because he had already been paid in advance.

He could hear the quickbeat of a mambo tune blaring from a radio somewhere. It seemed out of place. It was like "La Cucaracha" being played in a cemetery.

From behind a desk, Frederico asked a few questions. Cohen answered in his faltering Spanish. The guard offered several prolonged pauses, but made no effort more directed than that to increase the entry fee. Cohen could read nothing in his dark eyes. Lumbering to his feet, the man directed Cohen to raise his arms and frisked him halfheartedly. He poked around more carefully inside the large manila envelope Cohen was carrying, found nothing but paper and handed it back.

"Vamanos, Señor," he said, apparently satisfied. Cohen followed him, with the other two trailing behind.

All iron bars and slimy walls, dirt floors and the stench of decay, the dimly lit corridor widened after a turn to the left, then brightened a bit after another ten yards or so and a turn to the right. Cohen felt as if he were descending into his past, but was surprised to find a sense of anticipation overriding any feeling of dread. He was here for Elena, but *he* wanted some questions answered as well. He felt calm.

The mambo faded away, broken into little bits and pieces, barely heard. Moonlight began oozing in through open-air, barred windows at head level on both sides. A slight breeze helped lift the musty stench of the place and the underground corridor continued to emerge into the moonlight until the ground outside leveled off about chest high.

The passageway finally ended in the corridor's only cell, a large square space, surprisingly open and lit by two lamps on one side. It looked, Cohen thought, as if it were intended for four or five inmates, not one. A window of vertical bars ran the entire length of the cell's far wall, from halfway up, where it met ground level, to the ceiling. The outside view, which began about shoulder height, was a kind of gopher's-eye panorama of green grass dropping away toward lights that flickered like a city beneath an airliner, and the dark outline of mountains beyond. A distant corner of Lake Tocqual was visible. The rest of the lake and most of La Negra lay somewhere out of sight just over the curve of hillside.

The huge cell door, also constructed of vertical bars, was the same height and width as the corridor and opened into the middle of the cell. While Frederico fiddled with his keys, Cohen's eyes swept over the place, the dirt floor and the dark immaculately clean carpet that covered most of it, the empty slop buckets, straight-backed chairs and the bed up against the right-hand wall, a desk and chair beside it. Sitting at this desk, his back to the door and unresponsive to the sound of keys, was a man. Presumably Richter. He appeared to be writing something.

As the guard swung the door open and Cohen stepped warily into the cell, the man turned from his work and stood up. It was a bit of a shock. Though Cohen had seen Richter in court, he had never studied him up close before. In the confined space the man emanated energy. He was Cohen's height, maybe a little taller. Up close, the thin scar that cut across his left cheekbone seemed more dramatic. The cold blue eyes under his high, brooding forehead were focused intently on Cohen, who experienced a sudden unexpected nervousness.

The guard relocked the cell door and left. Richter broke the ensuing silence. "You must be Cohen. Elena told me about you," he said, looking faintly amused. The word "Elena" jolted Cohen out of his nervousness and put him back on task. "I am Johann Richter," the prisoner said. The voice was deeper than expected. There was no German accent. He sounded like an Englishman, thought Cohen, only slightly surprised Richter had elected to speak in something other than his native tongue.

They shook hands. Richter's grip was strong and firm. "Please sit down," he said. An Oxford don to his first-year charge. He motioned Cohen toward the bed, the only convenient place to sit anywhere near the desk. Cohen laid his envelope on a small bedside table. Richter looked at him intently, an evaluating stare.

"We have a mutual acquaintance, I believe," Cohen said finally, to break the ice.

Richter continued to eye him carefully. "And who might that be?"

"A man named Terry Harper."

"An Englishman? Who lives in New York."

"He did. Now he's dead."

Richter showed no surprise. "He was eccentric, but rather charming. Seemed a good man. He wanted to write about me. I told him more than I meant to."

"He did write about you," Cohen said. "Now I'm supposed to be writing about you."

"So I hear."

"I haven't written a word yet."

Richter smiled slightly. "Hard to get a handle on, eh?"

"Something like that. I've been listening to testimony, watching you for days. But I don't know as much about you as Terry Harper did. Assuming you told him the truth."

"Oh, I told him the truth. Perhaps with a little garnish – and I didn't tell him everything. He was a former journalist, as I recall, but he didn't always ask the right questions." Richter gave Cohen an almost playful look. "Do you want to ask me any questions, Mr. Cohen?"

Cohen's response was instinctive. "How do you live with the guilt?" he said. It sounded like an attack, he thought, but he didn't intend it that way. Not entirely, anyhow. It was a question he had struggled with in his own life.

Richter, in a deceptively quick move, jumped up and began pacing the cell, the hint of a smile still pasted on his face. "I don't expect objectivity from you, Cohen. If I were in your shoes – gone through what you've gone through – I'd probably hate my bloody guts too."

As the man spoke, Cohen had to remind himself he was German, not English, the understated accent was so perfect.

"I understand how it must appear to you," Richter said. His pacing seemed a bit hyperactive to Cohen. "I know I don't have to tell you, Cohen, about the camps. My wife was in one. I got a good look at it myself. It's remarkable what we humans are capable of doing to one another. And you are quite correct. There is plenty of guilt to go around from those days. I am a Catholic; I understand guilt. I am a strong believer in individual responsibility. Even with something that was basically unstoppable, like what Hitler did to the Jews."

"That wasn't unstoppable. You and your friends could have stopped it," Cohen said.

"My friends and I tried to stop it. My father tried to stop it, at great cost." Richter's voice trailed off. He quit pacing. The mask of detached amusement had disappeared. "I am quite willing to accept any guilt I deserve from those days – and I'm sure I earned some. But I will not accept Adolf Hitler's. Not for everything, anyway."

Though Richter still stared at him, it was with eyes now focused in somber contemplation somewhere behind Cohen's head. "Father Hidalgo," he said, "tells me that if your motives are pure and without guilt, then so are you. Moral intent, he says, does not guarantee a moral result. We did our best to kill Hitler. Father Hidalgo says any deed performed out of a pure intent is in essence an act of God, and is therefore divine fate, regardless of its outcome. That it is, by definition, redemptive."

This short speech Cohen thought somewhat remarkable given his two-minute acquaintance with the man. The talk of guilt and redemption struck an uncomfortable chord in him, made him wonder if there were a formula that could lead to his own salvation. Oddly enough, he found himself feeling more at ease.

"I heard you did kill Hitler," he said, not knowing what this might provoke. He wanted to gauge, perhaps, just how out of touch with reality Richter might be.

"Sorry?" Richter looked at him sternly, as if assessing his sincerity.

"Or at least thought you killed him."

"Who told you that?"

"Terry Harper."

Richter looked away. "Claus von Stauffenberg," he said in a muted voice, "thought he killed him too. Hitler was a hard man to kill."

The answer, for all its evasion, didn't strike Cohen as particularly delusional.

"He was the Devil. He would not stay dead," Richter added with something resembling a low chuckle.

That sounded more delusional, Cohen thought.

"How about the two murders you're being tried for?" he said. "Do you accept responsibility for those?"

Richter managed a half-smile, but his stare remained focused elsewhere. "I do," he said. "But not in the way Anne Johns, or even Marie Renault, is implying."

Cohen wondered what that was supposed to mean.

"Of the two deaths," Richter said, "I regret only Christine's."

"Why is that?"

"Christine died trying to help me. I didn't kill her, but I used her in a way that probably got her killed. I accept the responsibility, and the guilt, for that."

The smile was gone now. Richter's voice was tinged with melancholy. "Yvonne Duchamps, on the other hand, died trying to kill me. And she undoubtedly helped kill von Stauffenberg and the rest. Helped *me* kill them. I miscalculated with her. Badly. I thought she hated the Nazis. I thought her husband was a POW, held by us. And she had that beautiful child. . ."

"What happened?"

Richter gave him a long hard look. "How do I know you're not with British Intelligence?"

"You don't," Cohen said. "If you don't want to talk about it, that's your prerogative."

Richter shook his head and eyed Cohen obliquely. "I suppose it doesn't matter. Unless you're here to kill me." He almost smiled. "Are you?"

"Not exactly." Though it's not such a bad idea, Cohen thought.

Richter laughed. *"Not exactly,"* he repeated.

"So what happened?" Cohen persisted.

"With Yvonne Duchamps?" Richter shrugged, apparently in acquiescence. "I don't know why I trusted her, really. Marie tried to warn me, said something didn't seem right about her. But I just thought Marie was jealous. The male ego" – this time Richter did smile – "It never fails to get us in trouble.

"She was a good actress, Yvonne was. When I first told her we planned to kill Hitler, she looked at me as if I were out of my bloody mind," Richter laughed again. This time a laugh without humor. *Was* he crazy? Cohen wondered. "But she knew," Richter said. "She knew early on what we planned to do. And she passed it along to the British. Simply put, she sold us out.

"As did others. We were undercut from everywhere – the true believers, the officers too timid or too ambitious to go after the Fuhrer, the Allies with their 'unconditional surrender,' their determination to conquer Germany and subjugate her." Richter's tone remained even, but Cohen caught a fleeting glimpse of something behind the reasonable facade, something less under control. "And by the Communists," he tacked on.

"The Communists?"

"British Intelligence, in particular, was riddled with them."

"What would you know about that?" Cohen said. He recalled just the day before he had heard this same theory from Leland Powell and John Weaver. Was it really possible the two hadn't had any contact with Richter on the subject?

"It is my belief," Richter said, "that an agent named Anders Hardy was the ringleader. Though he may have worked with, or even been run by, another agent in place working for the Soviets, a man named Philby. And these moles aren't done yet. They're still out there. Two of them fled to Russia just last year. Some are still on active service with the British."

So Richter might be as valuable to MI6 and the CIA as Powell and Weaver hoped he would be, Cohen thought. If he could name names, and it appeared he could. For starters, he knew about Hardy and Philby, their two prime suspects.

"But why did that make any difference to you during the war, to your plans for Hitler?" Cohen asked.

"The Communist elements inside British Intelligence were actively undermining our attempts to kill Hitler. This is not something I knew during most of my time in England. Christine Johns told me shortly before I left. It's why she had to be killed."

"By whom?"

"By MI6. Anders Hardy, most likely. He's the one she knew for sure."

"That's all pretty far-fetched, isn't it?" Cohen said, though he was beginning to wonder. It matched up pretty well with what Weaver and the two Englishmen had said the day before.

"It wouldn't seem so far-fetched if you knew Anders Hardy," Richter said.

"I do know Anders Hardy."

Now it was Richter's turn to look skeptical. Cohen wanted to ask him the same question he had asked Leland Powell – why the Communists, why Stalin of all people, would want to protect Hitler – but suddenly he heard voices down the corridor and realized he'd better state his business. He couldn't believe he had set Elena's fate aside even for a few minutes.

"I have a message for you," he said, a little under his breath. "And I believe it's from him. Hardy." Cohen didn't know if the guards were coming for him yet, but he couldn't risk beating around the bush. He knew he had to speed things up.

Richter's eyes had taken on an intensity that hinted he already had a good idea what the message might be. He absentmindedly rubbed his cheekbone where the scar cut across it.

"Hardy or whoever it is, says he has your wife and daughter and won't let them go until you're dead." Cohen's voice was a monotone. It was a way he had handled things in the camps. But he didn't feel as detached as he had thought he would delivering the demand that Richter kill himself.

He searched the man's face for a reaction. Richter said nothing, merely frowned and turned away toward the barred windows.

Momentarily distracted, Cohen scanned the desk, topped with scattered handwritten pages filled with a disciplined penmanship. For the first time, he noticed what looked to be a small opened bag of coca leaves on the desk. Had Elena Stein smuggled it in?

Cohen found himself listening for a coca edge in Richter's voice, as the prisoner, his back to Cohen, said, "I will do whatever it takes to save my family."

This response got to Cohen, regardless of its inspiration.

"Where is Tomas?" Richter said.

"With your priest at my hotel."

Richter turned back to him. "Father Hidalgo?"

"Yes. He's the one who delivered the message to me," Cohen said. "He says you should ignore it. . . That you shouldn't give up hope," he added perfunctorily. He wanted to say *Save your wife and children – Kill yourself*, but reined in the impulse.

"Why did he come to you?"

"He was told to. They seem to think I have some special connection to you. Maybe they think I would appreciate the chance for a little revenge."

Richter stared at him. His eyes were icy now. "And would you?"

Cohen had no answer. He merely returned the stare.

Richter's eyes hardened even more. "Would you?" he repeated forcefully.

Cohen felt a momentary flashback – a German officer, an order, the chilling fear. For an instant he wanted to kill Richter himself. But then he remembered why he was there and held his emotions in check.

"Swear to me by all who died at Dachau that you aren't lying to me about any of this," Richter said.

Cohen was jarred by the mention of Dachau. "It's the truth so far as I know it," he shot back. "The priest told it to me. Nothing was written, he said. Your wife and daughter were taken while they were with him."

Richter continued to stare at him.

"Yes. . . I swear," he said finally.

Then he remembered the ring. He pulled it from his pocket and handed it to Richter. "He gave me this to show you."

Richter cradled the ring in the palm of his hand, staring at it as if trying to make it disappear. He held it up to the light for a moment, appearing to inspect the initials inside the band, then turned again to look out over the city.

For some reason, Cohen's thoughts turned to the kiss he had shared with Elena the night before. The wild mix of emotions it had evoked flooded through him again.

A cloud passed in front of the moon. When it had drifted back into the dark mass of sky, Richter turned once more to Cohen. His eyes had a softer focus. "They are all that's left. Everyone else is gone. My wife, my children, they're my redemption. Without them, there would be no point to anything."

He put his hand on Cohen's shoulder, a move so startling Cohen instinctively recoiled. But Richter held onto him, searching his eyes. This time he was not focused on anything else. "If anything happens to me, will you see to Elena? And if something happens to her, will you look after our children? Take them back to the States with you. Be sure they are properly cared for."

Cohen was speechless. Was it fate that was laying this offer at his feet? He felt a sudden, totally unexpected connection to Richter, aware at the same moment of the impossible chasm between them.

"Why are you asking me this?" he said, wondering how desperate this man could be, to ask him such a thing.

"Because of what you've been through," Richter said. "Elena told me about your father, your family, your friend Rachel."

When Cohen said nothing, Richter continued. "I had actually heard that name once, 'Rachel Stern,' at Kaisenher, before Elena ever mentioned her. It stuck with me because it was from the mouth of Heinrich Mueller, the camp commandant, and it sounded Jewish. And because a young girl Mueller wanted, Muriel, was being compared to her."

Cohen was too stunned to respond.

"I'm sorry about your Rachel," Richter said. "Mueller was a swine. But you've been in the camps. Elena has been in the camps. I know I can trust you."

To Cohen this seemed the final word on Richter's alleged involvement with Heinrich Mueller. And, by extension, with Rachel. It wasn't what he had expected, but the evidence, incredible as some of it was, seemed to add up. Any disappointment he might've once felt, was now gone.

"So what do you think, Cohen?"

Cohen had to regroup for a moment before he could remember what he was being asked. It was unreal, this request. And yet there was only one answer he could give, he knew. An answer not for Richter, but for Elena Stein. Maybe even for Rachel. In this, Richter's reasoning had been perfect.

"Yes," he said simply.

"Yes you will do it?"

"Yes."

"That's a firm pledge?"

"It is."

"Thank you." Richter dropped the hand from Cohen's shoulder. "I have some resources that will help you. In the event of my death, or of Elena's, ask Father Hidalgo. He will explain, and take care of everything."

Cohen heard voices down the long corridor again. This time they were definitely drawing closer. "I have one more question," he said.

Richter waited.

"Would you really have killed Hitler?"

"Wouldn't you have?" Richter returned.

"What?"

"If you'd had the chance, been in my position in 1944, wouldn't you have killed him?" Richter had a strange look in his eye Cohen could not read.

"Yes, I suppose I would have, if I'd had the guts."

"Good. We agree on one thing, at least." Richter broke off as the mambo tunes from a distant radio became audible again, then were interrupted by voices, louder this time and continuing to grow closer. He and Cohen waited in silence, inspecting each other one more time, each for his own reasons, each from his own world.

"It is time," Frederico said, approaching with another guard. He exchanged a companionable smile with Richter as he let Cohen out of the cell.

"You forgot something," Richter said, picking up the manila envelope from the bedside table.

"That's for you," Cohen said. "A copy of what Terry Harper wrote. I was hoping you might tell me how much of it's true." He suddenly realized how ridiculous this must sound, given the nature of the message he had just delivered.

"Editing my own obituary, eh," Richter said.

As he headed down the corridor, Cohen looked back. Richter was staring at him with a distant, worried look.

"Don't do it," Cohen said, the words escaping his lips without thought. "There is always hope." *Where did that come from*, he wondered, shocked at himself.

Frederico looked at him kindly, as if the message was meant for him. "You are right, Señor," he said. "There is always hope."

Richter smiled. Cohen turned a corner and lost sight of him.

"20 July 1944"

Johann Richter ran his fingers lightly across the smooth flanks of Yvonne Duchamps, who lay on her side, her back to him. Last night, they had become lovers. For several reasons, Richter would never forget the date: 5 June 1944. Though he had felt a pang of guilt toward Christine's memory and toward Marie, it had all seemed so inevitable, so natural, the guilt had been easily sublimated. The sudden release, he thought afterwards, had in part been a response to his father informing him he was no longer to be Hitler's assassin. The idea that his own death was no longer a foregone conclusion had filled him with a bursting new appetite for life.

And it was Yvonne who had taken the initiative, almost as if she'd understood all this. Her lovemaking had reminded him uneasily of Christine, a kind of attack, a frenzied whirlwind more furious than loving, at one remove emotionally. Now her naked body, half covered by sheets in the morning sun, erased the rest of the world. His inflated arousal wiped out any argument there could be something wrong with what they were doing. Nothing else was in his thoughts. Only the woman in this bed.

He nuzzled the nape of her neck, eliciting a murmur of pleasure. She stretched softly and reached back to touch his erection, which he had slid between her thighs, producing a low guttural sound from her. Gently, he rolled her around to face him, pressing her lips, breasts and loins to his in the damp summer heat.

He ran his hands softly and slowly up and down her thighs, and she parted slightly for him. She brushed her free hand across his face and hair, the back of his neck, sending shivers of pleasure through his body. They played these games until neither could stand it any longer and she whispered she wanted him inside her. When he bunched the sheets beneath her and lifted her to him, slowly at first, then faster, then more slowly again, she began to moan. The animal-like sounds gave beat to the rise and fall of hips building toward a sweat-soaked crescendo.

The explosion came and passed. The two bodies ground to a halt like a piece of overheated machinery. As his breathing returned to normal, the full length of his body still pressed to hers, Richter had a vision of Christine. It gave him a moment of wistful longing. He rolled off and offered a shoulder to nestle on. With Yvonne in the crook of his arm, whatever contentment he felt would be transitory, he knew. Their lovemaking was a tiny island of tranquillity in a sea of tumult, in danger of obliteration at any moment. Right then, however, he had no idea how quickly that moment was about to arrive.

Two hours later, following a morning gallop through heavy mist cut by a soft summer sun, they listened while German national radio announced the Americans and British had finally landed in France. Reports were confused as to where the Wehrmacht was to absorb the main blow and hurl the invaders back into the sea. At first it appeared to be Calais, but there were also reports of fighting on the beaches near Caen and Saint-Lo. The only constant was that the Americans and British and their allies faced certain defeat by the gallant, battle-tested troops of the hero of North Africa, Field Marshal Erwin Rommel, who now held the major field command on the Western Front.

Unknown to *Radio Deutschlandsender* or to Richter, however, was that Rommel considered the war already lost and was by now offering at least tacit support for the plot to kill Hitler.

* * * *

In the days that followed, Richter awaited in growing tension word on the assassination plot. Frustrated he didn't have a more direct role, he thought he could at least contribute. Even if France were to be only a sideshow to the main event, he knew it could be a key to ultimate success. Or failure. German troop strength in the West was at its highest level since the blitzkrieg into France and the Low Countries in 1940. Control of these troops was all-important, and the plotters had either active or passive commitments from many of the key generals in the West.

In particular, General Karl Heinrich von Stulpnagel, Military Governor of France, was an active, energetic member of the plot. He had command of the troops in Paris. The most difficult and important task would be to neutralize the SS and Gestapo, both fanatically loyal to Hitler. Stulpnagel would be a central figure in that effort. With those two groups out of the picture, and the generals firmly in control in the West, something could be accomplished even if the coup attempt ran aground in Berlin or elsewhere.

On 12 June the first V-1 rocket, the long-awaited "Wunderwaffe," armed with a ton of high explosive, was launched toward London from a base near Calais on the French coast. Richter held his breath as reports of the damage and terror caused by these first so-called reprisal weapons filtered back. The guilt he had felt in London three years earlier returned, but he thanked God the rockets appeared to have only conventional explosives and no nerve gas or newly invented instrument of destruction. Though the first V-1s would be followed by thousands more, and eventually by the even more deadly V-2, it was not enough to turn the tide. London suffered nearly 60,000 casualties but Allied troops continued to advance on Germany.

Through June and the early part of July, as the Allies stabilized and expanded their beachheads at Caen and Saint-Lo, Richter and Yvonne Duchamps continued as lovers, but slept together only sporadically in spite of what appeared to be a growing interest on her part. Richter remained infatuated with her, but was increasingly distracted by having to deal with the restless civilian population of St. Sentione. He was caught between trying to protect his troops and avoiding carnage and anarchy in the streets. He and Marie Renault, meanwhile, had settled into an uneasy truce of their own. He still trusted and confided in her, talked his problems out with her, in everything but the plot against Hitler.

In early July, Richter told Marie she must return to Paris, to stay with friends there or take lodgings where no one would be likely to find her. The Allies would liberate Paris soon; she should have to conceal herself for only a matter of weeks. He made arrangements to ensure her safe transit. She departed with a final warning to him to beware Yvonne Duchamps.

When he tried to convince Yvonne to leave, she steadfastly refused. Saying she would send three-year-old Giselle somewhere safer the moment it seemed too dangerous in St. Sentione, Yvonne insisted she herself would stay by his side. Now more than ever, she said, he needed someone he could confide in, someone who could ease his worries. Richter hesitated, but eventually accepted this explanation.

In the meantime he remained completely in the dark about what the plotters were up to. He didn't know that on 11 July, Claus von Stauffenberg, standing in for Colonel-General Fritz Fromm, commander in chief of the Replacement Army, had reported to Hitler at his Alpine aerie in Berchtesgaden with a bomb in his briefcase. He refrained from detonating it only because neither Himmler nor Goring were present. In Berlin, the plotters had already set Valkyrie in motion in anticipation of Hitler's death. They had to scramble to convince the Gestapo it had been a test run, designed only to prepare for street rioting should it ever occur.

On 15 July, at Rastenburg in East Prussia, Stauffenberg again carried a bomb into Hitler's presence, and this time was dissuaded from setting it off by fellow conspirators who wanted at least Himmler eliminated along with the Fuhrer.

Back in Berlin, an emotionally drained Stauffenberg vented his frustrations on his colleagues and won support for the idea that to kill Hitler alone should be enough to ignite the coup d'état attempt. Next time, the plotters agreed, the bomb must be detonated without concern for who was or was not with Hitler at the time.

It was not until 20 July that Richter became aware of any of the plot's culminating events. In the months and years ahead, he would often think back and wonder if he could've done anything that day to change the outcome, given that the plotters had come closest to success in occupied France. But on 20 July itself, he would later remind himself over and over again, he'd had no idea what was going on.

Early that morning Stauffenberg and his brother Berthold, a fellow conspirator, were driven through the bombed-out streets of Berlin, out through the relatively unscathed southern suburbs to a military airstrip at Rangsdorf. It looked peaceful enough right now, he thought, but if he and his co-conspirators did not succeed today, these Berliners would soon be fighting for their lives.

At Rangsdorf, Claus said good-bye to his brother, then he and his adjutant Lieutenant Werner von Haeften boarded an ancient Heinkel fighter-bomber with General Stieff and his adjutant, a Major Roll. Stauffenberg chuckled as he contemplated himself and his companions and sized them up for the momentous mission they were undertaking. The remnants of the Reich. He had left behind his right hand and forearm, two fingers from his left hand, and his left eye, in North Africa. In honest moments, he knew this physical devastation had added a touch of desperation to his personal mission. Perhaps it was a necessary ingredient, he thought. In spite of a wife and five children he loved dearly, getting himself killed at this point was not something that worried him overly much.

He looked over at Stieff, a short man with a hunchback, nearly a dwarf, chief of the Organization Section of the Wehrmacht's General Staff. The man was noted for his caustic and often pornographic wit. Nothing could be more pornographic than the Third Reich right now, Stauffenberg thought.

Once aloft, Stieff handed two parcels to Haeften, who put them in his briefcase. Stieff lit up a cigar, as if in premature celebration. The rest of the three-hour trip was uneventful, intermittent napping punctuated by small talk. Stauffenberg daydreamed of a Germany without Hitler, of salvaging a postwar world by stopping the war now. He regretted he had been unable to reach his wife by phone the previous evening, but thanked God she and the children were safely tucked away on vacation in Lautlingen. He wondered how they and the rest of the world would eventually look back on this day. What would they see?

The tarmac at Rastenburg airfield in East Prussia was baking in a hot summer sun. The day was beautiful, the sky perfectly clear above a thin summer haze. It would be a good day to die, if it came to that, Stauffenberg thought. The four officers sat in silence as they were driven the nine miles to the Wolfsschanze "Wolf's Lair," heavily camouflaged in a dark forest.

After clearing two sets of checkpoints manned by Hitler's personal SS bodyguard, Stauffenberg and Haeften took a late breakfast in the officer's mess then reported to the Wehrmacht Chief of Staff, Field Marshal Wilhelm Keitel. Keitel informed them the Fuhrer's briefing conference had been moved forward a half hour, to 12:30, because Hitler that afternoon was due to host a visit from Mussolini, recently rescued by the SS from imprisonment at the hands of his own countrymen.

Stauffenberg asked one of Keitel's staff officers where he might wash up a bit and change his shirt, and the officer offered his own quarters. Once they were alone, Haeften unwrapped one of the two parcels Stieff had given him, snipped the timed-delay fuse and put the bomb into Stauffenberg's briefcase. It was set to go off in ten to fifteen minutes. Stepping outside, the two officers were immediately accosted by Keitel, who said the meeting had already begun and they had to hurry. Stauffenberg followed Keitel through a phalanx of SS guards and into a wooden barracks conference room, in use that day rather than the concrete bunker nearby because of the heat.

Hitler was standing at a large map table listening to a report on what was happening on the Eastern Front. The news, as usual, was not good, but was being sugarcoated for the Fuhrer. He appeared to be in a reasonably good mood, perhaps in anticipation of his meeting with Mussolini, for whom he had always had a soft spot. Stauffenberg, now that he was here with the bomb in hand, felt the calm of battle, when all concerns short of life and death cease to matter.

At a pause, Keitel requested Hitler's permission for Stauffenberg to deliver his report on the status of the Replacement Army – he called it the Home Army – once the current discussion was done. Hitler nodded his assent.

Stauffenberg, standing only six feet from Hitler, carefully placed the lethal briefcase on the floor and edged it under the table with his foot. A sudden pain shot through the stump of his right arm and made him clench his teeth. Fighting for control, he told the officer beside him he had to make an urgent call to Berlin, but would be back before it was his turn to speak. As Stauffenberg stepped quickly outside, Colonel Heinz Brandt, an operations officer on the General Staff who the year before had unknowingly carried the brandy bottles containing bombs aboard Hitler's plane in Russia, accidentally kicked Stauffenberg's briefcase. It was in his way. He moved it slightly to the right, putting one of the heavy wooden supports of the map table between Hitler and the briefcase.

Several minutes after Stauffenberg had stepped out of the barracks, a shattering explosion ripped the building apart. It killed four men, including Brandt, and wounded a number of others, but left the Fuhrer only shaken up and still very much alive. He had been saved by the heavy supports of the map table and the wooden walls of the building, which had diffused much of the explosion's force. Hitler was euphoric, thinking he had survived an enemy air attack. He announced that he had been spared by fate to see the war through to a successful conclusion. Later, his mood would darken.

With Hitler at first presumed dead by Stauffenberg and the others, Valkyrie was now sounded in Military District headquarters throughout occupied Europe. Some commanders swung quickly into action, while others, too many others as it turned out, cautiously awaited confirmation of Hitler's death. Communications from the Wolfsschanze, which were supposed to be cut, were not. Colonel-General Fromm, who occupied a key position in Berlin for the coup's success, balked when Keitel informed him by radio-telephone the Fuhrer was still alive and only slightly injured. Though the plotters briefly placed Fromm under house arrest in the War Offices at the Bendlerblock, he would soon return to haunt them.

In addition, the intercession of Nazi Propaganda Minister Josef Goebbels, who was in Berlin and got through to Hitler by telephone, persuaded Major Otto Ernst Remer, commander of the elite local guards regiment Wachbataillon Grossdeutschland, to resist, rather than join, the plotters. Hitler promoted Remer to colonel on the spot and ordered him to put down the uprising in Berlin. Remer would succeed so well he would soon win appointment to the rank of major general.

By that evening, these developments had essentially doomed the plot, at least in Berlin. On Fromm's orders, Stauffenberg and Haeften – who had flown back to the capital immediately after the briefcase bomb had exploded – and two other major figures in the conspiracy, were lined up against a courtyard wall illuminated by headlights and shot. Mercifully, as it turned out.

Stauffenberg's last words were "Long live our sacred Germany." As the shots rang out, he whispered a prayer that someone else would step up to kill Hitler – soon, while there was still hope for Germany.

By the end of the day, it appeared that among the top-ranking plotters only Colonel-General Erich Hoepner and General Karl von Richter had survived capture or death. Hoepner was later arrested and publicly humiliated by the Nazis, tortured, and subsequently hanged on 8 August 1944. His imprisonment and presumed complicity were widely publicized.

There was no word on the fate of Karl von Richter.

The events of 20 July caught Johann Richter by surprise. He was sipping a quiet afternoon cognac at a cafe in the center of St. Sentione when his command first received the Valkyrie signal. Though he had been expecting the assassination attempt, he'd somehow expected more warning. By the time he reached the troop compound, the communications center had already received an order from Hitler's Supreme Headquarters and signed by Keitel. It countermanded Valkyrie and the follow-up directives of General Hoepner, who Richter knew to be with his father in Berlin. Though it now appeared Hitler might not have been killed, Richter knew the die had been cast for his father and the others. He mobilized what troops he had immediately on hand and organized transport. This took about an hour. For the next six hours, he sat in the front of a troop-transport truck, helpless, on the road to Paris with his men.

Had Rommel, sympathetic to the disaffected officers and eager to negotiate with the Allies, been active on 20 July, the German armies in the West might well have joined the plotters even with Hitler still alive. But three days earlier Rommel had been wounded when his staff car, motoring between two army field headquarters in northern France, was strafed by Allied dive-bombers. His injuries had knocked him out of any active role on 20 July. And that left the day in the West, where the plotters would be the best organized and meet the least resistance, up to Field Marshal Gunther Hans von Kluge, Rommel's nominal senior officer.

In the early evening hours of 20 July – while Richter and his men were still on the road to Paris and the insurrection was already beginning to break down in Berlin – General Stulpnagel, as military governor of France, presented Kluge with the fait accompli of having rounded up and imprisoned virtually all members of the SS and Gestapo stationed in Paris. More than a thousand of them altogether. Most communications between Paris and Berlin had been cut. Occupied France, as well as the entire German front in the West, was ripe for revolution against Hitler and the Nazis.

Kluge, however, was a fence-sitter. He had been generally sympathetic to those who plotted against Hitler, but had always been unwilling to fully commit himself until success had been assured by Hitler's death. On the evening of 20 July, Kluge, upon receiving word Hitler was still alive, was finally forced to make a choice. It was a crucial one. When he declined to support the plot, it collapsed. Kluge would pay the full price anyway. Five weeks later, recalled to Berlin, he would poison himself before the Nazis could send him before the infamous "People's Court" of Roland Freisler.

Richter's small convoy made the trip from St. Sentione to Paris without major incident, arriving to deserted streets in the occupied French capital about ten o'clock in the evening. Once in Paris, he transferred effective command of his troops to Colonel Friedrich von Teuchert, a member of Stulpnagel's staff, then went looking for General Stulpnagel himself. He found him at the Hotel Raphael, a headquarters of sorts for the conspirators.

A dispirited Stulpnagel, sitting calmly at a table drinking schnapps, told Richter the revolt was over. They had lost their gamble. "And our lives," he added, somewhat too matter-of-factly it seemed to Richter. He asked Stulpnagel if there were any chance at all they could still pull it off, at least in Paris. Stulpnagel – who after the failure of the putsch would try unsuccessfully to kill himself, then be nursed back to health, tried before the People's Court and hanged – said, "No. There is no way out. We are trapped. The cowards among us have doomed us all."

The General looked up at Richter, not unkindly, and smiled. "Give your father my regards if you see him again," he said, dismissing him.

Walking back through the eerie, nearly silent streets of Paris, Richter agonized over what his father's fate might be. After consulting with Teuchert and an officer from Kluge's staff, however, he was convinced there was nothing more he could do in Paris that would be of any use to Karl Richter. He therefore reassumed command of his men, who appeared thoroughly confused by the situation, and returned with them to St. Sentione.

Before morning broke, he went into hiding in a forest to the north of that city.

"An Arrival and a Departure"

The next few weeks and months were uncertain ones for the German army and German people. Many of the key plotters, the ones who had not been shot or hadn't killed themselves on 20 July, were quickly arrested. Among them was Admiral Wilhelm Canaris, former head of the Abwehr, who would be shunted from prison to prison until he was eventually hanged at the Flossenburg concentration camp a month before the war ended.

Others were caught up later in a huge net thrown by the SS and Gestapo over a wide range of what they considered unreliable elements within the German military and body politic. "Twenty July" was used by the Nazis as an excuse to finish off what little remained of their social and political opposition. The extermination of anti-Nazi elements went on throughout the latter half of 1944, and continued right up until the war's last shots were fired in May 1945. Fritz Fromm, who had tried to cover his tracks on 20 July by ordering the deaths of Stauffenberg, Haeften, General Friedrich Olbricht and Colonel Mertz von Quirnheim, did not succeed. He was brought before the People's Court and shot to death in Brandenburg Prison on 19 March 1945.

Some of the plotters killed themselves before they fell into the hands of the SS or Gestapo. A few of the more prominent ones, like Rommel, were encouraged to take their own lives when it was considered in the best interests of the Nazis for them to do so. Inducements included the continued survival and well-being of the victims' wives and children, mothers, fathers, brothers and sisters.

Perhaps the eeriest existences in the days following 20 July were lived by those who had been involved on only the periphery of the plot or who had only family connections with its members. The SS and Gestapo, spurred on by Hitler and led by Himmler, initiated a policy of "sippenhaft," the detention of kith and kin of the plotters, but the targets of this policy didn't know for certain what was in store for them beforehand. Few of these unfortunates knew whether the Nazis would arrest them or not. In most cases, instead of attempting flight, or at least hiding out, they stayed put and hoped for the best. In most cases, this was a mistake. Sooner or later they were arrested, tortured and – if not executed immediately – were more often than not killed before the end of the war, often just weeks or days before they would've been liberated by the Allied armies. Only a very few survived the war.

Johann Richter's status, however, was not much in doubt. If his father was implicated, and he assumed that to be the case, then so was he. He also had concerns about his mother and sister, and about Erich Borchers. And Elena Stein. What would happen to them? The possibilities were chilling.

Upon his return from Paris, he took possession of an old abandoned hunters cabin in the woods north of St. Sentione. There he brooded over the plot's failure. He wondered if the deeply religious Claus von Stauffenberg had been given the last rites as he had stood in the glow of headlights about to be mowed down by a hail of bullets outside the War Office. He could not clear his mind of Stauffenberg and his fate. It made him sad and furious all at once. And it made him wonder over and over about his father, and where he might be right now.

* * * *

Richter had left knowledge of his general whereabouts with only one trusted aide, a Wehrmacht major. Several days after 20 July, through this aide, he tried to contact Yvonne Duchamps. The major discovered Yvonne's young daughter had been left on the front steps of the St. Sentione prefecture the morning after the coup attempt, apparently abandoned. He had been told a local family had taken her in. Yvonne Duchamps herself was nowhere to be found, he said.

Two days later, worried about her fate, Richter dressed in civilian clothes and slipped back into the city, to the inn where Yvonne and Marie had lived.

He still had a key to Yvonne's flat. When no one answered the door, he let himself in, careful to relock it behind him, and explored the familiar rooms for a clue to what had happened to her. The place appeared undisturbed. Her personal effects, her clothes, jewelry, toiletries, were still in place, as were Giselle's books, toys and other belongings. Nothing appeared to have been tampered with. A faint smell of cigarette smoke still lingered. There was no evidence Yvonne had departed. But where was she?

He searched as quickly and efficiently as possible without leaving a trail of evidence. For nearly an hour, he turned up nothing. Then finally, in a dresser drawer beneath a pile of sheets and towels, he discovered a false bottom that opened onto a small compartment with an unlocked strongbox full of papers.

Inside, he found his clue. It was a shocker. Two encoded messages from England. Bletchley Park. From his own experience on the periphery of MI6, he knew they had originated with British Intelligence. He couldn't have decoded them, but as luck would have it they were conveniently decoded for him, in Yvonne's stylish handwriting. Not very prudent spycraft, he reflected.

Find out what the General is telling X about their army's plans for Hitler. If Hitler were eliminated, what would they do? Continue fighting? Accept a peace? On what terms? We need whatever you can find out.

Confirm. Go after the details of Valkyrie. Who is involved? Particularly generals or field marshals. What are their plans if successful? Of utmost importance that we know ASAP. You are our best source right now. Good show.

There were no decoded dates or sign-offs on either of the two directives, but the message was clear: Yvonne had told them about Valkyrie. The British had been using her – and worse, she had been using Richter – to infiltrate the plot against Hitler. To what purpose, he was too dazed to even hazard a guess. But he knew it was unlikely to have been anything beneficial to the plotters. If he had to bet on it, he'd bet the British, perhaps even Yvonne herself, were in contact with somebody loyal to Hitler about Valkyrie.

He remembered the warnings from Marie Renault. If Marie had known about the plot against Hitler, she might've connected some of the dots about Yvonne for him. But Richter had kept her in the dark, on the idea she was the greater risk.

Thinking back on his return to Germany, he recognized another painful irony. In relaying Christine's information to his father, he had helped shut down MI6 contacts inside the Wehrmacht, but the British had simply tapped him instead, through Yvonne Duchamps. Incredible. The simple fact, though he hadn't entirely accepted it yet, was that he had unwittingly betrayed his father and all the others. That it had been unintentional gave him no comfort.

Feeling sick at heart, Richter picked up the one other item inside the strongbox, a packet of letters. As he untied the string that bound them together, he noticed something that kicked his sense of unreality up another notch. The envelopes, every one of them, were addressed to a Lady Sarah Davies, at Cambridge. He recognized the handwriting. It belonged to Christine Johns.

He opened one. It was dated 28 September 1942.

My Lovely Sarah,

How I miss you. My days in London are filled with a combination of subterfuge and silliness. Sometimes it seems to me as if wars are waged simply to give men a chance to play at being boys again, only this time with real bullets, bombs, et cetera. My contact at you-know-where, who must still remain nameless, sorry, alternates between weary directives, ordering me about and loving to do so, and his tiresome and seemingly tireless efforts to get me into bed. Don't worry, I haven't succumbed, and I shan't. I let him dream a little – it makes him take it easier on me – but further than that, I shall never (again, anyway) go.

As for X, he seems to grow more disenchanted daily about the war and his own role in it. He says it has nothing to do with them finally starting to look as if they might lose, but quite frankly I wonder. I believe some of his basic Teuton heritage may be coming to the fore. He has started to talk about wanting to return home – which is not only absurd, given the current state of affairs, but would also leave me sitting here with nothing useful to do for the war effort. How boring.

The letter veered off into personal realms unfamiliar to Richter. Mutual friends at Cambridge and the like; who was doing what and where to whom, or with whom. He skimmed the rest of the letters, all in the same vein, all written in '41 or '42. There was an allusion in one of them that implied this Lady Sarah Davies person had leftist leanings. That she was in sympathy with Stalin and the Soviet Union.

She was not the only one. In the same letter there was also mention of one "Kim Philby." It took Richter a moment to place the name, but then he remembered Philby from Clay Johns' engagement party at Croyden Castle five years earlier. A *Times* correspondent who had eventually joined MI6. The man had some shadowy connections with Anders Hardy, Richter recalled, and like Hardy, had been a reputed admirer of the Soviets during the '30s. Richter had to remind himself a lot of people sympathized with the Soviets before the war, as well as in the early war years when it appeared Hitler was about to defeat them.

Philby had known Clay and Anne back before their marriage. The letter referenced a sexual liaison Christine apparently suspected the married Philby of having had with a friend of hers. Richter couldn't remember ever hearing of this friend before.

As he read the letters, it gradually dawned on him that Lady Sarah Davies must have been Yvonne Duchamps, in some earlier incarnation.

She had known Christine. Yvonne Duchamps had known Christine Johns. More than known her. Had apparently slept with her. Had Marie Renault known about all this? Is that what her warnings had been about?

And it appeared Yvonne – "Lady Sarah" – had known Richter had had a relationship with Christine as well. Had that been in her thoughts while he and she were together, riding, talking, making love? That they had both loved Christine; that he was the man everyone thought had killed her? This was not something he'd ever discussed with Yvonne – certainly nothing about that fateful last night at Croyden Castle, nothing about the suspicions that had fallen on him in the aftermath.

In an early letter, he chanced onto one more piece of relevant information. Yvonne, or Lady Sarah or whoever, had apparently also known Anne Weldon Johns. First at Cambridge, then in London. It was difficult to tell from the letter the tenor of their relationship, but Christine appeared to be responding to some concern of Yvonne's about the nature of Christine's own relations with Anne Johns. "She only dabbles with the likes of us," she assured Yvonne about her new sister-in-law. "For her, it's a kind of extended youthful indiscretion, a bit dangerous and thus quite thrilling."

It all made sense, but also flooded Richter with painful memories.

He returned the packet of letters to the strongbox and placed the box back in its hidden compartment. Confused and depressed, he sank down into a chair in the living room with the two encoded messages and reread them again and again.

Veiled references in the letters from Christine had pretty much confirmed she'd been assigned early in the war to keep an eye on him, presumably for MI6. But that was no real surprise. It was Yvonne's role that was the stunner. He wondered whether it had been patriotism or revenge, or perhaps even some kind of Soviet-ordered assignment, that had motivated her. Caused her to seek him out and try to destroy him, and Germany's last best hope along with him. How could he have been so blind? He tortured himself remembering all he could to confirm his suspicion that her work for British Intelligence had been aimed at undercutting the Wehrmacht's efforts to remove Hitler. He felt a perverse need to reach this conclusion, and dismissed any reordering of events that might've led to some other, less painful, determination.

He stared at the failing light outside the windows. The day was nearly done. It had started to rain. He wracked his brains trying to remember Christine or Anne Johns ever mentioning a Lady Sarah Davies. He couldn't recall a thing about anyone by that name. The harder he tried to remember, the more everything seemed to cloud over.

He didn't know how long he had been sitting there like that, when suddenly he heard a noise from the bedroom. Rising carefully and quietly – tensed, but almost relieved to be diverted from his thoughts – he turned out the lights and moved toward the room, his army-issue Luger drawn, the safety off.

The sound had stopped. So had the rain. It was too dark to see much. Flicking on a small flashlight he had with him, he moved its narrow beam slowly around the room: the familiar double bed, the dresser, a desk, two chairs.

He shined it under the bed. Nothing there.

It had to be the closet. Setting the flashlight on a corner of the bed, its beam at an oblique angle to the sliding closet doors, Richter backed away with the pistol held ready.

"Come out of there!" he shouted – in French, not having any idea who it might be. His voice cut the silence like a knife. "I know you're in there. Come out now or you're a dead man."

The answer was an explosion of gunfire from a bathroom doorway to the right of the closet. It was aimed at the flashlight, but the unexpected angle sent several rounds uncomfortably close to Richter, tumbling a floor lamp and shattering a window in a tinkle of broken glass. The flashlight was knocked to the floor and out of action, but enough moonlight lit the bathroom window that Richter caught a glimpse of his assailant. It was a woman.

If it was Yvonne, why was she shooting at him?

As long as no soldiers or SS were near, he knew nobody would arrive to investigate the gunshot. It was too dangerous these days.

Meanwhile, he wasn't taking any chances. He remained silent. Staying close to the floor, he belly-crawled to one side of the bathroom door. Grabbing a heavy glass ashtray from an end table, he tossed it at a lamp on the far side of the room. As the lamp hit the floor, another shot rang out from the bathroom. Richter sprang at the exposed pistol, which the woman was holding halfway out the door. He knocked it from her hand, grabbed her wrist and wrestled her to the tile floor of the bathroom. She was strong. She fought like a tiger, until suddenly she stopped completely. "Johann? It is you?" she said, in a voice that sent a shiver down Richter's spine.

"Elena?"

Their struggle turned into an embrace. They lay together on the hard bathroom floor, laughing and holding onto one another for dear life.

"I don't believe this," he said, as they propped themselves against the wall, shoulder to shoulder. "This isn't exactly how I envisioned our reunion."

"It is good my shooting is so bad. I almost kill you," she said.

More seriously, she added, "If that happen, I kill myself," and he knew she meant it.

"I'm just glad you're still alive," he said. "How the bloody hell did you find this place?"

"I ask some French people, when I arrive. Most of them tell me nothing, but one man, he tell me to try here. When I find no one here, I just walk in. The door is not locked, and I am desperate. I lock it, because I am nervous, and then I am here, just waiting. But Johann, I do not think it is you when you come in. And I do not recognize your voice, not in French. Your French is so bad, Johann. Worse than my English, I think."

Richter laughed again. He had tears in his eyes. "The professors at Heidelberg were always appalled at my French. If I'd known it would almost cost me my life one day, I would've studied harder."

She laughed. He had only heard her do that as a child, years ago.

"Why did you leave Orienbad?" he asked.

"Your father, he telephone to your mother right after the bombing against Hitler. He says to her that I must leave at once. For my own safety. He sends a message for you, that your mother tells me. He says you must escape now, any way you can. Even surrender to the Americans or the British, if that is the only way. Hitler is killing everybody connected to the bombing, he says."

"What about my father? Where is he now?"

"He says not to worry about him. What is necessary, he will do, he tells your mother."

"What does that mean?"

"He does not say. Or your mother does not tell me. But he helps her to get me train tickets, and I have my papers of identification still, that you give to me—"

"Wait!" Richter put a hand gently over her mouth. Someone was at the front door. He leapt to his feet and pulled her up with him.

"Stay here," he whispered, shutting the bedroom door behind him. He made it to the small kitchen just as the front door opened.

Crouched behind a breakfast counter that opened onto the living room, he watched a young woman stumble merrily into the apartment with an officer who had the distinctive double lightning bolts of the SS at his collar. It was an officer he recognized. The man had connections to the Sicherheitsdienst, the SD, the Nazi Party's dreaded secret police who were as much feared as the Gestapo. The SD had long been the Abwehr's biggest rival among the Nazis' intelligence services, and it was almost certainly now Hitler's most trusted weapon against those who had tried to kill him.

They were both a little unsteady on their feet. The SS officer leaned against the back of the couch, cradling the woman, a tall brunette, in his arms. There was something familiar about her, Richter thought, something in the way she carried herself. Then she spoke, just a few words and in French, but it was enough. This was Yvonne Duchamps, he suddenly realized. In disguise.

At the same moment, he became aware he didn't have the Luger with him. How stupid, he thought. He could see the two encoded messages on the end table between him and the couch. They were directly in Yvonne's line of sight. He braced for her sudden recognition of what they were and what their being out of the secret compartment might mean.

But Yvonne had other things on her mind. With her help, her companion shed his uniform jacket and unstrapped his sidearm. They embraced again, and she tugged impatiently at the bottom of his shirt, apparently in a hurry to get him undressed.

The man asked her if she had any liquor in the house. His voice had the blurred edge of one drink too many already. Reluctantly, Yvonne pulled away from him, tugging off her brown wig and tossing it into a corner. She ran her fingers through her blond tresses, then reached down to the end table for a cigarette and distractedly picked up the two messages Richter had left behind.

She stared at them with an air of puzzlement as she headed for the kitchen, still playing with her hair.

There was nowhere for Richter to hide. As Yvonne entered the kitchen he stood up to meet her. For a split second he saw in her eyes a look of panic or astonishment. Perhaps a bit of both. The encoded messages fluttered from her hands. Then she screamed. Richter shoved past her and dove for the SS officer before the man could recover his pistol. They tumbled across the couch and onto the floor. As they grappled, Richter could smell the alcohol on the man. That his adversary was drunk gave Richter an edge, though the man was heavy and strong as an ox.

They struggled to their feet and butted together again like two rams locked in mortal combat. The man got a front chokehold on Richter, but Richter broke it with a quick rabbit punch to the ribs. As the man stumbled backward, Richter caught him with a short right uppercut to the jaw hard enough to snap his head back against the wall. While his foe was dazed, Richter hit him with a knockout punch that sent him down, his head smashing against the floor.

The fight was over. Or should have been. From the corner of his eye, Richter caught Yvonne Duchamps leveling the SS man's pistol at him.

He heard two explosions almost simultaneously. A hot flash shot through his left side. The lights seemed to dim as he slumped to the floor. He looked for Yvonne, wondering if she were about to finish him off. Before he could find her, the lights went out completely.

When they went back on, he was lying on the couch, his head cushioned by a pillow. His shirt was off and Elena was kneeling beside him, cleaning his wound. She looked into his eyes, her emotions stripped bare with concern. "Thank God," she said, and smiled encouragement.

Richter raised his head, wincing at the pain the effort cost him. Yvonne Duchamps lay on the floor, her head turned at an awkward angle away from him, as if she had broken her neck. "I kill her. I am sorry," Elena said. "But she tries to kill you."

Richter could see just the legs of the SS officer. He was on the floor near the kitchen.

"Have you checked him?" he said, pointing. "He might be ready to wake up."

"His skull is broken," she said. "He will not wake up."

Richter took a deep breath, which hurt so much it forced his head back down onto the pillow. He tried to get a grip on things, but no rational order presented itself to his jumbled thoughts. He felt bad about Yvonne, or whoever she was, but she had earned her fate. His next thought was more analytical. The two bodies would have to be disposed of quietly. He knew where he could get help to do it.

"Hold still a minute," Elena said, dabbing at his wound with alcohol as he pulled away in reflex. It hurt. He clenched his teeth and could feel sweat break out on his forehead. To distract himself, he watched Elena as she tended him. She had filled back out a little during her time at Orienbad, but she was still thin, her features drawn. There remained the haunted look of the camps about her. But she also radiated a unique strength. And she was, he suddenly realized, a woman now. In all ways, he thought. A quite beautiful woman. It was something of a revelation.

"It will be all right," he said, answering an unspoken question that hovered between them. "I promise."

She looked down at him tenderly, as if she appreciated the promise, however impossible it might be to keep. The irony of his making it to the woman who had just saved his life did not strike her. She knew only that for the first time she could remember, she was right where she wanted to be.

CHAPTER XXII

When Cohen returned to his rooms at the Miranda, he found Father Hidalgo surrounded by a small contingent of British Intelligence agents.

John Weaver, the American exception, greeted him as if he were hosting a little get-together and Cohen was just joining the party. "How did it go with Richter?" he asked, speaking around the Camel dangling from his lips.

"I delivered the message. I suppose you already know about it."

The priest answered before Weaver could. "These gentlemen have been in touch with me for some time. I hope you don't mind that I've brought them into this."

Cohen shrugged. "Was there any choice?"

Nobody answered. That was answer enough. Cohen did not feel particularly put out. The truth was, on his return walk from the prison and his meeting with Richter he had already toyed with the idea of contacting Weaver and his friends. It appeared he was going to have to choose sides, and though any contact with MI6 still made him a little queasy, he was beginning to get used to it.

"Where's Tomas?" he asked.

"Asleep in the other room."

Leland Powell came in from the balcony with two men Cohen had never seen before.

"Cohen." Powell held out his hand; Cohen gripped it briefly.

Powell handed him a piece of paper that looked torn from a notebook. "We took the liberty," he said. "It was stuck under your door."

Phone this number immediately, the note said. It listed a number.

"This came with it," Powell said. He handed Cohen a snapshot of Elena Stein and Teresa. Elena looked more sad than scared. The flash-bulb had illuminated a few nondescript feet of background. The rest was totally black, as if the photo had been taken at night. No clues.

"That's undoubtedly from our boy Anders Hardy," Powell said. "He'll want to work out the details of whatever he's up to. That's what the number is for."

"He wants Richter to kill himself," Cohen said with another flash of anger at Hardy's choice of blackmail strategy.

"Yes, we know. We would've preferred that particular message not be delivered. However, since you were the chosen messenger, it opens up some possibilities."

Powell began pacing, holding his chin between forefinger and thumb, deep in thought. "We'd like you to deliver a counter-message for us when you make that call, if you would, Cohen."

He had the distinct feeling Powell was reading from a script.

"We'd like you to tell Hardy that before Richter will go through with his part of the bargain, he wants you to make sure his wife and daughter are safe and unharmed. Make it clear that you must actually see them. In person." He looked up. "Are you game, old boy?"

Cohen hesitated. A plan had obviously been worked out already. The British were always very thorough. He remembered that. Not always right, but always thorough. He wondered again if the hidden message was *Do this, if you want us to forget what you did in Israel.* How ironic would that be? When he was the one who couldn't forget what he did in Israel. But it was a good reminder. This time he would do whatever it took. Whatever it took to save Elena Stein.

"Don't do it for Richter, if that's what's bothering you," Powell said, as if divining his thoughts. "Do it for Elena Stein and her child. We need them alive and well if Richter's going to help us out."

The man knew which levers to pull. Whatever this group had in mind, Cohen thought, it had to offer more hope for Elena and Teresa than whatever Anders Hardy was planning.

He took a deep breath. "I'll do it," he said. "I'll do it if you can promise me, if you will swear to me, that you will do everything you possibly can to keep the woman and her baby from getting hurt. And that you'll see to their welfare afterwards, whatever happens."

"Done," said Powell. "Splendid."

"And will you add your personal guarantee to that, John?" Cohen asked Weaver.

"I will," Weaver responded without missing a beat.

"I need to think a minute. I'm going outside." Cohen stepped out onto the balcony. There was no fog. The moon draped its incendiary luminescence over La Negra. A part of him wanted to respond to the beauty, but he could not. Another day, perhaps.

All right, he thought. So I phone Hardy. I tell him I've got to see Elena and Teresa. In person. With any luck, he agrees. We work out a rendezvous. I meet them somewhere. Then what? These were professionals. They weren't going to set up a meet where they could be trapped. So how was this going to work?

He felt tugged in opposite directions. Why had he told Richter not to give up hope? That hadn't been prompted by Father Hidalgo. It had been an impulse, born of Richter's pleas that he look after Elena and the children. He had been thrown off balance. Richter, he thought, was starting to seem like a human being to him. A troubling thought.

The kicker, Cohen knew, was that he'd come to think of Elena as some sort of reincarnation of Rachel Stern, her children standing in for Rachel's unborn baby. When he had told Elena about Rachel and the child she'd been expecting when she died, the pain of losing them both, she had said she understood. And she *had* seemed to understand. Almost as if she'd been through something similar herself.

As difficult as it might be, she said, he had to go on with his life.

The connection he felt to her complicated things, but at least it narrowed his focus to the problem at hand. Much as it had done in Israel, with Rachel. That had not ended well, and this predicament seemed unlikely to as well. He weighed the options. They all appeared equally hazardous. But he had not been able to save Rachel, he reflected, and this felt almost like a second chance. He would not let it slip away.

When the glass partition slid open behind him, he had no idea how long he had been standing out there. It was John Weaver with a shot of tequila in either hand. He handed Cohen one. "Cheers, amigo," he said. "Thought maybe you could use a little jolt."

They downed the tequila, Cohen suddenly aware of the cool night breeze. "Thanks," he said. The liquor shot a hot streak directly to his gut.

"Don't mention it. I'll leave you alone now." Weaver started to walk away.

"That's all right," Cohen said. "There's not much else to think about. I'm ready."

Inside, he asked Leland Powell how this setup was going to do anybody any good.

"We need you as a go-between. Someone they might trust, at least a little."

"And?"

"And we propose to be there when you meet with them. On the QT, of course. We'll be with you all the way."

"That'll be a little tricky, won't it?"

"Trust me. We'll be there."

"You'll be there," Cohen repeated dully.

"We've gotta find'em," Weaver said, "and soon. We tried to trace the phone number, but these fellows are too sophisticated to allow for that. They're using a virtually untraceable relay switch to divert calls to wherever they are."

"Believe it or not," Powell returned to theme, "this really is for the woman and the child as much as it is for Richter. These turncoats cannot be trusted."

Cohen wasn't sure anyone down here could be trusted, but he kept the thought to himself.

"If you've a better idea, Cohen, I'm all ears."

He did not. He dialed the phone.

A voice answered in Spanish. "Un momento."

Cohen held on. On the phone, he could hear indistinct voices in the background. Behind him in the room, he could hear Father Hidalgo taking his leave. This surprised him but he was too distracted to worry about it.

"Cohen?" It was Anders Hardy.

"Yes."

"What did Richter say?" Hardy plunged right in, as if he and Cohen were simply continuing a recent discussion.

"He said he has to know his wife and daughter are safe, before he does anything."

"They're safe. You can speak with her, if you need proof."

"Richter says he wants me to see them, with my own eyes. He says that's the only way he'll go through with this."

The other end of the line went silent for a moment. "What's your number there?" Hardy said. Cohen gave it to him. "Wait there. I'll ring you back in twenty minutes."

He rang back in ten.

"We'll meet you at the Marina de Espana, in two hours. At twelve-thirty," Hardy said. "Don't write this down." He gave Cohen directions to a dock area along the lake. Cohen wrote it down.

"Oh, and Cohen," he said. "I know you met with Leland Powell and his CIA flunky. I'm giving you the benefit of the doubt here. Do not tell anyone about this, and do not try to bring anyone with you, or not only will we kill the woman and her child, we'll kill you. Sorry to be so blunt, old boy, but it's important."

"Thanks so much." Cohen couldn't keep the sarcasm out of his voice.

"And just to be sure we understand one another," Hardy said, "we have left you a little something. Look outside on your balcony. Cheers." He hung up.

"What did he say?" asked Leland Powell.

"He suggested I come alone. I hope you guys are good at this."

"Don't worry," Powell said. "But just in case you encounter any difficulties, we have a little present for you." He turned to one of his agents, who handed Cohen a small object wrapped in plain brown paper.

He unwrapped it. It gleamed darkly in its box. It was a pistol, so small it looked like a toy.

"A derringer-style weapon, courtesy of the British government, via the old Walther firearms firm and the Federal Republic of Germany," Powell said. "Walther used to make them for us on special order. Somewhat ironically, perhaps."

Cohen picked up the tiny pistol and turned it over several times. It was incredibly light but nicely balanced.

"Careful. It's loaded," John Weaver said.

Cohen knew that from the weight. He checked the chambers. The pistol was indeed loaded.

"Only two rounds, so use them with care," Powell said.

"You get another present too, pardner," Weaver said, holding out a large shoebox. "Make you feel like a real American."

Cohen opened it. Inside was a pair of dark leather cowboy boots. He took them out. The right one was heavier than the left.

"Lemme have the left one," Weaver said. He turned the heel of the boot 90 degrees and revealed a compact hollowed-out compartment. "We knew you were right-handed. If you sit with your foot resting on your right knee, you'll be able to grab the pistol with your right hand." He took the Derringer and fitted it perfectly into the space. When he rotated the heel back into place, nothing showed. An ordinary cowboy boot.

"The other one is weighted with lead, to compensate," Weaver said, handing the boot to Cohen. "Try'em on. We need to make sure you don't walk funny." Cohen remembered Tomas' observation. He already walked funny.

The boots fit snugly. They were heavy. When Cohen tried walking in them without looking like an idiot, Weaver piped up with a grin, "You look like a gen-u-wine cowboy."

"I hope I don't have to make a break for it in these things," Cohen said. Were they trying to protect him, or get him killed, he wondered half-seriously.

Weaver looked at Powell.

"Cohen, your role here is simply to get us to Anders Hardy," Powell said. "The weapon is strictly for self-defense. For use only in an emergency."

He and Cohen locked stares. "Understood?" Powell said.

"Ummm," Cohen murmured his grudging assent.

"Splendid." Powell looked around at his men as if gauging his performance in this little give and take. The gesture made Cohen uneasy. "Right, then," Powell said. "Let's have a look at those directions."

"I just remembered," Cohen said. "Hardy said he left me something. Out on the balcony."

He led the way through the sliding glass doors. There was nothing on the balcony. He was about to go back inside, when one of Powell's men said, "What's that down on the street?"

Powell took a look. "Go fetch it," he told the man. "With extreme delicacy."

A minute later the man was back in Richter's rooms with a satchel the size of a small laundry bag, which he placed very carefully on a rickety table. Powell and Weaver inspected it just as carefully. For a moment, Cohen wondered if it could be the 10,000 pounds Hardy had offered earlier.

"I don't think it's wired," Weaver said.

"Nor do I," Powell agreed. "We'll know soon enough. Stand back."

With everyone else standing at the fringes of the room, Powell slowly and deliberately undid the drawstrings and peered inside.

He said nothing. Just stepped away from the bag.

"What is it?" Weaver said.

"Who is it, is the question," Powell replied.

Cohen had a sinking feeling in his gut. He stepped forward to see which version of his worst fears might be confirmed.

None of them, as it turned out. He would never have guessed. It took him a few seconds to puzzle it out, but once he did, he recognized the head of Cisco Rojas, the young bellhop's eyes popped open in abject terror.

* * * *

Pacing his cell, anxiously awaiting an escape attempt as likely to end his life as save it, Johann Richter found himself reviewing a parade of old friends and acquaintances, familiar ghosts to him in the years since the war.

Erich Borchers, as he so often did, led the procession. Richter had once suspected Borchers of setting him up in the aborted attempts to kill Hitler, but had since uncovered convincing evidence to the contrary. His old best friend had somehow managed to sidestep Hitler's wrath after 20 July, and had wound up playing a leading role in the last-gasp defense of Berlin during the final spring of the war. Wounded and captured by the Russians, he was hauled off to Siberia, where he had eventually been killed in some minor rebellion over conditions in the gulag where he labored. Like Stauffenberg, he had held onto his courage and his belief in God to the end, it was said.

When he had heard of Borcher's death through the expatriate pipeline he still had access to at the time, Richter had broken down and wept. The news had hit him harder than he would ever have imagined.

Few of the 20 July plotters had lasted as long as Borchers. Richter at times still felt possessed by Stauffenberg and all the others who had died. In spite of his efforts to redeem himself later, he still felt guilt toward them. And he had never been able to shake a deep sense of remorse and frustration over how close it had all come to turning out so differently. *If Hitler had been killed in the bomb blast. . . If communications from Rastenburg had been cut. . . If even a few key generals like Fromm in Berlin or Kluge in Paris had gone along.*

The only silver lining was that the sacrifice of Stauffenberg and the rest that had once seemed such a waste, no longer seemed so. A sliver of Germany's national honor had been preserved in the bloodshed. The world had been put on notice, and history would record, that the nation had tried to rid itself of the scourge of Hitler. And that Germans had given their lives in the attempt.

On the other hand, plenty of Nazi true believers had survived and prospered, usually after undergoing chameleon-like transformations. Richter's own family offered a good example. Like Borchers, his sister Ellen's major general husband had been captured and shipped off to a Soviet prison camp, but unlike Richter's old friend, his in-law had reportedly bought into the indoctrination there and eventually been "rehabilitated." He was now serving as a Communist functionary of some sort in Stalin's East Germany – the "German Democratic Republic," they called it – with Ellen still by his side, as far as Richter knew.

Sitting down on the side of his bed, Richter laughed out loud. Hitler's old dream of a battle to the death between East and West, of a coalition of western nations fighting the evils of Communism, had come true. It was the driving force behind the desire of British Intelligence to free him. And as such, it seemed almost as odd as some of their MI6 colleagues helping keep Hitler alive during the war.

These fellows trying to spring him now had somehow managed to enlist everyone from the prison warden to Frederico. And Father Hidalgo. The priest had hinted Rivera and his guerrilla fighters would take part in the breakout attempt. Even this Michael Cohen appeared to be at least partially under their sway. Richter felt a little like Jake Barnes in Hemingway's novel of the Lost Generation after the First World War, an impotent spectator to all the maneuverings and counter-maneuverings going on around him.

But he knew what they wanted. They wanted to know about Soviet moles inside MI6 – Kim Philby, or whoever Anders Hardy was trying to protect. He might not know much, Richter thought, but what he did know – or they *thought* he knew – was valuable in the eyes of the British and Americans. And a danger to Hardy and his cohorts. It was the key that was opening the cell door for him.

It was also the key that might kill him.

Anders Hardy was a dangerous man. That much he knew. Now the former MI6 agent, backed into a corner, wanted him dead. Hardy would kill Elena and Teresa if necessary, according to Cohen, and Richter believed it. Twenty minutes ago, on the other hand, Father Hidalgo had relayed assurances from MI6 that Elena and Teresa would be safer if he remained alive. The only decision to be made was whether they were right. His best bet, he had decided, was to escape and go after Hardy himself. Elena and Teresa were not the only reasons. There was also Christine.

He prayed it was the right decision and that he was making it for the right reasons. The main thing was to protect his family, not exact revenge. He had to keep his emotions in check to be effective. But the prospect of derailing Hardy was, he had to admit, a compelling one in and of itself. It would give him great satisfaction.

He might die anyway. He was skeptical they could pull off this escape. A hundred things could go wrong, and any one of them could mean the end for him. He tried to reconcile himself to the possibility. If the attempt did fail, and he was killed, he consoled himself that perhaps Hardy would keep his word and release Elena and Teresa unharmed.

Even so, what would happen after that still worried him. When Michael Cohen was here, he had instinctively trusted the man. Had felt compelled to tell him about MI6, the Communists and the rest. But that he had made this total stranger – a man who was writing about him for a magazine, for God's sake – promise to look after his family had given him pause for thought afterwards. It had been an act of pure instinct on his part, a desperate act.

MI6 and the CIA had made similar promises, but Richter was uncomfortable with them. Cohen had been through the camps. To survive the death camps had to impart some kind of humanity to the survivor, he thought. A kinship with fellow survivors. Cohen would not betray Elena. Such had been Richter's thinking. But now he wasn't so sure. Distrust had seeped back into his thoughts. Even a touch of jealousy. It made him less prepared to die.

His depressed mood put him in mind of Muriel, the woman who had killed herself in the commandant's quarters at Kaisenher. Thoughts of her often came to him when he felt this way. The memory gave him an empty feeling at the pit of his stomach. He felt as if he had known her, somehow, and was still mourning her death, the impact all the greater because it was always tangled up with his memories of Christine. Today, though, it almost made him feel better. Perhaps after all, he thought morosely, there might be a touch of poetic justice in leaving Elena in the care of a fellow survivor if it came to that.

He would do his best to make sure it didn't come to that. So far at least, he felt little sense of fatalism, or even fear. Instead he felt a building anticipation. He had a score to settle. Richter pricked up his ears at a sound from the passageway. He stood and gathered up the last of the writing he had been working on and put it in a small valise he planned to carry. He waited. There was a voice. Father Hidalgo's. *This is it,* he thought. He looked toward the ceiling and closed his eyes. *Blessed Holy Father,* he whispered. *Please. . .* The attempt at prayer froze on his lips as he awaited deliverance.

CHAPTER XXIII

Luckily the air was clear and the moon was out. Otherwise, Cohen thought, he would never have found the rendezvous point. The docks Hardy had directed him to were a series of modest wood-planked pilings anchoring a string of small fishing boats used by the locals to take a meager living from Lake Tocqual.

In the moonlight, he recognized the dock Hardy had described. It stood out from the rest because an old-fashioned yacht was tied to the end of it. He was to go out and wait beside the yacht. He looked around as he cleared the last buildings before the lake, rows of small tin-roofed huts that housed the fishermen and others of the city's underclass. No one was about. He couldn't see Powell's men. So far, so good.

The dock appeared to be deserted. The cool night wind sounded a distracting whistle in his ears. Cohen walked toward a path of moonlight that shimmered across the water behind the yacht. The boat itself was dark. There was no other craft like it in the vicinity.

He stood at the end of the pier, where it formed a "T", and scanned the shoreline to both sides. To his left along the edge of the lake, modest stucco structures of the Spanish era emanated a warm light. To his right, in stark contrast, the line of modern high-rises he had wondered about from his balcony started half a mile away and glittered silent and cold along the waterfront for miles, seeming almost to touch the peaks on the far horizon. A world apart. Apparently half empty, if the scattered lights were any indication.

Cohen felt uneasy and strangely restless. He could not shake the gruesome picture of Cisco Rojas. An innocent bystander who had been caught up in all this craziness. A casualty of Hitler's war as surely as the first Polish fighter to die at the start of September 1939. Hardy must truly be a madman, he thought.

He remembered the warning Terry Harper had left behind for him, to watch his back down here. Earlier, he had wondered if he were choosing the right side. He'd worried he might betray the memory of his family by helping Johann Richter. But now saving Elena Stein came before all else. The fate of Cisco Rojas had ended all doubt. Whatever Richter's crimes might be, what Hardy had done to the boy had made Cohen's decision much easier. Now he felt almost a common cause with Richter. If he could help bring Hardy down, he would, even at the risk that MI6 might turn on him one day.

The breeze had softened and was beating a soothing tattoo against his skull, but it didn't alleviate the tension he felt building up inside him, the reluctant opening of a compartment long shut. The kidnapping of Elena and her baby had cracked it open. Now the severed head of the young bellhop, like a terrifying flashback, had blown the doors apart.

The last time Cohen had experienced a combination of adrenaline-fueled rage and recklessness as intense as what he felt now had been in Israel, when Rachel was killed. There, however, his anger had quickly given way to sadness and heartbreak. The doors opening now took him back further, to Dachau, the night of the retaliation. One of the *kapos* there, a Ukrainian, had sold out to the SS. He was gradually chipping away at an escape plot by turning in anyone he had even the vaguest suspicion was involved. Prisoners who were turned in were shot or otherwise disposed of. The Ukrainian's role had been uncovered by chance, when another prisoner overheard him talking with an SS guard. He was now the suspected source of a leak that had doomed the earlier escape try by Cohen's father and several others, all of whom had been killed.

Those who were planning the new breakout attempt unanimously voted a death penalty for the Ukrainian. They drew straws to determine who would carry it out. The short straw was drawn by a jeweler from Dusseldorf, the man who had said the Talmud over Cohen's father and would one day meet Cohen again in Palestine. The jeweler was a small man who could barely see without the pair of glasses he no longer possessed. He didn't protest, but Cohen could see he was shaken. The deed was to be done with a knife. The Ukrainian was a sizable man. The nearsighted jeweler was not strong enough, unless perhaps he caught the Ukrainian asleep, an incredibly dangerous endeavor because the *kapo* slept in a separate compound.

Cohen, whose father had been slain just weeks before, his severed head skewered on a spike and still on display in the camp yard, told the jeweler to give him the knife. He would do it. The grateful man handed the weapon over and offered to help in any way he could.

Cohen and the jeweler made a plan. The jeweler told the Ukrainian that, for a price, he would find out for him who was involved in the escape plot and who was leading it. The jeweler was an unthreatening figure, convincing in his need to please. On the appointed night, the Ukrainian, who had freedom of movement in the camp, met the jeweler in a machine shop near the jeweler's compound. Cohen was waiting, hiding behind machinery that turned out bullets for the Wehrmacht. As the jeweler started listing prospective escapees for the Ukrainian, who slowly and laboriously wrote each name on a piece of paper, Cohen crept up on him with the same combination of adrenaline and fear that would assault him again ten years later on a dock in La Negra. He had been advised to go for the jugular vein, to bury the blade as hard as he could then pull it across the neck in one quick, hard stroke. The man had lit up a cigarette, one more distraction in Cohen's favor.

His attack was a complete surprise. The Ukrainian made the only reaction he could as the knife was plunged into his neck. He jammed the pen he had been using into Cohen's right leg. Cohen stifled a yell and pressed his attack, making a second slash at the man's neck. The Ukrainian's horrified realization of what was happening came too late to save his life, but was just in time to freeze his features into a mask of animal ferocity. The second thrust severed his jugular, turning the start of a yell into a dying gurgle. Miraculously, his clinched teeth still held the cigarette in place.

Cohen had gone into immediate shock. All he could remember later was the splash of blood that covered him as he killed the man. It was the jeweler who got him safely back to their compound and cleaned him up. It was also the jeweler who bribed a guard for sulfa drugs when Cohen's leg became infected, saving his limb and probably his life, though he was left with a constant low-grade pain and a limp that would never leave him.

As luck would have it, by the time the SS came poking around about the killing, Cohen had regained his health and wits enough to deflect their suspicions. As far as he knew, there was never any official retribution for the killing of the Ukrainian. Normally the SS would have lined up and shot at least ten prisoners, at random if necessary, as a deterrent. Cohen always suspected the Ukrainian had become a nuisance, even for the SS. Among other things, he knew too much about which SS guards had lolly-boy favorites among the homosexual prisoners, and too much about the strictly forbidden heterosexual couplings that were traded for favors, or survival. The SS was probably happy to be rid of him, Cohen thought.

A few days after the Ukrainian was killed, the prisoners were ordered to bury the rotting heads of Cohen's father and the others. That was it, he thought. His mother. His father. Nicolette. Jeremiah. All gone.

Trying to shake his memories, Cohen scoured the shoreline of Lake Tocqual again. He could hear a distant explosion, and realized there had been several others he had been too distracted to register over the past few minutes. They were reminiscent of what he'd heard two nights earlier, the ones Elena had said were dynamite being set off by rebels. These seemed sharper, though. A little louder.

There was still no sign of Powell or Weaver and their men. They must be out there somewhere, he thought. It showed how good they were at this, he hoped, that he couldn't spot them.

Suddenly he became aware of movement behind him. He started to turn, but was stopped by an ice-cold voice. *"Don't move. Keep your bloody eyes on the shore."* The muzzle of an automatic weapon was stuck into his lower back for emphasis. Somebody threw a hood over his head. It was claustrophobic. It made him think of death. There was a mouth hole to breathe through, but he couldn't hear much through the heavy material.

Someone frisked him from the front, while someone else handcuffed his hands behind his back. They felt his boots, but in their apparent haste found nothing. Roughly, they shoved him over toward the end of the dock and down into the yacht. Twin diesels roared to life. Cohen could hear the throaty engine growl even through the thick hood as he was pushed into a seat. The boat pulled away from its moorings and plowed out into the lake.

They left him out in the wind – it felt like somewhere on the fantail – with someone beside him who reminded him he was there from time to time by shoving a pistol into Cohen's ribs. The use of a boat was clever, he thought. These guys, he reminded himself, were just as experienced at this sort of thing as Powell's outfit. He wondered whether his erstwhile protectors would be able to follow them.

The wind and the deep growl of the engine were steady for about twenty minutes, the yacht bucking slightly in a light chop, then the throttle was eased back and the boat rode its own swells into a new mooring. Cohen was yanked from his seat up onto a dock and led ashore.

He and his escorts entered a building. He could hear the door, then the echo of their footsteps along a long tiled hallway. They stopped and waited a minute, then entered what he assumed to be an elevator. Without visual bearings, he felt weightless and slightly nauseous as the elevator shot rapidly skyward.

At the end of this ride, a little woozy, he was led across a thick carpet, then halted abruptly, his handcuffs and hood removed. For several seconds, maybe longer, he could not regain his bearings. He seemed to be in midair, as if he were flying. A thousand stars etched a blinking mural across the sky, giving him a queasy sense of movement. A panorama of more earthly lights faded away toward his left, far below, while a dark void dominated all else straight ahead and to the right.

As he rubbed some life back into his wrists and hands, Cohen tried to sort it out. He must be in one of the high-rises along the lake, and those must be the lights of La Negra off to the left, he thought. The rest would be Lake Tocqual. While he watched, a sudden yellow flash lit up the darkness above the lake. No, that was an illusion, he decided, some kind of weird reflection. But then a second flash followed the first, down toward the old part of the city, down near where Richter's prison must be. The flashes were followed by what appeared to be smoke and flames, and by yet another distant explosion, this one muffled by the walls of the high-rise but detectable. For a brief moment, Cohen had the eerie sensation he was standing on some dead planet and looking out into the cold darkness of space. Down below was the exploding chaos of the universe.

He reached out and tapped a huge picture window so unblemished it hardly seemed there at all. Barely turning his head, he could make out the plush decor of a large room through the dim lighting. From somewhere behind him blew a gentle breeze. The window's incredible panorama continued to mesmerize him. It seemed a million miles away, with the expanding fire its brightest star.

"Quite the view, eh?"

Cohen turned toward the voice of Anders Hardy. There were two other men in the spacious sitting room as well. One was a huge man with a gut, the other a slim, swarthy character with a crooked jaw and a dangerous look. He thought he could hear someone else moving around off a hallway back beyond the private elevator entrance.

"What's going on down there?" Cohen said, nodding toward the fire.

"I don't know," Hardy said. "No cause for alarm. The oxygen here is insufficient for fires to get too big before they die out." He sounded uninterested. "Care for a drink, Mr. Cohen?"

"Something with vodka, if you have it." The subtle jab behind the choice of liquor was apparently lost on his host.

Hardy was already behind the bar with a drink of his own. He said nothing more until he mixed one for Cohen and handed it to him. "Sit down. Please," he said.

Cohen, still a little unsteady on his feet, welcomed the invitation. He walked slowly and deliberately across the room, the heavy boots a reminder, and sat in a straight-backed chair upholstered in dark suede. The picture window that overlooked Lake Tocqual was now at his back. As casually as he could, he placed his left boot over his right knee, gauging how quickly he could reach the pistol.

"Did you receive our little gift?" Hardy asked.

Cohen could detect no emotion in the reference, presumably to Cisco Rojas. "Yes, I received it," he said. "Was that necessary?"

Hardy sat on the arm of a stylish beige sofa across from him. He appeared calm, perfectly in control. "Beastly unpleasant, I agree," he said. "It was simply a matter of killing two birds with one stone."

"How is that?"

"We had enlisted the boy to deliver messages for us. We had reason to believe he was betraying our trust."

"So you killed him?"

"He had a little accident, you might say." Hardy sipped at his drink. "Rather unfortunate. But then, since he was already dead, and

I thought you and your 'colleagues' might need some encouragement. . ." He gave an almost imperceptible shrug.

So poor Cisco Rojas had just been in the wrong place at the wrong time. Cohen felt as if he were plunging back into the world of the Third Reich. Hardy was definite Gestapo material. For only the second time in his life, Cohen wanted to kill a man.

Feeling restless, he got up to stretch his legs. The two bodyguards moved toward him, but Hardy waved them off. Cohen returned to the picture window, where the distant flames now lit up a portion of the night sky. They appeared to have peaked, and were already beginning to shrink back toward the relative darkness of La Negra.

Looking out over the blank canvas of the lake, Cohen thought, *Where is God when you need Him?* Perhaps the human sacrifices were no longer being made in His name, but had they ever really given Him pause when they had been? It was not the first time he'd had this thought.

He stood there lost in another world. *At least with God the game had had rules.*

Hardy did not press him. Eventually, without prompting, he returned to his chair.

"So, old sport. Is Richter going to keep his end of the bargain?"

"That depends," Cohen said, wanting to leverage this exchange for any advantage he could gain, any little stall he could get away with. He felt relatively protected. Hardy needed him, as well as Elena and Teresa. At least for now. "What guarantees can you offer that his wife and daughter will be safe, once he's gone?"

"He has my word," Hardy said without apparent irony.

"Pardon my frankness, but I think he wants something more concrete than that. It's his life you're bargaining for, after all. I'm sure you understand."

Hardy had already polished off his drink. He returned to the bar. "Another vodka gimlet, Cohen?"

"I'm fine, thank you." In fact, he already had something of a buzz and was wondering if Hardy could've spiked his drink.

Hardy mixed himself another. A gin and something, Cohen noted. When he was done, he lifted his glass. "These were a favorite at the old 'Golf Club and Chess Society' at Bletchley during the war," he said. "Helped us break the Enigma Code." He drained a long swallow and added with force, "It's a little bloody ironic, don't you think, you sticking up for a Nazi. By all rights, you should want the rotter dead as much as we do."

The man had a point, Cohen thought, though his sense of Richter's guilt had dulled since his arrival in La Negra. Maybe if they hadn't killed Cisco Rojas the logic might have hit home a little harder.

When Cohen didn't reply, Hardy changed tack. "We have no desire to harm his family," he said. "We'll bring the priest in. Have him oversee things. Richter knows the priest. He trusts him. We might even have used the priest in your place, if we hadn't considered him compromised by. . .Well, let's just say by the 'other side.' That doesn't really matter anymore now."

He stared intently at Cohen, assessing his reaction. "But this has to happen quickly. No more than twenty-four hours. If Richter is not dead by then–" He shrugged. "In the meantime. . ." He nodded to one of his henchmen, the small dark one with the crooked chin, who promptly disappeared down the hallway. A moment later he and a new man, this one tall and unshaven, appeared with Elena Stein, who carried a sleeping Teresa in her arms.

Elena's eyes lit up cautiously when she caught sight of Cohen.

He stood up, unsure how to greet her. He had no idea if they could expect help. Delay was all he could think to do.

"Are you all right?" he asked.

"Yes," she said, in a flat voice devoid of emotion.

"Your husband wanted to be sure."

Elena lowered her eyes. For a moment, Cohen thought she was going to faint. Suddenly, however, she lifted her head and shouted, "Tell Johann not to do it! Do not do what they say. Please–" Hardy slapped her across the face, hard. She nearly dropped the baby, who started crying. The tall unshaven man took her by the elbow as if to lead her away. Cohen instinctively stepped forward, but was grabbed by the big guy with the gut. Crooked Chin produced a pistol and held it to Cohen's temple. So much for feeling protected, he thought.

"Listen to that, Cohen," Hardy said, "and you'll be as dead as Richter. We aren't here for our bloody health. Or for yours." He grabbed the infant out of Elena's arms and tossed it carelessly on the couch. "C'mere," he said to her. "You remember what it was like in the camps?" Elena did not respond. "No? Then perhaps you need a reminder, *Juden.*"

With the tall guy holding Elena, Hardy started to slap her. He hit her a little harder each time. She didn't cry out, but groaned softly. Cohen was desperate. He searched frantically for an opening. When Elena was nearly unconscious, Hardy grabbed her and let her drop to the floor, ripping part of her shirt away in the process. The sight of the purple scar that cut across her upper right chest and shoulder tore through Cohen like a knife, a reminder of Rachel. His guilt and his inability to save her.

Dropping to his knees, Hardy held out his hand. Crooked Chin, like a surgeon's assistant with a scalpel, produced a long sharp blade from a sheath belted to his back. Hardy took it and started tracing the skin just above Elena's breastbone, as if sketching a design of where he would cut.

During this macabre pantomime, Cohen tried with all his strength to focus. Hardy was a good fifteen feet away. His three men were distracted by what their boss was doing down on the floor in front of them. Suddenly Elena, who had seemed barely conscious, snapped her head like a snake striking its prey. She bit into Hardy's mouth and cheek. He bellowed, dropped the knife and started pummeling her with his fists.

The instant Crooked Chin leaned down to help, Cohen made his move. He wrenched away from the big guy and leapt at Hardy. The two larger goons were on him again in a flash, tearing him away and hurling him up against the plate glass window. Elena screamed. For a brief moment Cohen thought he was going through the glass. A rush of adrenaline prepared him to die. He could hear Teresa crying somewhere far away. The glass cracked but didn't break. He was able to push up and off it. It gave some more, but held. Bleeding from a deep cut on his shoulder, he rolled away from his pursuers. The tall unshaven one, with a grimly determined look, pulled a knife.

"Hurt him if necessary, but take him alive," Hardy commanded.

Still on the floor, Cohen groped at the heel of his boot. He got it half turned, but the guy with the knife was on him before he could release the Derringer. Cohen managed to push himself nearly out of the arc of the man's swing, receiving a slash across his left cheekbone just below the eye. The slice was so clean he could feel only the warm stream of blood running down his face. No pain.

His head swam and his eyes blurred, then cleared. *Thank God*, he thought. He scooted backward and reached again for the heel of his boot. The two men had him cornered now. The tall one handed the knife to the stocky one, hesitated a second, then lunged at Cohen. His body shielded the Derringer from the others. Cohen couldn't get a proper grip on the tiny pistol, but managed to fire at point-blank range. The report, muffled by the man's body, got the attention of everyone in the room.

His attacker slid to the floor, gut-shot. Cohen did not hesitate. He pumped his second and last round into another advancing target, the man with the belly. It didn't stop his momentum. The man fell on him, driving the knife toward his face. Cohen dropped the pistol to fend him off. He stopped the knife inches above his right eye, as the big man exerted tremendous strength to drive it home. A part of Cohen was ready to give in, surrender to death. But Elena half-naked on the floor was a reminder that too much had happened. At Dachau. In Israel. All his life, it seemed. Death would have to beat him. He would never surrender to it.

He held on. Gradually the pressure lessened. The knife fell to the carpet. The dying man slumped onto Cohen, who rolled out from under him only to discover Hardy standing above him with the Derringer in one hand, a snub-nosed pistol in the other.

"You'll pay for this, Cohen," Hardy said, cold as ice. Blood streamed down his right cheek and the look in his eyes was even wilder than before. Crooked Chin stood brandishing an automatic rifle near Elena. Another man with a drawn pistol had entered the room as well. Hardy backed away for a moment to confer quietly with this new arrival, who handed him a towel for the blood on his face as Hardy examined the empty Derringer with an abstract air.

Cohen wondered if their fates were now sealed. If he and Elena were about to die. Maybe even the baby. The possibility made him feel empty. Slightly queasy. Perhaps he was actually starting to fear death again. The notion both cheered and frightened him.

The phone rang as if on cue, unexpected and jarring. Hardy holstered his pistol and picked up the receiver. He listened for a moment before a sinister smile creased his face.

He hung up. "That was the word on our old friend Herr Richter," he said directly to Cohen, the smile still in place. "Our dearly departed Herr Richter, I must sadly report. May he rest in peace. He was evidently killed during an escape attempt." Hardy glanced around at the half-destroyed room. "So our little row here, you see, was quite unnecessary."

Elena let out an anguished moan. Cohen found the news hard to believe. He had no clue whether it would help them – if anything could help them now – or truly seal their fate. He staggered to his feet. Blood caked his face. In the background, Teresa continued to cry.

Hardy looked at the baby as if he were going to shoot her, but abruptly she stopped crying and he returned his attention to her mother. He pocketed the Derringer and gave his two remaining henchmen a nod in Cohen's direction. "Shoot him if he moves," he said. "And shoot to kill."

"You got what you wanted," Cohen said. "You don't need us anymore."

Hardy still had the slightly crazed look in his eyes. "But our Herr Richter didn't really keep his part of the bargain, now did he Cohen. And you. You have killed two of my men. I have something in mind for you, but first I think this one" – he nodded at Elena Stein – "needs a little object lesson."

Hardy grabbed Elena by the hair and brought her face up to his. She made no move to resist and gave Cohen a look reminiscent of the camps. Devoid of hope. A look of farewell. "I'm going to give you a present," Hardy said to her. "Something to remember us by."

He picked up the knife again and looked at Cohen. "This reminds me of one of my old lovers. Sometimes only the blade of a knife gets through to them," he said, as if instructing his prisoner on the finer points of handling women.

"Christine Johns?"

Hardy registered mild surprise. "Very astute, Mr. Cohen."

"Did you kill her?" Cohen said, desperate to stall Hardy as the man dropped to his knees beside Elena. There seemed nothing left to lose at this point.

Hardy looked up. He shook his head and laughed. "Cohen, Cohen, Cohen. You sound just like Anne Wheldon – oh, pardon me, Anne Wheldon *Johns*. She asked me that once. Jealous bitch."

"Christine Johns knew you were spying for the Soviets," Cohen said, prepared to grab at any straw even if he had to dream it up. "She told Richter. She told him about you and Philby. Your moles inside MI6. Everything."

Hardy looked slightly sick behind a cracked smile, though all this could hardly have been news to him.

"Is that what got to you?" Cohen pressed. "Or was it that she was sleeping with him. Was that why you killed her? *Old boy.*"

The smile disappeared. "Didn't you learn anything at Dachau, Cohen? It's dangerous to know too much in this world. And it's even more dangerous to spout off about it. You may think you've nothing left to lose, old sport, but believe me, you do." He glanced around a moment, distracted. As if he had misplaced something. "Just wait your turn," he said, his voice flat, not looking back at Cohen.

Refocusing himself, Hardy nodded to Crooked Chin, who put down his rifle with an eager grin as Elena tried to sit up, grabbed her from behind by the elbows and wrestled her back to the floor. Elena struggled in silence.

This go-around, Hardy wasted no time. Like some Aztec priest readying to extract a beating heart, he cut a quick shallow strip of blood down the middle of her breastbone, then wiped the knife clean on his trousers in preparation for a second cut. His movements were precise, as if he had done this before.

Watching this display, Cohen experienced a flashback so strong his mind went totally blank. He was suddenly back at Dachau, beyond premeditation, in no need of a cue or rational assessment of his chances. On automatic pilot. Ignoring the pistol trained on him, he bolted for Hardy. In slow motion, he saw Hardy's head come up and from the corner of his eye saw Crooked Chin and the man with the pistol start to move. There was a gunshot. Cohen did not feel anything hit him. He also did not hear a loud thumping at the door on the far side of the elevator entrance. Hardy was in a half-crouch by the time Cohen hit him with a roundhouse right. He staggered but didn't fall. Cohen hit him again. Just as he did, there was another gunshot, then a burst of shots. Cohen felt something tear into his right shoulder and heard all hell breaking loose behind him. Shouts. Breaking glass.

Everything after that was a dream. A slow, nightmarish dream. The sounds of battle were muted as the room filled with SS camp guards, *kapo* stooges, heads dangling from bodies. Cisco Rojas' among them. He searched for his father's, but could not find it. Somewhere behind this grisly panorama was an excruciating pain, but Cohen felt above it all. Looking down, he could see himself on the floor, lying on his side, watching Leland Powell, Elliot Johns and a man in uniform hovering over Elena Stein. While Johns placed a jacket over her, Powell checked her pulse and breathing.

She was alive. Cohen could tell by their reactions. He felt an immense sense of relief. It was the end of the war all over again. She was alive. He was alive. They had survived. That was all. He had no idea where the others had come from. He thought he heard a voice that sounded like John Weaver's, but it quickly faded.

His eyes glued on Elena, desperate for more clues to her condition, he was hit for an instant by an overpowering sense that Johann Richter was somewhere near. His image hovering just beyond reach, surrounded by a wall of fire but unscathed. He knew this could not be. That Elena and her children were his responsibility now. This thought was what was keeping him afloat. While he held onto it, everything else began to disappear into a murky haze. He closed his eyes and blended in with his own image on the floor. The world receded. He drifted away, wondering if this time he was escaping for good.

"Heinrich Mueller"

Elena Stein nursed Johann Richter back to health in the hunters shack outside St. Sentione he had chosen as a hideout. It was an open question whether they were in more danger from the Gestapo and SS or from the French Resistance. For a while it hardly seemed to matter, as Richter drifted in and out of consciousness, with Elena by his side around the clock, leaving only once to buy drugs on the black market to tend him with. She thanked God she had learned the rudiments of medicine from Jewish doctors imprisoned with her at Kaisenher.

Gradually, after about a week, Richter started pulling out of his tailspin. He could sit up and drink soup she made for him over an open fire. She gave him rubdowns with mineral oil to make him relax and ease the pain. Nights, they would lie together side by side, she waking every few hours to check on him as if he were a newborn baby.

On a second foray into St. Sentione, Elena, who spoke excellent French, learned Yvonne Duchamps' whereabouts were as yet unknown. There were rumors she had disappeared with the garrison commander, one Oberstleutnant Johann von Richter, or with a high-ranking SS officer who was also missing, but no one knew for certain. When Elena brought this news to Richter, he breathed a sigh of relief. Hopefully it would help throw the Germans, at least, off the trail.

As Richter's health returned, they began talking more, bringing each other up to date in a way they had not done the year before. Richter told her about his undercover work in England. He told her everything, almost, except about Christine, a subject he would not broach for several years more. He told her of the plot to kill Hitler, of his own involvement in it and his father's leadership role. He said he had, through Yvonne's treachery, betrayed the plot. That he'd had ample warning from a friend, but had ignored it. When he told her he was plagued with guilt, Elena did her best to assuage it.

For her part, she told Richter her life at Orienbad had been a blessing that had restored her, body and soul. It had allowed her to become a human being again. She told him about her long walks in the woods, where she would often spend hours alone, reading or just sitting and thinking. She told him of the special relationship she had formed with his old mare, Sacha, after his mother had told her how much the horse had meant to him when he was growing up. Frau Richter had been exceptionally kind to her at Orienbad, she said.

She told him of the visit by the Gestapo after the attempt on Hitler's life, of how Frau Richter had made certain Elena remained out of view while they were there. How when she had handed Elena the long-distance train pass, worth its weight in gold, and told her to go to Johann in France, she had also told her that whatever she did, whatever happened, she was not to return to Orienbad. That it would be too dangerous.

When Frau Richter had bid her farewell, she'd made an allusion to Elena's safety that startled the younger woman. She had known Elena was a Jew. Had apparently known it all along. When Elena asked her about it, Frau Richter had politely cut her off. She kissed her departing house guest and wished her luck, then went back inside the house as Elena pulled away in a chauffeured military vehicle Frau Richter had somehow managed to finagle for the trip to the train station.

For the first time, too, Elena told Richter about Kaisenher. About the terror of living in a prison with the daily knowledge you could die at any moment for any triviality. Or for no reason at all. How, with some, the law of the jungle prevailed, but with others compassion had ruled, at times evoking a quiet heroism that could bring death in its wake.

And because she had never been able to speak of it before, she told him about Erhardt, a German-born Aryan who was in the camp because he was a homosexual. Early on, she and Erhardt had become friends. He did her many little favors, which she did her best to return.

But one favor she could never repay. He had come to her rescue one night when she was attacked and raped by a *kapo*, a Latvian who hated Jews and had been assigned to barracks patrol. Erhardt had surprised the man and killed him by a blow to the head with a rock. They hid the man's body, but the deed was soon discovered. In response, Heinrich Mueller called the camp's en-tire inmate population out into the yards at daybreak and over loudspeakers ordered the killer to come forward, or he would start shooting prisoners, one each minute.

Mueller had killed before. Everyone knew he would not hesitate to kill again.

The several thousand standing in ranks were totally silent, holding their collective breath. Mueller had ten women cut from the ranks, took the youngest and prettiest first and placed the barrel of his Luger against her temple.

Erhardt stepped forward before the trigger was pulled. But Mueller just laughed and shot the girl anyway. Without a sound, she slumped to the ground, the top of her head blown away.

Mueller ordered Erhardt, who wore the pink triangle of the homosexual on his sleeve, stripped naked and tied to a post. With the entire camp bearing witness, Mueller took out the huge knife he carried and approached Erhardt, who had shut his eyes and appeared to be praying. At that moment Elena stepped forward and said Erhardt had only been protecting her from the *kapo*, who had raped her. As if in assent, a low murmur rose from the assembled throng until it was cut short by an order from the loudspeakers to be silent.

"So the pervert at least had the balls to kill a man," Mueller said. "And to protect a woman. How ironic." He arched a theatrical eyebrow as he said this, and looked around, seeming to challenge anyone to stop him. Perhaps wondering at his own power to do whatever he wanted to.

"Such decisions, however, are mine to make. And mine alone," he said to Elena. "Remember that, Jew, next time you think to tamper with my authority."

Mueller ordered two guards to hold her in front of Erhardt. "Watch carefully," he said, and proceeded to disembowel the man. Erhardt's screams were mercifully cut short by unconsciousness.

Mueller approached Elena, his eyes wild and distant. He took her face in his hands and with an unsettling tenderness covered her with Erhardt's blood. He ordered her back into ranks. As the two guards led her back, her mind barely registered the single pistol shot that ended the agony for Erhardt.

From that day on, she was singled out by Mueller for special attention. To him, the gruesome episode in the camp courtyard had apparently cemented some odd kind of bond between them.

One day, with no warning, she was taken to Dr. Roark and subjected to a lengthy physical examination. The exam was extraordinarily thorough, with a focus primarily on her reproductive parts. The following evening, she was led by a tall, silent SS guard to Mueller's personal quarters. There she was given over to two maids of Estonian extraction who took her into a bathroom, stripped her and washed her impersonally, as if she were a piece of food about to be cooked.

She tried to talk with them, but they didn't understand her German or French. When they had cleaned and perfumed her, they dressed her in a soft white cotton chemise, with fancy lace at the edges and belted at the waist, and led her into the dining room where a sumptuous dinner was set.

She sat there alone for half an hour, with a dish that resembled duck or chicken, heaps of potatoes and vegetables in front of her, not daring to eat though she was literally starving. There was no evidence of Rachel Stern, the young prisoner she'd heard Heinrich Mueller was sleeping with. No evidence of anyone, save the servants. She noticed a row of tiny drops down one side of the dress she was wearing. It looked like dried blood. She wondered who else had worn this dress.

When Mueller stomped into the house in a uniform half-unbuttoned and covered with dust, he looked at her as if wondering who she was. "Ah," he suddenly seemed to remember. "I must change into something more appropriate. Do not eat. I do not want to dine alone. But drink all you want."

He left. A servant stood by and poured a French champagne – it wasn't food, but it filled her stomach – into her glass each time she would empty it. This ritual was repeated many times before Mueller finally returned, freshly bathed and in a clean uniform. Elena was by then feeling extremely light-headed.

"Eat," he said, sitting at the head of the table just to her right. The food was cold, but it didn't matter. Between her inebriated state and her acute hunger, she barely noticed. Mueller ate with an appetite that rivaled her own, and with better manners than she would've expected. While they ate, he said little, but watched her closely.

The servant brought a dessert of chocolate mousse. Mueller had a second serving and offered one to Elena, which she ate in grateful silence.

They had continued drinking champagne, the only liquid offered, all through dinner. By the time they were done, Mueller was a little drunk himself. Elena had no idea what time it was, but in Kaisenher time was not important. Only that you were alive to live another day.

At the end of the meal she sat silently staring at her plate, feeling disoriented and slightly guilty.

Mueller's mood was one she would not have thought was in his emotional repertoire. Warmed by the afterglow of two bottles of champagne, he was expansive, almost friendly.

He spoke to her as if she were an equal. He seemed determined she should know and understand him.

"I know I frighten you," he said. He enunciated the words carefully, slowly – whether to help her understand, or because of the wine, she didn't know. "You should not be afraid of me," he said. "I am a man, like any other. I am a human being."

This pronouncement chilled her more than if he had announced he was a Bengal Tiger and intended to devour her. Elena could feel a trembling down deep inside, a physical manifestation of exactly the fear Mueller was talking about. She clamped her teeth together. She was determined to show no emotion. Especially fear.

"I did not ask to come here," Mueller said. "I was, I suppose, something of a ne'er-do-well in my youth. My mother was alone and had little control over me. In Garmisch, where we lived, I drank and I skied and I chased women. I joined the SS because to me it was like an exclusive club, something to aspire to. Something to straighten me out. I wanted to be SD, counterintelligence. Apparently Heydrich and Schellenberg and my immediate superiors did not think me qualified. They were going to assign me to an Einsatzgruppen squad in Poland. The idea horrified me. Instead I 'volunteered' for camp duty. They must have been hard up when they appointed me commandant. . . Unfortunately, once a man has served in the 'Death's Head' he is good for nothing else. We are the damned. We can never leave."

He eyed her again. She tried not to look at him. "So here I am," he said. "In Hell. As stuck with you, as you are with me."

He motioned for more wine. The servant poured it for both of them. Mueller held up his glass. "To the end of this goddamned war," he said, making a toast. "This fucking goddamned war. . ."

Elena looked at her glass. She felt dizzy. "Drink it," he said.

She drank the wine. All of it. Suddenly she bounded up from the table and headed for the bathroom where the women had bathed her a few hours before. She made it to the toilet, where she threw up. Later she would remember slumping to the hard tile, seeking comfort from its cold reality. Then nothing.

She was not fully conscious of anything else until she awoke in the dark on a bed, with a splitting head and unformed memories of something awful happening to her. She was naked. Her entire pelvic area throbbed with pain. She reached down and discovered a sticky substance leaking from her, both front and back. Everything down there was sensitive to the touch. She sniffed at the substance on her fingers. It had no smell, only a slight aroma of the perfumed oils she had been anointed with earlier in the day.

She was alone in the bed. There was no sign of Mueller, no sign of anyone. She was afraid to move. Finally, however, desperate to use the bathroom, she got up and limped painfully across the room. In the dim light she found that she had been bleeding. It hurt to urinate. She cleaned herself off at the sink as best she could, then found the white dress from the night before hung neatly in a closet. There were no other clothes, no underwear, shoes, anything. She put the dress on. It felt absurdly formal and pristine, but it was soft and at least covered her nakedness.

By this time dawn was beginning to break. Elena explored the house. The only person there was one of the Estonian women, cleaning the kitchen. The passage of twelve hours had not cured her inability to communicate. The woman, visibly nervous when Elena tried to speak with her, quickly finished her work and departed. Elena scoured the kitchen for food. She found some black bread and cheese, which she ate.

She tried to formulate a plan. She could think of nothing that would work. Perhaps she would simply kill herself.

Mueller didn't return until late in the evening. He was in a foul mood. "It has not been a good day," he said to her, as if he were an overworked husband returning home to a wife who would understand and soothe him.

That Elena didn't respond did not seem to matter to him. He rambled on about production delays and "asinine directives" from Berlin. It was bad enough before, he said, but since Heydrich had been killed it had gotten worse. "Now those idiots want it all," he moaned. "Production quotas met, while they starve and kill the workers essential to production. Their theory is that a steady stream of workers from their 'unlimited supply' in the East should make up for the ones that die. But they don't think of things like training, indoctrination, and the time it takes to simply move people in. And bodies out."

He didn't seem to require anything more of her than that she listen to him. She sat silently through a more informal dinner than the night before and let him do most of the drinking. She hoped he would get too drunk to bother with her, but it didn't happen. In bed, he wasted no kisses on her. Handling her more impersonally than roughly, he turned her over and jammed a grainy lubricant of some sort up both openings, not seeming to care which one he used when he mounted her.

When he was done, he passed out on top of her. As she lay there, the loathing she felt eased the pain and helped sustain her. Afraid at first to move and disturb him, she finally, very slowly and carefully, managed to wriggle out from under him. She didn't sleep until he left her in the morning.

In the following weeks and months he continued to treat her as half wife, half whore. He beat her up, but only twice, and only in drunken rages that seemed to have nothing to do with her. The second time, he had thrown her through a flimsy glass partition in the bathroom and Dr. Roarke had been required to stop the bleeding with sutures. This had left her with a long scar across her upper chest and shoulder. Mueller had shown some contrition the next day, but she did not want kindnesses from him. Not ever. She didn't want to have to respond to him on any human level. In general that was no problem. With few exceptions, he did not require her to be a human being with him, to reveal herself in any way. For this at least she was grateful.

During this time Elena had no contact with the general population of the camp. It was only from Mueller's often disjointed monologues that she understood camp operations, including the random killings and torture, were continuing to speed up. She herself was now classified as a political prisoner rather than a Jew, he told her. This was to protect them both, he said one night in the kind of calmer inebriated state in which he also sometimes talked about Rachel Stern. "She was a haughty little bitch when she arrived," he said of Elena's predecessor. "It was a quality that never quite left her, in spite of everything," he said. "I helped her preserve it, because I liked it. Added some spice to this hell-hole. Our time together was–" He paused, as if searching for the right way to say it. "Perhaps 'interesting' is the best word. When it was done, I sent her to Dachau for her own safety. And possibly for my own," he laughed without mirth. "But I can't do that again. Can't afford to be labeled a Jew lover."

Elena returned again and again to the idea of killing herself. It would be easy, she thought. She was left to her own devices for hours each day. There were cleaning fluids and other poisons in the house. Even knives, though only of the dull-edged table variety, were left unguarded in the kitchen.

Then one day rummaging around under the kitchen sink she found something even better. An ice pick. This discovery led to daydreams of killing Mueller. She taped the ice pick up under the frame of the bed, where she could easily reach it when he was asleep.

To kill him would mean her own death, she knew, but she felt prepared for that. One cold night after a particularly brutal round of sex she went so far as to bring the ice pick up into bed with her, watching him for hours, his chest heaving in rhythm with a drunken snore, carefully choosing where to plunge the sharpened instrument home. But shortly before daybreak, with a pounding rain as cover, she replaced the ice pick under the bed and feigned sleep until Mueller left. Then she lay awake and wondered what her hesitation might eventually cost her. Why hadn't she done it? Given the opportunity, Rachel Stern would've followed through, she was convinced. But not her. She couldn't do it. What had stopped her, she finally decided, was the certainty of the bloodbath that would have followed. Hundreds, maybe thousands, of prisoners would've been slaughtered in retaliation. It would have meant many more deaths besides her own, and in the final analysis she was not prepared for that.

She found another use for the ice pick. After a couple of months with Mueller, she started getting sick on a daily basis. When Dr. Roarke examined her, he informed her she was pregnant. She begged him to abort the baby. He was sympathetic, but refused. That night she did the job herself with the ice pick, thinking she would probably die in the process. Mueller found her on the floor in a pool of blood, and Roarke managed to save her. He saved her twice. Once by stopping the hemorrhaging, and again by not telling Mueller why it had happened. She herself would never tell anyone but Richter about it.

After that she went through her days in a haze, and Mueller, as if he sensed something were broken inside her, left her increasingly alone.

One day after about four months in the house, Elena was approached by one of Mueller's aides, handed the dirty, drab uniform of the camp and ordered to put it on. Then without a word from Mueller, she was marched back into camp life as if she had never left it.

Once again, she expected to die. Or perhaps follow Rachel Stern to Dachau in spite of Mueller's claim he couldn't send them another refugee from his bed. But neither happened. She heard later a girl of fourteen from Riga had replaced her in Mueller's quarters. He never spoke to Elena again and ignored her the few times he passed by her in camp. But other prisoners told her that her stint in the house had earned her an immunity of sorts, that she now had Mueller's personal protection and everyone knew it. The guards, she was told, had been warned neither they nor anyone else would be allowed to molest her. She may have been discarded, but Mueller still considered her his personal property it seemed.

Her hair, which had grown back to nearly shoulder length, was not shaved off when she returned to the compound, so she had one of her few remaining friends shave it off for her. She tried to use what little leverage she had to help others, particularly the women of the camp. Most of these efforts were rejected by her fellow prisoners, who resented her and considered her tainted by her contact with Mueller.

Despite her protected status, her health had continued to deteriorate until the day Richter arrived, Elena said. On that day, Dr. Roarke had given her a final inspection then personally delivered her to Richter. It had taken several more days, however, before she had allowed herself to believe she might truly escape Kaisenher.

"And now," she said, still nursing Richter's wounds in their forest hideout near St. Sentione, "Now we must both escape."

Richter's face had frozen into a mask. "We will," he promised. "But first there is something I have to do."

"Hitler's Assassin"

Despite Elena's objections, as soon as he was well enough Richter made arrangements for her safety then headed back into Germany alone. He had tried to devise a plan. Had tried to figure some way he might use the failed plot against Hitler as a way to penetrate the Nazi upper echelon. Every scheme he came up with, however, had seemed too risky, not only for him, but for the safety of any plotters still seeking to evade the SS and Gestapo. Every one of them, including himself, was a potential source of information about the others for the Nazis. He would have to play it by ear, he ultimately decided.

Alternating his Wehrmacht uniform with civilian clothes, as needed, he stayed away from the larger cities and traveled any way he could. As the Allies continued to apply pressure on the Western Front, movement in the rear echelons was becoming a helter-skelter combination of tightened restrictions, usually under control of the SS, or of no restrictions and no control at all. He used trains, trucks, hitched rides, even commandeered an army motorcycle at one point. The jolting motorcycle ride reopened the wound in his side and forced him to take nearly a day of rest in a barn less than twenty miles short of his destination.

When he reached Orienbad, he was relieved to find his family home still intact. The neighborhood had not been bombed at all. It looked much as he remembered it from a year ago. But at the door he received an unpleasant shock. The house was occupied by people he had never seen before. Immediately on guard, he identified himself only as a friend of the owners. Politely enough, these strangers informed him the "former owners" had been condemned as unfit to own property. They knew nothing more about them, they said.

Risking discovery, Richter made inquiries in the area. A discreet and sympathetic neighbor, an old friend of the family's, pulled him inside and hugged him warmly. The woman sat him down and told him his mother had been interrogated by the Gestapo, after which she had supposedly committed suicide. That was the official line. This had happened only two weeks ago, the woman said. She knew nothing about his father, though there had been rumors he too was dead, or about Johann's surviving sister Ellen.

Even Sacha had disappeared from Orienbad. There was nothing left for Richter there. Hitler's men had seen to that.

By this time, the hangings of members of the 20 July plot had begun in Berlin. They were well publicized, though not all details appeared in the press, not even in the Goebbels mouthpiece *Der Angriff* or the Nazi daily, the *Volkischer Beobachter*.

These were no ordinary hangings. The condemned men were suspended from butcher's hooks with piano wire, where they dangled in midair and died a slow horrible death, sometimes alone, sometimes to the accompaniment of one another's screams. Films of their helpless drawn-out tortures were sent to Hitler for his personal amusement.

Richter holed up in a second-rate country inn not far from Orienbad. His wound ached and he had some difficulty breathing. He was deeply depressed. The world once again seemed turned upside down, and he had apparently played a role in it, however unwittingly, giving Yvonne Duchamps and British Intelligence all they'd needed on the plot against Hitler. Though it hadn't stopped the assassination attempt itself, MI6 was now throwing all the fuel it could on the Nazi firestorm of paranoia over who might have been involved. Even publicly, particularly on the BBC, the British were tossing names around left and right for the Gestapo's benefit.

He could not believe he had been duped so easily. For now, he tried not to think about what had been going on between Yvonne and Christine Johns, or how Anne Wheldon Johns might have been assisting MI6. He had more than enough to feed his guilt and depression already. Hitler was alive. Stauffenberg was dead. As were Olbricht, Mertz, Haeften, **Stülpnagel** and so many others. The Wehrmacht would mount no more attempts on Hitler's life. The Fuhrer would live to drag Germany down with him.

Richter's own family, he feared, was gone. Gretchen had died two years ago, Ellen and her major general husband he had written off, and now his mother was almost certainly dead. But what about his father? He had seen no mention of him in the newspapers, heard nothing on the radio. What had happened to him?

He had to find out. He had to know whether his father was dead or alive. And he had to do it in a way that would not jeopardize him if he were still alive. He needed help. Richter could think of only one person, if he had not been implicated himself, who could provide such help and be counted on not to compromise him or his father.

He paid one more visit to Orienbad, this time at night with a flashlight to retrieve a Remington Model 700 rifle with telescopic sights from an outbuilding where his father, for reasons of his own, kept it tucked away along with a supply of 7.62 mm ammunition. It was supposedly a hunting rifle, but it could be broken down and fit snugly into an inconspicuous carrying case, which had always led Richter to wonder about its true purpose. He knew a patch of woods nearby where he could test-fire it.

Before he left, he also dug up a tin box full of Reichsmarks he had buried there the year before for emergency use. One final gift from this beloved soil.

Getting to Berlin was relatively simple. He commandeered a bicycle and rode it in, dressed in civilian clothes. His left lung still hurt as he bounced along bomb-damaged roads, but it was worth it. Bicycles attracted little attention these days, especially among civilians. Every day more two-wheelers appeared on the streets, replacing motorized transport that no longer operated due to rapidly escalating shortages in auto parts and fuel.

Stretches of Berlin were no longer navigable to motor vehicles anyway. The serious destruction, begun the previous November, was being augmented by daily bombing raids. Parts of the city looked more like the ruins of an ancient civilization than the capital of a nation so recently bent on conquering half the world. People went about their business with grim determination, a pall of impending defeat heavy in the air. Joy was absent even in the few children left behind in the exodus to the suburbs and countryside. Richter tried to block it all out and stay focused on his mission.

* * * *

Erich Borchers, it turned out, was still at the War Offices in the Bendlerblock, the same building from which Stauffenberg, Mertz, Olbricht and Haeften had been taken and shot on the night of 20 July. Richter reached him by phone and Borchers, betraying no hint of nervousness, agreed to meet him near the Zoobunker in the Tiergarten.

Richter marveled at the mammoth Zoobunker as he walked past. It must have taken a beating since he and Borchers had taken shelter in it more than a year ago, but even direct hits from the British and American bombers had merely chipped its massive walls. The Tiergarten's expansive wooded areas appeared to be taking more hits from the residents of Berlin than from the Allies. Against regulations, patches of trees had been clear-cut to provide fuel for a freezing populace, a phenomenon Richter had heard about during his posting in France. One more winter and the place would look like a desert, he thought.

Sitting on a low wall at the appointed spot in an obscure section of the park, Richter began having second thoughts. He worried about his old friend's seeming nonchalance on the telephone. Was there a danger of being set up? On the other hand, he reasoned, Borchers had always had a cool head. He'd been the only fencer at Heidelberg Richter had known who had prided himself on *not* receiving a dueling scar – a competitor who prized his skill with epee and foil and his reputation for cautious tactics above any wound, however prestigious.

Gently massaging his own Heidelberg scar, Richter wondered how Borchers had managed to survive 20 July.

Before he could worry this question through to a conclusion, or decide to leave, his old friend approached, looking commanding in his Wehrmacht uniform with full colonel's insignia. Borchers ignored his proffered hand. Instead, he hugged him with a genuine emotion that immediately put Richter's fears to rest.

"Are you all right?" Borchers said as Richter grimaced at his embrace.

"I'm fine. Just a little surface wound for the cause." Richter gently patted his left side, fighting off another grimace.

Borchers took this in, seemingly satisfied with the explanation. "Good. I am happy to see you, my old friend. Especially since I assumed you would be dead by now." He said this in a casual tone. "I have been praying for you to be admitted to heaven in spite of your many and well-documented sins."

Richter smiled at this, but time was short. He came straight to the point. "What has happened to my father, Erich? There has been no word of him since. . . since the events of 20 July." He held his breath. The answer could be anything. And could mean everything.

Borchers looked him squarely in the eye. "It's bad news, I'm afraid."

Richter braced himself.

"He and I were both at the Bendlerblock on 20 July," Borchers said. "Myself off and on; your father, the entire day and evening. He acquitted himself with honor. He held things together until von Stauffenberg arrived. Then they both did their best to rally the troops, but once we knew Hitler had survived the blast the initiative was lost and so was the battle. Earlier in the day we had seemed so close to success. . ." Borcher's voice was heavy with despair.

"And my father?"

"Your father, the next morning, when everything was still crazy and up in the air, was offered – by Fromm, I believe – the opportunity to take his own life. Instead, he drew his sidearm and marched down the hall to a conference room where Goebbels was meeting with someone. Goebbels, the little swine, had of course played a key role in putting down our attempted coup the night before.

"Your father walked into the conference room with his service revolver and aimed it right at Goebbels. Those present said later that he had two or three seconds to pull the trigger, but was killed before he fired a shot. No one knows whether he was actually going to shoot him or was choosing this way to commit suicide.

Goebbels had always been intimidated by your father and was apparently terrified during the encounter. It was all kept as quiet as possible. They didn't want an attack on Goebbels by a figure as prominent as your father to get out. Bad for morale of the *volk*. The press, in fact, has not dealt with your father's death at all."

Richter stared across the broad pathway at a surviving stand of trees long a favorite of lovers looking for privacy. He took a deep breath to settle his emotions. Borchers' words only confirmed what he'd already known, deep down, had to be true. That his father was dead. He felt a small consolation of pride at the way he had died.

"But then there are a lot of aspects of the coup attempt they haven't dealt with, or have lied about," Borchers said. "I was there. Von Stauffenberg died with God and Germany on his lips. He and the others all died bravely, but the press is saying they were sniveling cowards with a personal lust for power."

Richter tried hard not to picture his old friend watching from the shadows as Stauffenberg and the others were shot.

"And my mother?" he said, finally.

"Poison," Borchers replied. "She poisoned herself. I'm not sure she was given a choice. But she at least was allowed a funeral. Many of us who would've attended your father's funeral, if he had been allowed one, went to your mother's. Including me. It was quite a crowd in spite of the risk."

"Thank you. Thank you for going." Richter was genuinely grateful, but something was sticking in his craw. It was hard for him to believe Borchers had been at the Bendlerblock and somehow managed to survive 20 July and its aftermath.

Borchers read his mind. "Yes, I know what you're thinking. Why am I still alive? I was used primarily as a liaison that day, between the Bendlerblock and other members of Valkyrie placed at key points around Berlin. It saved my life. Fromm had no idea I was involved. And during the mop-up operations I befriended Major Remer, whose guard unit had defeated us, and he personally vouched for my conduct afterwards. . . Our best men died on 20 July, or are dying now. I'm not proud I survived, but my rationale is that I may yet be of service to Germany."

"No, it's better that you survived, Erich," Richter said, relieved that Borchers had an explanation. "Your death would have accomplished nothing."

Borchers acknowledged with a wan smile. "And now you, my friend, must try to leave Germany," he said. "My own position is still precarious. I had to be very careful coming here today. But I will help if I can. Do you need money?"

Richter returned his own tired smile of appreciation. "I need a uniform," he said. "I left mine in the woods this morning."

"I'll give you one of mine. It should be a reasonable fit. We're still about the same size. Like Heidelberg, remember? Trading our fencing uniforms back and forth when the laundering was too expensive?"

"Yes, I remember."

"I'll give you a set of my insignia as well."

"That would be a quick promotion. I was just made a lieutenant colonel."

"Well now you're a colonel. Congratulations."

"Erich, are you in touch with any of the plotters anymore, any that are still free?"

"Not really. The underground is in total disarray. We have reason to believe we were infiltrated somehow. Betrayed. The Gestapo seem to know who to go after."

Richter's gut churned at the possibility he might have been responsible for the leak. Borchers, however, had another suspect in mind. "Otto Sprague, your father's adjutant," he said, "was at your mother's funeral. I think he was, uh, 'enamored' with her. But I was never sure of his reliability."

While Richter absorbed this, Borchers continued, "In any case, Hitler's survival has put everyone who was not captured or killed on ice for the time being."

"And where is Hitler now?"

"He is supposedly still at Rastenberg, carrying on the good fight. Some say he's considering an offensive in the West." Borchers eyed him closely. "But since 20 July, no one can get near him. No one who is not with his immediate entourage. Everything is done by wireless or telephone. The Liebstandarte Adolf Hitler and another full SS division have completely sealed him off."

"Why do you say 'supposedly'?"

"I have reason to believe he has gone to Berchtesgaden. To lick his wounds."

"How certain are you of that?"

"Fairly certain." Borchers' look turned into one of concern. "Johann, if you have some idea of going after Hitler, put it out of your mind. Please, I beg you." He placed a hand on Richter's shoulder for emphasis. "Since the attempt on his life, Hitler has been on a rampage. He wants only destruction now. Nothing is immune. He's ordered von Choltitz, who made a name for himself at the siege at Sevastopol, to Paris to destroy the city before the Allies arrive. Here in Berlin, Heinrich Muller and the Gestapo are having a heyday settling old scores. You would only be sacrificing yourself. For nothing. The war is almost over."

The name Muller jogged something in Richter's memory, though he could not for the moment put his finger on it. He stared absentmindedly at Borchers. "Perhaps you're right," he said. "Thank you. I'll still need a uniform, however."

Borchers continued to look worried, but he agreed. "I'll bring you the uniform tonight. Here, at nine or as close to nine as I can manage. But watch yourself. With the blackouts on, it's dangerous in here at night. Do you have a firearm?"

Richter nodded.

"Bring it with you tonight and be on your guard. I'll see you at nine."

Richter watched his old friend walk away. An ineffable sense of sadness settled over him like a heavy cloud. He felt much as his father must have felt during the last moments of his life. He knew what he had to do. He picked up the carrying case with the rifle in it and followed Borchers out of the Tiergarten.

* * * *

Richter stared at the devastation outside the window. His train was passing through Munich. Or what was left of it, after two years of Allied bombing raids. His country was dying alongside his family. He felt a smothering sense of loss and despair. Of hopelessness. And a personal sense of guilt compounded by his share of the greater guilt of Germany. The only silver lining was that all this was shoring up his resolve to do what he had to do.

Borchers fortunately had brought him not only a uniform complete with sidearm and colonel's insignia, but also a high priority military travel pass. Their final exchange in the darkened Tiergarten had been eerie but had gone off without a hitch. The farewell had been particularly heartfelt, each of them knowing they were never likely to meet again.

Richter had requested one last favor. He had asked Borchers to use his connections to plant an obituary – not for his father but for him. "Give me a couple weeks, then have them run it," he'd asked. "It might give me some cover. Or for that matter, it might be true by then."

Borchers shook his head and gave him a pained look, and they had parted.

The train ride south had been interrupted repeatedly by sightings of enemy aircraft and work on bomb-damaged tracks. There had been no *razzias*, however, no police checks for identification. Richter had encountered little suspicion so far. People for the most part paid scant attention to his uniform or his new, more exalted, rank. Most of his fellow travelers appeared preoccupied, presumably with some aspect of the world crumbling all around them. With things starting to fall apart, the SS and Gestapo had dropped all subtleties and were clamping their control down even tighter.

But Anschluss with Austria gave him one advantage at least. As the train entered the Alps and "Ostmark," as the Nazis now called the former nation to their south, there was only a perfunctory border check. Everything from this point on was totally new territory to Richter. Having been told the rail lines north of Berchtesgaden had been heavily bombed the week before, he got off the train in Salzburg. It had been Hitler's custom to board the train here in the years before he had ordered an expansive new station built for his convenience at Berchtesgaden. Richter knew this from his father, who had visited nearby Berchtesgaden many times.

He chose a small hotel with no front desk – guests had to ring up a clerk for assistance – that was perched where the city ran its back up against the mountains, signing in under an assumed name. The top floor room he checked into commanded a view of the entire town. An impressive castle loomed off to the right above a river that bisected the valley. The train station was directly below the hotel. Richter broke out the Remington and reassembled it. Before he had test-fired it two nights ago, he'd never shot this particular model before. But now the rifle felt comfortable as he tucked it up against his shoulder. He focused the telescopic sight on a woman standing outside the train station. He could tell she had blue eyes. That should be good enough.

His first day in Salzburg, he purchased a pair of binoculars and talked an elderly Austrian woman into renting him her battered old Ford motorcar. She wasn't driving it anymore anyway, she said, and seemed happy he didn't simply requisition it for the Wehrmacht.

Nursing the ancient noisy machine and two cans of petrol the woman had managed to hoard, Richter drove the fifteen miles to Berchtesgaden through a gauntlet of majestic mountains. On guard for roadblocks, he didn't notice a thick white cloud blanketing the hills up ahead until he plowed right into it on the outskirts of town. Coughing, his eyes immediately beginning to water, he rolled up the windows and pulled over, wondering at the cause of his discomfort. As the heavy mist gradually dissipated, it revealed a sky painted the deep red of a spectacular sunset – but in the wrong direction, over mountains to the north.

Out on the streets of Berchtesgaden, his throat still a little sore, Richter asked the first person he met about the acrid haze he had just driven through. The woman gave him a quizzical look. "Oh, the 'Fuhrer fog,' you mean," she said.

"The *what* fog?"

"The Fuhrer's artificial clouds. The SS makes them with pressurized chemicals. They release them from big metal canisters whenever Allied aircraft approach Obersalzburg." She made a face. "You don't want to breathe it in," she said. "It goes right to the lungs, almost like poison gas."

Talking with others, Richter was told the fiery "sunset," not uncommon these days, was fueled by the fires of bombed cities to the north, and that the cloud-like haze was produced by an SS detachment they referred to as "fog soldiers." The object was to protect Obersalzburg, where Hitler and the other top Nazis had built homes on a mountainside to the east of Berchtesgaden. Richter could see no bomb damage. He had evidently missed the air raid sirens and the *ack-ack-ack* of antiaircraft fire earlier.

One more surreal footnote to this insane war, he thought.

After clearing that mystery up, he wandered around chatting amiably with anyone he encountered who was not in uniform, gathering what little he could on Hitler's whereabouts. The villagers – most of them women at this point in the war – were not given to loose talk about their infamous neighbor up the mountain, but they weren't impolite about it. Richter managed to engage several in enough small talk to paste together a few conclusions. The track north of Berchtesgaden had indeed been badly damaged, and it appeared Erich Borchers' information had been correct as well, that Hitler was here at his Alpine retreat, the Berghof.

Approaching a river and bridge near the middle of town, he was stopped by a pair of SS guards who asked to see his orders. Richter handed them the set of fake orders Borchers had given him. After a tense few minutes of questioning, the guards returned his papers and waved him on. Breathing a sigh of relief, Richter distanced himself from the bridge as quickly as possible.

At the edge of town, he climbed a hillside until he was sure he could not be seen. Taking the small pair of binoculars from his travel case, he scanned the surrounding mountains. On one of the highest, far above Berchtesgaden, he could make out the Berghof and Eagle's Nest, Hitler's mountaintop aeries, their swastika flags snapping in the stiff mountain wind. Both were accessible only by a narrow road with miles of hairpin turns cut into the mountainside. To reach Eagle's Nest, the higher of the two, required an additional elevator ride of nearly four hundred vertical feet. Together they were an impregnable fortress to anything short of a crack division of mountain troops, and too distant for sniper fire.

He wondered what Hitler was thinking about up there on his Mount Olympus with his shrinking empire imploding all around him. Was he seeking solace in the arms of Eva Braun or one of the other mistresses he was rumored to keep? And what did the Fuhrer of the German Reich make of the death of General Karl von Richter? Though they had never been close, Richter's father had been with Hitler for so long, had been through so much with him, there should have been a reaction, Richter thought. Possibly even a sense of loss.

Or perhaps it was more as it had been when Rudolf Hess had made his startling solo flight to England three years ago, shortly before the invasion of Russia. By all accounts Hitler had been deeply and personally wounded by what he perceived as the defection of his deputy fuhrer, but had quickly turned that emotion on its head, excoriating Hess nonstop for hours on end and declaring him insane.

Expecting a more conventional human reaction from Adolf Hitler was probably more insane than Hess ever was, Richter decided finally, and returned his focus to the task at hand.

* * * *

Richter returned to Salzburg and waited. For the next six days he waited, revisiting Berchtesgaden every other day to look and listen for signs of when Hitler might leave. The altitude was rough on his injured lung but the protracted wait gave him a chance to rest and husband his energy. Meanwhile he also cultivated several contacts in the surprisingly large number of restaurants and bars that remained open in Salzburg after five years of war. The city renowned as the birthplace of Wolfgang Amadeus Mozart was holding up well, all things considered. Perhaps Hitler's meetings with Mussolini here had boosted the local economy, Richter thought. Last year the Fuhrer had tried to shore up Il Duce's will to fight and the Italian dictator, beset by workers' strikes and talk of revolution, had tried to convince Hitler to make peace with the Soviets. Neither had succeeded.

For six days his efforts paid little dividend, other than to confirm the rail lines to the north between Berchtesgaden and Munich remained impassable. Doubts began to creep in. But late in the afternoon of day six he was finally rewarded. The sister of a woman whose husband was on the maintenance staff at the Berghof, who Richter met on a Berchtesgaden park bench, said the Fuhrer would leave in the morning. Refreshed and ready once again for the rigors of carrying the war on his shoulders, she declared. The woman, an attractive well-fed Bavarian in her mid-thirties, was still a true believer. Interrupting herself several times to shout warnings at her three young children playing nearby, she quizzed Richter as much as he quizzed her. Where had he fought? How had he gotten that scar? Was it true the Russians were raping and killing women and children on the Eastern Front?

Richter thought her information rang true, though he knew Hitler, a late riser, rarely did anything in the morning so dramatic as start a train trip. He parried her questions as best he could, trying to arouse as little suspicion as possible. His uniform and rank this time proved useful. She accorded it a certain respect, almost deference, in spite of the rather personal questions she continued to ask. He hoped its effect would cloud her perceptions of his obvious interest in her Fuhrer and his travel plans.

Back in Salzburg, Richter worried the woman had seen through him and would give him away. Even if they couldn't find him, it could ruin his plans if Hitler were warned. If he were truly committed to his course of action, he thought, he would have lured her somewhere secluded and killed her to ensure her silence. But he knew he could never have done it. So now he was relegated to waiting it out, hoping she had bought his line. And hoping she was right about Hitler's plans.

He barely slept that night. He stayed in a chair by the window that had the best view of the train station, fully dressed, fitfully dozing in and out of a half-sleep. During one such foggy interlude, he dreamed of a row of bodies dangling like marionettes, bleeding and screaming in an agonizing cacophony of death. When he suddenly realized the horribly mutilated body screaming the loudest was his father, he awoke in a tremor, bathed in sweat. The instant he regained his senses and realized where he was, he panicked that he might have missed Hitler's train.

Dawn was breaking on what promised to be a beautiful day. People were starting to move about on the streets below. Richter decided to take a chance. He splashed water on his face, quickly shaved, straightened his uniform and descended the four floors to the street. At an open market that displayed a pitifully meager assortment of fruits and vegetables at exorbitant prices – against pricing regulations, he noted – he bought a few items and kept his ears open.

When that produced nothing, he asked one vendor, an old man, if he had heard the Fuhrer was coming through town today.

The old man nodded, just barely. "So I hear." He said it cautiously, a civilian carefully guarding his words with a Wehrmacht colonel. But Richter decided the man wasn't just parroting the question. It was corroboration enough. He beat a hasty retreat back up to his room and resumed his watch, periodically scanning the station and the area around it with the binoculars.

The hours passed and Hitler did not show. Richter's left lung throbbed. He was unable to find a position that eased the pain. As the day wore on, one aspect of his intentions started to eat away at him. Was trying to kill Hitler at long range, without looking him in the eye, a coward's way out? No satisfactory answer came to him, but he began to realize, perhaps as justification, there was a good chance he was about to commit suicide. He had not much dwelled on the possibility before. But now as he searched out possible exit routes with his binoculars, the odds for escape seemed remote. At least Borchers would be standing by with his obituary, he thought ruefully.

He dwelled briefly on Elena Stein and all the other reasons he was here, but quickly banished such thoughts. He could not afford any distractions. He checked and rechecked the Remington a dozen times, thinking briefly to jury-rig a silencer but rejecting the idea for fear it might affect his accuracy. There was irony, he thought, in its being a weapon of American manufacture. His father had never shared Hitler's down-the-nose attitude toward Americans and their products. And he had kept the rifle in excellent condition. The more likely problem would be his own marksmanship. He had slacked off on his practice sessions after he'd been told he was not to be Hitler's assassin. It would be a difficult shot. He would need luck, as well as a steady hand.

Doubts continued to assail him. By five o'clock in the afternoon he had all but decided the Fuhrer, a notorious eleventh-hour changer of plans, must have postponed his departure. If he arrived much later today, he would be covered by darkness. Richter wasn't sure whether he felt more depressed or relieved by the prospect.

Finally, though, shortly after 5:45, with the sun still strong, a motorized escort pulled into the parking lot of the train station.

Dozens of SS men flanked four limousines that disgorged a small torrent of military VIPs. Richter held his breath to flatten out any potential shakiness. His left lung still ached. He tried to pick Hitler apart from the rest with the Remington's sniper sight. When he didn't spot him, he had to force himself not to panic. He could hear his own strained breathing. Each time he inhaled, he grew more nauseous at the smell of gun grease from the well-oiled rifle cradled against his cheek.

For an instant he thought he recognized Otto Sprague, his father's adjutant, down among the uniformed crowd on the station platform, stopping to light up a cigarette. This immediately rekindled doubts. How could Sprague be here if Karl Richter had been shot trying to remove Hitler from power? Or were Erich Borchers' suspicions right, that Sprague had sold Valkyrie out?

This was not the moment to falter. There was no time to confirm whether it was Sprague. The first of the high-ranking officers were already nearing the station building when from out of nowhere Adolf Hitler suddenly appeared in Richter's sights. He felt as if he knew the man, in spite of having seen him only once before, at a distance. He drew a bead on the instantly recognizable profile, asking God to forgive him for what he was about to do. His body relaxed and an immense feeling of relief flooded through him. An outside force, it seemed, had taken control of the rifle.

But as he touched his finger to the trigger and slowly, carefully increased the pressure, the telescopic sight abruptly turned fire-red. Hitler's profile had been replaced by the brick wall of the station building. Richter had missed his chance. Maybe his only chance. He was furious, frantic.

Then very quickly it appeared he would have one more opening, as Hitler's entourage began moving out from the protective cover of the building and down along the open platform toward the rear of the train.

He scanned the crowd of uniforms. Hitler was about to enter the train but had stopped to confer with a Kriegsmarine admiral. This time the Fuhrer was facing Richter directly. He looked somehow different. Heavier, perhaps, more jowly. Aiming at the bridge of his nose, Richter experienced one last wave of doubt. He remembered what Heinrich Mueller had said about aiming at a live target. Palms sweating, fingers icy, unable to make the final irrevocable decision, he pictured his father, his mother and all the others who were gone and finally let his finger move against the trigger.

For a split second, perhaps hearing the gun's report, Hitler stared straight up the sniper sight, a look of startled recognition on his face, almost as if he had been expecting this moment. The Remington kicked hard against Richter's shoulder, its recoil knocking the sight askew. He retrained it on his target, now sprawled on the station platform, and squeezed off two more shots before the rifle jammed. He surveyed the scene with his binoculars. Most of the others had scrambled for cover, but he could make out several knots of SS men appearing to shout and point in his general direction. It seemed odd Hitler's body remained unattended. Perhaps that's how destiny treats a tyrant at the end, he thought. Even an Adolf Hitler.

One group of SS did in fact now move to retrieve the body while several others, Richter could see, were scrambling into the streets that led toward him. He felt a little groggy and weak in the knees but otherwise remarkably calm.

He scanned the rest of Salzburg with the binoculars, gauging which avenues of retreat might still be open. It was time to leave. He had done what he had come to do. All but one thing. If he escaped Salzburg, he would finish the job. One more death. And if this one today didn't cost him his life the next one almost certainly would.

"End Game"

Richter managed to exit the hotel and cover nearly four blocks before he encountered the first contingent of SS snaking their way up the narrow street he was on. Relying on his borrowed uniform and rank, he beckoned them to follow him back up the hill. SS men could not always be counted on to take orders from a Wehrmacht officer, even a colonel, but it appeared he'd guessed correctly Hitler's bodyguards would be accustomed to dealing with high-ranking army officers. And right now, with what had just happened, they were likely to listen to anyone ready to take charge.

At the crest of the hill, in front of the hotel where he'd just left behind all the evidence they would need to piece things together – the Remington, empty cartridges, the binoculars – he told the ten men or so who had followed him he planned to split them up and send them in flanking movements to either side of the building. It was the most likely spot anywhere in the vicinity from which someone could have fired shots at the train station. Anyone could see that, and he needed his pursuers to have faith in him for at least a few more minutes.

Unholstering his Luger, he ordered the men to make sure no one left the premises, and to wait five minutes then converge on the hotel in unison. He would use a back entrance and scout out what was happening inside while they tightened the noose, he said.

The moment they were deployed and out of sight, Richter wheeled and headed back down the hill at a quick but deliberate pace. Halfway down, he found a side street that cut a right angle across the hillside and made his way along it. He was twice forced to stop to avoid more SS patrols, the first time ducking into a doorway, the second into an alleyway. There was no way to get to his car. When he reached a quieter part of town, he requisitioned a bicycle whose owner was nowhere to be seen and pedaled out into the countryside, where he was soon covered by nightfall.

His wounded lung feeling ready to burst, Richter made his way by the light of a full moon to a nearby village. There he approached the driver of a reasonably sturdy-looking Opel sedan – the only vehicle on the street this time of night – and offered him a generous sum for a ride. He added an appeal to the man's patriotism. That didn't work, but a backup threat convinced the unsympathetic burgher it was in his own best interest to comply. As they got underway, Richter told himself he would have to warn the man to be discreet about their destination. He asked about the radio, but his driver informed him it was broken.

Still a bit shell-shocked from Salzburg, he was genuinely surprised he had managed to escape. It wasn't until several hours into the journey, watching another beautiful dawn break through the treetops of a familiar stretch of forest, that the enormity of what had transpired started to sink in. If he had killed Hitler, as he thought he had, it opened up a whole new world of possibilities for Germany. Now he could only hope Goering, Himmler and the other top Nazis would keep it quiet as long as possible, while they wrestled one another for power in the wake of their Fuhrer's demise.

He was amazed how little he had thought it out in advance, in political terms. He had killed Hitler for personal reasons. To strike a blow for his father and mother, his sister, Claus von Stauffenberg and all the others, as well as Elena Stein and her family. Hitler deserved to die. But his crimes went far beyond these few. Added together they had brought unprecedented shame and destruction to Germany. Now hopefully all that he had unleashed would stop. The Pandora's Box of new bombs, rockets and gas would be closed and locked, maybe forever. In spite of the Allies' insistence on unconditional surrender, a peace agreement was now possible. Everything could change. All because one man was gone. The Fuhrer. Richter remembered the twinge of conscience he had felt when he pulled the trigger. He felt no such remorse today.

Though Stalin remained a dark cloud on the horizon, the future did indeed look brighter. But he couldn't dwell on the prospects right now. He had more immediate concerns. As the sky began to lighten, and the forest deepened in the same dark, depressing way it had last time he was here, he felt incapable of formulating a rational plan for what lay ahead. In Salzburg, in spite of the odds against him, he'd had a chance. This time he really could not picture how he was going to escape once the deed was done. It would take a small army to back him up. The sidearm and dagger he carried weren't going to be nearly enough.

He tried to console himself that it would be similar to Rastenburg, where Stauffenberg had pulled off everything but the assassination itself.

Of course Stauffenberg had also paid with his life. He would just have to play it by ear again. Not a comforting thought.

* * * *

Military etiquette was still lax at the camp gate, but Richter's new rank was shown more deference than the civilian world had given it. Heinrich Mueller was summoned immediately.

The commandant of Kaisenher did not appear immediately, however. This didn't surprise Richter. He cooled his heels while the SS guards grew increasingly nervous in his presence. The senior man phoned a second time, and finally a third, and Richter began to show his impatience, as he had often seen his father and other general officers do to get things done. Trying to ignore the jabbing pain in his side, he sat tapping the riding crop Borchers had tossed into his kit as a joke, a gesture from Heidelberg days, hitting it with authority against his boot. He glanced at his watch and glowered at anyone who dared meet his eyes. Nobody did it more than once.

He had the distinct impression no one here knew about Hitler's death yet, thank God.

Finally Mueller appeared. Richter was startled at the change in his appearance. He remembered him as a dangerous man, on the edge of instability, but also as shifty and alert, with a focused energy and a certain polish. Now he looked disheveled, his uniform sloppy, his once-handsome features gone slack. He needed a shave. His eyes were bloodshot. From the moment he opened his mouth, it was obvious he was at least slightly drunk.

His greeting had a note of challenge in it. "Richter. I thought it might be you. S'funny, though. I remember you as a captain. Your career must be taking off."

"Congratulations on your own promotion, Standartenfuhrer," Richter countered. Mueller was remembering his former rank incorrectly, but it made no difference. Here was one advantage, at least, of the news blackout on his father. Mueller was almost certainly chalking up Richter's rapid rise in rank to the General's influence. Mueller's, Richter assumed, rested on the productivity and life he continued to squeeze from his prisoners.

"What can I do for you 'Colonel'?" Mueller didn't bother to hide his sarcasm.

"I have confidential instructions for you, from Berlin," Richter said. This was about as far as he had gotten in formulating a plan.

Mueller gave him an odd look Richter could not interpret. "Let us, then," he said, "adjourn to my quarters. S'tha only 'confidential' place that exists in this hellhole."

Hell was exactly what Richter had in mind as he and Mueller crossed the compound trailed by two guards, the sky beginning to darken. The camp's SS detachment looked depleted since his visit of the year before. Other than that the place looked the same, like some too-familiar nightmare, a Dante's Inferno even worse the second time around. Its mere existence was enough to challenge anyone's faith, but Richter said a quick prayer of thanks that Elena Stein, at least, was no longer here.

"Drink?" Mueller offered, when they were alone in the main room of his quarters. The SS guards, as before, had posted themselves outside. "I have no more hard liquor. A great deprivation. I do, however, have enough wine to conduct Mass for the Pope."

Richter accepted a glass of dark red wine – "direct from Paris," his host assured him. Maybe it would ease the pain, he thought. Mueller's drinking habit was apparently not hampered much by the shortage of hard liquor. He noticed several empty bottles of schnapps left carelessly about the room, one of them lying on its side like a mantlepiece ornament above the fireplace.

Mueller placed the bottle of wine beside him and raised his own full glass, still sober enough to play the host, however reluctantly. His speech seemed to be back under control. "To Berlin," he said. "To 'confidential instructions' from Berlin." He downed half the glass to back up this latest jab at Richter.

The wine was excellent, a prewar French vintage. Richter began to wonder, as he and his host eyed one another warily, whether he had the stomach for this – in spite of what the man had done, including to Elena, and in spite of what he might yet do. If he were going to do it, Richter thought, he would have to pull it off quickly and quietly somehow or he would be just as dead, just as fast, as Mueller. It would not be easy.

Then Mueller hit him with a sledgehammer. "You know, Richter," he said, pointedly omitting the courtesy of addressing him by rank, "you're my first visitor from the outside since last week. Tell me what you know of this odd little incident in Salzburg yesterday."

Richter's veins turned to ice. Not because of the mention of it, but because Mueller's words raised the immediate thought that Hitler might not be dead. The Fuhrer's death would certainly be no "odd little incident."

"What happened in Salzburg?" he said.

"You've not heard?" Mueller gave him a quizzical look. "Usually if I've heard about something in here, the whole world has heard of it."

"I've been rather out of touch lately."

"Evidently." Mueller looked skeptical. "Why am I not surprised."

"So what happened in Salzburg?"

Mueller studied him a moment, as if looking for clues. "Somebody shot Hitler's 'double' yesterday at the train depot there. Very impressive actually. A clean shot right between the eyes at several hundred meters, as I understand it. Almost as impressive as your little demonstration of marksmanship last time you were here."

"Hitler's what?"

"His double. It was news to me as well. Evidently the Fuhrer has, or had, a stand-in, a lookalike double, just as Churchill does. Just as Stalin does. He may have others. I suppose it makes sense. Decoys. For just such an occasion as this."

Mueller snorted. "Now this one, poor wretch, has given his all for the Fuhrer." He took a swig of wine. "Heil Hitler."

Richter's mind was reeling. He held onto a thread of hope, but it was a thin one. His gut told him Mueller was right. That Erich Borchers had – unintentionally, he hoped – tapped into disinformation put out to protect the Fuhrer in the wake of 20 July. It would explain the way the man in his sniper sight had looked, puffier and more jowly than he remembered Hitler. And the way his body was left unattended at first. Hitler would have been surrounded immediately. No shots but the first would ever have reached him.

"Richter?"

He shook his thoughts out as best he could. Mueller was still staring at him, now with a suspicious look. Did he suspect him of the shooting?

"I was just thinking," Richter said. "So close on the heels of 20 July. The Fuhrer must have some determined enemies." He wondered if the woman on the park bench in Berchtesgaden could have given him away. Or Borchers, perhaps, but he quickly dismissed that thought.

Mueller's reply was a surprise. "The Fuhrer's worst enemies are those who surround him. His inner circle. They're turning him down paths that may soon be the end of us all." Mueller eyed him again. "I am telling you this in strictest confidence, of course."

"Of course." Richter was distracted. All he could think about was Salzburg. If Hitler had indeed survived yesterday, after 20 July and all the other attempts on his life, he must in fact be the Devil incarnate. He had created, after all, a nether world here on earth, the proof of which was just outside Mueller's door. Perhaps the man could not be killed by mere mortals. Perhaps his role was to lead Germany to some sort of cleansing Armageddon. Maybe all this was God's will, he thought.

Mueller meanwhile had launched into a vitriolic diatribe, of which Richter had missed the start. He was letting loose a torrent of complaints.

"...I don't think Berlin fully appreciates what is happening in the camps," Mueller was saying. "Our resources are cut back while our production quotas go up. I continue to receive new workers, but they die faster than they're replaced. Including my most trained people. No one knows how to run the factories anymore. We need more of everything. There is very little food. Even Jews and Slavs need food. Disease is rampant. Particularly typhus. Our one real doctor, Roarke – you remember Roarke – died last month from typhus and his replacement is incompetent."

Mueller looked at his visitor. "Are you listening to me, Richter?"

"You're not getting enough support from Berlin," Richter said. "Is that what you're trying to say?" Mueller's old confidence, his downright cockiness about the campaign to rid Europe of its Jews, appeared to have eroded since last year. The quickly shrinking distance to the Allied lines likely had something to do with that, Richter thought.

"That would be an understatement," Mueller retorted. "And Kaisener is not alone. They say the camps are a priority, but they drain us of troops. The prisoners at Treblinka practically took over the place last year. At Auschwitz, they destroyed a crematorium. The Allies have even bombed a few camps. Buchenwald took a big hit and it affected morale there. Their commandant started making deals. The prisoners' committees had him eating out of their hands. He was cashiered, but it's hard to blame him for protecting himself in case we lose the war."

Richter could not stomach any more. "The camps were a mistake from the start," he said. "They never should have existed. We are paying the price."

Mueller raised an eyebrow at such heresy but didn't let it stop his train of thought. "Put yourself in my place, Richter. When the Allies come waltzing in what do you suppose I should tell them? 'This is a labor camp. We don't kill anybody here. We just put them to work.' Think that will do the trick?"

"What *will* you tell them, Mueller?" Richter felt a brief stab of satisfaction picturing his predicament.

Mueller ignored the question and concentrated on his wine, in communion with his own thoughts. When he finally looked up, he changed tack. "So what's this confidential message from Berlin?" he said with a trace of venom.

Richter had not gotten this far in his planning. Mueller was supposed to be dead by now. He was too tired to think straight.

"Well?" Mueller demanded sharply. He had the look of a man ready to snap. It served as a reminder of what he was capable of doing.

Words did not come to Richter. When he could think of no other response he unsnapped his holster and took out the Luger. He rested it on his lap, pointed about five degrees to the right of his host.

Mueller stared at him with a dumb, slightly drunken incredulity. "Is that the message from Berlin?" he said. He did not sound nervous.

"There is no message from Berlin," Richter replied.

"I didn't think so," Mueller said. "I don't know what game you're playing, Richter, but you are in enough trouble already. I have a notice from the Gestapo, directing me to arrest you on sight. You are considered suspect in your loyalty to the Fuhrer. A possible accomplice in the 20 July conspiracy."

Richter had to stifle an impulse to laugh. He remembered his old suspicion Mueller might be related to Heinrich Muller, head of the Gestapo. He had neglected to look into it, but it hardly mattered now. "And what do you think, Mueller? Am I a traitor to the cause?"

"I think you are your father's son. My guess is he has been implicated too. That he can't protect you anymore." Mueller grinned and finished off his wine.

"I should add, perhaps, that they put the word out on you – something about having deserted your post in France – before what happened in Salzburg yesterday. But not many men could've made that shot. I'm sure the Gestapo would be interested in how good you are with a rifle."

Mueller stared at his glass, as if puzzled it had emptied itself so quickly.

"Another drink?" he said.

"No thank you."

Mueller poured himself another and without delay began draining it.

They were silent a moment, each warily inspecting the other.

"You know, Richter," Mueller broke the uneasy pause, "I've wondered from time to time how it turned out for you and our little Jewess." His look was balanced between confrontational and glassy-eyed. "Isn't that why you're really here? Something to do with her."

The mere mention of Elena from the lips of this man recharged Richter's urge to kill him. Right behind that impulse, however, he suddenly felt a countervailing one just as strong. To live, to see her again.

"What happened to her?" Mueller persisted.

"What difference does it make to you?" Richter said, remembering something that had confused him. "You protected her, Mueller. Would you really have killed her?"

"It was a spur of the moment thing. I just wanted to see how far I could push you." Mueller, his eye for a moment on the ceiling, appeared to consider the matter further. "I, uh, had her here in the house for a time. She interested me," he said, as if confessing to something slightly vulgar.

"But she's a Jew, Mueller. How can a Jew interest an SS officer?"

Mueller studied Richter, trying to figure out if he was being baited. "She interested you, didn't she?" he said. "It's something beyond race, I suppose. I'm not a scientist, or a philosopher. I just do my job. To serve Germany. That's all."

"Not the Fuhrer?"

"And the Fuhrer, of course."

The two men stared at each other.

"So where is she? Is she still alive?" Mueller said.

"She is still alive," Richter said.

Mueller continued to look at him, bleary-eyed, waiting for more. "That's all?" he said finally.

"That's all."

Mueller's look, almost crestfallen, reminded Richter of the end of his previous visit to Kaisenher. "I think about someone too from time to time," he said. "Do you remember the prisoner, the young woman, who killed herself here in your kitchen?"

Mueller's stare was immediately more focused, more intense. "All I have to do is yell, Richter. In ten seconds, you are dead."

Richter responded by rotating the Luger to point directly at Mueller, keeping his finger on the trigger. "Do you remember her name? Or was she simply one of so many, you have no idea."

Mueller poured himself another glass of wine. He touched it to his lips, but put it back down without drinking. "Muriel," he said. "Muriel was her name."

"Do you ever think about her?"

Mueller snorted. "Yes, I think about her. So what?"

"What do you think about, when you think of her?"

"That's none of your affair Richter."

"I'll tell you what I think about, then, when I think of her. I think about how unnecessary it was. That she died because of your lust for Jewesses. Is it because they're forbidden fruit, Mueller? Or perhaps you are a secret admirer of the Jews."

"Why don't you ask your Jewess, Richter? She would know."

Richter lost track of time for a moment his thoughts were so clouded by rage. He stood up, not knowing his own intentions. "Let's go. It's time we took a walk," he said, his reflexes on full automatic pilot.

Mueller grinned in defiance but stood up, a bit wobbly with drink. "You won't get ten meters outside the door," he said.

Keeping the Luger trained on Mueller, Richter slipped his ceremonial dagger from its sheath. "Turn around," he ordered.

When Mueller obeyed, Richter hit him on the back of the head, hard, with the butt of the pistol. A searing pain shot through his left side. He had totally forgotten his wound. As Mueller crumpled to the floor, Richter wondered if he had killed him. He could not believe he had gone this far with no thought whatsoever for what came next.

He knelt beside the body. It still had a pulse. Remembering Elena and her ice pick, he thought for a moment to finish Mueller off with the dagger. He had come here to kill him, hadn't he? In all likelihood the SS would take it out on the camp whether

Mueller survived or not. But the moment passed. For whatever reason, the impulse died before he acted on it. He wondered if he would regret that later.

Now what? he thought.

Richter calculated he'd need at least twenty minutes to clear the gates of Kaisenher before anyone was alerted. More, if there were any holdups. He left Mueller where he lay, and scoured the kitchen cabinets for rope. There was no rope, but finding some strong twine and old rags, he used these to bind Mueller's hands and feet behind him. The Standartenfuhrer appeared to be still unconscious, but to be certain Richter gagged him as well. Fighting the pain in his wounded lung, he dragged Mueller into a bedroom and managed to get him up onto the bed, where he pulled the covers up to his neck.

Somebody would be in for a nasty surprise in a few hours, he thought.

Richter straightened his uniform and composed his thoughts as best he could. Then he stepped outside.

It was raining. He had not noticed until now. He welcomed it. It was good cover. The guards outside Mueller's quarters, huddled in their foul weather gear, did not challenge him. He strode across the compound with the air of a senior officer headed somewhere important.

The same SS sergeant in charge of the front gate detachment upon his arrival was still on duty. A stroke of luck. The man had been so nervous at Mueller's long delay in greeting Richter, he had no inclination now to question the Wehrmacht colonel on why he was departing without an escort.

He did ask if Mueller was still in quarters, to which Richter responded, "The Standartenfuhrer is unfortunately 'indisposed' for the moment. I'm sure he will be available in a few hours, if you need him."

"Thank you, Colonel," the sergeant replied. Richter thought he detected a hint of amusement in the man's eyes. Presumably at his commandant's little-disguised love of the bottle.

Richter returned the guard's salute, and with a crisp "Good day, Sergeant," was out the gate and on the way to his hired car.

Five minutes later, with his reluctant chauffeur at the wheel, he began the first leg of his return journey to France and Elena Stein.

For an hour or more, Richter nursed his pain and stared through the steady downpour at the passing Bavarian countryside, trying somehow to make sense of things. Earlier he could not quite believe he had killed Hitler. Now it was difficult to believe he had not killed him. Perhaps Mueller had been mistaken after all and Borchers' information had been accurate about Berchtesgaden. Maybe the Nazi hierarchy *was* trying to cover things up while they battled among themselves to fill Hitler's shoes.

But with each new rationalization, he became more certain Mueller was correct. A decoy was dead. The Fuhrer was alive. It was a depressing thought. If not for Elena Stein – and a desire to return to her that unsettled him in its growing intensity – he would have turned around and gone after Hitler again whatever the odds. It came to him, really for the first time, how little he had considered what would've happened to Elena had he been killed.

It seemed appropriate Kaisenher should be his point of departure from Germany. The place filled him with despair and foreboding. Germany would indeed pay the price for what was being done there; another depressing thought. What had happened to the country he loved? No amount of trying to find a logic for it would work. Finally he gave up and started thinking again about Elena, and escape.

At a brief stop, these thoughts gained new urgency. A shopkeeper, deferring to Richter's authority, asked him what he thought would happen now that the Allies had taken Paris.

Richter asked him what he had heard. Von Choltitz had apparently surrendered the city intact with hardly a fight, the man said.

Good for von Choltitz, he thought, happy that Paris had been spared. Things were falling apart even faster than he'd anticipated. He had to reach St. Sentione before that city too was in Allied hands.

Staring out across a jagged set of mountains to the south, Richter had a sudden, disconcertingly real premonition of death. His own. He might escape Hitler's revenge, but how could he possibly escape the Fuhrer's sins. The nation's sins. Kaisenher, Dachau, Auschwitz and the rest would surely catch up to all Germans in the end. His own motives had been good, but ultimately he had hurt rather than helped the fight against the Nazis and their crimes.

In anguish, he forced his thoughts back to Elena. The one positive entry in his wartime ledger, she now seemed his only remaining hope. His one chance for redemption. His one way out. Out of this war, out of everything. But when he closed his eyes and tried to picture a future with her, all he could see was Adolf Hitler in the crosshairs of his sniper scope.

Such an easy target, he thought as he climbed back into the car. Hitler should have been easy to kill.

There had been so many opportunities.

How could we have missed?

finis

{"Killing Hitler" is dedicated to Claus von Stauffenberg and all those, including Johann Richter and his father Karl von Richter, who tried to shed the yoke of Nazi tyranny – most of whom paid the ultimate price. M.C.}

CHAPTER XXIV

From his hospital bed, Michael Cohen, propped up and with bandages covering half his face and his right shoulder, could see the afternoon sun gleaming off the surface of Lake Tocqual. He could also see the starkly lit row of high-rises off to his right, but tried not to look at them.

"Strange how beautiful this city can be, eh," John Weaver said, standing at the window. Weaver had just told him Richter was dead. He had offered no elaboration, and had not answered when Cohen asked about Elena Stein. The extended pause was answer enough, Cohen thought, feeling a stab at his heart. An all too familiar chill. Only the woman was different.

Looking back at Cohen, Weaver reluctantly confirmed the worst. "I'm afraid she's gone too, my friend," he said. "Shot when we busted in last night and all hell was breaking loose."

Twice in one lifetime was too much, Cohen thought. She had not been his to lose, really, but somehow that didn't matter. It was Rachel all over again.

"Shot straight through the heart." Weaver looked genuinely sorry. "She didn't suffer."

She had already done her suffering, Cohen thought, unconsoled. Maybe this time he was not as much to blame, but that hardly seemed to matter either. She was gone. Just like Rachel. That was all that mattered. "I thought she'd made it," he said. "I thought she was still alive."

"She was conscious a few minutes. Long enough to tell us you tried to save her," Weaver said. "At the end, for what it's worth, it appeared she was trying to return the favor."

Cohen winced, anguish momentarily preempting his physical pain. His grief was mixed with anger toward their would-be rescuers for taking so long to show up.

Weaver produced a pack of Camels. He tapped one out and lit up. He had long since quit trying to offer them to Cohen. "Also for what it's worth, we got her killer. We got all of them."

Cohen barely heard this last. He said the first thing that came to mind – about anything but Elena. "That wasn't Richter I saw at the high-rise last night then?"

"No, it probably was. He was there. He insisted on it," Weaver said, directing a plume of smoke toward the open window. Faint sounds of street life wafted up from below.

"Before you got there, somebody phoned that Richter was dead, killed trying to escape. Hardy seemed to believe it."

"That was us." Weaver looked down and shook his head. "We had a plant, a mole of our own inside Hardy's little band of renegades. Unfortunately our guy wasn't able to leave the high-rise until you arrived last night. By the time he got word to us, we were desperate. We didn't think we could reach you in time."

"So you phoned."

"He had the number and a code word. They trusted him. It was a roll of the dice."

"How *did* Richter die?"

Weaver studied the ceiling. He appeared to be assessing how much he could divulge. "He, uh, went after Anders Hardy the minute we cleared the elevator. Knocked him flat up against that glass wall or window, whatever it was. So hard, they broke right through. Both of them." He shook his head. "At least that sorry son-of-a-bitch Hardy got his."

Cohen remembered a sound that could've been glass giving way. He hoped Hardy'd had time to think about it before he hit the ground. He had earned a glimpse of Hell. Cohen also recalled more gunshots after the one that had hit him. Any one of which might have killed Elena.

He needed to think about something else.

Weaver looked at his watch. "The good news," he said, "is the baby girl survived. She and the boy are being flown to the States today."

This struck a chord in Cohen. "Richter and I had an agreement," he said without hesitation. "About his family. If he didn't make it, he wanted me to look after them."

Weaver looked surprised. "No, no. Sorry Cohen. Those kids are gonna disappear. For their own safety."

"I promised him. . ." Cohen tried to put his anger to use, but the truncated protest sounded weak, even to him. The whole idea wasn't the same without Elena as part of the package.

"Well, we promised him too." Weaver's tone was firm. "And I'm afraid our agreement takes precedence. We made the same promise to you, I might remind you. At your request. We told you we'd take care of his family. Remember?"

When Cohen didn't answer, Weaver said in a softer voice, "Don't worry. We'll find them a good home. A safe one."

Taking a last long drag on his Camel, he gave Cohen a meaningful look. "I don't need to remind you, I'm sure, how sensitive all this is. We're telling the locals the whole family, including Richter, died in last night's fire. The one Rivera and his boys set in a munitions dump to distract the *federales* while Richter escaped."

"Why?"

"It's cleaner that way. Easier to tidy up. The press is already nosing around for more details. This gives them something to hang their hats on. Hardy's fate we're keeping under wraps for now."

Cohen noted Weaver wasn't lumping him in with "the press." It didn't surprise him. To Weaver, he was a survivor of the camps and perhaps a veteran of sorts of MI6. Anything else he probably considered immaterial, Cohen thought, flinching as a sudden, stabbing pain shot through his shoulder.

Weaver, staring out the window again, did not notice. "It might interest you to know, by the way," he said, abruptly switching gears, "that Anne Johns, with Hardy out of the picture, immediately stepped to the plate and cleared up a few things for us. Claims before she testified down here Hardy threatened her not to say certain things. Swears her husband didn't know about it. She admits now she may have 'pushed the truth' a bit here and there. As in, for instance, that she was raped by Richter. She wasn't, she says now, not technically anyway. It just felt like she was, she said."

"She's also told us the elusive 'Yvonne Duchamps' was in fact a Lady Sarah Davies, an Englishwoman working undercover for MI6, tasked with milking Richter for inside information about the Wehrmacht officers' plots against Hitler. A rather easy recruit, according to Mrs. Johns, as apparently the woman bought the party line that Richter had killed Christine Johns. Her lover. Mrs. Johns wasn't overly forthcoming about how she knew all this. Evidently some kind of Cambridge connection. You know those upper-class Brits."

Cohen grimaced at another jolt of pain.

This time Weaver saw it. "Should I call a doctor?"

"It's all right." Cohen gritted his teeth and the pain started to subside. "Go on."

"According to Mrs. Johns," Weaver picked up, keeping a close eye on Cohen, "this Lady Sarah took special pleasure in going after Richter. She wasn't able to tell us anything, unfortunately, about the woman's fate in St. Sentione after 20 July. Only that she'd heard MI6 gave her a new assignment shortly after Richter disappeared."

Looking contemplative, Weaver extracted another Camel.

"So what happens now?" Cohen struggled to stay focused against an undertow tugging his thoughts back to Elena Stein.

"Nothing," Weaver said, toying with the cigarette without lighting it. "The British don't wanta shine a light on anything involving Richter right now. They won't go after Anne Johns. She and her husband've already left for England."

"History's a funny thing," he added. "How long ago was it the Nazis were the ultimate evil? Now we're climbing into bed with them, with the Commies out there. So the Rosenbergs get cooked, but someone like Richter has a fighting chance. Or had, anyway."

"I'm assuming you know what was in that package you left me this morning from Richter," Cohen said, referring to an earlier visit from Weaver before Cohen had returned to the land of the living a few hours ago.

"His prison notes. The story of his life. As he saw it, at any rate. We've copied them, of course. But you have everything. I saw to it nothing was deleted. My boss didn't think you should get anything at all, but I talked him around."

"Thank you."

"Thank Richter. He left explicit instructions. He wanted you to have them. I figured we owed it to you. Maybe even to him. . . Again, I can't stress enough how careful you need to be with this material."

Weaver punctuated his reminder with a short laugh, but there was no mistaking it was an order, not a request. "If you decide to write about any of this for *World Horizons*, or anyone else, you'll have to let us vet it for you. That way hopefully nobody gets hurt. Including me and my career. I'll leave you a contact number."

Cohen took this in, but did not respond.

"All this secrecy, it's not just to protect us bureaucrats, you know," Weaver said. "We don't wanta tip our hand to any of our moles, set off a stampede to Moscow. And it's to protect you too, believe it or not."

He did believe it. Cisco Rojas had been a relative innocent caught up in all this intrigue. His gruesome fate, so reminiscent of his own father's, would be forever etched in Cohen's mind.

Weaver, finally lighting his Camel, gave Cohen a sideways glance. "All the brouhaha yesterday, by the way, attracted attention from the local authorities. They're reviewing the passports and backgrounds of all 'civilians' – anyone not CIA or MI6 who could've been involved in Richter's escape. . . That includes you," he tacked on with an apologetic grin. "They've assured us you'll have your passport back by tomorrow. Next day at the latest."

"I don't think I'll need it before then," Cohen managed.

Weaver smiled, a smile that turned into a full-blown grin as Cohen's night nurse walked in. The woman was beautiful. Botticelli's Venus with flawless brown skin.

"Well pardner, I see you're in good hands," Weaver said. "I gotta be moseyin' along anyhow. Things to do. People to see. Lies to spread." He ground the barely smoked remains of his cigarette into an ashtray.

At the door, he turned and said, "We appreciate what you did for us down here. You need anything, let me know. I'll be in town for at least another day or two. Maybe longer. I'll be in touch before I leave."

"Thanks. And thanks for picking up the pieces last night," Cohen said, thinking, *Even if you were too damn late to save Elena.* He braced himself. He could feel the pain returning.

"No problem, amigo. Hasta luego."

As the CIA man's footsteps receded down the tiled hallway, Cohen looked at the nurse, who had stood by patiently during their farewells. She smiled at him in a way that made Cohen wonder how much she had understood. More than he'd thought, was his guess.

He hoped he was indeed in good hands. Weaver said the doctors had assured him Cohen would recover okay, that his body should be fully operative again within a few months. The nurse rolled him over onto his uninjured shoulder, pulled his pajama bottoms down and stuck a needle in him. "For the pain," she said in English. Rolling him back, she shook a thermometer and placed it under his tongue, then felt his forehead and took his pulse with a light touch that cut through the pain like a healing balm. A hopeful sign, he thought.

She removed the thermometer, looked at it without expression and left the room saying she would be back shortly.

Cohen took a deep breath. The high-rises along the lake were already steeped in shadow. Looking at them made him sad and wistful, anxious to leave La Negra and return home to New York. But first, perhaps, a detour. During his semiconscious slumber last night he had dreamed of Israel. It had been a beautiful and soothing dream. Immediately upon awaking, he'd begun to toy with the idea of paying a visit.

There were people there he would like to see. The jeweler from Dusseldorf and Dachau. Others. Not least among them, Maria Zamora, Rachel's best friend who had tried to comfort him after her death. Any return to Israel would be fraught with unwelcome memories. Elena's death had reopened the unhealed wound of Rachel's loss, compounding the pain but also opening up a door to new possibilities. To walk through that door he needed to confront his demons. And where better to do that than in Israel, with all its painful associations and powerful promise?

In some ways, for him, Israel *was* Rachel now, and he longed to see her again.

As he stared out over the lake, he marveled that his physical pain, at least, had already dissipated. Most of his anger had gone with it. Whatever the nurse had given him must be working. Better than booze, he thought, realizing suddenly he felt no craving for alcohol. Maybe he had finally turned that corner. And perhaps, he thought, as his head began to nod toward sleep, perhaps now it was time to turn another. In Israel.

* * * *

To the stewardess, it made no difference if the passenger in seat 56C moved to an aisle seat nearer the front of the plane. He had occupied 56C since their stopover in Caracas. Tall and good-looking, probably about thirty-five, he was someone she ordinarily might have bantered with. But there was something about him. The scar below his eye, a pallid complexion, his distant look, made him seem a little sinister. Not a man to kid around with.

She took a perfunctory look at his ticket. A Mr. Michael Cohen of New York City. "That's fine, Mr. Cohen," she said. "Just let me make sure it's okay with the woman in 36A."

"Ma'am, there's a gentleman in the rear of the aircraft who would like to take this aisle seat, if you don't mind. Would that be all right?" The woman she addressed was staring at the sea of white clouds outside the window. In spite of the sunglasses she wore, it was obvious the right side of her face was swollen black and blue. She held a sleeping baby in her lap. In the seat between her and the aisle seat a young boy was paging through a picture book.

"No, is okay," she said, and returned to her cloud-gazing.

The stewardess gave the man a little beckoning wave, and he came forward, carrying a slim briefcase with him.

"Good afternoon," he said to the woman in sunglasses as he sat down and put the briefcase in his lap.

"Good afternoon," she returned.

The stewardess, who happened to see this exchange, wondered if the woman would react to the man as she had. She hoped he didn't make her nervous. She did not notice the pair's quick handclasp across the middle seat, or the gentle pat on the head the man gave the small boy.

"You can put your briefcase up there," the woman said, pointing to the overhead luggage racks. "Is more comfortable, maybe."

"Thank you," he said, doing as she suggested.

Had she heard it, the stewardess would have been surprised, no doubt, by the implied intimacy of the next exchange between the two.

"How do you feel?" he said.

"Much better," the woman replied. She took off her sunglasses. Her right eye was swollen almost shut. The quizzical, slightly lopsided look she gave him made him reach out to touch her, but he pulled back with a quick look around.

"Our friend from Dachau is going to be all right," he said. "I have been assured he will recover quite nicely, with no more than a mild scar on his face."

"Thank God," she said.

"It will only make him more handsome, I'm sure." He smiled and touched the scar on his own face for emphasis. "We owe him a great deal. Even my name, for the moment," he said, patting the shirt pocket that held Cohen's passport doctored with his own photo. He winced slightly as he made the gesture.

"You are all right?" she asked.

"It's just the old wound. I must've strained it last night."

Elena Stein reached over and squeezed his hand. She did not feel so good herself. Hardy had left his mark. Their rescuers had promised her a doctor as soon as they touched down in the United States.

She leaned back against the headrest, thinking about last night and its aftermath. Most of it was still fuzzy to her, but she had rebounded quicker than anyone, including herself, had thought she would. She'd been relieved earlier today when informed Father Hidalgo – protected by the Church's political pull – was safe and that Rivera and his fighters had made it through with no significant casualties.

Her relief over the news Michael Cohen would recover was more personal. The last she remembered from the high-rise was Cohen on the floor, spilling blood. She had tried to reach him but blacked out. This morning Leland Powell and John Weaver had rejected her plea to visit the hospital where Cohen had been taken. She'd hated leaving him behind like that, with no explanation or farewell and without knowing his fate. With Johann's support, she had exacted a solemn promise that Powell or Weaver would one day, when it was safer, tell Cohen – as well as Rivera and Father Hidalgo – the truth. That she and Johann had survived La Negra after all.

From the very start, she had been confused in her response to Cohen. Encountering a fellow survivor of the KZs had thrown her off balance. Then two nights ago she'd found out about Cohen and Rachel Stern, her predecessor with Heinrich Mueller at Kaisener, and it had knocked her flat. Though they'd never met, the woman had always loomed large in her imagination whenever unwelcome memories of those times broke through her defenses. When Cohen described to her how he'd lost Rachel and their unborn baby in Jerusalem, it had pricked her heart with thoughts of her own lost child, the baby dead in her womb at Kaisenher. The memory had triggered a wave of long-suppressed emotion and a response to Cohen's kiss more intimate and more passionate than she had intended.

She knew Cohen had feelings for her, and admitted to herself it was not entirely a one-way street. Their connection was elemental, perhaps even a kind of love, but if he was seeking something more from her, she didn't have it to give. She and Johann had a bond anchored and strengthened by personal history and events. Together, they had cheated death and created life. Two lives they cherished more than their own. No one could give her more than what she already had, not even this long-lost brother of the death camps who'd miraculously materialized to help them escape.

In any event, what Michael Cohen wanted was Rachel Stern. And in spite of the remarkable confluence of events, she couldn't be Rachel for him. Unfortunately she couldn't absolve him of Rachel's death either.

An abrupt cry from a hungry Teresa cut this reverie short. In an instant, Elena's troubled thoughts evaporated and she turned her full attention to her daughter.

Johann Richter too had been thinking about Michael Cohen. By all accounts, Cohen had been a key player, possibly *the* key player, in keeping Elena and Teresa alive at the high-rise. He wished he'd had more to say to him at the prison last night, the one time they had met. He truly did owe the man. Something. Several hours earlier, he had made the one significant gesture he could think to make. Cohen was a writer. He'd said he wanted to write about Richter. Through John Weaver, Richter had left him the notes he had been preparing on his life. Loaded with opinion and speculation, the material had wound up ranging far beyond what would've been needed to defend himself in the trials he had expected to face in Europe. Now, if all went as planned, there would be no trials. Leland Powell was telling him the word would be put out – to everyone, without exception – that Richter and his family had been killed in the escape attempt. This would allow MI6 to close the books on his case, Powell said.

Meanwhile, Weaver and the CIA were promising a new life. They would give him a new home, a new identity, plus around-the-clock protection. In the U.S. he and Elena would become just another suburban couple – "blending in with the landscape," as Weaver put it –

with two kids, a big fluffy dog, a nice little house and out grilling burgers in the back yard every night. That would be their cover. Ozzie and Harriet.

All this in return for whatever help he could give them with Soviet spies and infiltrators. Particularly the suspected nest of moles inside MI6, where the infamous "third man" was thought still to be lurking.

His "death" would make a lot of people happy, but their cover story was bound to spring a few leaks. Richter glanced over his shoulder at Powell, in an aisle seat seven or eight rows back. Powell would hand them off to American authorities, then hop the Pond to London where he would spearhead any damage control that might be necessary.

Powell gave him a smile of acknowledgment. Richter hoped the man could be trusted.

Elena had discreetly opened her blouse for Teresa. Richter breathed the scene in, at once gratified they were all together again and anxious that it remain that way. He prayed her apparent recovery from last night was as complete as it appeared to be. His own pain, the old familiar sharp stabbing sensation in his side reactivated in the tussle with Hardy last night, only underscored how lucky he felt right now.

After a moment, he looked out the window, his restless thoughts continuing to bounce from present to past to an uncertain future.

* * * *

The nurse returned. She put a hand behind Cohen's back to coax him forward and allow her to unbutton the pajama top cut away to accommodate his heavily bandaged right shoulder. As she slipped it off him, he began to wonder what she was up to. Smiling again, this time reassuringly, she wheeled a cart in from the hallway. On it was a bowl of steaming water, washcloths and a pile of towels. She dipped a washcloth into the bowl, squeezed the excess water out and began to wash the unbandaged portion of his back. The damp heat untied his knotted muscles and soothed his aching mind.

She saved his chest for last. Here, it was as if she were massaging his heart, gently coaxing it back to life. When she was done, she touched his forehead gently with the back of her hand and walked away, an apparition vaporizing at the edge of his consciousness.

Cohen felt totally relaxed, but didn't fall asleep as he normally would've. He could not stop thinking about Elena. Her haunted look just before the end kept returning to him. It echoed an expression he knew from Dachau, a mix of fear and defiance, a look of acceptance in the face of death that lent dignity to the farewell. Mourning her loss, he was beginning to feel a sadness over Richter's death as well, something that caught him by surprise. His preconceptions had been ripped apart. With what he knew now, and what Richter's prison notes were likely to tell him, he suspected the man who emerged from the story he was about to write would bear little resemblance to the one he'd originally expected to encounter in La Negra.

It would take a little poetic license, but to the best of his ability, Cohen promised himself, he would tell that story as true to life as possible. He had all the ingredients he needed: Elena's point of view, the recorded courtroom testimony, his own impressions garnered in La Negra. In addition to Richter's extensive notes, he had Terry Harper's manuscript, which Richter had returned with "Not bad" scribbled across the top and several corrections noted in the margins. Beside the account of his telling Harper about killing Hitler, Richter had written, "Wishful thinking."

He would change only one thing. He wasn't going to be allowed to write the real ending anyway. MI6 and the CIA would want Richter and his family killed in the fire. It was "cleaner," as Weaver said. So he would write it his own way. The options, he thought, were to stop short of La Negra or make up his own more palatable version of it. Either way, at the end, Elena would not die. Nor would Richter. Perhaps they could escape and disappear into the landscape. With some hope. That would feel better, less depressing. He couldn't imagine how it could compromise anything.

But MI6 and the CIA were not going to like that ending any more than the real one. They'd want everything tied up in a neat little bow. Richter and Elena and their children dead in a fire. Nobody snooping around for them. *World Horizons* wasn't going to endorse Cohen's flight of fantasy either, no matter how strategically harmless it might seem. He could practically hear Jack Ames now – *You are a journalist, not a novelist* – each word enunciated slowly and deliberately so it would sink through his thick skull.

Jack Ames needn't worry. Cohen already knew he was going to have to go with Option Number One. He would have to stop short of La Negra. Stick with the truth. Leave out the grim ending.

No wishful thinking.

He smiled and gave a nod toward the heavens, thinking Terry Harper, at least, would have appreciated his feelings on the subject. Cohen's empathy with Elena and Richter, particularly Richter, would've suited the Englishman's sense of irony.

With his left hand, he picked up Richter's thick sheaf of notes from the bedside table and started leafing through them. They were written in English and they were fascinating. Earlier, he'd read about ten pages and skimmed the rest looking for an assassination attempt on Hitler. He had not been disappointed. "Killing Hitler" was the title he had in mind for Richter's story.

In spite of his agitated state, Cohen was fired up. He felt a burst of life, of animating energy and purpose, surging through him. He could wait no longer. In his mind, he began to compose what was destined to be the first of many drafts –

Johann von Richter was born in 1918 on a large estate outside Tilsit, East Prussia, and raised there until the age of six. From the very start, his father, a future member of the Wehrmacht's General Staff, instilled in him a sense of right and wrong that transcended the politics of the day. . .

* * * *

They had been in the air for several hours and Richter was asleep when the pilot announced over the intercom, "Ladies and gentlemen, if you look out about forty-five degrees from the port side of the aircraft, you should be able to make out a chain of small islands on the horizon. . . Right there, with that first island on your far left, is where the U.S. begins. Or ends, depending on which way you're flying." The pilot credited his own observation with a short laugh. "That's Key West and the Florida Keys. Welcome, folks, to the United States of America."

Elena Stein listened to this message in a mental fog, thinking of Rachel Stern again for some reason. The pilot's words had awakened her from a nightmare about Heinrich Mueller, her old tormentor at Kaisenher. In the dream, Mueller had tied her face-down on a bed and was making some kind of preparations behind her she couldn't see but that terrified her. Her only hope was another woman, one whose face she couldn't quite make out, hovering above them both, the long sharp spike of an ice pick gleaming in a hand Elena almost felt was her own. Thankfully she had awakened before anything more had happened, and hadn't disturbed Teresa, now sleeping peacefully in a small hamper beside Tomas on the next seat.

At the shock of waking, with the aches and pains of last night's beating making her nightmare all too real, Elena had to remind herself that while the commandant of Kaisenher had survived the rap on the head Johann had given him, he had not survived the war. As Allied troops had neared the camp in the spring of 1945 and his guards had begun to desert, Mueller had reportedly taken to wandering among the prisoners in a drunken stupor, sometimes berating them, other times commiserating with them. The temptation had proven too much, and one day a group of prisoners had cornered him alone and unprotected and stoned him to death.

She closed her eyes and let that sink in a moment, then took off her sunglasses for a better look at the islands below. On the horizon, the setting sun was framed by an "Emerald Drop," a ring of green light. In her native folklore this was a sign of good luck. She hoped it augured well for what lay ahead.

Despite her physical discomfort, for the first time since Johann had been imprisoned she felt good enough, and secure enough, to contemplate the prospect of starting over. She began daydreaming about a cozy little house in the country. Perhaps in New England; she had heard it was beautiful there. Or maybe out West. Somewhere they could be a family again. Find some peace, a safe haven.

That it was to be in Michael Cohen's homeland added a wistful note to the prospect. She knew she had to place Cohen firmly in the past and move on. La Negra was already receding like a bad dream, a hazy shadow world between Riberalta and a new, hopefully better life. Maybe Cohen would fade away in similar fashion. She was saying a short prayer for him, trying to make it a farewell, when she felt a hand on her cheek. Her husband was awake and brushing away a tear she hadn't known was there. Tears did not come easily to her. She smiled.

"Happy?" he said.

She shook her head, unable to speak.

He lifted their son across to her. "Let Tomas have a look at his new home." The boy gazed out the window, intent but silent. When she put him back in his seat with the picture book, he promptly fell asleep. His parents smiled at him, and at their sleeping daughter in the hamper beside him. Perhaps the war was finally over, these looks seemed to say. Maybe this new home would be their last, Richter thought.

It was hard to get last night out of his mind. The escape had been amazingly smooth. Rivera and his rebels had raided a government armory and munitions stockpile near the prison, setting fire to it to provide a diversion. But the key had been Father Hidalgo. Richter had been shepherded out disguised in an extra set of clerical robes smuggled in by the priest, aided by a bribed guard.

Father Hidalgo, as the one least likely to be killed or imprisoned in retaliation, had volunteered to remain behind. He was to impersonate the prisoner asleep in his cell, then eventually turn himself in to Frederico, whose shift would begin at 8 a.m. Leland Powell had pledged the priest would not be left holding the bag, as he and his team hustled Richter over to one of the tall buildings lining Lake Tocqual. There they'd joined a CIA man named Weaver and some others for a quick briefing on what was going on, or thought to be going on, inside, and Richter had convinced Powell to let him join the rescue attempt.

When they had burst into the suite where Anders Hardy was holding Elena and Teresa, the first thing Richter had seen was Hardy reaching for an automatic rifle propped against the wall. With a running start, he drove Hardy up against a plate glass window with a huge crack in it, forcing him to drop the weapon. For a split second it felt as if they were detached from the room, suspended in thin air. With instinctive reflexes and good luck, Richter grabbed onto the arm of a sofa and managed to pull himself back from the precipice.

Momentarily distracted by the battle in the room behind him, he saw at least two of Hardy's men and one of Powell's were down, evidently dead or wounded. Friendly forces with weapons at the ready were pouring through the door beside the elevator. He did not see Elena or Teresa.

A groan from Hardy made him turn back around. The damaged window, with Hardy enfolded, had bowed outward but so far was holding. Richter's old nemesis was trying to push himself back up into the room, but each time he did, the bowing plate glass rasped and gave way a little more. He was caught in a glass bowl whose bottom was slowly dropping out.

"Help me, Richter, damn you," he barked, reaching out his hand. It was more an order than a plea. Richter glanced around again, but still couldn't spot Elena. He looked back at Hardy, whose hand remained outstretched. Richter stared at him and waited.

Hardy's features contorted in anger. With a primitive growl, he made one final lunge at Richter and when he did the window finally, moving like molasses, gave way. The two men locked eyes, as in slow motion the shattered but still intact plate glass formed a tear-like droplet around Hardy. The capsule hung frozen in midair for a few seconds, then finally broke away with Hardy inside, carrying him to a silent end somewhere out of sight far below.

"Good riddance," said a voice at Richter's side. It was Powell. "I think your woman is going to be all right," he said. "I'm not so sure about our young friend over there," he added, nodding toward the prostrate body of Michael Cohen being ministered to by John Weaver and several others.

Richter barely took this in. Spotting Elena half-naked and bloody on the floor, being tended by a man in hospital garb, he bolted for her.

That was the last he had seen of Cohen. This morning, as the sleek new Douglas DC-6 banked over La Negra, Richter had been moved by the remains of the armory fire still smoldering down below. They owed their rescue to a lot of people, he thought, as he had watched first La Negra and then the peaks that guarded it fade into the distance. That a major portion of the credit belonged to a survivor of the death camps seemed surreal. He'd supported Elena's request that morning to visit Cohen in the hospital, but to no avail.

Cohen would never dream they had escaped. They were supposed to have died in the armory fire. That's what everyone was being told. Cohen would probably be happy Richter was gone – but maybe not entirely. He remembered the man's last words to him in El Morro: *Don't do it. . . There is always hope.* And his willingness to look after Elena and the children. Richter looked around again and wished he could give Cohen this more hopeful ending. Though it too seemed unreal. More like the closing scene of a novel or a film someone might dream up.

Maybe someday, he thought with a twinge of guilt.

Still a little groggy with sleep, Richter leaned toward the window and stared out across a dark sea just starting to pick up enough moonlight to balance the dimming sky. On the horizon, a band of orange clouds cut by a ribbon of mist separated the two vast panels of blue. The island farthest to his left winked at him in the last brilliant sun of the dying day. He let his eyes pan up the chain of islands toward a mainland not yet in sight and felt an eager anticipation growing inside him.

A new life. He felt like a pioneer, trading the Old World for the New; hopefully the old order for something different. He didn't know what to expect. Only that there would be new dangers to face. There always were. But it had to be better than what had come before. He remembered the stark premonition of death he'd had shortly after his attempt on Hitler and his last visit to Kaisenher. How real it had seemed. He was amazed it hadn't caught up to him yet.

His old life, however, was not about to let go so easily. The sense of guilt and futility – of complicity in the failure of 20 July, of betraying his father and the others, then failing to avenge them – would never entirely leave him. He knew that. Nor would the sense of loss. These things he would carry with him forever, wherever he went.

Hitler could not be banished so easily either. The Fuhrer might be done with this world, but it wasn't done with him. Like an evil Lazarus, he seemed to keep rising from the dead. As Richter had skimmed through Terry Harper's manuscript after Cohen left the prison last night, he had been struck by Harper's idea the Soviets had found Hitler's remains outside the Chancellery bunker in destroyed Berlin and kept it secret, eventually reburying him, along with Eva Braun, only a short distance away in Magdeburg.

This was a startling hypothesis. If Hitler had a grave, it would become a shrine one day. He would have followers again. It might not happen for a hundred years, but it would happen. To some variety of twisted soul, someday, his crimes would be an inspiration. The sands of time could smooth over nearly anything, but it would be an eternity, Richter thought, before history would erase what Adolf Hitler had done. Stalin of all people, with the blood of millions on his own hands, should understand that. Crimes of such magnitude cannot simply be buried and forgotten.

The same proposition applied to the German people, he thought. No German, including himself, could truly escape the stain of the *Einsatzgruppen* and the death camps, in spite of what he had told Cohen last night. There was only the possibility of atonement. To kill Hitler had been his own attempt at it. After his abortive try, he had gone through periods of denial. Wishful thinking that had hardened into fabrications. Particularly during the first few years afterwards. Terry Harper had caught him during one of those periods. To tell the man, or imply to the man, he had killed Hitler had hardly seemed a lie at the time.

Richter had in fact been told by old Abwehr sources his attempt on the Fuhrer's life had played a major role in driving him underground, first at Rastenburg and then the Berlin bunker. Hitler had been blind with fury he had never been caught, they said. Any consolation this provided was undercut, however, by knowing the killing in the KZs and on the front lines hadn't stopped until Hitler was really dead.

Dead by his own hand. On his darkest nights Richter still agonized over how easy it should have been to kill him earlier. With so many chances, how in God's name could he, Stauffenberg and all the rest have failed? The question confounded him. He had no answer. In the notes he had just passed along to Cohen, he had underlined it – *How could we have missed?*

Immersed in such thoughts, he was suddenly jolted up and out of himself by a touch on his arm. Tomas was awake and standing on the seat beside him, his clear blue eyes looking for reassurance. For a moment Richter saw something of his father in those eyes. He lifted Tomas onto his lap. It was hard to believe the boy in his arms was real. That this was not all a dream. Tomas laid his head against his father's chest and closed his eyes.

Richter watched his son with a sense of wonder and love. He had felt it before, but never at this level of intensity. Holding onto him and glancing over at Elena, with Teresa asleep in the hamper beside her, making certain one more time they too were really there, he closed his own eyes and drifted off again.

Somewhere in his sleep, he dreamed he was riding Sacha through a field of tall spring grass. It was late afternoon of a clear blue day. All around him spread the eternal Promised Land of milk and honey longed for by every dispossessed tribe and nation of every time. The sheer beauty of it filled him with joy and hope until he spotted his father up ahead on a hill on his favorite mount, a huge dapple-gray, distracted by something on the opposite slope.

As Richter reached the top of the hill, he peered down into the hazy valley at what his father could see. Far below, a KZ that looked like Kaisenher, only infinitely bigger, stretched to the horizon in never-ending rows of smokestacks belching a thick white ash.

His father looked at him with a profound sadness. Richter waited for him to speak, but he said nothing as they stared up at the ashes turning the dark blue sky a chalky white.

The wind began to rise. After a moment, Richter wheeled Sacha around and rode away. He stopped once to look back. His father's figure remained etched like a statue on top of the hill, eyes still glued to the heavens, the long spring grass beating in waves of green all around him. With a heavy heart, Richter pointed Sacha into the wind and rode toward the one thin strip of blue left beneath the spreading canopy of white.

Postscript

In 1956, Harold "Kim" Philby, the infamous Third Man, having dodged accusations he was a Soviet spy, was reinstated by MI6 under the cover of a journalist posted to Beirut, Lebanon. Two years later, he started providing information to the Russians again. When a Soviet defector to the West jeopardized his position in 1963, he was smuggled aboard a ship bound for Odessa on the Black Sea. In Moscow, he was set up with an apartment, a job and a pension. He was buried with highest state honors when he died in 1988.

Eventually declassified CIA and MI6 documents would indicate that a former member of the German Abwehr had been warning the U.S. and Great Britain about Philby since 1952.

When the Russians overran the Fuhrerbunker in Berlin on 2 May 1945, they found the body of a man they believed to be Adolf Hitler. Three days later, however, another "Hitler," burned beyond immediate recognition, was exhumed from a shallow grave along with the charred remains of a woman thought to be Eva Braun. Working from dental records, the Soviets determined the body discovered on 5 May was actually Hitler's, and that the first body was that of a stand-in. Diehard Nazis had planned to use this Hitler double – a replacement for one killed by an unknown assassin in Salzburg the year before – as a decoy in Berlin if their Fuhrer decided to make a break for it to the Alps. There, the idea went, German forces still held a stretch of mountain terrain sufficiently tenable for the Third Reich to make a final stand.

Russian archives opened after the collapse of the Soviet Union in the late 1980s and early 1990s revealed that in 1970, with neo-Nazism on the rise in divided Germany, Communist Party Chairman Leonid I. Brezhnev had the remains of Hitler and Eva Braun dug up from their unmarked grave in Magdeburg. On Brezhnev's order, the remains were cremated and the dust of their bones scattered to the winds. Only Hitler's teeth and a portion of skull containing the hole from the bullet that killed him were preserved. Some modern historians dispute whether the skull fragment is actually Hitler's. A few argue that he didn't die in the Berlin bunker at all, but instead escaped to a remote area of Argentina where he lived out his life in peace and security, undetected by the world he had almost destroyed.

A Florida native who attended Dartmouth and served in the U.S. Navy, David Bergengren has taught English composition at universities in New England and Florida, has been a skiwear merchandiser in San Francisco, a desk clerk in Key West, an Associated Press desk jockey in New York City and has worked as a newspaper reporter in Massachusetts, where he and his wife now live. *Hitler's Assassin* is his first novel.

38824454R00262

Made in the USA
Middletown, DE
28 December 2016